DOC AND FLUFF

✧DOC AND FLUFF✧

THE DISTOPIAN TALE
OF A GIRL AND HER BIKER

by
Pat Califia

Boston: Alyson Publications

Cover design © 1990 by F. Ronald Fowler.

This is a paperback original from
Alyson Publications, 40 Plympton Street, Boston, MA 02118.
Distributed in the U.K. by
GMP Publishers, P.O. Box 247, London, N17 9QR, England.

First edition, first printing, May 1990.

ISBN 1-55583-176-1

ACKNOWLEDGMENTS

My heartfelt thanks to the following people, who assisted me by reading all or part of the manuscript and offering invaluable comments. Some of them were even more generous, and allowed me to borrow and tamper with incidents taken from their own lives.

Dorothy Allison

Nell Barber

Beth Brown

Jan Brown

Carlos Omar

Edward Goehring

Bettie Harlow

Pam Lane

Alix Layman

Jesse G. Merril

Shadow Morton

Sky Renfro

Jane Santos

Lamar VanDyke

A special thanks to Stuart Kellogg and Devon Clayton, my editors at *The Advocate*, for being understanding when I missed their deadlines so that I could meet this one.

This book is for J. C. Collins,
Who persuaded me to give dykes
One more chance—
Starting with her.

✦Part One: The Road

1 ⋄

So how good are you at sucking cock?" Mendoza sneered.

Doc pushed her steel-rimmed glasses back up her nose, smoothed down her hair in back (where it was too short to get messed up, anyway), and ran her fingers through the top, making sure it still stood up in bloody little platinum spikes. She was already irritable. Today's long ride had made her sciatica kick up, and a hot wire of pain ran down the left side of her butt, the middle of her thigh, and buried itself in her calf. Her lower back ached from bending over the table where Mendoza had planted Sunny's butt, and invited her to prove that he did not know how to eat pussy. True, *she* was the one who had said to him, "Because you straight boys don't know how to go down on your girls," but *he* was the one who had asked her, "How come a dyke like you gets to party with the Angels?"

She suspected Mendoza of sour grapes. The back of his denim overlay was conspicuously empty, waiting for the Angel skull-and-wings logo and Alamo Chapter patch. Within five minutes of meeting him, she knew that he would never get his own set of colors. Mendoza was just the Angels' waterboy. Sunny was one of the things he used to try to buy a membership on the team. He seemed to have three or four other girls on tap, too. But he would have gotten more respect if he'd done his own ass-licking, Doc told herself.

She hadn't wanted to compete with Mendoza. Well, that was a lie. She was just pissed off about how long it had taken for Sunny to declare her the winner. She suspected the bitch of sneaking in a couple extra orgasms. It wasn't like it was a fair fight, pitting an old diesel like herself against a dude who probably hadn't even read *The Joy of Sex*.

She didn't want to fight with Mendoza either (uh huh), but the boy (all three hundred–plus greasy and unshaven pounds of him) was a poor loser, and had been needling her ever since they both stood up and wiped their faces. Now he had finally said something so foul that she couldn't think of any appropriate reply.

So she cocked her right arm. Mendoza beamed and put up his dukes. This wasn't a fair fight, either. Goddess, what a dumb fuck. Doc almost felt bad about kicking him in the nuts.

The pain knocked the breath out of him. He couldn't even scream. Clutching his crotch, Mendoza reeled back and hit the kitchen cabinets hard. His head whacked a door, and he slid peacefully to the ground. "You fool," she snarled, and drank the beer somebody handed her, the whole thing, in a dozen big glugs. It washed the taste of Sunny's pussy right out of her mouth. "You wanna fight with me, boy, you better get me to drink a whole lot more or drink a whole lot less yourself. Call me a cocksucker, you stupid prick! I'll tear you a new asshole!"

There was quite a crowd — anybody who wasn't too fucked up to come and watch the fight — and most of the bikers and their women were laughing and jeering at Mendoza, who was in no condition to keep track of who his friends were, anyway. A girl in tight jeans who wore only a leather vest over her formidable tits stooped beside the unconscious man, held his head steady by taking hold of his unclean beard, and drew little x's over his eyes with her lipstick. That really made everyone howl.

"Sit on his face now, Lydia," Doc suggested. "I bet he's a better time when he's unconscious." When it looked like Lydia was going to take her suggestion, Doc turned her back.

"Good party, Doc."

That made her jump. It was the Prez. He was smiling, and standing just a little too close. You never wanted to let these boys make you back up. It wasn't safe. So Doc closed the distance completely, and whacked him on the back.

"Yeah," she said, smiling right back. If he'd been chewing tobacco, that slap between his shoulder blades would have made him swallow it. "It's been too long since I got y'all fucked up, huh?"

He was not a small man, and she figured he only had a couple of inches and about forty pounds on her. Must be tough, to have to look a woman in the eye. Although the Prez never acted like it was any skin off his back. It was one of the reasons she kept taking care of his jones — that, and the cash, and the network she needed to keep her own bike in spare parts and her face on funny papers. These Harley boys, she thought, they will still be here when everything else has fallen apart, taking care of their own. Praise the Goddess, I'm just a poor relation who sometimes comes in handy.

The Prez hit her lightly on the upper arm. "Man's a sore loser," he said. "It's a bad idea to make a bet you can't win. If Mendoza could keep his own women satisfied, he wouldn't have to keep on loaning them out to other people. I just got myself a ringside seat, and figured I would look at you and learn. Now I got me a doctorate in the school of Doc-ology, and I'll never have no woman trouble ever again." He laughed to himself, holding his own sides, rocking back on his heels. Then he stuck his tongue out, made it vibrate like a buzzsaw, and laughed even harder. His black beard was shiny as a rabbit's pelt. He had clean white teeth (except for a gold one on one side) and no beer gut, didn't wear any leftovers or patches on his clothes. This was a man who took care of himself — or took good enough care of a woman to make her want to look after him.

Doc was laughing back, looking at his turquoise and silver bracelet, the silver hoops in his ears. He was a handsome bastard. Packs almost as big a dick as mine, Doc thought, playing with the blonde corners of her mustache. Of course, his is the inconvenient kind you can't leave in your saddlebags or trade down a size or two to accommodate a virgin, if you ever meet one of them mythical-type creatures. Her mustache was a little crusty. "Yeah, well, I think I better go wash my face," she said, to forestall the next comment, which would not be as crude as a direct invitation to give him some private lessons (after all, he was the Prez, the man had political cunning), but would push things one more step toward the moment when she'd have to be rude to him.

That really made him laugh. "Shall I send Sunny in to take care of you?" he asked — not sure exactly what that would look like, but sure of the proper way to treat a guest under his roof.

"Uh, thanks, I think I got all the help from her I needed," Doc demurred. "Where's the can?"

"Upstairs, to the right. If somebody's gone and passed out in there, just holler and we'll pitch 'em out."

"Not a problem. Whoever's standing in line can just catch 'em if they bounce."

Doc found the stairs, grabbed the bannister, and pushed her steel-toed engineer boots up, over, and down onto them. Fuckers felt like they weighed a ton. Got to stop sampling my own wares, she thought. I know they can't have wallpaper this pretty in a broken-into, burned-out farmhouse. I don't even want to think about how the original inhabitants got run off. Was it cancer from the insecticides and fertilizers, the land-grabbers at Del Monte, or a marauding gang of quarantine camp escapees? The troubles aren't over yet, I don't care what they say on the evening news. You wouldn't catch me living out here unless I was behind ten-foot walls and a pack of mean dogs. Let's just hope nobody decides to have a baby tonight, okay? Or needs a bullet dug out of some place delicate that's gonna spurt and bleed all over my face like that bitch Sunny. Mendoza sure thought he was butch comin' up with her tampon string in his teeth. I'd like to see him wallow that way in his own blood. Thinking about his piece scrubbing herself off on me gives me goosebumps. I got pussy-burn from ear to ear for sure. Thought she was gonna swallow my whole head. Glad I kept my jacket on, that mama has claws like a Bengal tiger. Acted like my scalp was the stairway to heaven. That must be what they mean by the thrill of victory.

There was, for a minor miracle, nobody in the bathroom. The microdot was probably putting people off their beer, keeping them from puking — or maybe just making them forget that they oughta puke in the john. Don't look behind the sofa, Mrs. Jones. She bent over the sink and rinsed off her face and neck, turned her head, and drank several mouthfuls of cold water. Her cunt hurt. People were gittin' nekkid downstairs, and an odd sort of orgy had evolved. There was sex, but it had a distracted quality, as if they couldn't stay focused on why they were doing this. Sooner or later the group mind would get going and then it could get ugly. Doc figured she would kick before then, find a place a few miles down the highway and board herself in for the night.

It wasn't that the spectacle of some bitch getting screwed a couple times by most of the men present bothered her. Gang-fucks weren't usually that hostile, unless the gash in question was a real pig. It was more of a sporting event, a contest, not unlike the one she had just won. And it wasn't as if she hadn't participated, when encouraged with the right chemicals and a fox who looked halfway decent. No, she definitely got a rush out of showing the boys that a whole hand really could fit in there, that's right, junior, and what are you gonna do with your dick now — hang it out to dry?

There just ought to be more to sex than getting straight bitches off to spite their men, she thought, and straightened up to dry her face. She almost jumped back into the sink when somebody else tweaked the bandana out of her back pocket and thrust it into her hands. Doc was half-blind from water in her eyes, but it didn't smell like a man was in the room, and it wasn't the kind of gesture one of them would make anyway.

"Thanks," she said, figuring it always paid to be polite.

"You're most kindly welcome," her benefactor said gravely. It was a soft Georgia drawl. Ooh, honey, Doc thought, does this Yankee peddler have anything you might like?

Then she got her eyes working and took a look. It was a child — a thin-faced, long-haired, large-breasted child with legs that went all the way up to Canada and blue eyes the size of the Great Salt Lake. What was she — sixteen? Oh-oh, maybe younger. And she was wearing a laced-up, short-sleeved leather dress that barely covered her butt. Her hair was longer than her skirt, curly, such a light brown that it was almost blonde.

"Like what you see?" the child breathed. Her hands went down to the ragged edge of her skirt. The leather was yellow, form-fitting, and looked very soft. Was it deerskin? Doc barely had time to register the fact that the bathroom door was closed and hooked shut. This was a quiet bitch. Sneaky, even. From between her shapely and slender limbs the child drew what seemed to be a g-string. "I saw what you did to Sunny," the girl murmured. "It sure looked like she was having herself the joyride of her life. Breaking every speed limit and not using her turn signal before she changed lanes." She pulled the yellow leather strip between her fingers. Doc noticed that the nails on one of her hands were unpainted, cut short and straight across. The other hand bore Mandarin claws, painted bright red, of course.

Then the girl stepped close up to her, so Doc could see the top of her head, the clean part between the two halves of her hair. She automatically put her hands out and clasped the girl's waist. It felt like spring steel. That was a hard little body, all muscle, like a snake. The tips of her fingers almost met around the girl. And, yes, the g-string was made out of the same leather as the dress. She knew because she could feel the same soft nap on her palms and on her face. The center of the strap was a little sticky, and she caught it in her teeth and shook her head. The girl pulled the piece of leather, pretending to take it away, and Doc began to growl.

She pivoted, lifted the child, and set her down on the edge of the cabinet that held the washbasin.

"Do you like what you smell?" The kid was laughing, kicking her legs in the air. "I got some more of that for you, if you can take it away from me."

She was barefooted, her legs lightly tanned, and there were fine little hairs on her ankles and up her calves. The hair at the top of her thighs was darker and much, much thicker, curlier than the hair on her head. It was a woman's cunt, trapped between the legs of a little girl, and Doc stuck her tongue into it and fucked the juice out of it so she could get a good taste. Then she lifted her head and said, "I don't think I'm gonna have to take anything away from you, you're gonna just bring it to me and wring it out for me, aren't you, baby?"

The girl wrapped her fists in Doc's short, white-blonde hair and pulled hard, making the older woman shake her head and growl again into that fragrant bush. The thighs around her neck trembled. Doc took the meaty morsel of the clitoris between her teeth and chewed just a little, as an experiment. The experiment was a hyperventilating, thigh-quaking success. So she licked up and around the outside of the inner lips, pushed her tongue back into the hole that by now was very slick, wetter than her mouth, and nibbled her way back up to the top of the slit, spreading it all out tight with her big hands, tight enough to make it hurt.

"Do it, do it, do it," a disembodied female voice said above her. The girl shoved Doc's face deeper and deeper into that delicious snatch, shook her by the back of her neck. Strong legs clamped around Doc's head and threatened to smother her. When the girl came, she bucked around so much that she accidentally turned on the hot water faucet. Doc pried her thighs apart just in time to hear, "Ouch! Goddammit! I've scalded my own butt!"

They separated laughing, but the minx wasn't done with Doc. She studied Doc for just a split second, while she reached behind herself to turn off the offending tap and slid to the floor. Then she jammed the g-string, which she still had clutched in her hand, in between Doc's surprised teeth, which immediately clamped down on the intruding hand. "Let go of me," she gritted, and punched Doc, hard, on the pecs, on the ribs. Doc shook her head no, bit down a little harder. "Fuck you then," the girl spit, and fisted the buttons on Doc's jeans open. When Doc resisted, the kid slammed her knee up into her crotch, doubling her over. Yep. Sneaky bitch. Coulda told you so.

Doc's chaps were cut so low on the thigh and that hand was so small that it had no trouble getting between Doc's legs without taking off her riding leathers, much less undressing her completely. This was something new for a bitch to try. Doc was so surprised she let her mouth open a bit, and the little cunt took her hand back and slapped her with it. "Keep your hands down," the girl insisted, as if Doc would hit another woman. Her tone was not nice. She was used to getting her own way. Doc tried to twist away, evade the hand that had a healthy grip on her pubic hair, before those sly fingers could determine just how wet she was. That was when the barefoot girl kicked her right heel and she tumbled to the floor.

Doc landed on her knees, balanced on her hands. Somehow the bitch was behind her, reaching forward to rub a palm full of cunt-juice over Doc's face. "You want it, and you're gonna let me have it," she said fiercely, splitting open the zippers on the outside of Doc's chaps. Doc found herself loosening the buckle, and not a moment too soon, because those small hands hauled at the back of chaps and jeans alike with the strength of a sailor, and would have had them down over her ass if it had meant taking skin with them.

"All right," she said, trying to pacify this little hellcat. "All right, you've got me."

"Never saw anything like you," the girl said, kneeling behind her, between her legs, "but I know what to do with you. Don't I? Don't I?"

The fist slid home, a perfect fit, and Doc started to come just from the sensation of it gliding all the way in. It was orbiting within her, touching every wall, rocking her cervix, she was too big and bad to be down on her knees getting fucked from behind by this child, who was probably somebody's prize bitch or even their half-grown daughter on her way to a wedding. She was trouble, trouble no matter how good it felt, no matter how good it felt, no matter how many times she was made to say she needed it and would do anything for it.

"Fuck me!" she shouted, and for a miracle, this little girl who could *not* be old enough — or queer enough — to know how to do this slowed down just a little but kept pumping hard until Doc came, and slid off her fist, and curled up around her with both hands on the deerskin dress and the whippet waist it enclosed.

"What do you want?" Doc whispered.

"I'm gonna take a piss, then I want you to get me out of here," the child whispered back. Their discretion seemed very funny after they had been crashing together like elephants, and Doc couldn't help but snort with laughter.

"I mean it," the girl insisted.

"Oh, honey," Doc said, and covered her face with a handful of that long, thick hair, "you look so good I'd put you on the back of my ride just any old time."

"I don't want to go for a ride, I want out of here. Permanently."

That southern accent certainly made it hard to take her seriously, Doc thought. Her hair smelled wonderful. It wasn't perfume, it must be, hmm, shampoo? Somebody really loved this child if she got fancy comforts like that. Well, what the fuck. If she stayed here a lot worse things were gonna happen to her than getting eaten out by an old dyke. Still, Doc didn't relish being given orders by this baby doll. Pretty girls don't usually take good care of their toys.

"I didn't plan to come back any time soon," Doc said lazily. "And I'm not no taxi service."

"I pay my own way," the girl said primly. "Now get over here."

"I thought you wanted to piss."

"I do," the girl said. "Put your mouth on me again."

Doc looked at her with renewed respect. "Who got to you at such a tender age and crossed your wires, honey? What makes you think I'm going to let you do that?"

"The look in your eyes," the girl crooned. Her fingers closed around Doc's windpipe, and she pulled. She obviously intended to continue pulling until she lifted Doc's trachea out of her throat. It was a difficult ploy to resist. "The look in your eyes when I shoved my cunt-strap in your mouth. The way you shoved your tongue up my pussy to drink me down. My piss is just part of me. Part of my sex. I tell you what. I'll make you all a little deal. You can have as much of me as you want and you just tell me it's too much, okay? Do we have us a bargain?"

But Doc was already drinking, and kneading a pair of the hardest little cheeks, covered with the softest skin, she had ever had the pleasure to imagine spanking in her life. Of course, she couldn't manage to catch all of it in her mouth. A fine spray of piss fanned out across her chest, soaking her T-shirt, and Doc knew some of it was getting in her hair. But getting dirty had never stopped Doc from getting some. In fact, she took a perverse pride in it. She wasn't any different from the biker boys about that.

And still it kept on coming. This sweet thing must have been letting her bladder back up for a week. The flow only stopped once, when Doc thrust a finger up the girl's ass and gently began to stroke her there, but there were only a few more drops to come anyway. Doc figured since the deal was she didn't have to stop until she'd had too much, there was no reason not to make this uppity piece come standing up, and see if she could keep to her feet.

She could not.

And would she beg for it? Laying with her head by the toilet, squirming on a floor that could not be clean? Just to keep the record straight, of course.

She would.

Well, that evened it up. Almost.

Then Doc got up, picked the bitch up, turned her over, and smacked her butt twice, leaving a big red hand-print on each cheek. "Payback's my middle name. Still want to come with me?" she asked cheerfully.

The girl rubbed her cheeks. Through gritted teeth, she said, "I want to leave. Now! It would take more than that to make me change my mind. You promised you'd help me. You going to keep your word or not?"

"Sure, princess, sure. I keep my word. All my gear's still on the bike. You need to go get your high heels or something? You got a jacket?"

"Next door."

They stopped for a pair of doeskin leggings that went under the dress (which was apparently really a shirt), some knee-high moccasins, and a white leather jacket with a lot of fringe on it. This outfit left a lot of bare skin hanging out. "Man who dresses you don't plan on droppin' you, does he?" Doc said disapprovingly.

"Guess not," the girl shrugged.

Doc figured she really ought to find out whose cookie jar she'd just busted, but it wasn't like she was gonna give this one back, so fuck it. Time to kick.

Doc's bike was a big, beautiful cruiser — a 1500 cc Medusa that could have hauled five people and their stuff around. It never (well, hardly ever) glitched. Doc usually kept her opinion about the reliability of Harley engineering to herself.

Much as she appreciated the mystique, she wanted something unique and more efficient. Her gear had not been fiddled with. Saddlebags, crossbow, quiver, sleeping bag — it was all in place. If you wanted what Doc had, you paid for it. She said so and the Prez said so. Enough examples had been made to make that a law. If you fucked with Doc, the next time you needed antibiotics or junk or an abortion, you could go fuck yourself.

Doc always stopped long enough to ogle her machine before she mounted it, giving its chrome and magenta lines a long, lusting look. She was convinced this courtship ritual kept the Medusa sweet on her. She touched the snake-haired head painted on the gas tank and tapped the beaded pouch that hung on the right side of the passenger's back-brace. She had acquired the grisly contents (a mummified male organ) a long time ago. It was a story she didn't tell very often. But nobody ever asked her what was in the bag, so it must still be giving out some heavy vibes. She got on, appreciating the lack of sway or sag as the Medusa took her weight like a lover. As Doc turned the key, she assessed the amount of room at her back. It was a good thing the bitch was skinny and didn't have any luggage, and she said so.

The girl was already tying up her hair, pinning it in place. She even had a big square of deerskin she knotted over her head. She took off her bracelet so she could put on her gloves. They went inside her sleeves (so they wouldn't fuck up the fringe, of course, but her forearms were gonna get chilly). Doc put down the rear pegs for her, and she swung up like a dancer. Damn silly jacket, though. This skimpy outfit was pretty at a party, but no good in a skid. Have to get this child some good boots and see how she looks in black.

"What's your name, honey?" Doc said.

The girl made a face. "Fluff," she said. She put her arms around Doc, and the big woman noticed, for the first time, that the bracelet she wore was turquoise and silver. In her mind's ear, she heard the sound of shit hitting the fan. "What's yours?"

"They call me Doc. But you can call me just about anything as long as you got me by the ears."

The garage door had been left open. Doc backed out between the other machines, turned her nose, and started eating road in a serious way. I want, she told herself, to get the fuck out of here. Where's my tricorder? Beam me up, Scotty.

✧

Back at the party, a few hours later, things were getting less colorful and a little more mean. The beer was running out, and what was left was warm. There wasn't enough firewood to last out the night, and nobody wanted to go bust up some more. The Prez had just made the rounds of the house, doing what he called checking his fences.

He went up to one of the women, his sergeant's old lady, Tina. "Where's Fluff?" he asked her.

Tina shrugged, making the Harley logo and the funeral wreath tattooed on her arm jump, then she looked worried. "Dunno," she said. She tipped her head back and started looking around, as if Fluff might be sitting on the ceiling.

Mendoza, who was parked at the kitchen table nursing his lumpy head against a tepid can of beer, said, "She was watching the pussy-eating contest. You shoulda seen the look on her face when Sunny started screaming, 'Doc wins, Doc wins!'"

"What?" The Prez turned toward him, balling up his fists.

Mendoza shrugged. "Know where I'd look for the bitch, is all I'm saying. With all due respect to your high office, an' all that crap." He smacked Sunny, who still looked inordinately pleased with herself. She ought to, she had Mendoza by the short hairs now. His other women could expect to be farmed out while Sunny took a little vacation on his lap.

The Prez grabbed his jacket, which was hanging off the back of the chair next to Mendoza. "Yeah? I told you to quit pussy-baiting Doc with that pack of tired old whores you cart around. If we needed entertainment, we coulda turned 'em loose in these hills and watched 'em run down wild dog dick and suck it. I do business with Doc. She is as close to being family as you can get without putting on colors. And I fucking well told you to leave her the fuck alone. So get your chaps on, asshole, and get your head on straight, and pray you are wrong."

"Whatsamatter, Prez, you sweet on that fat-ass butch? Getting too old for things to get ugly?"

The funny thing about the Prez was, you heard him better when he *wasn't* shouting. "If I thought I could make you any uglier than you are now, you'd be a dead man, Mendoza. But you are coming with me to take care of this now, since you have expressed an interest in my ability to cope, and as many of the rest of you useless drunks and dope fiends as can still sit on something that has two wheels instead of three had better be at my back as well if you ever want to see more of me than my ass, which you can kiss."

While he talked, he had been loading his piece. People were running all over the place — men throwing on riding clothes, bitches stuffing things into bags and emptying the refrigerator, more sober individuals rolling their friends over or kicking them awake. Somebody in the garage had started his bike before the Prez even finished talking and strapped on his holster. In ten minutes, the house was empty.

2.

It amused Doc to notice that Fluff had trouble getting her arms all the way around her chest. Or was it just that the girl wanted to try and mess with her nipples, even through a denim overlay, a heavy, lined leather jacket, and two sweaters? I know I don't wear any underwear, Doc thought, but a lost cause is a lost cause. Still, what can you tell somebody who saw the South rise again?

She pulled in the clutch and kicked up into fifth gear. It would be daylight in an hour or so, and she wanted to be off the road by then — holed up somewhere snug. Then it would be time to ask this child enough questions to figure out just how much this adventure was going to cost. She was nowhere near ready to sleep. The acid was still making the edges of her vision curl and bubble, and her jaw muscles felt like something was crawling along the bone.

Fluff was a good passenger — tucked her tiny head in between Doc's shoulderblades to stay out of the wind, went right over like a good girl on the corners, kept her sweet little whatsit pushed up against Doc's tailbone. It was kinda nice having somebody back there. Kept you warmer, anyway. She put one gloved hand back and patted Fluff's knee. Then thought, what the hell, and let her hand stay here, travel a little way up the thigh. Sweetcheeks had to be cold no matter how hot her blood ran, it wasn't good to haul somebody around in this wind dressed up like a showpiece hussy on her virgin run.

There were more houses now. Doc had deliberately gone for the outskirts of the town, figuring they had a better chance of hiding there than they did out in the open. There was always the chance some roving youth gang would find them, but it was hard to live off these abandoned suburbs. People were afraid of the toxic waste dumps they had been built on, and pickings were slim unless you had wheels. She wondered if Fluff knew how to shoot. Might be time to show her, it would be close-up work anyway, no need for a sniper's medal.

She took a couple of side roads, looking for a place that was intact but not too fancy. "Pick one," she finally yelled back at Fluff. "We gotta fold this bike up and lay down in our coffins."

Fluff turned her head and pointed at random. Doc took the driveway, and before she'd stopped, the girl had the garage open and was kicking on the door to the house. "It probably isn't locked," Doc said mildly, "so why break it?"

"Oh, yeah," Fluff said. It really had not occurred to her. She turned the knob.

"We shouldn't leave a whole lot of signs behind us," Doc added. "Would you close the garage door, please?" She walked the bike over to the back wall, cut the engine, and put the kickstand down. Then she picked up her gear, grunting when the full weight of the saddlebags hit her shoulders. "You're gettin' too much seniority for this job, you swaggerin' bulldagger," she told herself. "Wonder if my pension plan is all paid up. Maybe I'll take early retirement."

Fluff gave her an odd look. They walked into the house. It was eerie. Nobody had trashed it. But most everything that might have made it a home was gone. All the windows were intact. There was no furniture, but there were drapes and carpets. "Let's build a fire," Fluff said.

"No, I got some canned heat. We'll make us some cocoa. Just that and a bottle of Jack Daniels to keep us warm. No fire, no smoke. When these boys find us I want to know what kinda shitstorm I'll be dealing with. And I'd rather pick my ground if you don't mind."

Fluff's eyes got big. "You told me you'd get me away from there."

"Yeah, I did, simmer down. Nobody's going to make you go any place you don't want to go. But I have to find out what it's going to take to wrest you from their slimy clutches, honey. I mean is this something somebody has to die for, or can we buy our way out?"

They pulled the drapes almost entirely across the front window, so they could still see through part of the glass, and Doc wrapped her sleeping bag around them both. Fluff wasn't even shivering, came into her hands warm as toast. "Hard as nails, aren't you, honey?" she said, pleased with Fluff for being so tough.

"Give me that whiskey," Fluff said contemptuously. "I don't want any cocoa. I'm not a baby, and I'm sure not your honey."

Oh ho, Doc thought, but I might like it if you were my honey-babe. She handed her the flask. "So tell me about yourself, sugar-tits. If you ain't a baby, how old are you?"

Fluff shrugged. "I'm old enough to screw, if that's what you mean. I just look like jailbait."

Doc dumped instant cocoa into her metal canteen cup, filled it with water, and stuck it over some canned heat. "You sure you don't want some of this, honey? The sugar'll help you come down. You need the calories," she warned.

"God, I'm cold," Fluff complained, as if she had not heard her. "Let me drink some of your cocoa."

"There's only the one cup anyway." Doc blew on the liquid and held it to her lips. "Don't burn your tongue, now, honey, I might need it later."

Fluff actually spit cocoa back into the cup. "I don't eat pussy," she sputtered.

"Oh? I see." Doc laughed and grabbed her nipples. "You sure about that, now. Never put nothing nasty in that fine mouth of yours, huh?"

"That's business," Fluff said, indignant at her stupidity.

"Told you I'm no taxi."

"Oh. Oh."

Doc's thumbs and forefingers played grind-and-coax. Even tits this firm could stretch quite a bit. "Heard you was a girl paid her own way," she teased.

"Do — I do — oh!"

Doc slid one finger between soft animal skin and coarse muff-hair, and stroked the hard, wet ridge of the girl's sex. At first she got almost no response. But she was patient, and she had her tongue working in Fluff's mouth and throat. Her fingers barely moved, but they were in a very good location that finally began to move itself.

Now Fluff was trying to rip off her lips and eat them. Doc laughed inside her mouth. She deliberately concentrated her touch on the most sensitive spot, the peak of Fluff's clitoral hood, and put the tip of her little finger just barely inside the helplessly wet girl. "Get it over with," Fluff was hissing, thrashing. Doc shook her head no, kept playing. "Fuck me, damn you!"

"Suck my cunt, then."

"No!"

Doc crammed her own fist into her own jeans, grabbed Fluff's two skinny wrists with her other hand, and stuck her slippery, glittering fingers into Fluff's mouth. As soon as she pressed down on the back of the girl's tongue, Fluff started to suck automatically. "Tell me that doesn't taste better than a raunchy old dick," Doc told her, and tipped Fluff headfirst into her crotch. She held her down there while she stripped the lower half of her body. Fluff didn't really fight back, but the tension in her shoulders made it clear that she had to be pinned down — if only for reassurance.

"Go for it," Doc advised her, hooking her legs over the slim shoulders and winding Fluff's hair around her fists. "Put your face in it. Where your hand went in. Where you like it so much when I play with you. Lick me up and suck me off. Get yourself a reward if you show some talent, bitch." With the use of the word "bitch," all the tension went out of Fluff's body, and she began to earn her wings.

Talent, shit, the girl might be a genius. Doc came so hard she thought her toes might have shot off, but Fluff didn't stop. Why get off the train before you use up your ticket? Doc heard herself getting talkative and didn't feel like putting a cork in it. That word, "bitch," seemed to hit the bull's-eye, and she used it to hammer in each order and description. When she finally came again, she flipped them both over completely, so she was kneeling over Fluff's face, and she almost broke the girl's neck in her anxiety to peel herself off and check to make sure she was still breathing.

Her whole physical self felt so loose and blissful, Doc gathered up the fine-boned, adolescent body underneath her and hugged it to her, like a warm, clean shirt she was about to put on. She started licking Fluff's face, running her tongue wherever her own smell and taste lingered, even finding it deep within the girl's mouth, lining the inside of her cheeks, hiding beneath her tongue. "Honey, you are some good stuff," she breathed, and Fluff began to cry.

This was alarming. Doc didn't know anybody who cried. Tears belonged to another time, people too soft for her to afford. She shook the girl. "Hey. Hey. Whatsamatter? Did I break something?"

Fluff hit her in the side, punched her hard enough to leave a bruise, and rolled out of her arms. "Would you just fucking please not call me that?" she snapped.

"Call you what?" Doc shouted, getting indignant. "I'll call you any damn thing I please."

"Really. Will you really? No, I don't think so, or I'll get off your goddamn bike and walk back to the Angels, and tell them you were gonna sell me to a nigger pimp."

The world between Doc's ears got real quiet. "Don't you even think of doing me that way," she said. "I am a survivor. If I have a choice between you and me, I will always pick me. Don't ever force me to make that choice, Fluff."

The girl beat on the ground. "So why can't you call me that, you big, dumb animal? Call me Fluff. That's okay. The Prez started calling me that, I'll answer to it for you. Call me bitch. *Your* bitch if you wanna be sweet. I like that. You know that? I really like that. I know how to do that. I wouldn't mind bein' your bitch. But I am not a honey. I never had any name but that until I took out on my own. My name was Would You Honey. Get me a drink Would You Honey. Help me fix Would You Honey. Pick up my drugs, get me cigarettes, read to me, I need a backrub, where's my shoes, Daddy's got a hard-on, there's nothing to eat, I can't sleep, I think I'm gonna throw up, and Would You Honey is always supposed to jump up and take care of it. Well, fuck that."

"No," said Doc, grabbing her, rolling on top of her, putting a hand over her mouth. "No, I'll fuck you. You don't have to jump up at all. I mean, you can jump a little if you want to. But really all you have to do is just lay there and keep your legs spread open for me." She reached into one of the saddlebags and hauled out her dick. Fluff watched open-mouthed and wide-eyed as Doc fastened the straps of her harness. "You all sure do put your stuff right out there," she said, sounding amazed, amused, and a little proud. Doc wrapped her hand around the dildo. Her fingers barely met. It was a majestic piece of equipment, the closest thing to a horse-dick Doc figured she could wear without tipping over.

"Don't," Fluff said as Doc rubbed the head of it over her pussy, getting it slick. "I hate getting fucked in the cunt."

Do I take this seriously? Doc wondered. But Fluff's face was devoid of coyness or curiosity.

"That's for tricks, okay?" Fluff said, trying to explain. "Put it up my ass."

"Are you blind or just stupid? This ain't gonna go up your butt, little girl."

Fluff smiled. "Bet it will. I'm a little girl but I can take what you've got." She got into her jacket pocket and came out with a condom and a small, plastic bubble of lube. She applied both to Doc's tool, even loved it up a little with her hands.

Doc thought briefly of putting it down her throat but maybe that was too much like biz also. She didn't want to get interrupted again. So she got her hands on the back of Fluff's thighs just above the knee and hoisted her legs. "Put it in, then," she ordered.

Fluff reached down with professional detachment and got Doc's stick positioned at the gate. She let some of her weight hang from Doc's arms as she lifted and tilted her bottom and rocked onto its tip. "Uh—" she said as the head went in.

"Take it," Doc said softly. "Let me watch you take me all the way. Swallow it up, bitch. Does that hit the spot? Get you where you live? Feel like something you might want more of? This is all for you, sweet thing. Got your name on it all the way up to my belly. So work it. Open up, swallow it up, take it deep and let me ride you. Slut. Slut. Turn that thing inside out if you don't give it up. Maybe even if you do. You let me have a piece of this, and I'm never gonna turn it loose. Shit, girl, somebody who eats my pussy as nice as you do when you hate it, I just have to keep around. Imagine what you'll be like when you start developin' a taste for it."

The tiny buns flattened and stretched under her big hands, giving her a perfect view of the pink ring of muscle stretched wide by her intruding piston, drawn out to paper-thinness when she withdrew, tucked back in when she pushed. Fluff clawed at the rug, clutched at Doc, and sobbed in time to the pumping of her own hips. "Don't let me go," she cried. "Don't stop. Don't stop. Don't ever stop."

Doc got into that. There was enough speed in the acid to make perpetual motion seem like a distinct possibility. It took her a while to realize Fluff was leaving out the word "don't" and saying "please stop" instead. She pulled out, stripped off dick and harness, and came back to the girl, who was curled up on her side, shuddering and rubbing her belly.

She tucked them both back into the sleeping bag, pleased with the Goddess and all her gifts. But Fluff wasn't done with Doc, she had to worm and wiggle and pry her way down and between and go where she did not (Doc swore) belong, until it was less trouble to let the bitch have her way than it was to make her behave. The first glorious fuck had not been a fluke. That little hand was magic. Doc could barely focus when Fluff started waving her other hand around, demanding some kind of assistance.

"Wha—" she said blearily, barely able to lift her head.

"Cut these motherfuckers off," Fluff insisted, unfurling her red nails. "I could get both hands in, I swear it."

"You crazy little shit," Doc cussed. "You've already fucked all the come out of me, we're working on my quota of orgasms for my next life, which I'd like to save a few of to have then if it's all the same to you, and now you want to jam two hands up me? Save something for tomorrow night, okay?"

"Then I'm not gonna stop until you scream again."

"Again? I never screamed at all."

"Bullshit, bet your throat's sore."

"Yeah, where you grabbed it and almost tore it open."

"Scream."

It felt as if Fluff had her whole uterus in her hand. "No, I don't — I just don't — god *damn* you, child!"

They each had another shot of whiskey, then Doc made them up a bed. There wasn't room inside the sleeping bag for both of them, so she unzipped it and shook it out over them. "Keep your side tucked in," she grumbled, pulling Fluff up against her chest. "And keep this cute little fanny up against my belly, okay? So where'd you learn how to throw such a hard, mean fuck, huh, Princess?"

"Prez."

"What?"

But Fluff was already asleep. Well, well, thought Doc. So that's why she had that lopsided manicure. Do you like little girls, Prez, or just their little hands? You perverted bastard. We might stand a chance of getting out of this alive after all. Tomorrow we'll head for women's land. Think I got myself a plan. Not to mention a bitch of my own. Shit-howdy. Here comes sleep. But I know I ain't gonna dream, life is too unreal already.

✧

"Rise and shine," Doc said cheerfully. "Birdseed for breakfast."

Fluff pried her eyes open and grimaced at the daylight. Doc was standing over her, slugging back whiskey and eating something out of her hand. She swept the sleeping bag off her half-clothed, sticky body and sat up.

"Heat came on in the middle of the night," Doc said. "Just about fried us. Bet the hot water's still working too. Guess they never bothered to disconnect everything in this subdivision."

"Great. I can have a shower."

Doc laughed. "Sure. If you'd rather be clean than alive, go ahead. But I'm leaving. Want some of this?" She swung a plastic bag full of raisins, nuts, dried fruit, peels of coconut, and other atrocious objects in Fluff's face.

"Gack," the girl choked, pushing it away.

"That's all there is," Doc said grimly. "And we're leaving in five minutes."

"Yeah, okay, just let me wake up a little."

"Why don't you go wash your face and take a piss?" Doc suggested. "I'll pack us up. But we really gotta scoot, or things are going to get more interesting than this big, dumb animal can handle."

"Anybody tell you lately you're a great fuck?" Fluff said, grabbing Doc's hand and getting to her feet. Doc didn't say anything, just got busy stuffing the sleeping bag into its sack. Fluff stooped to kiss the back of her neck. "You really are, you know," she said.

Doc's hands tightened on a fistful of ripstop nylon and down. "Stop it," she snapped. "I can't be thinking with my cunt today."

Fluff jerked away and ran to the bathroom. Goddammit, Doc thought, I hurt her feelings. But I'm getting too sweet on that girl-child. Doesn't she realize I could spend all day banging her up against the wall and get nailed to it with a .357 magnum hollowpoint? Knowing Prez, he'd make her wear my brains while everybody in the club had a go at her, then they'd crucify her upside down on the garage door and leave her for the coyotes.

Goddammit, Fluff thought, as she perched on the toilet and a hard stream of piss scorched its way out of her, doesn't she know this is the only way I can thank her for taking me on? As if a couple of good fucks were enough to balance out the risk of having your head blown off. I can't help it, I don't want to just make use of her, but I was desperate. Why's she so pissed off? I thought we were jamming along just fine. Maybe it's different from hooking up with a dude. But I can't ask her how she likes her women to behave. I just better figure it out fast, or I'm going to get left here on my own. Sure hope we live long enough to do what we did last night again.

She came out, grabbed the bag of trail mix, and choked down as much of it as she could manage. The whiskey helped rinse the coconut flakes out of her throat. Doc had just come back from loading up the bike. She threw Fluff a bright yellow sweatshirt. "Put this on under your jacket," she said. "It'll cover up your butt and keep you warm. Looks like rain today."

"I don't mind getting wet," Fluff said, putting on Doc's gift. It looked like a muumuu on her.

"Oh, I know. I don't mind your getting wet either." Doc gave her a wicked grin.

Fluff grinned back. This felt better than being cranked at. "You ready to jam some wind up my nose?" she demanded.

"Only way to wake you up." Doc lunged at her, picked her up, and carried her out to the Medusa.

"Hey," Fluff said, adjusting her sore parts on the throbbing saddle, "you know when I called you a big, dumb animal?"

Doc was checking the gauges. "Yeah, honey?"

Fluff, who had been about to apologize, bristled. "Well, I don't think you're dumb," she said sarcastically.

Doc shrugged. "Two out of three ain't bad. Take these cute little pills, cutey."

"What are they?"

"What do you think? We have a hard day ahead of us, and if we're going to get where we need to be, we can't stop to eat or even piss. We have to ride as hard as we can, hold on tight, and pray for the Goddess to defend us."

Fluff let the weird religious comment pass, and handed the speed back. "I can't do this."

"Why the fuck not? It's good stuff, it won't hurt you."

"I'll hang on without it."

Doc saw there was no arguing with her, and swallowed the extra cap herself. "I'm not gonna feel sorry for you later," she said nastily, knowing she was lying.

Fluff squeezed her hard. "Don't worry about it, just go."

3.

On this particular run, the bikers of Alamo Chapter were accompanied by three vans and a couple of trucks that carted around groceries, spare parts, girls, and (if necessary) disabled Harleys and riders. Tina and Carmen had appropriated one of the trucks and loaded it down so there was no room for any of the loose women who had the hots for biker dick and followed the Angels around with insane desperation.

At the last minute, they relented and let Desiree, a redhead who was part of Mendoza's crew, sit in the back. Mendoza had a van for his dogs, a pair of Dobermans who'd been trained to do more than bite on command, and the girls. It was always crowded, but now it was unfriendly as well, since Sunny had replaced Desiree as Mendoza's favorite (and the driver).

Desiree was trying really hard to get out of the pool. She had figured out that Tina and Carmen were different. They never got left behind if they couldn't bum a ride. They always had a place to sleep and something to eat. And they didn't have to fuck any biker who asked them. As if anybody ever asked her. Horny Angels didn't even bother to talk to Desiree. They just grabbed her tits, crooked an eyebrow at Mendoza, and waited for his nod. It was enough to make any girl want to change her career. What she still didn't seem to realize was that women who rode with the Angels got that security if they scavenged, organized, and made the food, set up the tents or bedding indoors, and fucked only one man — or nobody.

"Her hair's gonna get messed up," Carmen said, looking in the rearview mirror.

"Yeah. Too bad, huh?"

They both laughed, not unkindly. These women had been friends for years. Some of the guys called them Salt and Pepper because Tina was a strawberry blonde and Carmen was dark-haired and as brown as you could be without being black.

Tina turned the ignition key. She especially had a soft spot for poor Desiree, trying to figure her life out and get a grip. Tina had once been part of a harem that another scumbag, Grizzly Bear (whose only personal asset was a dick like a beer can), kept available for the club's entertainment. She had lucked out and spent some time with the Prez, who she thought then was coming down with a bad case of the flu. She noticed he was getting twitchy, turning pale, sweating too much, and kept excusing himself to go to the john. Tina was the kind of person who fed stray cats and took broken-winged birds to the vet. So she intercepted him when he came out of the bathroom, where he had thrown up, and made him lay down. Instead of trying to jump his bones, she spent the night holding his head while he puked, rubbing his back when he shook from the fever, and even holding a pot for him when he had to shit and could not make it to the bathroom. His dick was hard practically the whole time this was going on, and toward morning, she made him come with her hand, just to put him to sleep. This went on for nearly a week. They didn't fuck until the last night, when he got hold of a bottle of tequila and took about eight hours to try her out on everything.

The next day, he took her to Anderson, a quiet ex-Marine who was so big he hardly ever had to crack heads in his capacity as sergeant-at-arms. Anderson was fanatically loyal to the Prez, and almost never picked out his own women. He was the conduit through which Prez phased girls out of his bed. But this was intended to be a little more than that, Prez let him know. "I think this one might do for you," he told his sergeant.

"See if she suits. There's more to her than pussy, but the pussy ain't bad."

Tina had been happy with Anderson. It was as if her life suddenly acquired a rock-solid foundation. He was not usually a passionate man, but when he wanted sex, he wanted a lot of it, now. Tina liked waiting for the mood to strike him. It was a good bet that after one of the mandatory marksmanship sessions Prez made everybody run through, Anderson would come home in heat from handing out the ammunition. He could hold his liquor, he was scrupulously fair, and he loved children. They had a boy and a girl, both conceived after Fourth of July fireworks-and-munitions displays. They were too little to come along on the autumn run, and had been left down south, at Alamo. In public, Anderson had a way that Tina loved of touching her on the hip, dragging her close if she was not standing right up against him. He seemed to be saying, this is mine.

When Prez had notified Grizzly Bear of the change in Tina's status, he had been indignant. "You got a lot of brass balls nerve. What're you going to give me for her?" he blustered.

"No, no, no, Bear, you don't understand. It don't work like that. What's mine is mine and what's yours is mine. You ain't no patch-holder. If you don't give up Tina you don't ride with us no more. Besides, I'm doing you a favor. That bitch is too smart for you. If you keep her you better give up sleeping because she's going to stick a knife in you some night and save me the trouble."

This was a story Anderson had repeated to her in bed, giggling in her neck like a little boy. "I knew you were that kind of girl, but it just makes me sleep better at night," he snickered, dragging her across the bed so he could put his head on her shoulder. "Now that I got you I guess I can forget about buyin' a pit bull." The next night she had found a blade under her pillow, a Ka-Bar. She wore it everywhere, strapped to her thigh, and valued it more than most women prize a wedding ring.

Carmen was one of the few old ladies who wore a real diamond ring. She kept a copy of her marriage license in her wallet to win bets with skeptics. She had been hitched to Michaels since high school. He had been riding with this club before Prez became the Prez, and he was the treasurer now, a little man with tattoos all over his arms and back and enough gold rings in his dick to provide Carmen with endless opportunities to tease him about where he kept the club's assets.

"So where do you think we're going?" Carmen asked, as Tina swung the wheel to follow the line of bewildered, angry bikers that were strung out on the road, straggling after Prez.

"Fucked if I know. Guess the Prez is going to sniff out a trail somehow."

"We could always start looking for girls with their skirts up and their legs in the air who've bitten their tongues off and have shit-eating grins on their faces," Carmen snickered.

"Doc spoor," Tina agreed.

"Uh huh."

They both laughed.

"Don't know if I like this," Carmen said when they quit laughing. "Prez and that kid … It makes me feel a little funny."

"Yeah, but then I think, how old was I when I started?"

"Well, sure, but that was with boys my own age. Mostly. Until I got smarter."

"Well," Tina said sadly, "Doc has fucked up good this time. Because Prez has a permanent hard-on for that Fluff, and he is not going to give her up."

"Shit," Carmen said, "that little bitch isn't worth three drops of Doc's blood." They rode for a while in silence.

Tina thought, I tell Carmen almost everything, but I am not going to tell her about that time I locked myself into a closet with Doc and she had to keep her hand over my mouth. I've never been fucked so hard, she almost had to make me pass out to keep me from screaming my fool head off. Got rid of my cramps, though.

Carmen thought, Michaels would kill me if I ever told Tina about the night I got Doc into bed with both of us, poor man couldn't get a dick or a tongue in edgewise until sunup when Doc staggered off to her own bedroll. Probably saved our marriage. Now all I have to do is get Doc a beer and I know we're going to wear a hole in the damn mattress.

"Well," Tina finally said, "she isn't worth three drops of the Prez's blood, either. I'm not sure Prez can take Doc, Carmen."

"Well, fuck, it ain't as if the man don't have backup."

"That's an ugly picture."

"Whooee, yeah. Sure is."

They contemplated its awfulness for a few minutes while Tina drove badly, shifting jerkily, even letting her wheels run across the lane dividers. These were women who understood the concept of female pride and honor, but in their eyes it was a fragile thing, easily destroyed. Prez was ruthless — and he was not the cruelest man in the club.

"Prez don't know where he's going," Carmen said in disgust. "He's just got to do something."

"Men," Tina agreed. "Follow their dicks anywhere."

"Up a tree."

"Up a little girl."

"I don't like it, Tina."

"A war with Doc is not going to be good for the club. Who's going to move all that crank for us? And where're we gonna get spare parts for the Shermans and the helicopters?"

"That's right," Carmen nodded.

"Okay, so we better do something about it."

"What can we do?"

"Well, the guys aren't going to listen. They wouldn't see anything wrong with Prez banging a ten-year-old girl, much less one with tits like Fluff's. But I bet you Josie isn't very thrilled." Josie was Scott Campbell's old lady. Campbell, the club secretary, had long hair, past his butt, and usually wore it braided into a club at the back of his neck to ride. There was something wrong with Josie — cancer, probably. This was likely to be her last run. So she was taking care of business now, doing exactly what she wanted to do, and would not be likely to mince words or shy away from a fight. *If* she thought they were right. With Josie, you never knew which side she would come down on. Even her old man couldn't count on her to back him all the time. If he got into a fight that she thought was stupid (for example, letting his hair down to do the Texas Two-Step with Michaels at a redneck bar), she was out of there. Consequently, Campbell had had his nose broken far less often than most of the men in the club.

Tina turned on the radio, got nothing but static, and turned it off. Carmen was talking again, adding up more names on her fingers.

"Paint probably thinks this is bullshit, too. Wouldn't give two cents for the whole thing. Want me to put a tape in?"

"Yeah, let's have some music and plan this thing out. Okay, so we have a meeting tonight. Just the ladies. Old ladies only?"

"Shit, no, we better get all the women together. I don't want Desiree's little friends going behind our backs. Nobody's going to listen to us as long as they've got tail hanging around to pat them on the back and spread their legs and make them think everything's just fine."

The search went nowhere. Everyone was exhausted, and it was freezing cold and threatening to rain. Prez finally flagged everybody down and told them to go back to the farmhouse. While traffic was stopped, Tina and Carmen got out and went up to every truck, van, or bike that carried women. "What the fuck has gotten into them?" Michaels demanded, as the chase vehicles peeled out. A few women on Harleys followed the cages.

"Oh, they probably just want to make sure there's some hot food waiting for us," Prez said, adjusting his goggles.

Instead, what the men found when they got home was a neatly-laid-out line of their gear, which they couldn't help but follow. It lead to the barn. The line ended with an arrowhead made out of several industrial-sized cans of beef stew, a can-opener, a box of wooden kitchen matches, a cardboard box of assorted bent, broken, or dirty utensils and plates, and the biggest cooking-pot in Tina's traveling pantry.

Prez kicked one of the cans, denting it. "What do these crazy bitches think they're doing?" he swore.

It was Mendoza who came sauntering up, reporting back from the farmhouse. "Bitches done pulled our spark plugs, Prez," he reported. "The keep-away's been nailed to the door."

That was a spectacle so dreadful that everybody had to wander back and take a look. The women had covered up the windows on the ground floor, giving the house a funereal air. "Guess they're all on the rag," Mendoza said mournfully, pointing at the bloody Kotex that had been pinned to the door with a ten-inch butcher knife. At least an inch of the blade's point was buried in the wood.

This ancient symbol of biker-women's wrath made everybody rock back on his heels and suck his teeth. The last time such a thing had been seen, it was because a renegade tattoo artist was counterfeiting the symbol that verified you'd gotten vaccinated against AIDS. Some dude who had been dumb enough to think this was a bargain had opted for the tattoo instead of just paying his ransom for the shot, and infected his wife. She found out about it when the baby she had with him got sick and died. The other women in the chapter (not Alamo, thank God) had decided that since he was going to die a lingering death anyway, it didn't make any difference if they got to him before the virus did. The videotape of that event sold really well in Europe, and had made the bitches a tall stack of cash that they gave away to some hospital that treated fade-away babies.

Somebody made a jocular remark about how it took more than a little blood to make his dick go down, but nobody seemed to take fire from his comment. Then a fierce gust of wind and rain scattered everybody, sent them running to get their sleeping bags out of the storm. When they dragged everything into the barn, Anderson was there ahead of them. He was heating up the stew. Prez was in a rage. "Well, you don't seem too surprised," he shouted, getting up in his face. "Did your fucking insubordinate, smartass, mouthy old lady Tina have something to do with this?"

Anderson looked at him calmly. "Well, you've known her longer than I have. Why don't you tell me?" He filled a bowl with stew and shoved it into Prez's hands, scorching them. "Just remember, motherfucker, you're talking about something you gave me."

Charisma has its limits, and Prez knew when he had hit his. He sat down and shut up. But he was still so mad, he stuck his fingers into the stew before it was cool enough to eat, and burned hell out of them. It almost felt good. But not as good as having Fluff bind his wrists with wire and throw her lithe body on top of him and his bound hands. Her sharp little teeth felt like they were punching holes in his neck, and she had chewed on his tits until they were perpetually sore. He checked them, pinching them surreptitiously. Yes. Still sore. Then she would wind more wire around his balls, and more around his wrists, so that every time he pulled on his dick it felt like he was going to cut it off. Next time, she said, it would be around his throat. Then she hoisted his legs into the air—

His face went hot and cold, hot and cold. Somebody was looking at him. He jerked his head up and met the cool blue eyes of Anderson, who was offering him a spoon. "Just found a few of these," his sergeant said. Anderson descended to a crouch in front of Prez, close enough to smell. One hand dangled between his legs, cupped his crotch. Prez shut his eyes and took the spoon. Anderson held onto it for just a second, made him pull a little harder to take it away. "Too many bodies down here," Anderson said. "I'm going to sleep in the loft. Want your bag taken up there?"

"Yeah," Prez said.

Anderson touched his face, his lips, so lightly he thought he imagined it, and when Prez opened his eyes, the man was standing in front of him, his hips at eye level. The denim was faded below and to one side of Anderson's fly, where the fat head of his uncut dick had worn it down. Prez closed his mouth.

Anderson had already turned and walked off. The sergeant whistled between his teeth as he gathered up his own bedding and Prez's blanket roll. He didn't catch that look of weakness and lust on Prez's face too often. And he didn't stop to analyze his own response — the strands of adulation and resentment that bound him to Prez had been twisted into a thick cable that would never be broken. Like most of the men here, Anderson lived by the credo that if you wanted something, you took it, and if other people got in your way, you ran over them.

He took one of the Coleman stoves up to the loft and set it up not too far from the sleeping bags. It wouldn't do shit to keep them warm. But Prez was about to generate enough heat for both of them, and he wanted enough light to see Prez sweat. Anderson grinned as he pulled his bone-handled boot knife and laid it on the grill. By the time Prez made the rounds and charmed everybody into forgetting how useless their cold, wet ride had been, and got his ass up here, the blade would be cherry-red. There had been something else useful in the cardboard box of utensils and supplies Tina had left the exiled men — a big can of Crisco, half full. He set it down by the head of Prez's sleeping bag, where the man would be sure to see it and equally sure to ignore it.

His own dick started to talk to him, letting him know it needed to sniff the breeze. He got it out and let it dangle. Soon it wanted to stretch, so he helped by pulling it a couple times. He couldn't resist picking up the knife and testing its point on his forearm. His own hair sizzled and curled into nothing. Mm-hmm. Getting there. He put it back over the flame.

Downstairs, everybody had gathered around Prez and a bottle of whiskey. Mendoza had taken one of the rusty farm implements off the wall and was sharpening it. The curved blade made an irritating noise, rasping against the stone. The sight of Mendoza made Prez's gut knot. Fluff really was gone. She hadn't just taken a little ride with Doc (and on Doc, if Prez knew that raunchy old bull-dyke). Mendoza, as the bearer of bad tidings, was the natural focal point for Prez's wrath. It was Mendoza's fault that Fluff had become aware of Doc's sexual prowess and stamina.

Prez genuinely liked Doc, but he had always been afraid that someday she would humiliate him. She knew too much about his weakness, the forbidden drug he needed more than he needed sex or power. Now Doc not only had his secret, she had a living witness to all the kinks in his libido. Fluff was probably singing her head off about all the weird and evil shit he'd made her do. *Made* her — come on, he had slapped her a few times, threatened her, but that wasn't deadly force, it was just priming the pump. Prez had been doing this long enough to know that you couldn't make a chick dominate or torture you, she had to be bent that way. All he'd done was point that bitch in the right direction and squeeze the trigger. You never knew what you'd get when you did that. Sometimes it was like cocking your thumb and forefinger at somebody. Sometimes it was like squirting a water pistol. But Fluff was a fuckin' howitzer.

And now somebody else had her. Prez averted his eyes so that Mendoza could not see the hatred percolating inside them.

Every one of the bros in the circle wanted to tell his fucking life story. Prez kept nodding and smiling, nodding and smiling, while his tits ached and his asshole itched, until he wanted to smash their heads together. Finally Michaels, who had come in from taking a leak, said, "Hey, leave the man alone, he's done in," and hoisted him to his feet.

Michaels pointed Prez in the direction of the ladder and pushed. Prez staggered into it and grabbed blindly for one of the rungs, still feeling Michaels's slap in the middle of his back. He was deeply grateful to the treasurer for replacing him in the circle, but wondered if the slap had not been a bit too forceful to be brotherly. And how the hell did Michaels know where he was bedding down?

He climbed the ladder heavily, wondering if this was not a mistake. The first time he had made it with Anderson, he'd gotten him good and drunk. But somewhere in the middle of the sex, he had opened his eyes and met that icy Viking gaze, and known it wasn't booze that made Anderson willing to take his ass down. The wolf on Anderson's face was mate to his own beast, and while it would never betray him, it meant to enjoy him completely.

Tonight, Anderson wasn't drunk at all. Prez took the whole scene in — the grease, the Coleman stove with its ominous burden, the big blond man airing his stiff dick — and almost disappeared back down the ladder. But Anderson was quicker, and darted over to the trapdoor as soon as he saw the top of Prez's head. "Come and get it," he said, slapping Prez's face with his hard meat. "Cocksucker, come and get it."

He hauled Prez the rest of the way up by his ears, put him on his knees, and kicked the trapdoor shut. He immobilized the dark-haired man by pulling his jacket down over his shoulders, trapping his arms in the sleeves. And with the hot knife, he slashed apart the T-shirt underneath it, leaving deep, bloody cuts and angry red burns beneath the ribbons of knit white cotton. Prez didn't scream, but his face was contorted like a gargoyle's. Then Anderson grabbed one of Prez's nipples between the knife and his thumb, and bore down. "Suck it," he said, pushing his hips into Prez's face. "Suck my cock or by God I'll cut this off."

The bearded mouth opened obediently, and Anderson sank into wet, responsive, submissive flesh. "Take off the rest of your clothes," Anderson hissed, "but stay on your knees, and don't stop suckin' my dick."

46 ❖

Prez stripped himself while Anderson wrapped his big hands around his head and face-fucked him. It had been a long time since Prez had sucked cock, and the shame of it, combined with Anderson's brutality, made his own dick as hard as Fluff ever got it.

"I'm not ready to come yet," Anderson told him. "So stop right there." He had to shove Prez off his cock. "Get on your back," he said, giving him another shove to help him get there.

They were pretty much of a size, but desire made Prez's limbs tremble so badly that he could not keep his hands still on the floor, or keep his knees from shaking. Anderson laughed at him. "You need this bad," he said, laying full-length on top of Prez. The sergeant bent his head to suck one of his commanding officer's nipples completely into his mouth. The cuts around it began to sting as Anderson's tongue opened them, and he sucked them hard enough to make the blood flow freely. Prez swallowed hard, trying to choke back cries of pain, and each time he swallowed, it seemed that the taste of Anderson's pre-cum and foreskin went down his throat again.

"Don't even need to tie you up," Anderson said. "Do I? Do I?"

Prez refused to answer, and Anderson's left hand went between his legs and hoisted his nuts high enough into the air for both of them to see. The knife, which had been laid on the stove again, was in Anderson's right hand. "So help me," Anderson said, "you'll answer to me here in private or to every single man that's sleeping downstairs."

"No, you don't have to tie me up," Prez said. He took a deep breath and let it out slowly, his chest heaving. Blood and shadows highlighted his pectoral muscles, his well-defined abdominals. He was strong, almost young, healthy, arrogant, and completely self-centered but afraid, and Anderson loved the look of him. "Not that I wouldn't like it anyway," Prez added, grinning.

"Oh, I like that smile," Anderson said. He touched the tip of the glowing knife to Prez's cockhead. The resulting scream made him grimace with satisfaction. "But I like making you eat it better," he decided, and ran the hot knife all the way up the underside of Prez's rigid shaft. "Like the way you keep it up under pressure, Prez, tells me just what a sick motherfucker you are." His compliment could barely be heard as Prez raged in agony.

Anderson got on his knees and raised the other man's legs. "Hand me that grease. Yeah. You think I'm going to shove my big, fat dick in you? You're right. But that ain't all we're gonna do. Play with your tits, you're going to need all the help you can get."

None of Anderson's parts were small. And he liked to have plenty of space to stretch out and make himself comfortable. He made room for himself inside of Prez's body with the same insolence he would display getting on a crowded elevator or taking his lane on the highway. "Give me these," he grunted, knocking Prez's hands away from the bleeding, throbbing nipples, and bit down on them with jaws like a beartrap. "Make you feel my dick in your throat," he promised, shoving home. "I've had bitches who didn't like to have their tits played with as much as you like it. And I've never had a bitch who took it up the ass as good as you."

Prez's eyes were half-closed, his head turned to the side. His hips responded to Anderson's insults and his cock, but his face did not acknowledge them. He might have been asleep. So Anderson pulled out, grabbed a handful of Crisco, and began to shove his fist up Prez's ass. The man under him came to life, staring and keening. "Grab your legs," Anderson warned him, "and keep 'em up, because nobody's going to stop me from getting into this. And you are going to know I've been there, I promise you. Every time you spread your legs for your Harley you're going to think about me."

Now Prez cried out, whimpered like a lost dog, and stared into Anderson's face as he ground his hips on the sleeping bags, which provided almost no padding between him and the bare wood floor of the hayloft. The fingers pointed within his sphincter belonged to a hand that was three times the size of Fluff's. But so was the muscle in that arm, and Prez knew if he did not open himself, Anderson would rip him apart. This wasn't about sex any more, maybe it never had been. There was too much blood-smell in the air between them, too much violence locked within them, hoarded for each other.

Then Anderson took Prez's left nut between the knife and his thumb, and Prez gave it up completely. The largest part of the sergeant's hand slid within the ring of muscle, and Prez screamed. That was when Anderson bent forward, covered his mouth with his own, and administered the ultimate indignity — a man's tongue, thrust deep enough to make Prez gag. "Swallow my spit," Anderson hissed at him, and hacked a large gob of it into his open mouth. "Pretend it's cum, if that makes it taste better. Cum out of my hard dick. You gonna scream again when I go in? Don't know if you sound more like a virgin or a butchered pig. But it's all music to my ears."

He tucked more grease inside his fist and gave it one final push. By the time Prez was done screaming, Anderson had his fist lodged securely in his butt, and was using it without mercy. "You go ahead, make all the noise you want," the sergeant told him. "We'll sell tickets. I'm beginning to get an inkling of what rings your chimes, Prez, and it ain't normal. Is it? There's a part of you really digs the idea of having your own club piss all over your face while I fist-fuck the shit out of you, just like there was a little part of you loved sticking your tongue up that little girl's asshole while she made you hurt and bleed. Was she the one opened your butt up enough to make room for me? I sure hope you had her using two hands, buddy, because the best is yet to come."

Anderson made Prez tilt his ass until it was pointing at the ceiling. Then he got up on his toes, as if he was doing pushups, and pushed his cock into his own inserted fist full of grease. Prez groaned like someone giving birth, and his dick shot a thin mixture of piss and cum that left a silvery puddle across his belly.

"Yes, that's right," Anderson said, his lean hips forcing his sex into the other man's body. "I'm jerking off in your ass, Prez. While I fist fuck you I'm jerking myself off inside you. I'm gonna cum inside you, make you take my load. Tell me you need it, tell me you want the whole thing, beg me for it or I'll pull out now and ruin you."

Prez's belly ejected another stream of piss and cum. His limp dick acted like a garden hose and sprayed it over both men. Anderson slapped him for that with his free hand, and stopped himself from doing it again, harder, only by the greatest effort of will. Prez would forgive this entire evening — reward him, more likely — but he would not forgive having to appear in public with a fat lip. Instead, Anderson went for the knife. "I'm gonna slice you open and your nuts are gonna drop into my hand," he said, and crushed the base of Prez's scrotum with the dull side of the blade. "Beg me to come, now, or you'll never come again."

As Prez screamed, "Come! Pleeeez!", Anderson drew the wrong side of the knife hard across Prez's ball-sac, and they both shot. The convulsions of Prez's asshole trapped Anderson's hand. So he just withdrew his cock and kept fucking the helpless body on the floor, fucking it during, through, and past its climax, and into another one while Prez chewed his own mouth bloody and beat his fists to pulp on the unforgiving planks.

When he finally extracted his hand, Prez had passed out. Anderson wiped himself off with the rags of the demolished and bloody T-shirt, then threw it into a corner. Anybody who found it would wonder what the fuck, but let them wonder. He drew a cover over Prez, stripped, and rolled himself into his own bag.

Sometime toward dawn, he woke up. Someone was moving around, bumping into stuff. "Prez?" he said. "Izzat you? What's the matter?"

"I'm in trouble," Prez said softly. "I forgot to do something last night."

Anderson got all the blankets off his face (he had a childish habit of wrapping his head up in the covers) and located the unhappy voice. His fearless leader was sitting next to the stove with a belt around his arm.

"Goddammit," Anderson said sadly. "Not that shit again. Prez, I thought you cleaned up."

"I did, for a long time."

"Yeah, I bet. How long has it been? Months?"

"Yeah, a couple."

"Why can't you shoot speed like everybody else, huh? One of these days you're gonna nod out on your bike and probably take two or three good dudes with you."

"Don't give me a fucking lecture, Anderson. I hate crystal. Things go too fast already. Too much happening." Prez sucked at his arm, where two or three drops of blood showed. "I can't find the damn vein. I can't show tracks, Anderson."

"Oh, come on. A man with your arms?" Anderson went over to him, knelt on one leg, and balanced Prez's arm on his other knee. The veins were like fat worms, bulging above and below his elbow. "You just like somebody else to stick it in," Anderson grinned. "Open your mouth." He put the end of Prez's belt between his teeth. "Bite down on that mother and pull, now."

"I'll remember you said that next time you shove your dick down my throat," Prez growled, following his orders.

"Shut up and take your medicine." Anderson hit blood, depressed the plunger. "Would this happen to be another one of Fluff's useful household skills?"

"That chick could find a vein in a turnip," Prez said softly. His eyes were luminous, his face completely relaxed. "Want me to fuck you now? Be quite a ride."

Anderson slammed a foot into his chest, knocking him down. It took a couple of kicks to roll Prez over. By then he had his own belt off, and wound around his hand and forearm. The leather cracked as it came down across Prez's shoulders. He used it again, and again. When a stray stroke hit the back of Prez's neck and his face, he covered his head with his folded arms. He lay quietly while Anderson beat him, only shuddering when the sergeant changed tactics and used the buckle. Then Anderson rolled him over again, dropped over his torso, and fucked his throat with enough careless force to bang the back of Prez's head on the floor and make him dig his fingers bruise-deep into Anderson's thighs in an attempt to throw him off and breathe. But Anderson had both hands wrapped around Prez's neck, and was too absorbed in his need to pour cum down Prez's gullet to be distracted by a few feeble attempts to break his hold. "You aren't even sucking my dick," he spit at Prez, "I'm just fucking your face the same way I fucked your ass. And you're going to take it because you can't help it, you can't make me stop, you can't do anything except let me use your throat like I'd use some bitch's cunt."

He came like a flamethrower, came as if a grenade had gone off in the small of his back. And almost immediately fell asleep. Prez rolled Anderson onto his side and kept his mouth around the limp cock, tucked the balls in with it, and jacked himself off, didn't come, nodded out, came to, and jacked himself off some more without coming. Anderson began to piss in his sleep, and Prez was swallowing avidly when the sergeant woke up a second time, said, "*You* are a *pervert*," kicked him away, and dragged blankets over them both.

But before he slept, it seemed to Prez that he heard Fluff somewhere behind him in the darkness, and she was laughing.

4

T his isn't a very smart thing to do," Sunny said defiantly, from the couch where Carmen and Desiree had tossed her. "I mean, we're going to get into big trouble locking them out this way." She tossed a strand of hair out of her eyes and looked hopefully at Mendoza's other girls, also on the couch, for support. Dee Ann, a zoftig brunette who had to take her time to figure things out and fought with a fifteen-foot piece of heavy chain when she was rushed, played with her pop-beads and pretended Sunny wasn't there. Rose, who was as skinny as Dee Ann was big and as quiet as Sunny was out-spoken, lit one cigarette off another and kept her own counsel. Her knees hurt. Nobody ever remembered what Rose's face looked like, probably because it was usually at belt-buckle level. Lydia just stared back, arms folded across her incredibly large tits. She wore, as usual, tight jeans and a leather vest with nothing underneath them. Desiree was no help at all, she was out in the kitchen with Carmen, hustling up refreshments, sucking up to the old ladies. Worthless cunt.

Tina laughed at Sunny's pique. "If you aren't ready for trouble, girl, take off your leathers and act like you're supposed to. This is not a movie of your life, and you don't get no stunt woman."

"Does the boys good to cook their own dinner every now and then," Josie said, lighting a joint. Her arms were painfully thin. The skin of her face was stretched unnaturally tight across her cheekbones. But she always wore a little smile. The only way you might have been able to tell she was in chronic pain was the brief gesture she sometimes made of laying a hand on one of her breasts and pressing it into her chest, and rocking back and forth. But she would swear loudly at anybody who caught her doing that.

"You shouldn't smoke that shit," Carmen said irritably, bringing a tray full of sandwiches in from the kitchen.

"What's it gonna do?" Josie asked her, cocking an eyebrow. "Kill me?" She took a deep hit, coughed, laughed, and toked again.

"I'm just glad that somebody had the balls to bring this up," Paint said bluntly. "I like Doc. Prez has got his pride, but it doesn't seem like blood ought to be spilled over some skirt that isn't big enough to come up to my throttle." Paint was the oldest woman present, a rangy blonde with a weathered red face who wore her hair in two pigtails done up with eagle feathers and Indian beads. Down south, she had a shop where she did customized paint jobs and some body work. Wherever she went, she took shit from no one and had sex only with young candidates for the club, whom she always informed, "I'm old enough to be your mama, and you damn well better treat me that way." She had gotten rid of the last one when he dumped his own bike for the third time and refused to ride behind her for the rest of the run. "I can drink you under the table, fuck you till it drops off, and ride circles around you so fast you'll think you're in the eye of a hurricane," she had told him, "and if you think you're going to turn my machine into modern art, you can stand by the side of the road and stick out your thumb." There wasn't a man in the club who didn't think her offer was more than generous, and all of them paused to call the boy an asshole before they gunned off and left him eating dirt.

"Exactly," Tina said. "But if we had found Doc today, somebody would've gotten killed, and then it would have been an eye for an eye."

Everybody said amen to that.

"Doc saved my little Susie," Tokyo said, fiddling with the Chinese buttons on her brocade dress. Her earrings were two long dragons cut out of gold foil. "She started coming out feet first. Had the cord wrapped around her neck. If Doc hadn't been there I might be dead too."

"No more killer weed from the dykes on that weird farm," Crystal said. Crystal was a bit of a joke between Tina and Carmen, she tried so hard to be the ultimate "biker chick," with her ironed-straight, honey-colored hair; her kittenish pout; her slit-up-the-sides leather skirts; her knee-high boots; her brass-knuckle belt buckle; and "so much black mascara you'd think she'd been cleaning the oven," as Carmen put it.

"Yeah, who's going to take all the crank into the city for us? We'll have to start dealing with those niggers directly," Crystal's best friend, Angel, said. Angel, despite her long hair, was known as "the butch" behind her back because of her chunky arms, thunder-thighs, and the panther tattoo that clawed blood along her biceps. She was extremely protective of Crystal, and very few men got into bed with one of these girls without taking the other one along.

"No more microdot," Crystal mourned.

"Remember the time Shorty went down and got gangrene, and Doc chained him up and cut his foot off, and cauterized the stump with a hot poker?" Tokyo said breathlessly.

"Yeah, and laughed like a maniac the whole time," Paint said caustically. "Shorty hasn't been right since."

"Well, yeah, but he was gonna die anyway." Tokyo's admiration for Doc's surgical savoir faire could not be swayed.

Paint snorted. "I dunno, I think I'd rather die than hear somebody laugh at me that way. It was just too cold to be human. Josie, are you saving that joint to pass on to your children?"

"There's some wine, too," Carmen said, putting a straw-wrapped jug in the middle of the floor with some paper cups.

"But I think somebody put the last of the acid in it. That blotter we had last month, you know? It looks like there's little pieces of paper in the bottom of the bottle."

"Oh, well, it keeps it from turning to vinegar," Angel said philosophically.

"You know, I heard pissing in it will do that, too," Josie said, passing her joint to Paint. Everybody laughed.

Angel downed half a cup of the wine and made a face. "This better have something extra in it because it tastes like somebody did piss in it."

"Prez," somebody — Rose — said softly, and they all drew in a shocked breath, then laughed nervously.

"Having sex with kids is just not right," Crystal said righteously. She took Angel's paper cup, filled it half full, and drank it down. "Oh, this isn't so bad. Makes me feel like I'm doing something healthy, like eating a salad."

"Child molesters and baby rapers," Angel said, "should be taken out and shot."

"Fluff isn't exactly a child," Tina demurred. "And she's been on her own for a long time. She knows what she's doing."

"But when I think about my own daughter..." Tokyo whispered. The rest of them heard the unspoken end of her sentence — "with Prez," and sighed their agreement.

"Seems like there are enough grown women here to go around, without Prez having to corner a little filly like that and drop a rope on her," Paint said disapprovingly.

They gabbed on, with almost everybody condemning the difference between the Prez and Fluff's ages. Somebody suggested that Doc should just give Fluff back and apologize, then they would send the girl down south to Alamo. Almost everybody thought that was a dandy idea. Only the girls on the couch were silent. This made Tina edgy. If all the women didn't present a united front on this, Prez would drag them into a war. Doc had friends who would be pissed off about her dying, friends powerful enough to guarantee that some bikers would go walking after her into the spirit land. She didn't want to think about what had happened when Smoky Joe went AWOL and raped one of the dykes on that farm. Or how the Jaguars dealt with another bike gang that sent them a batch of substandard crystal. None of Doc's friends were nice people.

"Well, Sunny," Tina said, in the hard-assed voice that could make even Prez cringe, "don't you have anything to contribute? I would think you'd have some recent fond memories of Doc you'd want to share, at the very least."

"You catty old ho," Sunny said viciously. Then she chuckled. "I am sick to death of you with your nose up in the air. Thinking you are better than anybody else. Just 'cause you got yourself a *ma-yun* you think is tied to your pussy hairs. I'm not the only split-tail here that Doc could find in the dark with nothing but her nose. Y'all are soft on her because she gives better head than any of your old men, and she's a better fuck, and never knocks anybody up or gives them the clap or beats them up. You never minded Prez making Fluff his property and using her like a piece of liver 'cause that meant none of you had to put up with his kinda sick sense of fun. This ain't about protecting no goddamn kid. That girl has been on her own since she was eleven. You can't kidnap her and send her any place. Who do you think you are, her fairy godmothers? You're all jealous, that's all. I say Doc deserves to have a little something keeping her bedroll warm. We oughta *give* her Fluff as a thank-you present from all the old ladies and the real ladies of the Angels. If Prez has his nose out of joint Doc can pay him a dowry like she would if Fluff was his daughter. As for what Prez deserves, if you ride long enough and far enough, you'll run into everything on the road, including a little justice."

The rest of the girls on the couch were clapping their hands like backup gospel singers. Desiree had betrayed the new alliance she was trying to make by clapping with them. Tina was laughing too, but it sounded a little forced.

"Well, why didn't you just *say* so?" she crowed. Privately, she thought, now I know who put Fluff on Doc's tail. And what does she know about Anderson that I don't? "You have more common sense in your little finger—" she began.

"Than you do in your clit," Sunny snickered. "Okay, so how are us girl geniuses going to persuade the club that this is the way to go?"

"If we have to, we can starve them into submission," Carmen said grimly, "but it's a mess, going on strike that way. Makes 'em real mad and I can't stand being horny that long."

"I think," Tina said, "by morning they will be more reasonable."

"Why don't we just appoint you two our representatives? Ask Prez to speak with him and the other officers in private," Paint suggested. "If you want to, me and Josie will go with you. If everybody else is agreeable."

There was a chorus of okay-fine's, and the last of the spiked wine went around. Then Paint contributed a bottle of bourbon to the circle. "I was savin' it to wash my socks in," she said, "but I'll just keep my damn boots on."

"I just want to announce," Sunny said, standing up with surprisingly little difficulty, "that if that contest had been between me and Doc instead of Doc and Mendoza, we might have kept the title in the club. And if anybody doesn't believe me, I am ready to make good my claim here and now." She gave each of the women present an insolent up-and-down examination, then chugged some more Old Overcoat.

Josie blew marijuana smoke out of her nose and turned a speculative eye on Sunny's big smile. She crossed the room and sat down beside her, making a shooing motion with her right hand. Dee Ann, Rose, and Lydia got up and obediently went elsewhere. "Been thinking about seeing what that's like," she said, taking the joint out of her mouth and turning it around. Sunny bent forward to let her blow smoke into her lungs.

Tina caught Carmen looking at her as she watched all this go on, and she made a little clucking noise, which Carmen promptly echoed.

Desiree was watching Josie and Sunny, too. She jumped when Paint put her hands around her neck from behind. "Do you know," she said in her ear, "I think I'm old enough to be your mother."

Oh-oh, Desiree thought, what does she think I am, a prospect? Well, in a manner of speaking, I guess I am. Paint's hands were reassuring — warm, dry, and strong. "Can we keep this private?" Desiree asked.

"Sure, why not?" Paint replied. "Where's your stuff? I already took mine upstairs."

That night, Carmen and Tina were just about the only ones who went to bed alone. But that was because each of them preferred her fantasies about her single encounter with Doc, coupled with the rapid action of her right hand, to any of the other women present.

In the morning, Carmen made a huge pot of coffee and several pans of cornbread. Then she woke everybody up. "I suggest we haul this out to the barn," she said.

"It's going to take more than hot coffee to put a smile on those faces," Sunny said.

"Blow jobs," Rose suggested. Lydia giggled and bumped hips with her. They turned to face each other and began to play pattycake, pattycake, baker's man.

"Yeah, well, the lucky girl in charge of cheering Prez up had better roll him over and work on the other side," Sunny said rudely, pushing between them. "Okay, Carmen, let me give you a hand. Let's do it for Doc, fastest tongue in the West."

"Second fastest," Josie said, hustling to take the other handle on the pot. "Let's haul this over before it gets cold."

The rest of the women, hung over and feeling a little strange about last night's party, staggered after them.

"This is not going to be a high school reunion," Crystal whined.

Angel laughed. "How would you know? If you ever showed up at your high school reunion, everybody'd think the local whorehouse was opening under new management and you were the free sample."

Crystal snapped, "I ain't hardly free."

"Oh, don't I know it," Angel drawled. "So tell me, honey, have you got rich yet?"

5.

Fluff had stopped trying to watch where they were going hours ago. In order to see around Doc, she had to lean perilously far to one side, crane her neck, and endure a gale force wind that snatched the breath from her lungs and drove the meat off her cheekbones. The evil blast chased tears from her eyes and froze them, making her feel as if someone had thrown a handful of sand into her face. Now she was content to huddle behind Doc. Still, the wind attacked any part of her it could reach. It congealed the muscles of her thighs and went up her sleeves, paralyzing her forearms. The muscles in her feet and calves were permanently cramped. She shifted from time to time to move the pain around, and wished for gloves with gauntlets. Doc was better dressed for this, but she didn't have anybody in front of her for a windbreak. Fluff was grateful for Doc's wide back and the pockets in her overlay. If only she weren't so sleepy. Fluff's terror of losing her grip was very real, because if she slipped, her weight would be enough to put the bike over.

Doc was humming to herself, watching the dials and counting white lines. So far it wasn't actually raining, and it seemed like they were riding away from the storm clouds. Miserable as this was, being soaking wet would make it worse. She touched Fluff frequently to make sure she was still alert. The arms around her were thin inside the white jacket, sweater, and deerskin dress. Bird-bones. The whole girl weighed as much as Doc's leathers.

She kept hearing Fluff say, "I never saw anything like you before but I know what to do with you, don't I?" I sure hope so, she thought, shivering, her teeth — her whole body — on edge with delicious anticipation. Because I never saw anything like you before either, and I *don't* know what to do with you. I'm just makin' this up as I go along. But I want you. I want you bad enough to jeopardize my whole business network and make some really nasty enemies. And all I can think about is how somebody ought to pay because I couldn't climb naked into bed with you this morning and lick you from your nose to your toes and beg you to let me drink your sweet piss and spread my tree-trunk thighs for your hummingbird fist.

The speed made euphoric busy-work out of every twitch of her eyeballs, made every thought seem to echo, rewind, and repeat itself fifty times. At some point she was going to have to give it a rest. How would Fluff deal with the irritable monster she became when she came off a run on crystal wheels?

What am I worried about? Doc thought in sudden exasperation. If we're both still on the planet, the bitch can lick my boots and damn well be grateful we're both here, even if I am climbing the walls and snarling at the sun for being rude enough to come up and the birds for being impolite enough to sing.

She touched Fluff's knee, slid her hand up her thigh, squeezed. The thin arms around her tightened. She turned her head. "You okay?" she shouted.

"Never better." The whisper of a shout reached her by the arbitrary grace of the wind.

They finally had to stop for gas. It was one of those huge, well-fortified places that survived along the interstate. The pumps were inside concrete bunkers, and gas was dispensed only if you fed cash or a magnetized credit strip into the slot. If you needed anything else, you had to check your weapons and go through a metal detector. The system was set up to avoid any contact between station employees and customers. Nevertheless, an attendant was strolling around outside. Probably got bored being cooped up in the fortress with nothing but stale candy bars and bottles of antifreeze for company. Doc admired the shoulder holster that housed his Uzi.

Fluff could barely walk to the bathroom. When she came back, Doc showed her where the .45 was and left her guarding the bike while she took her own turn. The attendant was visibly upset when she returned. He made a comment about it being dumb to leave her daughter alone.

"He thought you were my old man until you went into the ladies' room," Fluff explained. "So I told him you were my mom."

"Oh. Well. Huh." Doc wondered how she was going to explain the complexities of navigating through a straight world to this little airhead.

Fluff picked her teeth. "Better use the men's room next time."

Doc was nonplussed by her tone of flat practicality. "Good thought," she managed to say, then got them back on the freeway.

An hour later they caught up with a convoy. The storm clouds had thickened, turning the sky blue-black. It might as well have been dusk. Visibility sucked, and the impending storm seemed to threaten other catastrophes. There were a dozen ebony limousines leading four semis. The trucks were painted black, with big red-and-gold neon crosses on both sides and the back doors. Their loudspeakers broadcast religious music. The cars and trucks were escorted front and back with two camouflaged troop carriers full of mercenaries. Doc swore. It must be a traveling sideshow of evangelists from the Free Christian States on their way to the next big revival, faith-healing circus, and fleecing of the faithful in the pagan cities of California. They were going along at a good clip but she had to pass them. The wind the semis kicked up was dangerous, and they just weren't in as big a hurry as she was. It would be ironic to have built up such a good lead on Prez, et al., only to have these Bible-thumpers take them out.

Nothing for it. She moved into the left lane and went by, expecting any minute to hear an AK-47 going off. Who would care if two female bikers were found dead in pieces by the freeway?

But there was no response from the ghostly convoy. The soldiers did not even turn their heads. Were they real? Or were they dressed-up dummies meant to scare off trouble? Trust a bunch of falwells to put their faith in GI Joe ... and save the expense of keeping real soldiers on the payroll. Then she saw the Iwo Jima logo and the stenciled slogan, "The Only Good Defense," and knew they were definitely for real. These men were MacKenzie's Marines. A lot of the soldiers who had been guards at the AIDS camps went into that outfit when widespread rioting and the discovery of a vaccine shut down the quarantine system. Her hands were suddenly slick with cold sweat. Nothing makes you feel sicker, she thought, than living through a close call.

The ride got progressively grimmer. It was going to be dark in another hour, and they were going to run out of gas any second. They were on a two-lane county road, not well maintained, when she saw the scarecrone — a ten-foot-tall wicker statue of a woman. Doc took the turnoff it guarded. This was the only route into Harpy Farm. On the other three sides, it was bounded by a swamp and by minefields. The women watched this road and shot trespassers. Everyone in these parts knew men did not go past the wicker Amazon and the log cabins at her feet.

Doc had been dealing with these women for years. She had lived here briefly while she avoided taking sides in a price war between her coke wholesalers in the city. She had helped them set up a gun shop and lay the minefields and booby trap the swamp. When she left the farm, it was to act as intermediary for their biggest cash crop, sinsemilla. She also reorganized their system for artificial insemination. They were exposing far too many male babies and children with Down's syndrome.

Doc knew there was a market for male children (the white ones, anyway), but it would take a religious revolution or a corruptible High Priestess for her to be able to develop that as a profitable sideline. The boy babies were supposed to be unusually evil and potent male demons that had managed to overcome all the female energy poured into their conception so they could intrude on women's space, poison and pollute it, and ultimately destroy it.

Doc thought that the current High Priestess, Raven, would have been diagnosed as a schizophrenic and locked up any place else. Maybe she was just trying extra hard to compensate for being a former heterosexual who was dumped off at the edge of Harpy Farm by the men who had kept her for a couple of weeks and finally gotten tired of brutalizing her. She would have stayed in the special camp the Harpies had set aside for ex-hets if the Chief had not started looking for a partner there. Raven was the most presentable, the most assimilatable, of that whole bad lot. That was important because the Chief's lover was traditionally also the High Priestess.

Raven's predecessor, White Owl, had left Harpy Farm to live with someone from another settlement, Snake River. That had been a major scandal. Harpy Farm had been without a priestess for nearly a year. Then White Owl and her new lover came back to Harpy Farm during one of the holyday festivals, when any country dyke who had an itch to travel visited other women's land. The Chief had accidentally killed her rival during a wrestling match. White Owl had cursed her and everyone on the farm and placed all of them under blood guilt. Harpy Farm was still paying reparations to Snake River. The old women on the council, much displeased by the red ink in their ledgers, sent the Chief off to fast, dance, sit in a sweat-lodge, and dream her way out of this dilemma. There were several broad hints made that it might be time for her to see a vision of her successor. Instead, she came back with this crazy story that the Goddess wanted her to find a lover who lived in a tipi. The only women on Harpy Farm who still lived outside in tents were the ex-hets and the passing women. And the very notion of Chief with a butch was apparently too outlandish. Nobody said "another butch" because Harpies didn't condone role-playing. "We're trying to live without men," was what one of them had said to Doc when she had first gotten there and was trying to tell them all how good it felt to be with a bunch of butch women who weren't afraid to fend for themselves.

To everyone's surprise, Raven was seamlessly orthodox. She took up her duties as if she was a lesbian born of lesbians with four lesbian grandmothers. Doc had seen her smother male babies without turning a hair. Well, Raven certainly didn't have any reason to be fond of men. Did anybody?

Doc couldn't do anything about the Harpies offing the little pricks. But she knew that proper technique would reduce the incidence of retardation. It was her personal opinion that if you were going to get knocked up anyway and spend nine months doing an imitation of the Westair blimp you might as well put up with getting fucked for thirty seconds and increase your chances of having a healthy kid, but there was no talking to the Harpies about that. Now on the four holy-days, fertile women reported to the two-room ovulation huts and had Doc, or somebody she had trained, inseminate them. The huts were located near the scarecrone, so technically the men had not set foot on women's land. Most of the male volunteers were farmboys, truckers, soldiers, or bikers. They never saw the women whose children they fathered. They just walked into the dirt-floored room, jerked off into a sterile container, got paid, and left. It amused Doc no end that the Harpies wouldn't even give them a chair to sit down on. She had once pinned a porno centerfold to the wall, to help the poor bastards get it up, and the stink that had caused was unbelievable.

Up ahead, the pavement ended and became hard-packed dirt. Doc slowed down and explained the scarecrone and a few other things about the farm to Fluff.

"They're *all* lesbians?" Fluff demanded, clearly surprised there were that many in the whole world.

"Yep," Doc said. "They sorta prefer to be called dykes, though. Most of 'em never even been with a man. It was their great-grandmas that started this place up. There's a bunch of them all over the country. You oughta be here for a high holyday like Beltane or Samhain. They travel from farm to farm to visit each other, find new girlfriends, swap seeds, sell stuff. Everybody drinks homemade hooch and does mushrooms. There's big bonfires and rituals and dancing around naked. Getting sunburned, eating tons of food. Singing and running races and generally carrying on. It's a hoot."

"They think they're witches, don't they?"

"Yeah."

Fluff laughed. "You believe all that shit?"

"You think you know everything there is to know about why stuff happens?"

Fluff made a noise through her nose that sounded like a horse blowing out trail dust.

"You can think whatever you want about Harpy Farm and the Harpies," Doc said, "but if anybody can give you asylum from those Harley boys, honey, they are it. So just keep your snotty attitude to yourself, and let me do the talking, or we'll find ourselves in the swamp up to our necks in quicksand and alligator shit, trying to talk Prez into throwing us a rope."

Doc braked the bike. There was a tipi pitched near the road, and a woman with a shotgun stood just outside it. The mostly collie mutt beside her pricked up its ears and wagged its long, matted tail. The sentry kept the muzzle of her gun trained on them as she walked within earshot. As she came closer, Fluff got confused. This person had a beard, and was chewing something — tobacco? Was Doc wrong? Had men taken over the farm? Then she noticed that Doc's shoulders were down, relaxed, and she was talking to the sentry in a warm, bantering tone of voice that was completely different from the convivial but cool tones she used with men.

"Hey, Wally, keepin' your powder dry?" Doc asked.

Wally blew a large pink bubble, popped it, sucked all the gum back into her mouth, turned the wad over and chomped it with gusto. "My powder, my pussy. Raven does her best to keep us all pretty dry," she said. "The only thing around here that's wet and running free is the irrigation ditches."

"Trouble in paradise?" Doc asked.

Wally shrugged. "Old women say it was bound to happen when the Chief had that vision, and went looking for her life-mate in the tents of the ex-hets. It was such a terrible penance that everybody knows White Owl will have to lift her curse sometime soon, but it still didn't make the High Council have multiple orgasms."

"Wrong side of the tracks," Doc nodded. "Can't trust those ex-hets, you know. Gonna tempt the young 'uns away with tales about the wicked outside world."

"Yeah, all those titillating stories about the delights of being a battered wife," Wally said. "Pure pornography. Oughta keep it in town where it belongs."

"Or the conception cabins," Doc snickered. Wally snorted, and they shared a private joke.

"Too bad the charter says they gotta take in any female refugees who cross the boundary and ask for help," Wally said piously.

"Well, they gotta let them in, but there's nothing says they have to live in the big house like white folks," Doc murmured.

"Right-oh," Wally said. "You here with us for a while, Doc?"

"Well, I happen to be double-packing a refugee, myself."

Wally came closer and stared at Fluff, who stared back in horrified fascination. She had never seen a woman with so much facial hair. Doc's little blonde mustache did not compare.

"What's the matter, honey, you don't like my face? Or you want to sit on it before we've even been properly introduced?"

"Don't call her honey," Doc said automatically. "This is Fluff. Formerly the property of the Prez, Alamo Chapter of the Angels."

"Who are no doubt headed our way, ready to kick ass," Wally said sadly. "Doc, the Chief ain't going to like this. And Raven will want to hang you from the highest tree on the highest hill she can find on Harpy Farm."

A truck rumbled by them, lurching around the potholes which its feeble headlights barely picked out in the dirt road. The back was loaded down with big metal canisters. It smelled awful. Luckily, Wally waved it through, so it didn't even slow down.

"So you gonna try to sleep in the raven's nest, or do you want to bed down with us passing women? You know why they call us passing women here on Harpy Farm, right? It's because they'd like us all to pass away. But we're here to stay. That joke was for you, Fluff. Aw, don't laugh like that, it sounds like you've got internal injuries. This big girl been rearranging your insides?"

"Actually, she gives a good tune-up," Doc responded, before Fluff could say something hasty. Instead, she tucked her face into Doc's shoulderblades and shook with suppressed laughter.

Wally raised an eyebrow. "Well, it's about time. You been running on empty since Mahalia died."

"Stuff it, Wally."

"Sorry. I truly am sorry. Don't pay any attention to me, I'm just a butch old thing in charge of shooting lost farmboys and making the honey wagons run on time."

"So that's working out, huh?"

"Shit, yes, Doc. You were right about that too. Three-quarters of the farms around here don't have indoor plumbing that works anymore. They all got outhouses now. The locals are so glad to find somebody to clean their privies and haul the muck away, they pay us to do it, and we cart it up here, put it through the ponds, and use it on the fields. Cuts way down on the amount of chemical fertilizer we need, which was getting damned hard to find, anyway."

"And the High Council, Instrument of y'all's Collective Consciousness, can't hardly pitch any of you out for being ex-women or women-to-be when you are running such a vital and profitable and dirty part of Harpy Farm's economy."

"You got it, Doc."

"Aces."

They gave each other a thumb's up.

"So," Doc said, "I think I'll mosey on up to the big house and get the fireworks display started, ruin everybody's appetite for dinner. See if you can't let the friendlies know I'm here, huh? I could always use a little support from the sidelines. And if you got a place where I could bunk with my, uh—"

"Your mechanic," Wally said gravely.

"Yeah, my mechanic here, that would be right neighborly of you."

"Sure. We'll tuck you in. What's left of you. Look after your widow, too, Doc."

"You're a sport, Wally."

"Don't mention it, Doc."

This exchange, what she understood of it, filled Fluff with trepidation. She wanted to sit someplace quiet, with her legs together, and feel safe. She wasn't ready to face a crowd of strangers and argue for her right to take shelter among them, especially if all of them were going to have beards. There was no reason why these women should do her any favors. But there was no place else to go. She renewed her grip on Doc and tried to remember what Doc's face looked like, what she looked like without her clothes on. Those memories would not come into focus. But other memories would. Prez, his fist clenched, bending his elbow, pumping up his arm. Prez asking her, "When are you going to let me do you?" and not really meaning it, because no junkie likes to share his dope. But every time she punished him, hurt him, tortured him, pierced him and reached for his heart, she could feel the bile accreting in his muscles, in his soul, and knew it was only a matter of time before he turned on her and pretended he was entitled to take revenge.

I have no choice, she thought, and after that wished only to go to sleep.

6.

After the coffee and cornbread got distributed and everybody else broke down into groups or couples, to fight or to kiss and make up, Tina, Carmen, Josie, and Paint gathered Prez, Anderson, Michaels, Campbell, and the other officers of the club off to one side and said their piece. Actually, Tina said it. The other three women fell silent in the presence of the men they had locked out. Prez found himself watching Anderson's old lady — the way her hips moved unconsciously as her hands shaped the air. She had a nice mouth, too. But it was thin and muscular. It should be more relaxed — more swollen.

Anderson was distracted and didn't notice Prez's narrowed eyes or where they were focused. When he had seen Michaels, he automatically tried to drop his hand on his friend's shoulder. But the shorter man had moved away and cuffed at him. He had to go after him, grab him by the neck and half-wrestle him back into the circle. "Don't you want to hear what these rabid bitches have to say?" he kidded, then hissed, "What the fuck is the matter with you, anyway?"

Michaels felt like a block of concrete. By a visible effort, he made his body relax. "Nothin', man," he smiled. "What would you fucking do if you saw something as ugly as you comin' at yourself?"

Anderson forced himself to laugh. "That better be a compliment, you motherfucker," he said.

"Would you rather I said you were pretty?" Michaels said straight back, with no smile at all on his face.

"Hey," Anderson replied without thinking, "tell it like it is. If I look that good to you by all means let me know."

"I don't know, seems to me maybe somebody else looks that good to you," Michaels said to his boots. Then he moved to the other side of the circle, putting several men between them.

Now Anderson watched him and whistled while equal parts of rage and amusement tore around inside his head. Green-eyed monster has got you by the butt, Michaels, he thought. Only question is, which one of us are you crying yourself to sleep over? This could be a very interesting winter.

Tina's skirt had pulled up, and Prez saw the Ka-Bar on her thigh. Tina usually wore jeans, like all the other girls. Maybe she had decided to dress up today to make her big speech. Prez licked his upper lip, scratched the inside of his left arm. Tina caught him staring at her legs and flicked the hem of her dress down. She gave him a dirty look. "You haven't heard a word I've said," she snapped.

Josie shook her head, and Paint groaned. That was not the right tone to take with Prez. Carmen moved a little closer, protectively, toward Tina, and her fists were clenched.

"Sure I have," he said lazily. "You all felt like having a little pajama party, and when you got together and there was nobody but yourselves to talk to you felt so big and bad you thought you could tell me what to do. I'm not going to give you the back of my hand, Tina, because I think you are ridiculous. Nobody tells me what to do. My own officers don't tell me what to do. I'm sure Anderson has his reasons for letting you get so full of yourself. But he had better take a hint and keep you in line from now on. And if you ever try to pull this shit again, you brassy little cunt, I'll have to take matters into my own hands. Now get your asses out of here. Bitches do what they are told. If you don't know that by now, there's a lot of good men here who can show you why."

Paint said, "Prez, all the women voted to do this. Don't single Tina out."

The look he turned on her was like venom shot from the mouth of a pit viper. "Oh, don't worry, I've got all of you down in my little black book," he said. "Get out of my face. Now!"

They scattered. He noticed that Josie had put her hand on Carmen's arm and was gripping it hard enough to make the skin white around her fingers. So Carmen had been about to talk back to him as well. Of the four, only Josie had had the sense to keep her lip zipped. But Josie might as well be dead. There was a proverb in there somewhere. The only good bitch...

To his pique, dismissing the women was not the end of it. His officers were still standing there, looking at him as if they expected him to say or do something else. "What the fuck are you staring at?" he barked at Campbell.

"Christ, get off the rag," Campbell barked back. Josie hadn't braided his hair yet, and it hung almost to his knees. "I want to know what you really think about what we just heard."

"What do you mean, what do I really think? Since when do I have to ask the bitches' permission to go after somebody who has ripped us off?"

"What do you mean, *us*, white man?" Michaels said. His olive face was flushed. He actually seemed pissed off! "This is a personal matter that you have made club business, Prez. You got us all going after somebody who ripped you off. Nobody here wants his woman taking over his life. My old lady talks way too much about things she don't understand, and when I get tired of her running her mouth, I shut her up. But if you teach a hundred monkeys to type, one of them will write the maintenance manual for a softtail. Every now and then the bitch has a point. If I don't listen then, who's being stupid?"

"So I'm supposed to just let this go?" Prez said. "Let Doc take my old lady? How long are any of you going to back me if I start sending thank-you notes to my enemies?"

"Fluff wasn't your old lady, was she?" Anderson asked, talking in his usual slow, deliberate way. "I don't care about her being a kid, if they're old enough to fuck they're old enough to get hitched. But you never put your mark on her. Never said to the rest of us, hands off. You never kept a woman before."

"And how do you know what she told Doc?" Campbell asked. "Fluff wasn't around last time Doc rode with us a ways. Maybe she thought she was just picking up a hitchhiker, giving some scooter gypsy a ride to the next town."

"Nobody is asking you to forget this," Michaels chimed in. "Obviously the situation has to be made clear. Reparations are in order. But if Doc is willing to admit that a mistake was made and apologize, try to shake her down for a better deal. Make her give the bitch back or take a smaller cut in the biz. I don't see how she could turn it down. She doesn't want a war with us."

"And we don't want one with her?" Prez said bitterly. "One dyke has us all by the short hairs, is that how you see it, men?"

"Said yourself she was the closest thing you could be to one of us without puttin' on colors," Mendoza said. He had been hanging around on the edges of their powwow, ignoring baleful looks from the officers and staying just out of the range of Prez's right arm.

"I'm going to kill you," Prez said simply, and went for Mendoza's throat. It took a while for Campbell and Michaels to go in after him. And it looked like they hadn't actually decided that they should stop him, just slow him down a little. Anderson and the others just watched and laughed.

Paint reached the group clustered around what was left of breakfast, and grabbed Desiree. She shoved four pieces of cornbread in her face. "Hurry up and eat this," she ordered, then started eating herself and guzzling coffee as fast as she could. She had heard the argument brewing as she walked away with Tina, Carmen, and Josie. Now she heard Mendoza shouting, "You crazy fucker!" as Michaels pried Prez's fingers from his windpipe. Between the two of them, Campbell and Michaels couldn't get Prez completely off the man.

"There's not enough sex and too much violence around here," she told Desiree. "You want to stay for the free-for-all? It's ugly and fucked up now, but it's going to get worse. You got somebody to look after you?"

"Hell, no," Desiree said. "Nobody's going to take care of me."

"I will," Paint said. "I haven't had me a girl on my back pegs for a long time. Want to be an apprenti, honey? Show you how to be a big, bad biker lady when you grow up."

Desiree threw her head back and laughed. There were bruises on one side of her white throat.

Campbell and Michaels had lifted Prez off Mendoza. Now they let him go. Prez went after him again. They caught him, Michaels talked to him, Prez nodded, they let him go, and he was on Mendoza in a flash. "Get him the fuck out of here," Michaels shouted, and some of the other bikers got Mendoza up and started walking him out of the barn. Prez rested in Michaels's arms. The smaller man's head came up to his shoulder. Both of them were panting and soaking wet. There was a little froth at one corner of Prez's mouth. Campbell was in front of him, talking slowly and softly. Prez laughed, nodded, said, "I'm cool, I'm cool." He twisted out of Michaels's grasp, put one hand on Campbell's hip, and slid around him. Then he was running to the wall and taking something down. It was the scythe that Mendoza had sharpened last night, while everyone was sitting around talking. He had cleaned it up so carefully that there wasn't a trace of rust on the blade, and its edge was hair-fine.

Prez took off after Mendoza, and swung his weapon so hard that he turned himself completely around. Mendoza's head landed right at his feet. The noise it made coming off was unforgettable — a wet ripping thump. The exposed neck briefly showed bone — the yellow column of the severed spine —

before everything, neck and torso, was covered in blood. One of the bikers who had been helping Mendoza heard Prez coming and hit the dirt, but the other man was down on one knee with blood spurting from the truncated roots of his fingers. He hadn't even cried out, he was just staring with horrified fascination at the miniature fountains of his own blood and the little pieces of himself lying on the straw. Mendoza's body toppled over, still spurting blood. It landed on the uninjured biker, and the rest of the blood in the body spilled over him. He pushed at it but could not bring himself to touch it, made retching noises, and finally kicked himself away from the body. The heels of his boots dug up little mounds of straw and dirt. But he could not get far enough away to escape the death-smell of blood and shit; it made the hair on the back of his neck and his arms stand up, and curled his upper lip back to show his teeth.

Desiree had never seen anything quite like it. It certainly was the kind of thing that told a girl she should make up her mind pretty damn quick. "Well," she said, "I'm sure not going to stick around here and apply direct pressure to *that* wound. Let's git."

Prez was laughing and wiping blood out of his eyes. He was covered with gore. The muscles in his arms were pumped, bulging with his own blood, living blood, and he punched at the ceiling again and again. "Got you," he crowed. "Bleed on me, you dead pig. If you weren't dead already I'd fuck you." The injured biker was digging around, trying to pick up his severed fingers with his whole hand. Prez kicked him. "Leave them in the cow shit," he said. "You dumb fucker, you came between us. Be glad you didn't lose anything bigger than your goddamned fingers. The only person who'll miss them is your sow-faced, cow-titted, shit-encrusted twat of an old lady." The man kept scrabbling in the dirt, and Prez stepped on his injured hand and ground his heel into it. As he came off it, the man on his knees screamed, and Prez kicked him again, this time in the mouth. Then he kicked Mendoza's head into the thickest part of the crowd. It landed at Tina's feet. The open eyes were smeared with filth from the floor of the barn, and it wore an inappropriate snarl. Mendoza had died knowing Prez was coming for him and hating him, for all the good it did him.

"Here's a present for you, sweetheart," Prez crooned. "Just so you know I don't hold any grudges. Wanna play football? Touch football? Or should we play with full body contact? Wanna tackle me?"

He was walking toward her, and Tina was backing up, shaking her head, looking everywhere for Anderson. She wanted to throw up, but she couldn't stop, couldn't take the time to be sick now. And her eyes wouldn't focus — she could not see the door. Or Anderson. She just kept staggering backwards and bumping into people who pushed her away, and the only thing she could see was the cow manure in Mendoza's bloody hair, his twisted, furious, dead lips.

Anderson couldn't have cared less what happened to Tina just then. He was behind Prez, staring in fascination at the blood-soaked dirt floor. His dick was so hard it hurt. If it got any bigger it was going to split open like an overcooked hotdog.

Prez tripped over Mendoza's body before he could get to Tina, so he kicked it. And then he could not stop kicking it. The steel toes of his boots crushed tissue, broke ribs. It was bizarre to see the vicious kicks and hear their impact, but not hear anybody screaming as each one landed. Anderson's body jerked every time Prez's boot made contact with the corpse. Michaels came up behind him and grabbed him just above the elbows. "Coming in your pants?" Michaels asked, and the two men laughed in each other's faces. Michaels barked, and Anderson howled back. They hugged each other, grabbed somebody else, and made him howl too. It spread until the barn sounded like it had been invaded by a wolf-pack on a chicken hunt.

Paint and Desiree had brushed the crumbs off their clothes and left the barn. "We'll have to stop and pick up my gear," Paint groused.

"Oh, it's already on your bike," Desiree told her cheerfully. "I was, uh, kinda hoping maybe you would give me a ride. I mean, I was going to ask you, later. If you would pack me around today. It's cold in the back of that truck."

Paint threw an arm around her. "And I'm a little better company than watching Tina and Carmen through the back window, right?"

"Yeah, you are."

They were outside, where the bikes were parked. "Especially now," Paint said, frowning. She swung onto her Harley. "I wouldn't want to be in those girls' company now for all the weed on Harpy Farm. Which is where we're headed. And then who knows?"

They were long gone by the time Tina found the barn door and stumbled out, just a dozen steps ahead of the Prez. His bloody T-shirt was already drying in spots and sticking to his chest. The wet toes of his boots had picked up crusts of dirt. Tina ran to the truck, dug for her keys, and sobbed with dismay when she realized she was wearing a skirt, with no pockets for her keys. She slammed her fists into the door of the truck, dragged on the handle. Locked. It was locked. All of her stuff was still in the farmhouse. Without thinking, she turned and ran toward it.

Prez loped after her, not even breathing hard. He didn't want to catch her until she was inside. Nobody would be there — everyone was back in the barn. And he knew, he just *knew*, that nobody would interrupt them until he'd had time to get a little of his own back.

7.

S teady," Doc said over her shoulder. Fluff nodded, but her hands still shook uncontrollably against Doc's ribs. "You cold or scared?" Doc asked.

"Bit of both," Fluff replied honestly.

"Well, the least I can get us is a place out of the wind tonight. But it won't hurt if you look like somebody's been chasing you with an ax. I know it's out of character, but try to arouse these girls' protective instincts, okay?"

"I don't know where you got the idea that I'm such a hard case," Fluff said.

"Honey, anybody who could survive a night alone with the Prez, let alone keep that bastard entertained for several weeks on end, has got to be a hard case. I expect great things of you, Fluff. If you live long enough you'll probably be toppling nations instead of a fat old woman on a riceburner."

That made Fluff laugh. They were passing the duck pond, and all the birds woke up and started to gabble. "These craters are compliments of the U.S. Army," Doc said. "Congress got the military involved in the war on drugs, you know, so every now and then the boys from the nearest base would send a chopper over here to strafe the dykes. We got a little pissed when they started making holes in our land. But the fish and the ducks like 'em."

"How'd you stop them?" Fluff asked.

"Bless you, child, for assuming we could stop 'em," Doc said. "Seems that some sniper got the last chopper. Took out the tail rotor."

"Does modesty forbid you telling me who did that fancy piece of shooting?" Fluff giggled.

"No, but we just ran out of time. Got to cut to a commercial. Get ready to look wan and helpless."

Doc pulled up in front of the biggest house Fluff had ever seen. Actually, it looked something like a train. Because it wasn't so much a house as it was a series of rooms that had been built right next to one another. In some places it was two stories tall, in others one or three. The staircase was on the outside of the part that went up three floors. A banner hung from one second-story balcony. The wind lifted it and straightened it out enough for Fluff to see that it carried appliqued figures of two winged women, facing each other with clawed feet uplifted. One of them held something in her foot. She could not tell what it was. Atop the house, several chimneys made out of field-rock or brick were pouring out smoke. The smell of cooking food made Fluff's mouth fill with cold, thick water.

Women were coming out of screen doors, doors made out of heavy planks, steel bars that had been welded together to form a door, and a door or two that were really just heavy drapes of quilted fabric or leather. Dogs came prancing around the building, barking at the sight of such a crowd. Faces appeared at a few glass windows. Most of the windows were made out of several layers of plastic, and it was too dark for Fluff to see through them. Some of the women who came outside lit torches and stuck them into tall metal pipes that had been driven into the ground. The last women who came out of the house came down the outside staircase, and they all had long gray or white hair. One was carrying a small drum. Another carried a rattle. All the rest of the crones were walking with long staffs, topped with carved figures, clusters of feathers, bells, and ribbons. The old women all wore black or purple.

Fluff's stomach turned over like a pancake. These women did not look like Doc — or Wally. They looked like gypsy Indians. Almost all of them wore homemade skirts and had long hair that was tied back with bandanas or headbands. Only about a quarter of them had simple short haircuts, or were shaved down to the scalp. Here and there were leather pants or jeans. Almost everybody wore sturdy laced-up boots and long, colorful, padded vests with harpies appliqued or embroidered on the front panels or the back.

Fluff made herself look at faces, pay attention to what they were saying. There were lots of smiles, women calling out greetings. This was not a mob. Most of these women knew Doc, and many were her friends. Still, it was odd that nobody approached them. It was almost as if these women already knew why she and Doc were there.

The old women stayed on the stairs, above the crowd. There was music from the drum and rattle, and everyone gradually became quiet. One of the elders banged her staff on the stairs. "You bring the smell of trouble onto our land," she shouted at Doc. "Before we break bread with you and make you our guest, you must tell us what this trouble is."

"Haven't I broken bread with you many, many times?" Doc asked. "Haven't I been told I am always welcome at your table? I am more than a guest. Because some of what is on your table is the fruit of my labor, Aspen."

"It's true," someone in the crowd said, and there were soft cries of, "What she says is so."

The gray-haired speaker's mouth tightened. "You are more than a guest, but less than a daughter," she said. "You have not labored here for love, or for a permanent place among us. We have always repaid you well for your energy. What I seek to know now is the cost of whatever trouble you have brought us. I want to know the price for our hospitality."

"Yes, that's fair," the crowd echoed. "Doc, what's wrong? Tell us!"

Then a single voice soared up, and other women moved away so that Doc could see who the speaker was. It was a beautiful voice that carried well. That alone was enough to make the Council hate her guts, Doc thought. Raven had short black hair that she combed back from her face in two stiff wings. She outlined her eyes and lips with black, and despite her youth, she wore a tiered black-and-purple skirt, and her vest was black velvet. Her belt was a plain piece of rope, tied in a noose. Instead of a staff or a musical instrument, she carried a fly whisk made from scarlet-dyed horsehair. The handle was silver-banded ebony. As she talked, she swished it from side to side, beating her own shoulders.

"Who do you travel with, Doc?" Raven asked sweetly. "I will wager this, that the tale of that child is the tale we are all waiting for."

"You speak the truth, Raven," Doc began.

"Then tell us the rest," Raven interrupted. "You came before our evening meal. I am sure all of us would rather be inside where it's warm, taking a well-deserved rest, and listening to stories with much more pleasant endings."

"I would not dream of talking while you give us the benefit of your wisdom, Raven," Doc said sarcastically, and there were muffled giggles from the crowd. Even two of the crones were smiling. The High Priestess glared. Fluff bit her lip. She had thought that Raven was a potential ally until the High Priestess started talking to Doc as if she were four years old. This diminutive Harpy was arbitrary and touchy. Fluff hoped Doc would be careful — but then thought that when you are dealing with that much arrogance, being careful usually doesn't do you any good at all.

Then Doc surprised the shit out of her. "Every woman has to speak for herself," she said, drawing approving murmurs from the crowd. "This is Fluff's story. So she should tell it." She hissed, "Get down so they can see you, and talk to them, honey."

Fluff slid one foot off the peg, gasped with pain as she got her other leg out from around Doc, and half-fell to the ground. She gave Doc a bitter look, but the big biker was examining her nails.

"I — I don't know where to start," she said.

Nobody gave her any suggestions. But the women's faces (most of them, anyway) were open and relaxed. A few even smiled encouragingly. As she stood, rocking from foot to foot, there was movement in the crowd. Smaller women — children — were coming forward, arranging themselves in front of their mothers.

One of the older girls left the side of a large woman with short, salt-and-pepper hair, a woman who wore fringed buckskin pants and a vest, and had feathers in her hair. Her daughter was dressed exactly like her, down to the beaded armbands tied about her biceps and the blue spirals tattooed upon her breasts. The older woman nodded with approval as her daughter walked over to Fluff, took one of the feathers from behind her ear, and put it into Fluff's hand.

"I have heard it is otherwise elsewhere," the girl said. "But here we all have an equal voice, and I will stand here to make sure no one tries to stop you from having your say."

Doc smirked behind one hand, pretending to itch her nose. Leaping Salmon and Fluff made a cute couple in their butch-femme deerskin outfits. Like mother like daughter. The Chief's daughter had apparently taken quite a shine to Doc's girl. Raven wouldn't like that, either.

Fluff realized that she had to start talking even if she didn't have her thoughts properly organized. She had their attention now, and it was better to sound muddled and confused and honestly terrified than try to be glib and persuasive.

"This is all my fault," she said. "None of this was Doc's idea." As she said that, a weight seemed to come off her shoulders. She realized just how bad she had been feeling about putting Doc in this awful situation. At least she could take responsibility for doing it. "All Doc did was come do some business and party with these bikers. But they're not just any bikers. They're Angels, Alamo Chapter. And I asked her to take me with her when she left. She didn't know that it would make any trouble. So I guess I lied to her. At least, I didn't warn her. And I'm sorry for that. Maybe someday I'll get a chance to make up for that. But I had to get away. I never wanted to be with them anyway. And the one that was keeping me there, he was awful. Everybody felt sorry for me, the women did anyway, but nobody would do anything about it because he was the Prez, the head baboon, you know? I mean after a while I thought that it would have been better to belong to everybody in the club, the way he kept threatening he would do, turn me over to all of them, but I think he just liked to talk about it, describe how it would be, having all of them rape me, to get himself excited before he — made me do things to him."

As Fluff talked, one by one the other teenagers and girl-children came to stand behind or to the side of her. The Chief was staring at the ground and nodding, nodding in time to Fluff's speech. The old women had composed themselves, standing like a flock of crows, waiting for the water that had been stirred up and muddied here to settle. Raven was wringing her hands, staring at Fluff, while her black-rimmed eyes seemed to get bigger and her face even more pale.

"How did you come to fall among such evil men, child?" she asked in her musical voice. The tone was cloyingly sympathetic, but the implication that Fluff must have fucked up to get herself into so much trouble was plain. Fluff shook. She had no idea what their notions of right and wrong must be. Maybe they thought every woman who wasn't born here was sub-human, a natural victim. Better just tell the bare minimum truth and hope it would not offend.

"I was trying to get to the west coast," Fluff said. "I left home, that's Atlanta, because there was too much trouble. My mama is a drunk and she always has these bad news boyfriends. I got tired of her fighting with them and them beating up on her or hitting on me. But she kept trying to make me come back. She couldn't take care of me but she wouldn't let me go. So me and a friend, actually just this girl I worked with, we had caught a ride to California. She got sweet on the driver and I guess she was afraid he would start to like me too much, so she told him some bullshit story and they left me. I hitched my way out here and was trying to get south when the Angels found me by the freeway and chased me down until they caught me. They made me run for a long time, I thought one of them would run over me. They ripped all my clothes off. Picked me up by one hand, my hair, dragged me, threw me around. I thought I was lucky when one of them put a stop to the general hilarity and put me on the back of his bike. But like I said it might have been better to take all of them on. Maybe then they would have just fucked me and left me. Because once Prez got me he hardly ever let me out of his sight, and the things—"

If Raven doesn't stop doing that to her hands, Doc thought, she's gonna tear them off. She's about to see a vision or have a fit. Some of the children were crying. Then Raven's voice pealed, "Tell us what he made you do. You do not have to keep his secrets. There is healing in sharing such pain." Yeah, Doc thought, and I hope your thighs heal up quick after you get done rubbing them together over this child's awful history.

"He liked to be hurt. Only it made him angry. Like it was my fault that all these sick things got him hard. So he liked to be tied up with really skinny cord or wire, and have me burn him or cut him. He didn't like to be hit too much, he said it made too much noise, but I could bite him or stick needles in his dick. He made me suck him off while I shoved my fist up his ass. He wanted me to strangle him."

Only Doc heard the note of grim satisfaction in this speech. I am sure Prez will never know just how motivated you were to gratify his "sick" impulses, Doc thought. You were probably just pissed off that the whole thing was his idea, you sadistic little bitch, you light of my life, you.

"Stop!" one of the crones cried. "We all know that in the patriarchy women do not defend one another, not even their own children, and we all know that men are dangerous, diseased, sick, violent animals. But the children of Harpy Farm do not need to ride the nightmare tonight. We have heard enough to make a decision. If we hear any more of this it will bring our spirits down, and we need to have strong hearts if we are going to face this storm."

Doc saw Raven's lips move. Was she repeating the words "strangle him"? She took a closer look, saw Raven's belt, and shook her head. The Chief must have paid off her blood-guilt long ago if she had put herself into this one's hands. Then the Chief — for the first time — opened her own mouth, and it startled Doc so, she almost jumped off the Medusa.

"It is the duty of the Council to give us the benefit of their experience," the woman in buckskin said. "And the High Priestess reminds us of our duty to the Goddess, and helps us interpret Her will. But it is my duty to gather all of the people together between my hands and speak for them. And it is my belief that the women gathered here want to take Doc and Fluff in and protect them from their enemies, if the Goddess will give us the means to keep them safe."

"The borders of Harpy Farm are too wide," one of the crones protested. "We cannot keep these men off our land. Not forever. And they might make common cause with other men and bring them against us as well. This may cost many lives. Why should Harpies shed their blood for the sake of this stranger?"

There were howls of outrage from the darkness behind her, and this time Doc did jump off the Medusa. Every ex-het and passing woman on the land must be out there, just beyond the range of the torches.

"Sanctuary!" they were shouting. "This land is sanctuary!" And Raven was screaming, "Would you give this child back to the men who kidnapped and raped her?"

Then Wally was walking into the torchlight, with three other bulldaggers, all of them carrying shotguns. "This year I lost two of my sentinels," she shouted. "Two brave women who weren't born here. I don't think most of you ever even knew Lou and Andy's names. Both of them gut-shot and dead to keep intruders off *your* land. What did they die for, Aspen? And what exactly do you propose to do with Doc and Fluff — tie them up and hand them over like sacrificial hens? I think I speak for the whole patrol when I say that if you don't take on this fight and finish it, we'll lay down our guns and turn our backs the next time a drunk gang of truck drivers thinks it would be fun to burn your house down. If these Harley boys can come onto women's land and take Fluff and Doc off it, what's to stop them from coming after your daughters next?"

Left unspoken, Doc thought, was the threat that some of the less privileged residents might take it into *their* heads to burn the big house down.

The elders were looking at each other, shaking their heads. One was arguing fiercely with the others, even brandishing her fist. The Chief decided that this had gone on long enough.

"All who favor giving sanctuary, raise your hands," she said.

There was a sea of waving arms in the air.

"Council?"

One of the younger elders nudged the oldest woman present and whispered in her ear. She shook herself. Her frail voice could barely be heard. "The Council, as always, is bound by the will of all present. We will not block consensus. But we register a protest. Some of us feel this is not the wisest course."

That is, Doc thought sourly, exactly the same response I have heard you constipated senior citizens make every single time an important decision gets made around here. What the High Council needs is a high colonic.

"Thank you," the Chief said. "The High Priestess and I will confer with you privately later, to obtain your guidance. Doc, how long do you think it will take these motherfuckers to show?"

"Sometime tomorrow is my best guess," she shouted. "But I'd double the watch tonight."

"The Maidens claim this duty," the Chief's daughter, Leaping Salmon, said. "Wally, we'll find extra bodies for all your shifts."

"I'll stand a watch," Doc said.

"Bullshit," Wally retorted. "You can barely stand up. Wouldn't it be just peachy if the Angels torched our fields while you snored peacefully by the side of the road? Go inside and let them feed you. By the time you're done with dinner, I'll send somebody with a lantern to fetch you down to our camp and get you bedded down."

Doc clapped her hand on Wally's shoulder. "Thank you, buck, I really am done in."

"Well, I'm sure you'll get a lot of rest sleeping with your mechanic," Wally said, popping her gum. "I know I would."

"Excuse me," Doc said. The Chief's daughter was lifting Fluff's hand to her lips. "I'm grateful as all hell for your help, Leaping Salmon, but you can skip the gallantry."

"You are rude," Fluff hissed.

"I'm tired and hungry, crashing off of about a week on speed. I need a lot of protein and carbohydrates, a stiff drink and a quick fuck and about sixteen hours of sleep. I'm just too cranky to stand around waiting for you to get your hand kissed. So you are coming with me right now, hellcat honey." Doc picked Fluff up and carried her, giggling and screaming, toward the house.

"Don't feel bad, kid," Wally said. "You're going to grow at least another foot before you're done. Probably be able to throw Doc over your shoulder then."

"What for?" Leaping Salmon spat.

"Oh, boy, do you have a lot to learn," Wally sighed. "C'mon, let's eat, and set up some schedules. No telling how long we're going to have to keep this up."

"Don't call me a boy."

"Don't act like one."

They went off in the dark toward Wally's campfire, arguing loudly. Only when they were out of earshot of the big house and far from the torchlight did they start holding hands.

"But, Daddy," Leaping Salmon said, "I thought you wanted me to be your boy."

8.

Tina threw the door open so hard it bounced off the side of the house and hit her across the backside. She collided with the kitchen table, fell across its smooth surface, and lay there gasping. Then someone touched her on the back of her neck, and she screamed.

"Did you change your mind about keeping me out of here?" Prez said. His own laughter felt soft inside his throat, made it feel almost as good as Anderson's eight inches.

"Don't touch me!" she cried.

"But I already have touched you," he said lazily. "We've been a lot closer than this, in fact. Did you forget?" He lifted her by the arms and smashed her into the table. "Bitch, I should never have turned you loose. Fucking bitch. Forget your place. Try to tell me what to do. Troublemaking slut. You know, Tina, I didn't mind knowing I wasn't the first man who had you. But I think I might like being the last one. What do you think of that?"

He lifted her, turned her around, and slapped her with the front and then the back of his hand. "Answer me! Answer me!"

She said nothing sensible, just threw her head back and wailed. Prez dragged her further into the kitchen, toward the wood-burning stove. The front of it barely felt warm. He kept one hand around Tina's right wrist, opened one of the doors with his other hand, and threw several pieces of kindling onto the coals. As the stove door slammed shut, Tina lunged at him.

Prez had not been expecting an attack, but he responded quickly, dragging her to him, spinning her around, and wrapping one arm around her neck. While he cut her air off slowly, slowly, he bent her toward the floor. As she passed out, he let her go, and pulled the knife out of the sheath on her thigh. Tina came to just in time to see him lay it on one of the iron burner covers.

"Give it up, Tina," he said. "You are a slow learner. I'm going to do whatever I want to you, and I won't even have to tie you up to do it. I'm stronger than you are, bitch. And a lot more evil. You can't stop what's gonna happen or change any of it, but you can make it easier on yourself. Just let me hurt you. Let me do some damage. Get my way. I'm gonna take it anyway. But there'll be a little less blood if you don't make me angry. Believe me, Tina, I'm not angry right now. No. I even think I might like you a little. I don't even think I'd mind if you enjoyed some of this. Of course, that might be a little hard for you, learning how to play my game. But if you'd had a knack for my little ways, Tina, I wouldn't have had to dump you on Anderson."

He nudged her with the bloody toe of his boot, turned just enough to reach the knife and take it off the stove. "I know you're awake now. Get up on your knees. Take my dick out and kiss it like you love me. Or by God—" He reached out and touched the very tip of the hot knife to her face. "You won't even want to kiss your own reflection in the mirror."

She winced away from the glowing point. It left a tiny, livid triangle on her cheek. But she refused to touch him the way he told her to, and beat her fists on his thighs instead of unbuttoning his fly.

"You asked for this, Tina," Prez said, and slashed at her blouse, aiming for the flesh underneath. He got his fist wound in her hair and used it to move her around. Still she fought him, once almost taking out his eye. So he kicked her to the floor and choked her again, choked her until she passed out and had a little fit, her body spasming from the lack of oxygen. When she came to, he had his own dick out and in her face. He smiled at her tenderly and caught her nipple between his thumb and the edge of the blade. "You're bleeding," he crooned. "Please don't make me do this, Tina. I'll hate myself in the morning."

He was jacking himself off, watching the hate war with fear and pain in her face. Her pupils were dilated. She was obviously out of her mind. He pressed in on the nipple, cut into her breast. She shook her head, then seemed to reach some decision. Her mouth opened, and she bent her neck to reach him.

Prez twisted his knife-hand and pinched. Tina screamed so loudly that for a few seconds it made him go deaf. In total silence he watched his own hand pump his load all over her distorted face. "You dumb bitch," he said, "did you think I was stupid enough to let you get your teeth around my dick? No fucking way."

He let her cover the mutilated breast. Blood came up between her fingers. She gathered the rags of her shirt and tried to stuff them into the wound and stop the bleeding.

"What makes you think you're gonna live long enough to heal?" he asked roughly, hauling her hand away. "At least you're not trying to bargain your way out of this, trade a little pussy for an easy ride. But it's not a little pussy, is it, Tina? You're used to taking that big dick of Anderson's, aren't you?" He sucked air between his teeth and relished the look on her face, as she absorbed the familiar tone of his reference to Anderson's tool. "And you've dropped a couple of his pups, huh?" He clicked his tongue. "Bet it's not as tight as I remember."

He put his hand on her bleeding breast and squeezed it until his palm was full of blood. "Doesn't matter. I just came. Won't be able to get it up for another ten or fifteen minutes. But there's no reason why I shouldn't show you a good time despite my limitations. Spread your legs, Tina, or I will cut off your other nipple and make you eat it."

She believed him. Finally, she believed him. She pushed her legs apart, whimpering. Prez found the hole with his middle finger, and it didn't take a whole lot more time for the rest of his hand to follow. Something caught around the base of his thumb and tore. Oh, well. A little more blood would smooth the way. There was lots of soft, spongy tissue inside, strange parts for his fingers to rearrange and hurt. Tina was crying. No tears came out of her eyes, but she was crying anyway. The noise was a weird parody of the sounds bitches made just before they came. Did *he* sound like that when he was getting fucked? Damn. It wasn't going to take him any time at all to get it up again. Well, Anderson had shown him what to do about that.

And damned if Tina didn't find her Ka-Bar, just as he had his free hand busy trying to stuff his joint up where the other hand was trapped. He grabbed for her wrist, but didn't get control of the knife before she had slashed his cheek. Red rage boiled up the back of his neck and fogged his vision. His head was pulsing until he thought it would explode. A little taste of his own blood seeped into one corner of his mouth. He spat it back into her face and broke her wrist. He couldn't understand why he didn't kill her. While he slammed her head back against the floor, slammed it until she went limp and held still, while he cut off her other nipple and put it in his own mouth, while he lifted her by the hand that was buried in her cunt and rammed his aching sexual flesh into her ass, he couldn't figure that out, why he didn't just kill the bitch and have done with it. Why he fucked her instead, cut her and fucked her, made her body thrash in the thin sheet of her own blood that coated half of the kitchen floor. When he came again, the only thing that could have made it better was to cut her throat, and have her blood hit him in the face. So why didn't he do it, why—

His spent dick slipped out of her, he pulled his hand free, and Prez looked up to see Anderson standing in the door of the kitchen. Then he knew why he had left Tina alive. Because the look on Anderson's face was better than any ejaculation. Prez felt as if he had pissed up the very ass of God.

9

After setting up defenses and conferring with everyone who was at all anxious or needed to be told what her job was, the Chief went to the kitchen, grabbed a hunk of bread, some cheese, and a mug of beer. She could hear everyone else at dinner in the big hall, laughing at one of Doc's tall tales, and felt a pang of regret that she was not there to play her role of host and protector, and top Doc's outrageous lies with some of her own. Ever since the Raven had spread her wings over Harpy Farm, there had been precious few opportunities for the Chief to spread her own wings, throw out her chest, and be the proud leader that her mother had been and her daughter was destined to become. It made the cold cheese and dry bread that she gulped on her way to Raven's room stick in her throat. She did not want to go to this meeting, but if Raven listened to what she planned to say, it would be the last time she would ever have to make this frightening journey. Because she had made up her mind that it was over. She would rather leave Harpy Farm as an outcast and murderer than continue to be Raven's penitent.

The High Priestess's room had a real door. Without this barrier to keep sound in, the Chief wondered if she would ever have submitted to the things that Raven did in the name of cleansing, purification, and payment. She hated this place. High priestesses were always weird, if they had any magic at all, but the Chief suspected that some of Raven's visions did not come from the Goddess. This heresy made her feel much more guilty than watching her rival's neck snap on the edge of the wrestling platform.

She stopped and knocked on the door, waited for the soft "Come in." Raven never raised her voice. The Chief winced, remembering how she had been taught to listen for the priestess's faintest subvocalization. Out of respect, she touched her brow and bowed from the waist. "Priestess," she said. "I trust your vigil was successful." Raven had absented herself from Harpy Farm society for a week prior to Doc and Fluff's arrival, fasting at the sweat lodges up in the hills. It was these frequent quests for inspiration that had given the Chief enough breathing time to keep the farm going, heal her ravaged flesh, and regain sufficient self-esteem to keep herself from running away.

"The *Goddess* is always good to me," Raven said. Her emphasis on the divinity made it plain that She succeeded where mortal women failed miserably.

One wall of the room was lined completely with bird wings, severed from the hunters' kills or dead birds the children found. Raven claimed that they did not decompose, but the Chief imagined she smelled decay, nonetheless. Another wall was decorated with shards of broken glass, set in various colored batches of plaster and clay, with the points outermost. A third wall was a collage of magazine pictures of women's faces and nude bodies, torn up and rearranged in any order, spattered with bright red paint and dull brown stains. Iron manacles on short chains had been bolted into the wall. Around the door, which was in the fourth wall, Raven had hung assorted homemade implements, braided out of twine, cut and stitched from leather, or made specially by the farm's blacksmith. They were weapons that would have been useless on anyone who could fight back, tools for harvesting pain. These things had sharp edges, were studded with needles or tacks, had handles that turned long, piercing screws or closed tongs with crushing teeth. Most of them could be heated. The sight of them was enough to make the Chief long for something as simple, as humane, as the long black whip with plain, heavy lashes she had once seen coiled on top of Doc's saddlebags.

The room was lit by hand-dipped candles, a luxury item that Raven wasted shamelessly. The priestess sat on her bed in the midst of constantly moving, overlapping, golden fans of light. Only the Chief knew that her mattress was full of pebbles from the riverbed, and the comforter had been stuffed with thorns. The fact that Raven herself must sleep this way, after she sent the Chief back to her own bed, made the High Priestess even more horrifying to her victim and consort.

The Chief saw what Raven was plaiting out of wire in her small, white hands, the hands that had nails with black polish, and she shook her head no. She even said the word out loud. "No."

Raven raised her head from her work. Considering that inside this room she had never been refused anything before, her face was remarkably tranquil. The priestess laid down the hanging noose she was cinching snug.

"No?" she said. Her voice was gentle. "You know, then."

"Know what?" The speech that she had rehearsed churned below the Chief's diaphragm. But she managed to hold it back. Something strange was going on here. Let the lunatic unfold it.

"The Goddess has said to me, release the Chief of Harpy Farm. There is no stain upon you. But the tents must come down, She says, for all Her children must sleep warm and dry in the coming winter, which will be unusually hard. I will keep your enemies from the gates of Harpy Farm, the Goddess told me, only so long as you know your enemies from your new sisters, and give the stranger the first place at your fire, and feed her before you have fed yourselves."

"And you intend to say this to us all?" the Chief said. "This is your parting gift?"

"Yes," Raven answered. "Tonight. Before everyone leaves the hall. You need never come under my hands again. Because the Goddess has also said to me that I must leave this place. She has prepared a calf for me, a wild bullock that I must fatten for Solstice."

"What will we do for a high priestess?"

Raven shrugged. "That is your affair. But if She spoke to me, surely She will speak to anyone else She has truly chosen."

"So it ends," the Chief said. It seemed ... insufficient. Was this all she had suffered for?

"So it ends," Raven agreed. "Now do you wish to escort me below, so I can share this prophecy with everyone? Or do you wish, perhaps, some parting token of the many happy hours we have spent together?"

The Chief shook her head, retreated a few steps, then came back to give Raven her hand. "I wear enough of your feathers, Raven," she said, touching the scar of a brand.

"Do not hate me," Raven said, taking the hand and hauling upon it to lever herself up and out of bed. The Chief was surprised to see that she really needed help. And she was even more surprised to find herself upset when she saw that Raven had trouble walking to the door. "I have done what I was told to do," the priestess said. "Neither of us had a choice. More blood than yours has been spilled in this room. But you had someone to watch over your ordeals. When the Goddess wishes to be cruel to me, She only tells me what I must do, and then leaves. She knows I will obey her, so She does not even stay to watch."

"I do not think I have ever known anyone like you, Raven," the Chief said, and put a hand around her shoulders to steady her. It was the closest thing to tenderness they had ever shared.

"Pray to the Goddess She does not make many like me," Raven answered, and let herself be led downstairs and into the hall.

"Fire!" somebody shouted outside the farmhouse. It was a masculine voice gone treble with hysteria.

Michaels crowded into the doorway behind Anderson. "Fuck!" he cursed. "We must have used too much kerosene to get the stiff to catch fire." Carmen snorted. She was far more worried about what had happened inside this room than any catastrophe outside. Let the men handle that. The boys could clean up their own goddamn mess for a change.

Michaels needed only a glance at Tina and Prez to know he should try to keep his wife shielded behind him. But she was too quick for him. Anderson also started moving toward the body on the floor. Prez went wide of him and edged out the door. Carmen smelled him as he slunk by — cum, more than one person's blood, and the acrid sweat of insanity. Then she saw what she knew she would see, Tina ruined, not moving. Unlike the man who was still screaming "Fire! Fire!" outside, she did not panic. She shoved both men out of her way — first Michaels, then Anderson — knelt, and picked up as much of her friend as she could. Tina rolled over and folded herself up against Carmen's chest. Blood soaked through Carmen's blouse, sticking them together. Oh, sweet Virgin, Carmen thought, merciful Mary, bless you, bless you, I owe you a candle, I'll make a novena, she is alive, she is alive.

Anderson let her push him, just as he had let Prez ooze out of reach. He should have exploded after him, taken him down, cut his throat. But he had been paralyzed. Compared to that shame, it was a little thing to let a woman shove him around.

Everything around him was dissolving. Anderson had kept his life in dozens of small compartments, and what he did in one tiny cell of that honeycomb with Prez had not troubled him as long as there was another, he had assumed larger and more important room, filled with Tina and his children and the bros he did not fuck, never even thought of fucking. His history, his sexual history, unreeled in front of him like a maze full of mirrors. He saw many, many more images of himself rutting with women than he saw of himself getting blown, butt-fucking, beating men other than Prez. (And why were there so many mirrors showing him simply beating, punching, stabbing, kicking dudes to the ground, trashing their bikes and their enemy colors, in the middle of this movie that was supposed to be about sex — his hard dick spitting in his own fist or somebody else's hole?)

He frantically examined all the acts he had committed with women he had paid or seduced or forced. They were so normal, those acts, even if they were done without pity or permission. Surely they canceled out the strange, isolated things he found himself doing thoughtlessly to a few surprisingly available male bodies. Now something ugly and strange he had kept walled off, corralled, caged was on the loose, wreaking havoc in a place he had tried to keep sunlit and peaceful. He did not know how to cope — what to do. Suddenly the fences were down. His life was all of one piece. The honeycomb, the maze, had been an illusion. He had never had that much control. He had just been a lucky fool. What else could get loose — get mixed up — do damage — show itself to people who had no business knowing what he had done when he was too drunk or angry to be held responsible?

He had frozen, and he was still frozen, knowing he should have reacted quickly to the sight of Prez with Tina's blood on his hands. But the knife — how it had been used — the fact that his own hands had been wet with Prez's blood, soiled with his shit — him doing to Prez what Prez now did to Tina — whose fault was this anyway? The question was like a short in his ignition. He could not get past it, roar into action. He was like a bike up on its center stand with its wheels spinning, useless.

"Get our gear, first bedroom on the left at the top of the stairs," Carmen told Michaels. She unclipped keys from the belt-loop of her jeans and threw them over her shoulder without looking to see where they landed. "Go get the truck warmed up," she ordered Anderson. "And don't you fucking touch her. Where were you when this went down? Damn you. You useless son of a bitch. Don't you fucking try to touch her now."

The two chastened men went soberly to do exactly as she said. Michaels came back from packing up the truck and said, "Can you get her out there by yourself?"

"Tina, honey," Carmen said, "Cristina, querida mia, I'm going to let Michaels pick up your feet for me. I can't carry you all by myself. He's my man, he won't do nothing except what I say. But then I'm gonna put you in the truck and we're going to go get help. Just you and me, okay, honey? No, don't throw yourself around. Decansa, reposa. Rest, rest. I won't let nobody hurt you. Carmen is here. None of these pricks will touch you, nina."

Babbling reassurance in Spanish, she signaled for Michaels to hoist most of the injured woman's weight. Between the two of them, they carried her outside. Tina cringed away from Anderson, who was holding the truck door open, and his face crumpled. He moved back from the three of them, holding his hands up in the gesture of surrender. When they got Tina onto the passenger seat, he walked around to the driver's side and knocked on the window. Carmen rolled it down, and he passed her a loaded rifle and a spare magazine.

"Keep it under the seat," he said, but Carmen had already stashed it out of sight and away from Tina's mad hands. "We'll be right behind you. Uh, where do you think we should — you said you were going for help — where—" He started to cry. Michaels went over to the farmhouse and tried to punch a hole in its much-abused front door.

"I heard somebody say Doc was probably headed for Harpy Farm," Carmen said. She threw the truck into reverse. "That's the only clue I've got."

Michaels had come up to the window in time to hear what she said. "Makes sense to me," he said. "Drive like hell, baby, we'll keep up. Do you think Doc can do anything for her?"

That question was just too much. "How the fuck would I know?" Carmen shouted. "I can't even stand to look at her. No tiene remedio, no se puede remediar. Goddammit, let me out of here! Callarte. Apurate!" Tina was huddled up against the door, away from the angry noise. But Carmen couldn't leave yet. Anderson was rummaging in the back of the truck. He came up with a blanket and wadded it through the window.

"Wrap her up," he said helplessly. "And let's go."

Even in his anguish, he spared a look around the yard for Prez, but his chopper and most of the other bikes were already gone. The barn was burning noisily, snapping back at the wind. The big, fat sparks that flew off it were sure to catch the house on fire as well. This place could not be saved. Could not be saved.

"Come on!" Michaels yelled, pulling on his arm.

In her rear view mirror, Carmen saw the two men move like synchronized toys, hurrying to mount and start their machines. But she was already plowing down the driveway, not caring if she left them behind. She cursed their stupidity in Spanish, and used softer English to coax Tina to keep the blanket wrapped around her body and come over by her, where heat blew from the single vent in the cab.

Anderson was also aware of the way Michaels followed him, did what he did, backed him up. They were not at odds with one another any more, had not been since they dragged Mendoza's remains into the barnyard, piled up a makeshift funeral pyre, and poured kerosene over it all. Right there in front of God and everybody, he and Michaels had pulled out their aching cocks, taunted each other for being sick motherfuckers, and jacked off into the flames.

"How do you get it up with that much metal weighing your dick down?" he had teased.

"With all this hardware in my joint I don't need to get it up," Michaels had grunted.

"I don't believe you."

"Lemme show you."

Their loads and the piss from a dozen other Angel cocks had hit the fire together, but the flames had only leaped higher, as if they were pouring on more kerosene.

Yes. His body was full of flammable liquid that had just been ignited. Lemme show you, Anderson thought. Oh, Prez, let me show you. Bulldoze your firebreak. Light your backfire. No place in the world will hide you now. The place where we were together cannot be saved, nothing can be saved.

10.

T hen I wiped my hands on the front of his shirt," Doc said, laughing as hard as everyone else — and suddenly had the disconcerting experience of losing her audience.

It was the Chief, leading Raven into the dining hall. Everyone fell silent like bad kids surprised by their parents. Raven walked over to the fireplace and held her hand up. But she already had their attention.

"The Goddess has said this to me," she began, and someone opened a big book that sat at the head of one of the tables, and began to write. "Release the Chief of Harpy Farm. There is no stain upon her. Her sin was not the crime of woman-murder, but the most heinous kind of pride, an unwillingness to back down from a challenge even to prevent disaster. Because this led to a death, and because I need all of My warriors, you had to be taught to bow your neck and do another's will. This you have done, and soon My servant White Owl will return and lift her curse from you. Now show all present the proof, so they will know that it is so."

Her own scars were so familiar to her that the Chief hesitated only a second before stripping. She displayed her back in the firelight then walked slowly around the room. Everyone assembled gasped at the sight. Dozens of brands in the shape of a feather marked her back and upper buttocks. The brands had been arranged in the shape of wings. Leaping

Salmon had brought Wally in to have some hot food, and as her mother passed, she was careful not to let her face show a thing. She was awed, but it would detract from the Chief's pride to say so. It was more proper to behave as if it were a little matter to do what was right.

When the Chief was clothed, Raven raised her hand again, and everyone glanced at her neighbor and lent her ear. "The Goddess has said to me, the tents must come down. All of My children must sleep warm and dry in the coming winter, which will be unusually hard. I have sent you many daughters, the Goddess told me. They have come through the doorway of your road, covered with sweat and with their own blood, and through the gate between your legs, covered with your womb-water and blood. But you have not welcomed all of the children I have given you. Do not scorn the woman who runs to you on her own two legs, lest I seal up the gateways between all of your legs and deny you daughters born. I will keep your enemies from the gates of Harpy Farm only so long as you know your enemies from your new sisters, and give the stranger the first place at your fire, and feed her before you have fed yourselves."

This created no little stir, but Raven did not allow them time for discussion. She raised her hand again and went relentlessly on.

"The Goddess has said to me, leave this place. I have prepared a calf for you, a wild bullock that My servant Raven must fatten for Solstice."

Now true pandemonium reigned. Raven was not popular. No Harpy counted herself as Raven's friend or lover. But she was a high priestess of true inspiration and great power, and no one could stomach the thought of her leaving, especially not after the disaster that followed losing White Owl. A high priestess was supposed to live to be an old, terrible woman, and train her successor.

"You ready for bed, Doc?" Wally asked. She had worked her way over to them through the crowd of protesting, whistling, stamping Harpies.

"Shit, yes," Doc said with disgust. "Silly bitch interrupted one of my best stories."

"Yeah, but we've all heard it before," Wally said unsympathetically, "and nobody ever heard nothing like this. C'mon, I got two of the guys to give up their trailer for you honeymooners."

Wally stayed only long enough to get Doc and Fluff to the trailer and show them where the sanitary trench was, so they didn't fall into it in the dark, then she left to supervise her sentries. They could barely stagger up the stairs. Once inside, Doc headed for the nearest level surface and stretched out, but Fluff seemed to get a second wind. The trailer's usual occupants had left them some flowers in a glass jar on the kitchen table, and she just had to rearrange them. She seemed to feel a need to touch everything in the trailer, look in every cupboard and closet.

Doc huddled underneath the sleeping bag, wishing Fluff would quit fooling around with the kerosene heater and come to bed. Lucky for her the bed was narrow, so whatever was bugging the bitch, she would still have to put her butt up against Doc's belly and help her stay warm. The hot food and homemade beer, the laughing faces of so many good women, strong dykes who were going to help them, and a handful of Valium, made Doc so sleepy that she barely noticed the ache in her body, the speed jones that wanted to be fed. Fluff's determined chin, the thin arms and capable hands, and the way that cute little ass stuck out as the girl bent over the heater, cursing it and adjusting it to her exact specifications, filled Doc with a mixture of love and lust, and fear because that combination was a dangerous one, far more dangerous than any drug or any crazed Harley boy. So it occurred to her that she ought to find out for sure if Fluff was pissed off. Knowing women, she wouldn't be too tired to answer a question about how she was feeling.

"How are you feeling, honey?" Doc asked, and covered her head at the derisive noise that came out of Fluff's nose.

"What the fuck do you care?" Fluff snapped. "You haven't talked to me all night. *Nobody* talked to me. You didn't even notice I had to eat dinner off of your plate." Her accent was so thick Doc could barely understand her. Every word had at least four extra syllables.

"Are you still hungry, honey?" Doc said, anxious to placate Fluff, who was much angrier than she had imagined.

"Yes, I am still hungry. I never saw such weird food in my life. Spaghetti with squash and broccoli and no meatballs? That cheese with all the seeds in it? And crunchy-fried soybean snot? That beer everybody was swilling tasted like shoe polish. The room was full of smoke. But nobody offered me any. Everybody looked right through me, like I was one of your saddlebags or a dirty old boot."

"Hey, excuse me, princess," Doc said, no longer feeling much like placating her young passenger. "This place is on the brink of survival. Always on the edge of not making it. They don't have many luxuries. They put as many plates as they had on the table. We weren't the only ones sharing. And they don't eat much meat because this is a bad time of year for hunting. Pigs haven't been slaughtered and smoked yet. They need what they can save up for winter. So they eat all the vegetables that aren't going to keep because they can't be bottled or made into flour. As for the beer, it tastes a lot better now than it did when they first started making it. And we probably used up more than our share tonight. But they didn't stint us because they figured we all needed a little conviviality before we go to war. Fluff, some of those women might die for you in the next few days. How can you be angry at them?"

"Because they think I'm a Martian!" Fluff cried. "They look at my hair and my clothes, and they roll their eyes and look down their noses. I could never live here. Nobody would be my friend. Much less sleep with me."

"It's a real different place from what you're used to," Doc admitted. "But things are changing even on Harpy Farm. What did you think about Raven's farewell address?"

"I don't even understand what she was talking about," Fluff admitted.

"Come on over here and get under these covers," Doc said. "Come on. You're cold and scared, and you didn't get fed and petted as much as you want. Let me get you warm and settle you down."

"I don't want to be settled down."

"You want to sleep on the floor, be my guest," Doc said curtly, turning over. Her feelings were hurt. Try to save a bitch's life, look at the thanks you got. Life was nothing but sloppy seconds, after all.

Then Fluff's hands were on top of the sleeping bag, kneading her shoulders. "I'm sorry," she said. "I need to get some place safe before I can relax. And there just isn't any such place, Doc."

"Oh, baby," Doc said, turning over and fitting around her hips like a spoon, "I'm afraid this is as close as it gets. You must have had a real hard time with the Angels if you're that sensitive about strangers. Don't you feel safer here than you did with the leader of the pack?"

"Yeah, but I feel like I don't belong and I don't matter. At least with Prez and his bunch, I had some leverage. I hate Prez, but being attached to that bastard gave me a place. Rank hath its privileges, you know? Here I'd just be one more despised straight girl living in a leaky tent watching Harpy brats while the dykes made all the decisions and did all the important shit."

"Don't you think Raven's decree is going to change some of that?"

"Maybe. It didn't look like it made too many people happy."

"Well, yeah, you're right. But you have to look beneath the surface a little, Fluff. There's a lot of women at that table who have lovers in the tents. The fact that it's usually the ex-hets who wind up running herd on the brat-pack has its pluses and minuses. Little baby Harpies grow up thinking of some of those 'outsiders' as their mothers. The dykes don't make all the decisions, Fluff. When the ex-hets and the passing women came to the meeting, they got to speak their piece. One of the good things that could come out of this crisis is that the women who were born here might realize how bad they need the runaways and immigrants to defend their land. But the Harpies shouldn't just give their farm away to any desperate female who doesn't understand how to keep it running or how precious this land is."

"Nobody laughed at any of my jokes," Fluff said. Her voice was small. She rolled over to face Doc, whose back came out from under the blanket and hit a cold wall.

"You didn't make any."

"I started to. Twice. And you didn't stop talking."

"I was on a roll, honey. When you're hot, you're hot."

"Oh?" The bird-thin hand was a claw now, locked around Doc's throat. Fluff's fingers found old bruises and deepened them.

"Stop it, now," Doc sputtered. "I'm warning you. It'll be like fucking a corpse."

"Thought you were hot," Fluff said, and jabbed between her legs. "Think I spent all this time playing with that fucking bomb they call a heater so you could hide under your blankies all night long? If you don't let me get in between your legs I'm going to punch a hole in your throat."

"All right, all right, you know how much violence upsets me!" Doc wailed.

She was expecting penetration and dreading it a little, since she was dry. Five more minutes of being choked would have taken care of that, despite the methamphetamine. But Fluff was sliding down her body, stopping to lick at and then chew on her nipples, and that worked even better. The little hands were on her hips, turning her onto her back, and Fluff was on top of her, riding one of her thighs. She pushed her leg up at the girl, but Fluff said, "No, lay down, let me play," and so she held still, let the girl experiment. Then Fluff slid even further down, and her hands were plucking at Doc's thighs.

"Is this what your other girlfriends did for you?" Fluff said, really asking. She was licking Doc's thighs, persuading them apart. "Were they really good at it? Did you have to show them how? How do you like it? Tell me. Tell me."

She was separating Doc's lips, and her breath was hot on the chafed flesh. A long ride pounded hell out of your cunt. The constant vibration was a turn-on for the first hour, and after that it was a grinding tease. Doc ached, and the long, light strokes of Fluff's tongue chased the pain away. Made her feel new again, eased her, renewed her. The point of that tongue went deep within her, searched her out, and came back up to flick her clit, make her jump. "Do you jerk because you like it or because it's too much?" Fluff asked. "Too much," she decided, and sucked thoughtfully on the hood of Doc's clit, agitating the cord of nerve within it, but keeping just above the exposed peak of her glans. She kept at it, stopping only to lick a couple of fingers and slip them up where it was no longer dry, but still not wet enough for a fist. Fluff found a place that talked back to her on the roof of Doc's cunt, a hard knot that seemed to want pounding, so she tickled it and then pump-fucked up at it, made it bounce back, made the walls of Doc's channel close down hard. She kept her mouth gentle, persistent. It seemed to Fluff that maybe going down on another chick (Doc?) — well, another girl (Doc?) — well, whatever — that it couldn't be as rude as fucking. You had to be kind of delicate. But dedicated. You had to mean it.

Then Doc's hands came down on her head, gripping hard, and she figured that meant the same thing it meant when a guy grabbed you that way — "Don't stop or I'll kill you." Doc's hips were thrashing, plastering cunt across Fluff's nose and mouth so she couldn't breathe. She moved her tongue faster, harder, figuring it was okay now to let things get sloppy, and Doc told her who she was, what she was, but with those meaty thighs locked around her ears and a pool of cum in the palm of her hand, she really didn't need to hear it. She was home.

"Don't touch me," she said as Doc dragged her up, tucked the sleeping bag around her, and licked at her face. "I just want to feel exactly this way. Don't mess me around, okay?"

They slept so soundly that they didn't even wake up when Carmen's pickup truck barreled down the road, bouncing off ruts and rocks. She pulled into the yard, rousing dogs and chickens and Harpies and causing a slightly smaller repeat of last night's chattaqua. Carmen was so exhausted that it never occurred to her to ask for Doc when she did not see her in the crowd. It took a long time for them to coax Tina out of the truck and into the hall. She would not let anyone look at her injuries. Raven finally went into the kitchen, melted down some opium, and poured it into a glass of blackberry cordial. Carmen persuaded Tina to drink it.

While they waited for it to take effect, dawn came, and other women went into the kitchen to start making breakfast. A sentry came in to get thermoses of tea filled for the women outside, and volunteered to find Doc. It took a lot of pounding to rouse the two travelers. They came into the hall wrapped up in Doc's sleeping bag, still fuzzy from their long ride. Fluff pushed hopelessly at the mess of hair on her head, sniffed the odor of pancakes and maté tea, and decided what the hell, she would try to wake up. Then she spied familiar faces.

"Carmen! Tina!" Fluff was overjoyed to see regular girls, girls from the outside. Then she noticed the dark circles under Carmen's eyes, Tina's hunched posture and bloody face.

"Get my saddlebags," Doc said, and Fluff ran back to the bike.

Raven came up to Doc. "I've boiled some dressings," she said. "I think she is hurt inside."

"Probably," Doc said. She knelt in front of Tina and began to examine her. Carmen soothed her, but it never occurred to Tina to fend off those hands. Doc would make everything better. She always did.

"We don't need a crowd," Doc snapped. "Raven, get rid of all these voyeurs." Raven cleared the room with a hard look and a single shooing gesture. Fluff came panting back with all four of Doc's saddlebags. Doc told her what she wanted and where it was, and Raven went into the kitchen and brought back a bowl of steaming white cloths. "We're going to have to soak her shirt off," Doc said, so Raven lifted one of the cloths with chopsticks to let it cool. Fluff went to wash her hands. Doc and Raven applied warm compresses to Tina's blouse, and peeled it from her chest. There was a little renewed bleeding. Doc touched Tina's face, said, "Oh, honey, I'm going to kill that bastard for you."

"No," said Raven. "I will."

Doc spared her a glance. Raven's eyes glittered. A cold breeze went by. The short hairs on the back of Doc's neck lifted and crawled. "Deal," Doc said briefly. "Just put a hurting on him first. A serious hurting."

"Deal," Raven said.

Doc said, "Tina, can we clean you up? Let me have these towels, honey, they're dirty." She gently pried the rags from between her legs. "I need to look at you now, Tina. I'm going to try not to hurt you. Can I have another compress?"

Fluff wrung out a rag, handed it to her, and took the ones they had already used back to the kitchen to be boiled again. Doc let the warm water soak into Tina's pubic hair, then blotted away the dried blood. There was a long scratch between one of her outer and inner lips. The other inner lip was badly torn.

"Fluff, is that speculum clean?" Doc asked. But Fluff was in the kitchen. Raven went to get her and the implement. "Now,

Tina," she said to her patient, "how do you want to do this? You know I have to take a look. But I don't want to open you up if it's going to scare you. Do you want to put this in?" She showed her the metal blades. "It's not even cold."

"Um, sure, I'll put it in," Tina said. These were the first words she had spoken since Carmen found her, and her friend began to cry, shaken with sobs of helpless relief.

"Drink this," Raven said, and she gave Carmen what was left of the doctored cordial. "You were very brave, to get her here. Now let us take care of you a little." She moved behind Carmen, encouraged her to lean back on her, and massaged her upper arms and shoulders. At first Carmen was stiff beneath her hands, but Raven's touch was seductive, and soon she was slumped over, in a twilight state between sleep and waking. While Fluff handed Doc long cotton swabs, Raven lured Carmen out of the room and up the stairs to the room where the Chief was sleeping. She turned back one corner of the quilts, careful not to wake the sleeper, and Carmen slid beneath the covers. "Try to sleep," Raven whispered, tucking her in. "We will guard your friend with our lives."

That was a damned funny thing for a skinny little girl who wore even more mascara than Crystal to say, but Carmen believed her. Or dreamed she believed her, anyway.

"We're going to have to sew this up," Doc said, shining a flashlight between the speculum's blades. She had already splinted the broken wrist. There were too many little bones there. The Goddess knew that hand would never work right again. "Tina, can you stand it? I could give you some Lidocaine, but the shot is going to hurt as bad as the stitches."

"I stood having it done to me," Tina replied.

"Tough little bitch, aren't you?"

"I hope so."

"Squeeze my hand," Fluff suggested, handing Doc a tiny envelope that contained a curved, sterile needle and suturing thread. "When it hurts just squeeze my hand as hard as you want. It'll help the pain."

And that was how they did it, with Tina hissing and Fluff encouraging her to squeeze harder, harder, harder! Doc grunted and cursed the lack of sufficient light, and put her stitches in as quickly as she could. Then she took out the speculum and gave Tina's other injuries a second look. She cleaned out the scratch between her labia, but otherwise left it alone. The other lip, she pieced back together as best she could. Fluff loaned Tina her other hand. The nipples, however, had Doc stymied. Prez had gotten just the tip of one of them, but the other was gone completely, areola and all. Stitching was going to pull Tina's breasts into a weird shape, but she could not leave a wound that big open without inviting infection. Tina finally could not stand the anxiety of waiting, and snapped, "Just do it, I know it ain't going to be pretty. You think I care about being pretty now? Just sew the fucker up." Doc shook her head and did her best, although the crudity of the work made her own nipples hurt. The kind of plastic surgery Tina needed was beyond her. She finished by giving Tina a shot of penicillin in the hip.

"I know where she can rest," Raven said, wiping Doc's face. Doc and Fluff both jumped. Raven had not made a sound coming back into the room. How long had she been standing behind them?

As they assisted Tina out, they passed groups of women eating standing up. The kitchen crew had not been able to set up the hall for breakfast. They had inconvenienced everybody to give Tina privacy. Raven laid a finger across her lips, and nobody spoke. Several made the sign for healing, or for good wishes. Doc knew that the story of Tina's injuries and her heroic lover would spread all over Harpy Farm before anybody did their morning chores. It would stiffen everyone's resolve, make them mad. First child-rape — and now this! It would not occur to anyone, except perhaps the ex-hets, that

Tina and Carmen were not lovers. Straight women simply did not rescue each other. That was dyke behavior, dyke honor. Why, it even made Doc wonder.

Tina woke up enough when they tucked her into bed to grab Doc's arm and say, "Anderson and Michaels are coming. After Prez's scalp."

"Well, they can't stay here," Doc said. "If they come onto women's land, they'll be shot."

"Oh," said Tina. "Okay. Carmen has the keys to the truck. Just park it on the edge of the farm. Leave 'em a note. Their clothes and stuff are in the back. They can sleep in it. But bring back the keys, okay? Nobody else gets to drive our truck."

It was a tense day. Everyone expected Prez and his minions to show up any minute. Doc, who had more experience with the way things can get fucked up when you're traveling with a dozen temperamental all-American boys and their even more temperamental all-American bikes, wasn't surprised when suppertime came with no sign of trouble. She spent the day touring the farm with Wally, checking out the sinsemilla fields and the fish ponds. Fluff tagged after them a while, but stayed behind when they visited the machine shop. "You really make *guns* here?" Doc heard her ask Sahara, the tiny black woman who ran that operation. "Can you show me how to sharpen my knife?"

"Hell, I can show you how to sharpen all of them," Sahara grumbled. "Ain't nobody on this damn farm who isn't too lazy to sharpen her own knife. Got a pile of 'em on the bench as tall as my head."

Sahara had been carefully scraping black gunk off an engine part. She stopped long enough to find the knife-sharpening stand and its attachments and put them on the other end of her work bench. Fluff opened the first knife and screwed the blade into the clamp. Then she swept a ceramic rod across its cutting edge. The stand held both knife and sharpening stick at the correct angle, making the whole job pretty easy. It was repetitious and soothing.

"I like your vest," Fluff said.

"Uh huh," Sahara said absently, her small hands turning, cradling, and patiently cleaning the mysterious piece of metal.

"What are all those patches and things for? It looks kind of like colors."

Sahara gave her a brief look that said she didn't know what Fluff was talking about and had no time for nonsense.

"Colors are the denim vests that bikers wear over their leather jackets. They put their club patches on them, pins from runs, things like that. Those winged lion-women are harpies, right? So that means you're from Harpy Farm?"

"Yep." Sahara pushed her round spectacles back to the bridge of her button nose. Her compressed lips disapproved of Fluff's comparing her clothing to biker finery.

Fluff refused to give up. "But what's that patch with the gear on it?"

"Says I'm Nuts and Bolts Clan. We keep things running around here. You got a wheel, we make you run."

"So you're mechanics?"

"Oh, yes, all that and more. We're also the carpenters, roofers, plumbers, electricians. Anybody who isn't afraid of hard work and getting dirty. This little patch here that looks like a target, that's my marksmanship badge. It's purple because I'm an instructor. We got a rifle range out past the orchard, all the young 'uns got to do their time out there."

Fluff had turned the pocketknife over and sharpened the other side. She took it out of the clamp. "Test it on your arm," Sahara suggested. "If it shaves off those hairs, you got a good edge."

Fluff passed it gently, at an angle, up her forearm, and it harvested a fine spray of short, gold hairs. She closed it and put it to one side, then started sorting all the remaining knives into piles. Do the folders first, she planned, because they were the easiest. So she would practice on them. Then do the daggers. But this machete and that Khukri — she didn't see how they would fit into the stand.

"So what clan is the Chief?" she asked.

Sahara snorted. "She does have a name, although everyone seems to eschew it in lieu of her grand title. Her name is Eagle Wing, and she's Eagle Clan, of course. Buncha glorified vultures if you ask me. Like to flap their big wings and open their big beaks wide and scream at the rest of us. And I really don't know if it's a good idea for a mother to put so much pressure on her daughter to follow in her footsteps. Leaping Salmon's a good kid, but I'm not sure she's..." Sahara never did finish this sentence, so Fluff asked another question.

"So tell me more. What about Raven?"

"Snake Clan. They do a lot of magic stuff. Keep the bugs off the corn, weed the marijuana, you know. A lot of the potters and musicians are Snake Clan. Artistic types. They run the sweat lodges and the bathhouses, too. They have a friendly rivalry going with Cloud Clan, which does magic for rain, studies the almanacs, decides when to plant. Clouds douse for water and if they find it they dig the well. They also keep the irrigation ditches clean, although around here Wally and her guys seem to do a lot of that grunt work."

"So not everybody has the same jobs on every farm?"

"Goodness, no. And not all of the farms have the same clans. We don't have any Bee Clan here. Every time we go to a holyday, the Chief encourages us to try and seduce and entice somebody from Bee Clan to move here so we can put in some hives. Everybody has a sweet tooth and sugar is just too expensive. Besides, we have to argue with Snake Clan every time we order some. They say it's bad for our spiritual energy. Yeah, a farm that treats their Bee Clan right makes a lot of money. And nobody has a clan that handles optics. If we want eyeglasses we have to go outside. A lot of us order them from Doc.

"But we do have a very accomplished Shuttle Clan. They have a whole shed out there, where they do the weaving. We even have one power loom. Takes a long time to set it up, but when they hook it up to the generator, it makes a lot of cloth. Shuttle Clan's sewing machines clothe everybody on Harpy Farm and a lot of the women on other farms. Every summer they clip the sheep with Wolf Clan."

Fluff had finished with the pocketknives and was trying to get the clamp to grip a double-sided dagger. The middle of the blade was much thicker than the edge, and the clamp did not feel secure. But she kept fiddling with it, not wanting to interrupt Sahara, who was fitting a gasket over the edge of the part she had just cleaned.

"Wolf Clan raises sheep, goats, chickens, hogs. In the fall they hold the hog slaughter and smoke hams, bacon. Apple Blossom Clan helps them out. The rest of the time, Apple Blossom tends the orchards. When the fruit's ripe, they harvest it, put up jam, chutney. We make a fabulous salsa here. Makes your ears ring and your eyeballs sweat."

"What about the ex-hets and the passing women?" Fluff asked. "Are those clan names?"

Sahara pursed her lips. "No, they are not. If you ask me we'd be better off around here if we made all the newcomers take clan membership within six months. That's what the Maidens have to do when they become grown women. I have been pushing for that longer than I care to remember. There is Autumn Leaf Clan. They take in a lot of the ex-hets. Everybody likes to have babies around here, but nobody likes to raise them. They're noisy and they stink, and as soon as they learn to talk they start saying 'No.' Most everybody who has the patience to run herd on the brat pack is ex-hets. Autumn Leaf Clan orders us books, keeps a lending library circulating, and they teach. But pushing literacy on this farm is like trying to sell Japanese cars in Detroit. I keep saying we ought to have a mandatory badge for reading and writing, just like the marksmanship, but so far only one farm makes the young 'uns do that."

"So Wally and the guys don't have a clan?"

Sahara laughed. "Not unless you count what they get called behind their backs, 'Penis Clan' and 'Turd Clan.' That's about as funny as them referring to us as the 'Rabid Pussies' or 'Castrating Bitches.' But you know, not all the passing women come from outside. On every single piece of women's land, some of the children gravitate toward the more butch element. And their initiation process is no less severe because it is informal. Sometimes it's harder to join the outcasts than it is to fit into the mainstream. Then there's the children who leave us. We don't never talk about them."

The dagger seemed to be firmly in place. Fluff started putting an edge on it. It made a wonderful sound. She felt like she was stroking the blade, filling it up with potential violence. "Do you know women in Nuts and Bolts Clan on other land? Do you go visit with them when you travel?"

Sahara was hunting through a muffin tin for the right size screws. "Oh, my, yes. The clan system is one thing that preserves ties between different farms. Like, you might be at a festival and meet somebody cute you want to talk to, so you'd say, 'Oh, you got your farm vehicle maintenance badge, who was your teacher?' And she might say, 'Badger at Purple Mesa Pueblo.' So you'd say, 'Yeah, mine is from One-Eye, Trout Lake. But I live on Owl Farm now. They got a new tractor and wanted to take care of it right, so they recruited me. Owl Farm is friendly. I found me a sweetheart first night there. But she isn't with me on this trip!'"

That made Fluff smile. "Are there a lot of women's farms?" she asked. She was sharpening her third dagger. This one was an Arkansas toothpick, and it was a snap to work on.

"Well, there's Harpy Farm, Snake River, Owl Farm — that's one of the oldest, Trout Lake, Purple Mesa Pueblo, Green Valley. More besides. But not nearly enough to save all the women of the world. I have learned, however, that you can't save the unwilling."

Sahara gave Fluff a sharp look. "You're very good at getting a laconic old mechanic to bend your ear. So tell me why you wear all that stuff on your face. If you're going to a ritual, I'd advise you to make yourself a little more colorful. And if you aren't going to a ritual, why don't you let your skin breathe?"

They spent the rest of their time together exchanging information about life outside and on women's land.

When Doc got back to the big house, she found Fluff bustling around, returning an assortment of daggers and folders to their owners, dispensing a piece of advice here and there about not chipping a blade or being sure to keep it oiled. Women thanked her, even tolerated her advice. Doc chuckled and went to help set the tables and bring out food. The tables were made out of anything large and flat that could be set on trestles — a barn door sawed in half, corrugated aluminum siding, plastic sheets of roofing material. During the day, the tabletops were taken off and stacked with the trestles along one wall, to keep the room open.

Fluff was returning a switchblade to its rightful owner. Sahara had said, "Look for the one with pink-and-green hair. You can't miss her."

The little punk dyke who thanked her for the knife was wearing a leather jacket, but it was a lot more battered than Doc's, and seemed to be a size too big for her. She had transistors pinned all over it. "I love your hair," she told Fluff. "It's very radical to be so feminine here. I'm a former city dyke, you know, but I am *not* an ex-het. It's so hard to get the women here to make that distinction. Do you like my jacket? I'm Microchip Clan. I don't want to go the Nuts and Bolts route. This is the future, we gotta stop thinking *hard*ware. Software is female, we have to take it back from the dickhead computer nerds. That's my name, Software, Microchip Clan. Well, actually, there's only me. But I have a Wizard computer, her name is Gorgon, and a state-of-the-art Stardust printer, she doesn't have a name yet. We could publish a newsletter. But it would be so much easier if I could get everybody to see that we need computers and modems on every farm, then we could just telecommunicate. Start a BBS. If only I could convince a work crew to go out to the highway and tap into the phone cables. We could even have cable television! I want to talk to Doc about hustling a satellite dish. It wouldn't have to be a big one. We could bounce a signal off Tokyo Star. Goes overhead once every eight hours. That thing's so immense they'd have a hell of a time finding a pirated signal. Imagine — we could have our own TV station! I don't know, I think the idea is too radical for everybody here. They're coming from survival. But if push comes to shove none of us are gonna make it, so who cares? I live for media power. You got any tapes, CDs, wafers? It's been forever since I heard any new music."

"No, I'm sorry," Fluff said. "But Doc is over there, wrestling with the tables and things. I'm sure she'd love to get you all a satellite."

"Oh, thanks, wow, I really love her hair."

Doc and Fluff had eaten only the first few mouthfuls of their meal when the sound of motorcycles outside made everybody jump. Doc could have sworn that the woman across from her actually peed her pants. She knew just how she felt. But then common sense asserted itself. This was one machine, not a horde, and the sentries would have sent off flares if there had been any sign of Prez and company.

Paint strolled in, elbowed herself a place at one of the tables, tucked Desiree under the other elbow, and started feeding both of them. "How you been?" she said cheerfully to Doc. "Enjoying what little time you got left to live, I see."

"Same to you," Doc said.

"Hi," Desiree wiggled her fingers at Fluff. Fluff waved back, passed her a plate of rice cakes. "The spaghetti sauce isn't bad," she volunteered. "Just close your eyes and chew."

"Oh," Desiree said, looking at everybody else's plate. "I'm so hungry I think I could make dinner out of my shoes."

"The pink ones?" Fluff said.

"Yeah, I guess those are the ones I'd cook first if I was starving. You look happy."

"Making the best of what's left of my life," Fluff giggled.

"Me too," Desiree said. "Is this place weird or what?"

"I kind of like it," Fluff said. "You have to find a job to do."

"Well, Lord knows I'm a working girl from way back."

"Yeah, well, you work for me, now," Paint said, pulling her hair.

"Yes'm."

Fluff widened her eyes, and jabbed Doc's thigh. "What's the matter, you want me to pull your hair, too?" Doc said, reaching for it. But Fluff was quicker, and pulled Doc's head down to her mouth, where she could bite the back of her neck.

"Who do you work for?" she whispered in Doc's ear, and stroked her when she shivered.

"Going to have to make more tables," Sahara said, from another table, to no one in particular. She had no children, but was well known for visiting the tents of the ex-hets.

"Going to have to build some more rooms first," somebody else said.

"Before winter?"

"Better before winter than during. Got a pile of shingles out by the cowshed but beams are a problem. Could go tear some out of the old abandoned Johnson place."

The Harpies began to debate how best to bring everybody into the big house before the first snow. "Maybe it's time for another house," somebody said.

"I like having everybody here."

"What's the point of bringing everybody together if we just get split up again?"

"We could have a big common hall and little sleeping houses. More private."

"More private for what? Doing something you don't want us to know about?"

"Just don't see why everybody on the farm should know when I get lucky."

"Put your face in a pillow," someone suggested.

Bread was thrown.

After dinner, most of the women stayed in the common area to socialize. A few read or just talked, but Fluff noticed that almost everybody had their hands busy. They were knitting or crocheting, embroidering or carving wood. Very few seemed able to sit still and do nothing.

As it got later, Raven circulated with pipes full of weed. Everyone except those women who had sentry duty got pleasantly buzzed, and slept well.

11.

The next day, Doc went down to the truck. It was parked just outside the boundary of Harpy Farm. Two boys, one tall and blond, one short and dark, were bundled into it, sleeping side by side. Anderson was a little too long to fit the bed of the truck, so he had curled up around Michaels. Doc cleared her throat. "You fellas walk here?" she asked. They woke up looking scared and angry.

"I had a breakdown," Anderson said. "We had to leave her off the road, chained to a tree. So I got on back of Michaels, and what does his back tire do but spring a leak. My God, what a pain in the ass. Doc, is Tina here? Is she okay?"

"Yeah."

"Well, I want to go see her! Let's go!"

"You can't."

"What do you mean, I can't?"

"Anderson, you know the rules. She's too sick to travel. And you can't come onto the land. I'll send Carmen down a bit later and you can talk to her about it. She, uh, Tina isn't going to be herself, you know. Not for quite a while. Maybe never."

"My God, did he hurt her bad enough to cripple her?"

"Cripple her mind, I think. We're having a hard time keeping her on the planet, Anderson. Her spirit is injured. She doesn't want to be here. She's running a high fever and antibiotics aren't bringing it down. I don't think it's infection. I think she's just out of her body, trying to find her way home.

Carmen got her here really fast. May have saved her life. I'll try. But you shouldn't expect things to be the way they were before, bro."

"Don't think much of anything is going to be the way it was before," Michaels said solemnly. "Moping about Tina is not going to help her now, Anderson. Prez is on the way. You know that, right, Doc? And we have to turn him, Anderson. Put a stop to this shit."

"You could talk to a few of our people," Doc said carefully. "If you think you can mind your manners. It'd help if we knew what we were up against. How many men, what kind of weapons. Stuff that you'd know, being the sergeant-at-arms, Anderson."

It never even occurred to him that he was committing treason. "Anything you want to know," he said simply. "Anything at all."

"Then I'll send them down to talk," Doc said. "You boys are going to be camping here who knows how long. Why don't you get off your butts, make camp, get yourselves some coffee? It'll take a while for the sentries and everybody else to sort out who wants to parley with you."

Anderson stopped her from leaving. "Doc?" he said. His face was pathetic, bad-dog with no hope of redemption. "If Tina calls for me you would come and get me, right? Let me know?"

"Yeah. Sure. You bet." Doc punched at his arm and got the hell out of there. Tina wouldn't talk to anybody except Carmen, herself, Fluff, and Raven. When she wasn't out of her head with fever, she was listening to Raven's stories about the Goddess, how She made the world to win a bet with Her mother, how She made women because She was lonely and made men by mistake. When Tina talked about the future, it was about working in the garden, sewing herself some new clothes, being at the solstice celebration, cooking something special to thank everyone for helping her. It was clear to Doc that Tina was assuming she was staying right where she was, on Harpy Farm. Doc hadn't talked this over with Carmen. None of them were sure yet that Tina would live. She only kept down about half of what she ate.

It was good that Paint and Desiree had arrived. They were company for Fluff. And they were easing the separation between the born-Harpies and the women who had come there seeking sanctuary. Clearly, nobody was moving *them* out of the big house and down with the ex-hets. The women who had refugee lovers were bringing them in for supper, squeezing them in to sleeping places. Some of the tents had been moved closer to the big house. Paint was giving the older girls rides on her Harley, and was teaching a couple of them (including Desiree) how to ride. Doc wondered if they would be staying on Harpy Farm as well.

✧

It was two more days before the sentries' flares finally went off. In the pale light of dawn, they could barely be seen by the watchers at the big house. Nerves had been stretched so tight by the long wait that cheers and war-cries reverberated all over Harpy Farm. Everyone who had a gun grabbed it and headed for the scarecrone. Armed women would surround Raven, protect her, and serve as a warning to the bikers to stay on their own side of the line. Some women brought torches. A few stayed behind with the children, although there were no illusions about what would happen to them if this battle was lost.

The Chief led her archers into the forest, and these women carefully and quietly made their way through the trees, concealing themselves on either side of the enemy. The Harpies who were going to confront the bikers openly made as much noise as possible to draw attention away from them. Doc knew that those bows and arrows were no joke. The Harpies had cooked up some nasty poisons. A scratch from a dart treated with one of those was lethal. Even the sentinels, who all had rifles or shotguns, felt safer because they had this backup, as if Artemis Herself was behind them, nocking Her arrow.

On her way with everybody else, Doc was glad she had thought to move Carmen's truck closer to the house, within the boundary of the farm. Anderson and Michaels had put themselves a nice little camp together, hadn't needed it any more.

The Angels had gathered at the foot of the scarecrone. That guardian figure did not look any more pleased to see them than the Druids had been to see the Romans. Doc had a brief but pleasant fantasy of stuffing the wicker woman full of Angels and setting them on fire. I'd paint myself blue with woad to see that movie, she thought.

Prez stood in the middle of the road, and everyone else milled around behind him, as if he were an obstacle they could not pass. There weren't as many bikers with Prez as Doc had expected. But there were a hell of a lot of them. Most of the men were sporting sawed-off shotguns or pistols, but a few of them seemed to be unarmed. Then Doc noticed something even more incredible. Their women were with them! Not just the doxies and groupies — old ladies were there, standing next to their men. It was a biker maxim that you never let things get ugly in front of your wife. If you had to rock and roll, you sent her away first. The chase vehicles were parked behind the bikes, some of them off the road, so that they would block a retreat, if one was necessary. Doc shook her head in disbelief. Anderson would have cut their ears off for being so sloppy.

Either Prez was not thinking, or not everyone was minding. His officers should have been ranked around him, clearly identifiable and alert, his bodyguard. But two of his key men, Michaels and Anderson, were on the wrong side, standing just outside the border of Harpy Farm.

Doc saw the bikers notice that, and some of them scowled, and stared at the ground. They were used to having Anderson get them pumped up and primed, tell them they were the best, remind them of the strategy, the battle plan, tell them to take no prisoners. They were used to Michaels giving them a little speech about the order of plunder — what part belonged to the club, what had to be offered to Prez so he could take first pick, and what could be kept back for their own.

They were used to fighting other men. None of them liked dykes. All of them were afraid, and they resented being afraid of a fight with women. Dying at a woman's hands had no dignity. And they weren't sure what the fuck it was all for. This wasn't about drugs or money or territory. It was about a girl that none of them had thought Prez meant to keep. They had been waiting for the day when they'd all get to have her. If Prez was still secure in his role as their leader, everyone would have ignored that, rewritten history to make it sound as if his old lady had been abducted against her will, and pretended that was true.

But his position was not secure. Just killing Mendoza would not have been enough to make them doubt him. Mendoza wasn't patched, wasn't even a serious contender for club membership. But Prez had killed Mendoza for deriding Doc — Doc, the very person he had insisted was the enemy. And then what he had done to Anderson's old lady — well, that was bad for the club. It made the chicks uneasy, made every man look to what was his and swear that Prez had better not get any funny ideas about coming after it. It made no sense for him to do that to Anderson. Anderson was his second, a loyal and righteous officer. If that was his reward, what was the point in the entire hierarchy? Where did any of them belong? How should they behave?

Still, Doc knew, they were Angels first, and nothing else mattered more to them. Prez was nominally still their leader. Their grievances with him were a family matter. They would not let outsiders come between him and the rest of the club. But if there was some way to save face, to give them a compromise — if it became clear to Prez that he had to take that compromise or risk being ousted — maybe there was a chance to avoid a massacre.

"Doc!" Prez roared. "Come out here and tell me what the hell you thought you were doing, running off with something that belonged to me. Where is that little whore, Fluff? What have you done with her? I want her back *now*, Doc!"

"She's right here," Doc said. She did not mention Tina, Carmen, Paint, Desiree, Anderson, and Michaels. "Why should I give Fluff back to you, Prez? So you can do the same thing to her you did to Tina?"

"What I do with her is my affair! We've always been square with you, Doc. Made you a lot of money. Had some good times too. This isn't friendly, Doc. And it's damn bad business."

"I'm not coming back to you, Prez!" Fluff shouted. He jumped visibly at the sound of her voice. That would be bad for his image, Doc thought, laughing at the toes of her boots. "You never told me I was anything special to you, you bastard. Always told me you never took anybody special to keep for your own. Always told me you were just about ready to make me public property. When a girl sees a chance to better herself she has a right to take it, Prez. If you wanted to keep me, you ought to have said so."

That was pretty forward, but fair according to Angel ideas about how women ought to behave — or would have been if Doc had been a man. It was just that none of the boys would like being told so. Doc cleared her throat. It was time to remind Prez about a thing or two. "There's business and there's business," she said. "I figured the biz you and I did in private was just that, private. But if you are gonna come after me and mess with my private life, Prez, there's no reason for me to protect you."

"You're bluffing!" he shouted. "You don't know shit about me. This chapter knows I am its duly elected president, and they have every confidence in me. They wouldn't have ridden up here for nobody else but me, and there is nothing you can say to my bros that will make me less than I am in their eyes. *I am their leader!*"

You're a bold-as-brass liar, Doc thought, with a touch of her old admiration for his style and arrogance, the way he puffed himself up and went headlong after everything he wanted.

"Stop this. There will be silence!" Doc was riveted again by that musical, penetrating voice, by Raven's ability to be heard without shouting. Her voice seemed to come from outside the crowd. She walked out between Doc and Prez, and Doc began to sweat and pray. The woman was a damn fool to make herself a target that way. Don't let any of these bikers get trigger-happy now, Goddess. Doc had to force herself not to look for the snipers hidden in the woods. An ambush wouldn't work if she tipped these boys off.

"There is no resolution here," Raven said. She was wearing a very tight, black dress. She had dispensed with her shawl. The dress was low-cut and backless — something she showed off by turning around to make warning gestures, first at Doc, then at Prez. "We of Harpy Farm have no reason to fight with you. This conflict was brought to us. We did not ask for it. But we cannot let you come onto our land and take any woman off it. This is our place." She showed her teeth. "You know it is our place."

"Bullshit," Prez bellowed. "We've left you crazy bitches alone up to now, but if I give the order these bikes will roll over your goddamn farm and we will level it. We will torch your buildings and rip up your fields and carry off every woman here that we have a use for. The rest we will kill."

"There are children here," Raven said. "Would you kill them, also? Or do you have a use for them?"

Before he could answer, Doc shouted, "Some of these kids are *your* kids. Any of you want to stop and think about that? Some of these little girls are gonna look an awful lot like some of you. Just 'cause you never saw them get born and didn't help raise them doesn't mean you aren't their fathers. What kind of man kills his own children? And how are you gonna sort out the ones that are yours from the ones that are not?"

Doc saw with great satisfaction that *that* didn't make any of them very happy. Prez's war was not the stuff that legends are made of. If anybody ever did tell stories about it, the men who were here would be slow to admit it.

"Do not speak," Raven snapped. "Neither of you. Until I have had my say. I wish to know why such a powerful man, a man who has such a large tribe of his own, wishes to possess a woman — a child — who does not want him. Are there no women who desire you, Prez? Many women must pursue you. Couldn't you have any one of them that you wanted? And find her eager for you? Women must always be trying to attract your attention. Even women who don't know you. Strangers." She was running her hands up and down her sides, her hips. Prez was staring at her, licking his lips. She was sinuous, slender, shapely, small-breasted, with a pert ass, and tiny hands and feet. Child-like. Then he noticed her girdle. That silver hanging noose, carefully braided out of thin wire, fascinated him. It talked to him.

Finally he jerked his gaze away and glared at all of Doc's allies. "You say you can't let us come onto your land and take somebody off it. Well, then, you must understand that I can't let somebody walk into one of our celebrations and waltz out with a girl that's been traveling with me. If Doc had asked me for her, I might have given her away. But nobody asked."

"I never asked you for Deirdre," Doc said. "Or Jennifer. Or Kathleen."

"Deirdre?" she heard Fluff hiss. "Jennifer? Kathleen?" Doc hoped she got enough time to tell Fluff these girls meant nothing to her, before Fluff decided to seek revenge.

"You'd had every single one of them. Who knew that this was any different? Every time I ride with your club I wind up taking some broad out with me. Usually you think it's funny. Hell, do you want me to read you a list of everybody's old lady I've been down on? Come on, Prez, that's a pretty big club. I remember you telling some dude who woke me up with a

Mauser in my ear that it was too late to show his chick that he knew how to use his gun. You told him that after I broke his arm for him. I still got that Mauser, Prez. Why should my friends and your men die, because you lost your sense of humor?"

He was mud-stubborn. "You took something that didn't belong to you. You took something that was mine, and somebody has to pay."

"What is fair payment?" Raven asked. "Is one woman fair payment for another?" She crossed her arms, put her hands over her breasts. She leaned toward him.

"Maybe," Prez admitted.

Raven made brisk patterns in the air with her scarlet fly whisk. "Then we have something at last that we can talk about. Get off your machine. We will talk face to face. You, and one of your choosing. Fluff and Doc. Me to mediate the circle. Here. Where everyone can watch and hear, and see that there is no treachery."

Prez dismounted. He looked over his club, searching for a second to take into this negotiation with him. Anderson and Michaels moved toward him. He backed away from them. They shrugged and disappeared into the crowd, greeting buddies, answering questions. Because of what was going down, he could not stop them from rejoining their bros, as if nothing at all had happened. In the old days, a pair of traitors like those two would have gotten stomped. Prez ground his teeth. Josie came forward and wrapped her hand around Anderson's, asked him quietly about Tina. His answer made her hug him and cry.

Prez was forced to take Scott Campbell, an honest man but no Einstein, with him. He was still sick, weak, felt like he had the flu. His nose was runny and raw, and his bones complained about being shaken around inside the dry old bag of his skin. Right after the fire, he had stopped for gas and fixed in the men's room. He was in such a good mood, he had done just a little bit more smack than usual, and knew he was in big trouble before he got the needle out of his arm.

Luckily, some of the bros had come in with him to take a piss. Campbell knew CPR and had saved his life. But they all knew what had been in that needle, and none of them liked it much. If he had killed himself with an overdose of speed, there would have been no disgrace in that. But in the racist parlance of the Angels, smack was "that nigger drug." It was bad for your ride. Everybody did it once in a while, but the code said you had to be man enough not to get hooked. If they had still trusted him, they would have told him so. One of his officers would have taken him aside and given him a ten-second lecture, hit him between the shoulders, and encouraged him to get a grip. Instead, they avoided his eyes, and talked to each other. Behind his back. Behind *his* back!

Prez felt the absence of the loyalty of Michaels and Anderson like a cold wind up his jacket. It suddenly came to him that dealing with them was going to be a lot more difficult than this parley at Harpy Farm. The thought of all the damage he had done, damage he knew he could not repair, made him blindly furious at Doc. But it also made him urgently hungry for release, for yet another way to avoid facing the music. He knew now that he could not have Fluff. His session with Tina had sated his appetite to commit violence. Now he wanted to be small and weak, to be persecuted, hurt. Until that jones was taken care of, torturing Fluff or even killing her would not be very satisfying.

Besides, he was having a hard time remembering what Fluff's appeal had been. (This would have enraged Fluff, who was already pissed speechless at Doc, who had tried to make her wear baggy clothes and leave her hair uncombed before the meeting, so she wouldn't attract attention.) To Prez, this dark apparition with its sinister accessories — whip and noose — seemed to promise a more complete journey into subordination and degradation. This was not someone he would have to threaten or train. She would have ideas of her own. Things she wanted. Things he could not guess. And she was alien, utterly alien. A dyke, like Doc, but little, frail, crushable. When he turned on her (that inevitable and vicious reversal of roles that he anticipated even as he wallowed in some woman's piss, or bled around her fist, which sweetened and sharpened the pleasure of being her victim) the possibilities for revenge would be myriad, rich, reliable. The waistband of his jeans was chafing the tip of his cock. Prez whimpered. He stepped into the circle with the three women and his side man, and cut the worst deal of his life.

Doc did not like it. When she saw what was going to happen, she tried to argue with Raven. But the stubborn bitch had gotten them boxed in. Once she offered to take Fluff's place, Prez would settle for nothing less. He was not interested in Doc's offer to take a smaller cut as the courier for the speed the Angels manufactured. She was a broker for many other drugs and light industries. When she offered to let him in on some of that biz, Prez did not even pretend to listen.

The Harpies were still in shock from Raven's announcement that she was leaving them. It had not occurred to any of them that this was how their high priestess planned to go. Cries of outrage and whistled signals that meant, "Kill, kill!" were ringing out. It wasn't going to be possible to keep them under control much longer. So Doc gave up. She tried to give Raven a chance to survive. She made Prez give Anderson and Michaels amnesty. If those two let any harm come to Raven, she swore privately that she would have two more dehydrated dicks hanging from her Medusa. She also tried to get Prez to give Raven an official status, exchange public vows with her. He balked at that.

"Let us compromise," Raven said. She stood straight and slim in the sunlight, not a hair out of place, not a drop of sweat on her face. To the catcalls and ululation, she paid no heed. She might have been ordering dinner in a French restaurant instead of standing between a pack of bloodthirsty Amazons and their natural meat. "If we are still together for Solstice, we will exchange vows then."

Prez, ignorant of the witches' calendar, thought Solstice happened only in a Leap Year, and readily agreed. But Doc, who knew how they celebrated the longest night of the year on Harpy Farm, shuddered, and remembered Raven's promise.

While they bickered, Raven had instructed the women to bring jugs of wine down from the farm. The wine was doctored with sedatives. The Harpies placed the bottles midway between themselves and the bikers, and invited them to come and get them. "Talking is thirsty work," someone said, but her voice was not particularly friendly. The farmers circulated identical jugs (full of spring water) among themselves, to allay any suspicions about their intentions. By the time the negotiations were completed, Prez's people were crashing. Raven had signaled one of the Harpies to bring him his own jug of wine, and he had made frequent use of it. Even if he had wanted to, Prez couldn't have gotten ugly now. Campbell barely got him out of the circle and into the shade of a tree before he collapsed.

"At dawn," Raven promised. "I will come to you with the morning light." With a gesture, she gathered up her warriors. "We will return to the big house now," she said.

A voice that Doc recognized as belonging to the Chief rang out from the trees. "Down in front! Warning shot, fire now!"

As one, the Harpies around Raven folded to the ground. Some of them shielded her with their own bodies. A sheet of arrows arced out of the woods. Miraculously, not one landed in human flesh, although one biker stared, stupefied, at the shaft that had buried itself in his seat, landing between his crotch and the gas tank. But it was clear that no one would have escaped if that had been the archers' intent. Arrows had landed at many men's feet, and Prez was surrounded by a complete ring of them. Only the biker women had not been threatened.

Raven stood. Doc assisted her. As Fluff got up under her own power, she hissed, "Thanks a lot." Doc sighed. Never expect gratitude, expect abuse. That way you won't be disappointed.

Raven smiled at Prez, who could not seem to make sense out of the feathered shafts that ringed him in. Scott Campbell's face was chalky. He knew exactly what had almost happened here. "I will come to you of my own free will," Raven said sweetly, and gave her new flock a regal little wave before she turned her back and took the Harpies away.

✧

The meeting that followed was stormy. The Harpies had been upset enough by the notion that Raven would leave them. But the idea of her becoming a hostage to the same man who had sent Fluff and Tina to them for help stuck in the collective gorge. Several women suggested that it had been stupid not to poison the wine. Since it was too late to mend that error, they wanted to go back to the edge of the farm and use the men for target practice. "Let's finish them off now," one of the archers argued. "Then they can never threaten us again." Her proposal met with general agreement.

"And what will you do with their women?" Raven asked. "Will you orphan their children? None of us have been injured."

The Harpies had been cranked up to fight to the death, and all of them were disappointed that there was not going to be a pitched battle. Doc was sure there would be a few wrestling matches between the Harley boys who had gone easy on the wine and the sentries. That would blow off some steam. The bottom line was, the farmers did not want Raven to go off with the bikers. They perceived them as bestial, psychopathic, and filthy. Not too far wrong, Doc thought, just a mite optimistic.

Raven told them again that she had had a vision, that the Goddess had ordered her to leave Harpy Farm. "My word is not for you alone," the Goddess had told her. "My rule is not for women alone. Solstice is coming. I have brought you a calf. Now you must fatten him, and teach him to bend his knees when you twist his horns. I give this calf to you because I love you, and because I want you to spread My word among women who are too far away to ever hear of Harpy Farm."

"Don't you understand?" Raven said. "This is a sacred calling. I cannot deny it any more than I could deny becoming your high priestess. The Goddess will care for me. I am in Her hand. Sisters, do not weep for me. Even if I never return to you, you can trust in Her as I do. This is something I must do."

In the end, they could not compel Raven to stay on the farm any more than they could have ousted Fluff. It was not in them to force another woman to do anything. So they helped her pack medicines and other herbal concoctions, some of her magical paraphernalia, a few of the tools on her wall. But the thing she seemed to care most about packing was a box that she put together after a whispered consultation with Doc — a box that contained ketamine, syringes, catheters, and a high colonic tube.

12.

The raucous argument downstairs reached Tina's room and awakened her. But she was not alone. An enormous Woman towered over her bedside. She was as wide as She was tall, and looked very strong. Her feet were planted in the earth. Tina looked more closely at Her toes, too fascinated by this apparition to wonder where the bedroom floor had gone. The brown digits twined like tree roots, and disappeared into the soil. That was odd, but it also seemed appropriate for a Woman the size of a redwood tree.

She wore a robe that was green and blue and gray, and its hem seemed to dissolve, break, and reform like the waves of the sea. Despite Her height, Tina did not have to tilt her head back to see the Giantess's face. That was because the Woman had reached underneath her, put the silky skin of Her big hand between Tina's aching, itching body and the harsh, crawling sheets and lifted her up.

The Goddess (Tina just knew that it was Her) had a broad face. Sometimes it was brown, with cheekbones like Carmen's, and sometimes it seemed African. Her hair rippled like black topsoil turned back from the blade of a plow, and from the furrows Tina saw green sprouts starting. The tiny green shoots quickly became tall rows of corn, and the woman who held her in Her hand was blonde now, with a hooked nose, death-white skin, and a cruel, crimson mouth. Around Her brow was a silver fillet, which held a crescent moon between Her eyes. She smelled like apples ... or lemons. Her voice was like the wind inside a seashell, but it sometimes turned growly, like the speech of a lioness or a bear.

"My child," She said tenderly. "You are hurt." Tina nodded, and wept for herself.

"Do you want to return to Me? You would come into My bosom, into the earth, and you would not suffer any more."

The large, shining eyes regarded her with great compassion and complete neutrality. To live or die was Tina's choice alone. It was a privilege the Goddess rarely granted.

"No," Tina said finally. There was too much vitality running below the level of her injuries. And she was so curious about this new place, these women Carmen had given her to.

"Then be healed," the Great Mother said, and placed Her hands together, holding Tina cupped between them. In the darkness a miracle took place. Tina knew as it happened that she must remember. Her old self would want her to forget, but she must start looking at things for herself, look hard, be careful to remember everything she saw, and never again let somebody else tell her what was important and unimportant, what was real and unreal.

The crescent moon on the Woman's brow was waxing, and by its light Tina saw Her smile. Now She looked Chinese, or did She look like an Eskimo? "Here is a new being," the Goddess said. "She must have a new name. I name you Moon Rabbit, because the mother rabbit pulls fur from her own breast to make a nest for her young. You have showed Me again and again that you are willing to take food out of your own mouth and give it to someone you think is hungrier. I will give you the power to call rain out of the moon, just like the rabbit, by drumming on the dry ground. But you will have to learn how to kick first. I gave the rabbit strong hind legs to defend herself and big teeth to chew her way out of trouble. She is prolific and ingenious, one of my gentle warriors. It isn't enough to be a mother. You can't take care of your little ones if you don't know how to fight for them. If a pregnant rabbit knows there will be no safety for her children, she will absorb them, and use their flesh to make herself strong. She knows that her first duty is to survive."

The Goddess stopped to smooth out Tina's bed before putting her carefully back into it. As she descended, Tina saw a bow and quiver strung across the Woman's back. The upper part of Her dress was dark blue, and full of stars.

"Take good care of My children here," the Goddess said. "They are good girls but they get excited sometimes and forget to be kind to one another. Try to teach them compassion, Moon Rabbit. And get them to play sometimes. I don't hear enough laughter from Harpy Farm. I know it sounds like a lot of work, but don't let your new job frighten you. I will send you My servant White Owl. She has much to teach you."

"You're leaving me!"

"No, daughter. You chose to leave Me. But we will speak again. I wish you would stop eating so much red meat. It really isn't good for you. In fact, if you want to talk to Me, quit eating for a day, then go up in the hills and sleep on the ground. White Owl will show you how. It isn't very hard, but few of My children seem to want to visit with Me anymore."

For a moment, She looked very, very old. Then She was gone. Moon Rabbit looked around, blinked a few times, and fell asleep. She did not even need to touch her injuries to know they had vanished.

13.

A t dawn, Raven strolled into the bikers' poor excuse for a camp. She awakened Prez by kicking his boots. "My luggage," she said, dropping her gear at his feet. "We are leaving now. It's time to go south. To go home."

Everyone heaved a sigh of relief at that. They were road-weary, homesick, missing spouses or children who had not been able to come along. Winter would be chasing them all the way south as it was. This ridiculous quest after Prez's stolen skirt had been a bust.

Prez had barely enough sense left to go along with her. While the others checked their gear and got ready to travel, she took him a little deeper into the woods and told him to remove his jacket and shirt. Then she drove a needle through each of his nipples. She did it without preliminaries, without warning. Prez hated it, and hated her, but it made him as hard as a handlebar.

Then she stuck a gun in his mouth and brought him to his knees. From his perspective, the pistol barrel protruding from his lips seemed much bigger than any cock he had ever sucked. It was harder, too, hard enough to chip his teeth, rip the roof of his mouth, ruin his throat. It tasted like cold steel and gun oil. He thought about her fucking him with it, and his bowels were suddenly dangerously loose.

"You will wear these needles all day," she said. "Tomorrow you will wear more than two. I will hurt you whenever I want to. I will want to hurt you almost all of the time. You have a lot to learn, Prez, and a lot to pay for. And you will never touch yourself with a needle again, or I will blow your brains out. Trust me. Now get your clothes back on, and get me out of here."

Raven put the pistol back into its shoulder holster. She would be wearing it, waking and sleeping, until the last act of this sacred drama had been played out. She wondered why Doc had been so worried about her.

At Doc's urging, Paint and Desiree accompanied the Angels. It wasn't hard for Paint to tear herself away. She had discovered the shell of an old Rattlesnake in one of the sheds that dotted the Harpies' land, and was so excited about restoring it that she stuttered when she tried to talk about it. Carmen (who had been sleeping with the Chief ever since Raven tucked her into the leader's bed) seized upon this discovery as a good reason to make her own exit. If they could pry Paint's hands off the derelict bike long enough to get it into the truck bed, Carmen would be happy to ferry it back to Alamo. Desiree had discovered the shooting range and had begun the weapons training for young Harpies. She wasn't finished yet, so she didn't exactly want to leave. "That little target with the prick in the middle of it would look so cute on my overlay," she pouted. But Paint promised to bring her back in the spring. "And it ain't like I don't have any guns at home, girl," Paint told her. "You can shoot all the tin cans in my backyard that you want to, you crazy bitch. Gunpowder bug bit you for sure, you pistol-packing mama, you."

Unhappiest of all those taking leave were Anderson and Michaels. Carmen flatly refused to let either man ride with her in the truck, so the two friends were going to have to travel as a duo until they could find Anderson's abandoned, broken-down Harley and hopefully get it running again. "I don't know what the fuck I did," was Michaels's frequent refrain. "I can understand Anderson bein' in the doghouse, but I don't know what the fuck I did."

Anderson had refused to believe that Tina would not see him or go home with him. Doc was scared stiff that he would try to storm the big house, and catch holy hellfire from the Harpies who were grieving for Raven as if she were already dead. So she arranged for the two of them to meet briefly in one of the scarecrone huts, and it had scared him almost as much as seeing her body on the kitchen floor. She would not answer to her right name, insisted on being called some kind of silly witch thing. He tried to remind her of their kids, and she told him, "The Goddess has given me other children." Then she showed him her body, and he expected to see terrible injuries, stitches, but there was nothing — it was all pink and whole, healed (she said) by the touch of the Goddess.

"Don't think you can just come home now any time you get sick of playing house with these goddamned dykes," he said. She had left without even responding in anger, and that was not like his Tina at all.

It was Doc who reminded him that Prez had hurt her mind as well as her body. Instead of blaming Tina or the women who had taken her in, Doc suggested, he should think about getting his own back. If Tina knew Prez could never hurt her again, the world would probably look a whole lot different to her. She laid a geas on him to look after Raven. She also dropped a few hints to him about Solstice being a meaningful time, but these bikers usually didn't even know what day of the week it was, so who knew if he would remember?

By the time everybody left, Doc felt she had done everything she could to see that Prez collected his karma long before he would be eligible for social security. She felt a grudging respect for Raven, who was willing to trade her body for Fluff, and follow her visions no matter how dangerous they got. She still thought the woman was not right in the head. But if the combined forces of Paint, Desiree, Carmen, Anderson, and Michaels could not protect her, well, that's life. You swallow your spit and take your chances. We are all just straw dolls, burned at the Goddess's whim. Every spring she makes herself some brand new toys, and she doesn't miss us at all.

Doc looked forward to spending some uncomplicated time with Fluff. She wanted to rest up, get a little fat and lazy, and get to know this girl. Where the hell could they go from here? It was obvious that despite the settlement that had been made, she had better not follow the bikers to Alamo in southern California, where they made their winter camp. She was going to have to go up to the city and explain to certain powers that be why no more Angel speed was going to be forthcoming to keep the ice factories going. You didn't usually get to just peacefully resign as the middle in deals like this. Yes, she definitely needed to spend a little time on Harpy Farm before she could get it up to face that music.

She still could not comprehend what the hell had happened to Tina — uh, Moon Rabbit. It seemed that Harpy Farm had a new tradition that its High Priestess was a refugee. The only trace of the assault left on her body was a tiny scar on her cheek, shaped like a crescent moon. It made no sense whatsoever. If I was a real doctor, Doc thought, I'd write it up for the Journal of the American Medical Association of Assholes and make myself famous in circles I do not move in.

The Chief had been dramatically altered by her brief affair with Carmen. The look of perpetual pain, the tense set of her shoulders, was replaced with a kind of comfort and ease that made Doc's heart warm to see. It was only natural for the Chief to gravitate from Carmen to her friend, Ti — Moon Rabbit — and try to comfort her.

But Doc's hope for a vacation was not to be. Scandal erupted on Harpy Farm. Fluff unwittingly caused it by continuing to flirt with Leaping Salmon. Doc was able to view this with a certain amount of amusement. It irked Fluff that she couldn't get Leaping Salmon to pant after her mini-skirts and high-heeled boots. Fluff was just too new to lesbian ways to know about or understand a baby butch who wanted to be an older woman's boy. Leaping Salmon treated her with an infuriating mixture of courtliness and lewd curiosity.

While Doc watched Fluff fail to get something she wanted, and experienced a detached sense of enjoyment, Wally was beside herself. She could not stand to watch Fluff openly flirt with her secret lover. Doc suspected Wally was also nervous about the possibility that her boy might develop a taste for bossy femmes. One night, Wally caught Fluff sitting in Leaping Salmon's lap and yanked her out of it. "Keep your hands to yourself," she said brusquely.

"I will not," Fluff said. "I don't belong to you, and neither does she."

"You deserve a spanking," Wally said, and lunged for her. Fluff (who had continued to sharpen all the knives on the farm, and now wore, in various locations about her person, several blades that had not been claimed by prior owners) cut her across the face. Wally was so stunned that she could not figure out how to respond. Fluff had no such inhibitions. If Doc had not been there to sit on Fluff, the chief of sentries would have been turned into sushi.

Leaping Salmon panicked. "Daddy!" she wailed, and ran to tend her injured sweetheart. By nightfall the news of that affair was all over Harpy Farm, and all the implications of that single passionate love-word were being discussed more heatedly than the best method for curing bacon. Only the arrival of White Owl, who had been told by a vision to return to her former home and lift her curse, chased that piece of gossip from the front pages.

Doc took Wally aside and suggested that it might be a good idea for her to leave with White Owl to set up a sewage treatment system for Snake River. Wally responded that guests and fish smelled after two days. When the Chief echoed that sentiment, Doc took the hint. She put Fluff on the back of the bike and headed for the city, filled with misgivings about the unpredictable personality of her passenger.

"Try to bore me for a few days, okay?" she suggested. Fluff, of course, made no promises.

❖Part Two: The Town

14. ✧

They were sitting in Denny's, eating hamburgers. Doc had encouraged Fluff to order fried chicken with biscuits and gravy, but she had sniffed, "Yankees don't know how to make gravy."

Doc kept shifting around, trying to get comfortable. "Goddammit, sitting on your fist and that bike makes it motherfucking hard to sit any place else," she groused.

"Girl gets lucky, still complains," Fluff smirked.

"Watch your mouth, or I'll stick something besides a handful of french fries in there."

"I'm a little saddle-sore myself," Fluff reminded her. "Are we getting cranky now?"

"No, I'm just wondering where the hell we should go."

Fluff regarded her for a moment, spooning ice cream out of her malt glass. She wasn't sure how she felt about Doc's assumption that the two of them would keep on traveling together. Reassured? Irritated? So far, the words "I love you" had not been spoken. And how did she feel about that, considering what kind of requests usually followed the utterance of that trite phrase? Reassured? Irritated? Shit. "Well, where would you go if I wasn't with you?" she asked mildly.

"When I was a brave young buck, I would have said San Francisco. But that was before the third Ayatollah bombed Washington, D.C., and we got government by the Joint Chiefs of Staff, coming at you live, from the only underground capital city in the world."

"What the hell does that have to do with San Francisco?" Fluff asked.

"You don't know much about your world history outside of Dixie, do you, girlfriend? It was in the midst of all that confusion that the Free Christian States seceded from the union. When the generals finally stuck their heads out of the rubble and asked them how the hell they thought they were going to get away with that, the New Confederates said, what are you gonna do about it, bomb us? And so poor beleaguered San Francisco, which was already being starved to death because abortions were still legal there so they didn't get any federal money, and they wouldn't quarantine the queers, so they didn't get any state money, decided they would go ahead and do the same thing. And when the generals said, what the hell makes you think you can get away with that, and San Francisco said, what are you going to do, bomb us, they said damn straight, and called in the National Guard."

"I thought it was always just one big military base," Fluff said, "and that was why they had martial law there. National security. Yankee national security, that is."

"Yeah, well, this is why you should stay in school. When I was a little shaver, if you wanted to be a wild child and you couldn't run away to San Francisco, you went to Seattle. But that was before some rabid political entity in the Mid-East tried to nuke Seattle and missed, and fried a big chunk of Canada. Wasn't that fun, now, with Israel blaming the PLO and the PLO blaming Israel, and the Survivalists Party blaming Japan and calling for the repeal of all their offshore oil-drilling leases in California, and the Japanese blaming the Chinese, and the Chinese blaming the Russians. We never did find out where the hell that sucker came from."

"So you think you're so smart, I bet you don't know that there used to be a place called Mexico." Fluff licked chocolate malt off of her upper lip.

"Say what?"

"There used to be a whole country down south of Texas. But right after the Lone Star State seceded from the Free Christian States, the Texas Rangers just rode on down and annexed it. Didn't you ever wonder why most of the people in Texas speak Spanish?"

"No, I thought — well, never mind what I thought." It wouldn't do to set a bad example for Fluff, who had to be told at least once a day that she was a racist dog.

"But we aren't going to Texas," Fluff guessed.

"No, no, we aren't going to Texas. There's some mean people down there who would be way too glad to see me. We're gonna go north, up to Portland."

"Portland?"

"Yeah. I knew all along that's where we had to go. I don't want to go anywhere near the California coast anyway. Those glorified gas pumps the Japs have got running are causing too damn many earthquakes. Baja's already halfway to Hawaii. I keep forgetting that Portland's a big city now. It quadrupled in size when all the cultural and nuclear refugees from Seattle and San Francisco and even Vancouver streamed in. It's just that I gotta disappoint some people who really don't like to hear bad news. Well, if it gets too hot in Portland, we can always go to Canada."

"Canada won't accept my passport," Fluff said. "Not since the Klan lynched their ambassador for sleeping with white women. Figures they'd have to send us a ni — a black man."

"Don't worry about that, princess. As long as you're with me you can be the woman with a thousand faces. Think of an alias that isn't too exotic, okay? Scarlett O'Hara is a bad choice."

"Comedian. You want any dessert?"

"No, I'm getting too fat. Don't want my stomach to sit on the gas tank. C'mon, let's tip our waitress and git outa here. I don't like checking my blades at the door."

"I'll protect you," Fluff said, grinning.

"I'll just bet you would."

They laughed together. For some strange reason, security guards tended to wave Fluff through the metal detectors, even if she made them go off like church-bells. Doc thought it was a hoot, having such a dangerous traveling companion. It was like having a pet hand grenade.

"How many days to Portland?" Fluff asked as they got back on the Medusa.

"Two, if we stop fucking."

"Be realistic."

"They ain't gonna see our faces in the big city for at least two weeks."

"That's my big dumb animal."

"That's my honey."

They spied a couple going into the restaurant. The man was in a gray, pin-striped suit. The woman was wearing a flower-print dress and a scarf around her neck. When they saw the two bikers, the woman moved closer to the man, and he put one arm protectively around her. As one, Doc and Fluff turned and screamed at the top of their lungs. It sounded like they had just seen the most terrifying sight in the world, and it was loud enough to make people inside Denny's jump.

"I think they both peed," Doc said complacently.

"I would," Fluff said happily.

"Yeah, but you'd stomp over to the bike and piss on my boot."

Fluff hugged her tight, and settled into her back. Doc sighed and shifted on the seat. She really ought to stop and pack her leg in ice and rest for a few days. But the thought of how that would feel made staying on the bike seem like a better idea.

They didn't always travel together so harmoniously. One day, they came out of a grocery store where they'd bought cigarettes, a magazine for Fluff, and some sandwich fixings, and the Medusa would not start. Doc swore, and damn near ran the battery down trying to get it to turn over. Finally she gave up, heaved all the saddlebags and camping gear off the bike, and yanked up the seat. Nothing seemed to be amiss there. Then Fluff, who was around on the other side, said, "Aren't there supposed to be some hoses running from here to here?"

Doc took a look and swore again. Somebody who didn't like Japanese bikes, or bikers in general, or dykes, had reached into her engine and yanked out some vital parts. "Where the hell am I going to find spare parts in this Goddess-forsaken, one-horse town?" she shouted. "This had to happen in the middle of the sticks!" Her face was scarlet. Fluff thought Doc's eyeballs might pop out from the sheer pressure of her rage.

"At least we're not on the freeway," Fluff said.

Doc rounded on her. "Well, if we were driving on the freeway, this wouldn't have happened, would it?" she said nastily. "But we had to have our magazines and our snacks, didn't we?"

"You were as hungry as I was," Fluff said defensively. "Besides, this could have happened at a gas station."

Doc's only response was to throw a wrench over her shoulder, and swear some more.

"There's a pay phone over here," Fluff said.

"What the hell good will that do me? You want me to rip the phone out and fix the bike with it?"

"No, but I can look in the phone book and see if there's a—"

"There won't be any goddamn phone book in that goddamn phone booth," Doc said nastily. "Somebody will have ripped it off. I'd be surprised if there was a phone in there."

"Then I can call directory assistance."

"Oh? And what are you going to ask for? Dykes on bikes roadside service? Because there ain't none! And if you don't know the shop name they won't give you the number."

Fluff shook her head and walked over to the phone booth, more to get away from Doc than from any expectation of being helpful. Beneath the phone hung a thick book, stuck inside a metal binder. She flipped to the back and looked through the yellow pages. "Who makes the Medusa?" she asked, scanning the two pages of ads for motorcycle dealers.

What Doc screamed at her did not sound like the name of any manufacturer she knew, so Fluff started reading the ads. When she saw one that had the word "Medusa" in it, she dropped some coins into the phone and dialed.

When she walked back to the bike, Doc was staring at it, smoking, and muttering, "I knew I never should have bought this piece of shit."

"There's a dealer that handles Medusas not far from here," Fluff said. "I called a taxi."

"I don't have money to pay for taxis!" Doc shrieked.

"You're welcome," Fluff replied, thinking seriously about walking over to the road and sticking out her thumb. Luckily, the taxi arrived before she made up her mind. Doc walked off without the saddlebags, so Fluff picked them up and came after her. It was a struggle. "What's all this shit?" Doc demanded when Fluff presented them to her at the cab door.

"Wouldn't you like to have these with you?" Fluff asked.

Doc grunted, and dragged them onto her lap. "There just isn't any place to put all this stuff back here," she complained.

"So I'll sit with the driver!" Fluff snapped.

"Hey, lady, take it easy with my door, okay?" the driver said.

"Yeah," Doc told her. "You don't have to rip that thing off its hinges. This is an American-made car. The doors shut real easy."

By the time they got to the dealership, Doc was cheerfully whistling, and Fluff was seething. Doc gave her some change and told her to go play the video machines while she got her parts. Instead, Fluff cruised the clothing-and-accessories section and picked out a pair of goggles. She was looking at leather body suits when Doc found her.

"What the hell are you doing? I've been looking all over for you."

"You're always complaining about the way I'm dressed. I thought I'd see about getting something else. Look." She showed Doc a pair of engineer boots. "I think these'll fit me if I wear two pairs of socks."

Doc laughed.

"What's so funny?"

"Nothing, nothing."

Fluff felt her face getting hot. "You asshole. You better tell me right now what's making you laugh so hard."

"Well, it just doesn't seem to be your style, that's all."

"I see. So you're gonna give me a hard time for wearing a dress on your bike, but if I try to buy something else, you're gonna make fun of me?"

"Oh, for Chrissake, you don't have any money to go shopping anyway."

"I picked up the check for breakfast, didn't I? Wait for me outside," Fluff said.

"Wait for you? C'mon, I've got my stuff, I'm all ready to go."

Fluff threw a handful of change at her. "Go play the video games, why don't you? There's a game out there called Going Crazy. Seems to me it's just your style."

"Are you premenstrual or what?" Doc shook her head, shrugged her shoulders, and left, tromping on the scattered quarters.

Fluff wasn't sure if Doc would wait for her, but she took her time anyway. When she walked out, she was wearing a pair of black leather jeans with silver conchos on the side-seams, a black leather bodice with silver laces, and a pair of high-heeled boots with engraved silver toe-points. Her old deerskins were rolled up under her arm.

"Who'd you have to suck off to get that?" Doc demanded.

"Did you call us a cab?" Fluff asked.

"I said, who did you have to suck off to get that?"

"What do you care? Said I was a girl paid my own way. How I do it is my business, isn't it?" Fluff's Georgia drawl poured poisoned honey over Doc's head.

"Not any more."

"Oh, does that mean you're gonna let me in on your business? Tell me all about it? Make me a partner?"

"Hell, no!"

"Then shut the fuck up."

"I still want to know how the hell you got all those clothes. That is expensive shit."

"Well, you know that redhead at the service counter, the one who tried to sell you the wrong parts? Yeah, well, he gave it to me in the pussy while I gave his boss head. What's the matter? Aren't you gonna start jacking off? I mean, why let a good story go to waste?"

That was literally a blow below the belt. Doc loved to hear lurid stories about Fluff's kinkier clients when she was getting herself off. Doc felt herself fill up with steam, like an espresso machine. But she was just too angry to think of anything clever and biting to say. A cab went by, and Fluff hailed it. Her face was very pale, except for tiny spots of bright red in the middle of each cheek. Wish I was as cute as that when I get mad, Doc thought.

When they got back to the Medusa, Fluff reached into her white fringed jacket and took a roll of bills out of the inside pocket. "Do you all have change for a hundred? Oh, wait a minute, I got a fifty in here somewhere. You don't? No, I don't want to go into that awful old store again, it'll take too long. You all can just keep the change. Thank you for rescuing two ladies in distress."

Doc slid out of the cab. Fluff was waiting for her, and dropped her saddlebags on her feet. "You all play your cards right, some day I might take you shopping," she said sweetly. "If you ever figure out who you have to suck off to get what you want. No, don't bother to apologize. I'm just a whore, nobody has to apologize to me for nothin', I'm just supposed to spend my whole life bowin' and scrapin' to decent folk who overlook the foul nature of what I am. And now that I know you're one of the decent folk, I'll keep to my station in life, thank you, I really will."

She went over to the store, leaned on its front window, and opened her magazine. And she did not look up from it or budge while Doc repaired the Medusa's violated engine.

Later that night, Doc, trying to kiss and make up, said, "Are you going to stay mad forever? Look, if you want to, you can beat me for it."

Fluff looked at her with horror. "I never want to feel that way about you. It would be like what I did with Prez."

All Doc could feel was the horrible humiliation of being sexually rejected. This is what comes of letting girls get their hands on you, she thought. Being a stone butch is so much safer. I'm a fool. "Stupid bitch," she said harshly. "You can't even take a joke." Then she rolled over and cried herself to sleep, but soundlessly, the way she had taught herself to cry because making all that blubbering noise made her feel dirty.

They didn't have sex that night. The next day, Fluff made a joke about how her pussy was glad to take a vacation, but it did not want to become unemployed, and things were nearly back to normal.

But Doc smoldered with resentment. It had been a fucking crisis. What was she supposed to do, break into song? She knew she could have been more appreciative when Fluff found a place for them to get the parts, but who knew how to put the parts on, huh? Nobody said thank you to her for that. Her mechanical expertise was just taken for granted.

And Fluff smoldered with resentment. She didn't expect to have to take crap like that from another woman. In fact, she told herself, any man who dared talk to her that way would have found his own bloody balls in his hand. She knew Doc had saved her life, knew she ought to be grateful, but when Doc got abusive she felt like so much dirty laundry instead of a rare prize won in a dangerous battle. Besides, she had come through with practical assistance. Wasn't that worth a little credit?

It disturbed both of them to find themselves suddenly at war with one another. But it kept on happening, no matter how passionately they took each other after each battle. A residue of bitterness was left each time they wounded one another. It grew slowly, but it grew.

Another thing that bugged Doc was that Fluff would not get high with her. Oh, she would drink — some. But she would not smoke dope, pop speed, snort coke, drop acid, or allow Doc to medicate her with any of the delicious, illicit pharmaceuticals she carried, no matter how highly Doc praised them as spiritual aids, painkillers, sedatives, energizers, or aphrodisiacs.

Finally one night, they splurged on a motel room to get out of the rain. Fluff had horrible cramps. Doc insisted on knowing why she would not take any one of a half-dozen things she had that would make them go away.

Fluff tried to put her off with a little humor. "You think I got any brain cells to spare?" she asked.

"C'mon, I don't think you're stupid. You don't know a carburetor from a crankshaft, but that doesn't make you stupid. Suffering when you could just swallow a cap of this and make it all better is stupid."

"Why does it matter so much to you? We have a good time, don't we?"

"Yeah, we have a good time. But we aren't having one now. If you went to a doctor they would give you a prescription for this. Come on, let's get fucked up together. I don't feel like I really know somebody until I get high with them. It's one of the ways I bond with people."

Fluff said, "Let me show you how I bond with people," and tried to wrap the cord from her bathrobe around Doc's neck.

The big woman evaded her. "You think you're too good to get stoned with me. And you're afraid of losing control."

"Darlin'," Fluff said heavily, pressing her hands on her relentless abdomen, "you have no idea what you are messin' with."

Doc leaned over her and pinned her down. "Tell me."

Fluff started to cry. "Let me up, you big ox. You're hurting me."

Feeling ashamed and guilty, but also feeling like she hadn't really done anything wrong, Doc backed off. "Usually you like it when I'm forceful."

"Not now. Not now." Fluff struggled to control her tears, knowing they would upset Doc so much that she would get angry. She wanted to be comforted, but Doc was the person who had made her feel this way, and she did not want Doc to comfort her. When Doc held her and stroked her, it was all she could do to keep her hands at her side and not push her away.

Finally the words came. "My mama is a drunk. And I can't hold my liquor. Never could, and never will. I got a bellyful of her binges and hangovers, the upchucks and headaches and DTs. And her boyfriends were worse. She had a knack for pickin' up these losers and bringin' them home. Junkies and pillheads and potheads and crack freaks and even one guy with those wires in his head. Had himself a little button in the middle of his chest he could push any time he needed a jolt. And they took away her money, beat her, lied to her. Fucked her. I cannot tell you how much I hated doin' the laundry. Sheets and towels. I didn't even want to touch those sheets and towels.

"I used to make 'em come after me so they'd leave her alone. Hope she'd see what was happening and kick their sorry asses out. Then one day one of them gave me money. Twenty dollars. Can you believe it? And somehow she found out about it. She came up to me, said, 'I know Jerry gave you some money,' and twisted my arm until I gave it to her. So they could go out drinking. My money! As God is my witness.

"Well. I packed up and left home that night. I already had girlfriends who hustled. But I told myself I was a good girl. I was gonna stay home and take care of my mama. She used to tell me, loosen up, girl, you ain't any better than the rest of us so why do you act like it? If you think you're gonna be somebody special when you grow up you better get such ideas out of your head right now. Then she'd try to get me to have a nip out of her bottle. Sometimes I'd take it, you know, just to make her be quiet, but I have never liked the taste of the stuff. To me it tastes like all the things I wanted from her that I never got, that she would never give me."

"C'mon," Doc said. This story made her feel sick. She certainly did not want to start thinking about her own childhood. She wanted to put all of this far, far away. "It really makes me angry that because your mother was a wino we can't have a good time and get close to each other. You have to let the past go. Quit feeding your ghosts."

"Let it all go?" Fluff said. "Then what am I? All I have is these clothes on my back, a spare set of leathers, and my life. I can't afford to forget one little bit of it."

"You have me," Doc said.

Fluff knew that ought to be reassurance enough. But Doc's declaration didn't make her feel better. Fluff didn't believe she *would* have Doc forever, and anyway, she wasn't sure she wanted to be stuck with this blustering, unreasonable, irascible (and tall, gutsy, sexy, funny) woman for the rest of her life. Love didn't fix anything. It just complicated your life. It meant you had to pretend you weren't lonely, because there was somebody around all the time and you couldn't hurt their feelings. You had to pretend you trusted them, too, even while they crept closer and closer to the truth of your life and threatened to spill their own opinions and needs over what ought to be private and protected. Simple loneliness was scary, but maybe it was easier. Fluff didn't know anybody else who felt this way about romance, that it was an experience that combined as much blackmail and claustrophobia as it did lust and affection. There must be something wrong with her. Maybe her heart was just frost-bitten. Suddenly, she could not stand to feel so cold and ancient.

"All right," Fluff said, "Get me a glass of water. I just can't stand this any more. But leave me alone about that other shit, it reminds me of bad times."

Doc came back to her, not with a glass of water, but with a Jack Daniels and Coke. "It'll keep the chill off you," she said. Fluff sighed. Well, what was the difference? She swallowed the pills with a bitter, fizzy mouthful of liquid. Doc was turning on the TV and going through the channels looking for a movie. When she had it fixed the way she wanted it and settled into bed beside Fluff, she brought a joint with her. Fluff turned to say something, and Doc blew smoke in her face. She couldn't exactly be angry about a little weed after taking those pills, could she? So Fluff took the joint and had a couple of tokes. It wasn't the first time she had smoked pot, but all it seemed to do was make her cough and cough.

Fluff woke up with a start when Doc nudged her in the ribs. "You're a real party girl," Doc said. She was tired. Her voice sounded like shallow water running over little rocks. "I love the sound of you snoring. It's very romantic. Let's go to bed."

Fluff stripped and rolled under the covers. She reached over, but Doc was already asleep. Fluff felt as if she had made a mistake, done something wrong, and disappointed Doc, but what was it? What did Doc expect?

There was beautiful country on the way to Portland. Oregon had become the last stronghold of militant environmentalists, and they had preserved much of the wilderness. But the thick stands of pine cast shadows on the road, and the altitude made it cold. They found it more and more difficult to sleep outside. And Doc was hurting so much, she found it hard to keep the bike on the road all day.

Finally, Fluff said, "I'm tired of watching you limp around." She made them stop for a few days and rent a motel cabin with a kitchen. For three days, she kept Doc in bed with her leg propped up, cooked for her, and changed her ice packs. Doc was by turns effusively grateful or snappish about "being treated like a cripple."

Fluff sighed, and just kept feeding her Coke and Jack Daniels. Once Doc had become so unreasonable that Fluff went into the kitchen to mix her a drink, and spit in it. She felt so bad about it that before they went to bed, she confessed and apologized. It made Doc laugh like nothing had for days. "Wondered why it was so tasty," Doc said, rolled her over, and stuck her tongue up Fluff's asshole. They had a festive evening, and by the next morning, Doc pronounced herself well enough to travel.

Nevertheless, the last leg of the trip was a bear. When they saw a sign that said, "Portland 60 Miles," Fluff almost cried. She felt as if she would never get warm or clean again.

What she wanted was to go straight to a hotel room and stand in a hot shower for about two days. Instead, Doc took them on a freeway that ran by the Willamette river. "That side of the river is Richville," Doc explained. "Lotta fortified communities for the well-off, whole parts of town where you can't get in unless you got a pass says you are a loyal slave and have been duly fingerprinted, brainwashed, deloused, vaccinated, and butt-fucked by your masters. See all the checkpoints on the bridges?"

Fluff wondered just how many bridges there were. She counted at least twenty, and every one was different. There was an ancient-looking one built on square brick pilings, a railroad bridge made out of plain, functional steel girders, a modernis-tic suspension bridge, even one that floated on pontoons and a rickety-looking wooden one that could only be used by foot traffic. But each bridge, no matter how different its architec-ture, was divided in half by identical yellow-and-black booths that were full of guards checking people's papers.

"We aren't going to go over there to Richville, are we?" Fluff asked. She didn't want to try and explain herself to any cops. The river smelled terrible, but the colors were pretty, surges of dark green, purple, and red. From time to time, the sun struck the oily surface at just the right angle to make the whole river look like a rainbow. "Bet you could dissolve an entire car if you left it in there overnight," she called to Doc, feeling a little awe.

Doc laughed. "I doubt it would take that long. We're going to Poor Town, honey. I've gotta look up some old friends and see if we can find us a place to stay." It was hard to stay awake. Better continue the history lesson. "The old train station is in the middle of Richville. It's nearly two hundred years old. They think it's a landmark, but it looks like a Victorian prison to me. They might as well use it for a jail 'cause the trains don't run any more. Quarantine authority used to ship people through Union Station on their way to the racetrack that's just north of town. Portland Meadows was a hunger camp for a long time. Got shot to pieces during the troubles, railroad tracks got torn up by the mob. Later on they fixed up the racetrack so the ponies can run, but not the steel tracks for the iron horses. If you're a good girl we'll go to the races some day and lose our shirts."

"Uh huh," Fluff kept saying. "Uh huh." She appreciated Doc's monologue. She didn't want to think about how tired she was or feel the aches and pains in her back, arms, and thighs.

Doc finally left the freeway and wound her way through innumerable streets. In the residential areas, the houses were missing chunks of their porches or roofs, had peeling paint, and the yards sported old washing machines, cars, or snow plows. The business streets were lined with pawn shops, attorneys whose signs were in Chinese, Arabic, or Spanish, secondhand stores, junkyards full of auto parts, and fast food places. Almost all the people Fluff saw were black. Finally Doc pulled up outside a dingy, grimy building with a plastic sign that lit up from behind. Some of the bulbs back there had burned out, making it hard to read. Fluff spelled out, "Come 7 Come 11."

"Welcome to Craps," Doc said, and got off the bike. She did not wait to help Fluff down, just charged toward the bar. Fluff took a look around. There were several lounging, unsavory males of the type her mother called "gentlemen of leisure." One of them saw her, pursed his lips, and started walking toward the bike.

Fuck the saddlebags. Fluff folded her arms across her chest, and ran into the door where Doc had disappeared.

15.

J esus Christ," Michaels said, "I am really sick of you acting like a puppy that got its ass whipped. When are you gonna stop moping around like somebody ran off with your balls?" Anderson didn't say a word, he just went into the bathroom and locked the door. Michaels sighed loudly. If he'd had anything at hand, he would have thrown it at the damn bathroom door, but he wasn't about to get up and find something to use for a missile. He was too fucking tired.

They had spent a frustrating day trying to diagnose the problem with Anderson's bike, which for a wonder was where they had left it. Never underestimate the power of an Alamo Angels license plate. It's the best insurance policy against theft that a bike can have.

After dinking around with the unresponsive engine for two hours, they had finally given up and had it towed to the nearest dealership. Michaels was in a foul mood because Carmen had absolutely refused to help them, and he'd had to ask that old fart, Shorty, who drove the only other truck, to do him a favor. Of course the first thing the one-legged bastard had said was, "Why don't you get your wife to do it?"

Anderson had been quiet all day, not speaking unless spoken to. He wasn't taking any initiative at all. Michaels felt as if the whole thing had been dumped on his shoulders. Several times he had said to Anderson, "If you don't care about getting this taken care of, why should I?" and Anderson just stared at him out of big, hurt eyes and took another pull from his bottle of Southern Comfort. So Michaels just started giving him orders. Anderson did whatever his friend told him, but he moved slowly, as if he couldn't see his own hands or feet, and if you left him alone for very long, he ran down like a clock and just stood wherever he was, staring at nothing.

They had decided to stay in town, and had taken a room in a motel close to the Harley shop. Everybody else had gone on, and things were so bad in the club that it never occurred to anybody (including Carmen) to keep them company and make sure they had wheels so they could catch up with the pack tomorrow.

It was your generic cheap motel room — beds bolted to the floor, television bolted to its stand, hangers that wouldn't come off the clothes rod. Michaels wouldn't have been surprised to find the lightbulbs glued into their sockets and the towels stapled to the racks. There was an absolutely nauseating picture (bolted to the wall) of a ship sailing into the sunset. None of the colors were those you could find in nature. From where he was sitting on the bed, Michaels opened the top drawer in the stand between the two beds. Holy cow, the Gideon Bible wasn't chained up.

He lifted it out of the drawer and slid out his boot knife. One stroke removed a dozen pages. Grunting his satisfaction, he felt in his overlay for the plastic baggie full of marijuana, and rolled himself a joint with the first page of Genesis.

The smoke cooled his brain, took the edge off. Michaels started to feel ⸍ little more human. He reached down into his jeans and readjusted his balls. That new ring on the left side of his scrotum kept getting caught on a seam or something, and tugging everything down so it didn't sit comfortably in his pants. He checked his other rings and bars, more for the satisfaction of feeling all that gold and the memory of laughing his way through each piercing than because he thought any of the holes were infected.

Maybe he would see about ordering a pizza, get both of them fed. Shit, you couldn't blame Anderson for being blue, it wasn't every day your old lady got herself half-killed, then dumped you to join up with a bunch of queer turnip-turners.

He got up to flip on the television (which had "Property of the Econo-Inn, Red Bluff, Oregon" written on it with an electric engraving pen). But a dull thud from the bathroom made him turn around before he got his hand on the knob.

He tried the bathroom door. "Anderson!" he called. "Hey, are you all right in there?" He expected the stock response — "What can happen to me in the bathroom? You think something's gonna come up out of the toilet and eat me?" But there was no answer. He pounded on it hard enough to make the panels shiver. Well, fuck this. He had wanted to trash this place ever since they gave him his key.

Michaels kicked the door hard, twice, and the jamb split. The door sagged open enough for him to see a glimpse of Anderson slumped on the john. He shoved at the broken wood, and got a real good view of a sink full of blood. There was a Ka-Bar on the floor, a replica of the one Anderson had given Tina.

"Oh, you asshole," he exploded, and started looking for wounds. The throat wasn't cut, that was good, one wrist wasn't cut, that was good, one wrist was cut, no, it was the forearm, sliced all the way up, the long way, and that was fucked up, Jackson. He pushed the edges together, clamped his hands over the whole mess, and bellowed for help.

Somebody quit knocking on the front door of their room and unlocked it. "Just what do you think you're doing in here? What are you, some kind of wild animal? Just look at this. You're going to have to pay for all this damage," a prim female voice scolded.

"Get your ass in here," Michaels snapped. When nobody appeared, he took one hand off Anderson and leaned out the tiny bathroom far enough to grab the interloper. He reeled in a prissy, middle-aged lady in a blue-and-white striped dress and a yellow apron. The owner. Great.

"Press down on this," he said. "Press hard. Damn you, don't you get sick on me. We can save him if you help me."

She didn't say a word, just replaced him. Her face was grim, but she didn't seem to mind the blood that squeezed up between her fingers. Michaels sprinted into the other room and almost ripped the top flap off one of his saddlebags. Inside, on the bottom, wouldn't you fucking know it, was a sewing kit. He grabbed it and ran back into the bathroom.

It was pretty tight in there, and he tried to leave the mandatory half-inch between himself and the woman at all times. He tugged his belt out of its loops, cinched it above Anderson's elbow, and gave her the free end. "Keep it taut," he said. It slowed the bleeding immediately. Then he took a closer look at the cut.

Anderson had apparently passed out after making just one cut, and the slash wasn't as long as it had looked at first. If he had stayed conscious long enough to make it deeper and cross it with another one, there wouldn't have been anything anybody could do. "Okay, I've seen Doc do this a hundred times," he said out loud. "Come on, you clumsy bastard. Figure it out. We got to sew the ends of these tubes together, the ones where all the blood is coming out." He flipped the sewing kit open and jabbed some thread at one of the needles. It wouldn't go through. Goddammit, that was a little hole.

"Young man," said the biddy, "do you have any medical training? Because you certainly don't know how to sew!"

"Shut up, this is my friend. I have to save him."

"Oh, calm down. You can lose a lot more blood than this before it's going to kill you. Besides, your hands are filthy. He's probably got lockjaw just from having you stick your dirty fingers in there. Here. Hold onto this belt. Give me that."

She took the spool of thread away from him and dropped the needle on the floor. "We really should get a doctor," she said. "But I suppose we don't have time." Her wrinkled, age-spotted hands were busy between the lips of Anderson's self-inflicted injury. Michaels had to look away. He didn't want to see the insides of somebody he cared about. It was as if Anderson wasn't a person any more, just meat.

"That needle is useless," the old woman said. She took a pair of tweezers out of her apron and dug into Anderson's arm. "Come here, you. My, you're slippery. Got it." She wrapped thread around the ends of the tweezers and nudged it off. "One down, one to go." She repeated the procedure. "Now, I'm going to call my doctor."

She left the bathroom, fanning herself with her apron. Michaels heard her dial the phone and speak crisply into it. But he was too engrossed by the still-oozing blood to remember what she said. Should he loosen the tourniquet? Didn't you get gangrene if you kept it tight? He tried it, and was dismayed by the fresh blood that welled eagerly up.

"All this blood will never come out of this bedspread," she said from the other room. "I hope you know it will be on your bill."

He must have tracked blood into the other room. "Who the fuck cares?" Michaels shouted.

"Is this marijuana?" She appeared in the doorway, brandishing his baggie.

"Oh—" Michaels tried to think. Was pot illegal in this state? He looked at Anderson's arm. Was she going to call the cops? That would be a fitting climax to this fun, fun day.

"It is marijuana, isn't it? Don't you lie to me." She put it in her apron. "We'll just consider this a down payment on your repair bill."

Anderson was moving around. Michaels held his shoulders down. "Stay quiet, man, you're okay. Just leave that alone."

Someone knocked on the door and said they were Doctor Riley. Michaels went to let him in, but the portly gentleman with the black bag seemed reluctant to enter. Then Michaels remembered what he must look like. He had been too busy keeping Anderson quiet to wash his hands. There were bloody boot prints on the carpet and smears of red on the wall. "Place looks like hell, doesn't it?" he said, trying to be affable. "My friend got hurt real bad. Can you take a look at him?"

The motel owner raised her voice so she could be heard from the bathroom. "Get in here, Boyd," she said. "I know you charge by the hour."

The doctor opened his bag on the bathroom sink and cleaned out the wound. He gave an approving cluck at the tied-off veins, then got out his sutures. "All you left for me was the finishing touches, Ruth," he said.

She sniffed. "That's Mrs. Parker to you, Boyd."

After sewing up Anderson's arm and bandaging it, the doctor gave him a tetanus shot and left Michaels with a handful of Keflex and physicians' samples of various painkillers. Dr. Riley then accepted three twenty-dollar bills, and left them alone.

"You better keep him quiet," Mrs. Parker said. "I want you both out of here first thing tomorrow. I shouldn't let you stay the night, but the damage has already been done. No harm in letting you slumber in the ruins, I guess." She touched the mutilated Bible with her toe and clicked her tongue at him.

"Get out of here," Michaels told her. "Go add up my bill. And thanks for being such a good Samaritan."

"Young man," she said, "you don't know how lucky you are that I was cleaning out the ice machine and heard all of this racket." She left, fanning herself with her bloody apron.

Michaels guessed that she was right, and anyway, what did it cost him to let her have the last word? Might even be worth ten bucks off the bill. Besides, he was too busy getting Anderson on his feet and into bed to shout something vulgar at her starch-straight back.

The big blond man leaned heavily on him. At the bedside, Michaels tipped him over. He went onto his back with a groan.

Anderson was fully conscious now. "Why didn't you let me die?" he asked, staring hopelessly at the ceiling.

"That's a dumb-ass question. Even dumber than you trying to off yourself."

"I can't go on like this, Michaels. I can't do it. I'm no good to myself and I'm no good to anybody else. I can't stand feeling this way. You should have let me go."

"Fuck you," Michaels said. "Since when do you get to tell me what to do? Think you're some kind of master of the universe since you got Prez to bend over? Man, you were just putty in his hands. You ain't the boss of nothing."

"Leave me alone."

"Leave me alone," Michaels mimicked. "I left you alone and look what you did." He was slamming a fist into his palm, he was so angry.

"So what are you going to do, put my lights out?"

"Maybe I should."

"Maybe you should."

Michaels put his hands on Anderson's shoulders. "Man, I was just so afraid of … losing you. I know everything is all fucked up. If I had known the last run of the summer was going to be like this, I would have stayed home and grown tomatoes. I know you miss Tina. But would it be any better if she was like Carmen, here, but not with you? She's doing what she needs to do. You got to let her go. And you have to realize that you do have something to live for."

"Like what? What have I got to live for?"

"You got me," Michaels said, and kissed him.

Anderson could remember being a boy and having grown-ups plant unwelcome kisses on him. He could remember forcing Prez to accept his mouth and tongue and spit. You kissed women because they liked it. It was a way to distract them while you got their blouses unbuttoned. This was different. Something warm and … good … radiated from Michaels's mouth into the center of his being. He had been thinking of himself for days now as a shattered wasp's nest, a hall of cracked mirrors. But this kiss brought the shards and fragments together, heated them, sealed their edges, made them whole.

"I don't—"

"Shut up," Michaels said. "Just shut up."

The kiss went on, and became something else. Something that hurt, oh God, it hurt, but it was love.

16.

Fluff stopped by the door to let her eyes get used to the darkness inside. The room was filled with so much smoke, there must be a lot of people here, but they had gotten so quiet, the bar might as well have been empty. Her eyes focused enough to find Doc, and Fluff walked over to her. She hoped her hair wasn't a complete mess.

"Get me a drink," Doc said, without looking at her. Damn, the woman had eyes in the back of her head.

Fluff didn't like her tone. Then she managed to process what she was seeing, and figure out what kind of place this was. This was a hustler's bar, full of pimps and their women. She went meekly to the bar, ordered a drink for Doc, and paid for it. The bartender was a black faggot with a little mustache, a tiny diamond in one ear, and fingernails as long as some of the girls. She took her change and got a pack of Doc's cigarettes out of the vending machine.

She carried the drink and the smokes over to where Doc was sitting, talking to a dark and handsome gentleman in a purple velour suit. "Get yourself something," Doc said. So she went back to the bar and got a tomato juice. She gathered she was not supposed to sit down. So she hovered a few feet away from their table, coming forward once to put a clean ashtray by Doc's elbow.

In the meantime, she took a look around. It was a medium-sized bar. Most of the pinball machines in the back, between the doors to the men's and women's bathrooms, looked broken. In one of the back corners there was a window that led to a kitchen. The liquor-serving counter took up one side wall. That guy behind it was lucky he was working alone, Fluff thought, because the bar wasn't really long enough to accommodate two bartenders. There were square black bar stools, round red ones, a couple of brown ones, and even one made out of wicker. One round stool was missing its padded top, but someone had put a square, flat cushion on top of the bare metal. There were a lot of little tables and mismatched chairs, and that seemed to be where most people sat.

She was not the only white girl there, but most of the women were black. There was one table of girls who looked Vietnamese. They were playing poker. The other girls were resting, talking with each other, fixing their faces, complaining about their aching feet, and telling their men that they'd get their asses out and make some money in a minute, just hold your horses. A young woman in a short kimono was nursing a baby, whom she handed back to a woman whose gray hair had been braided and pinned in a crown around her head. The mother gave the older woman (her own mother?) more instructions about how to take care of that child than anybody could possibly remember.

The men were dressed in well-tailored business suits that were every color in the rainbow, except for one man who was wearing a black tuxedo with a red cummerbund, and another who was wearing a cowboy shirt and hat, a suede jacket, and some expensive snakeskin boots. Some of them had hats that matched the suits. Fluff knew that outside some of them would even have cars parked that matched their suits.

She loved looking at their jewelry. The pimps had big pocket watches, gold chains and pendants, earrings, and lots of diamond rings. The so-called nice people who went to church in exactly the same spirit that they went to work every day would turn their noses up at this gaudy stuff and declare it was in bad taste. Most of it was the flashy fake stuff you bought to make it look like you had more money than you did, but there was also some really ostentatious and expensive shit that said, "Fuck you, it's *my* money." That was what tickled her. The pimps specialized in rebellious elegance. They didn't try to hide who or what they were. Instead, they competed to find new ways to make their status even more obvious.

In about a half hour, Fluff knew, there would be no women in this bar at all. Some would scatter to work nearby streets. The pimps would drive others closer to downtown. Everybody had their territory, and girls were sometimes rotated to provide novelty, or to reward or punish them.

About ten o'clock, the pimps would go out cruising and check on their strings, take in the cash that had been made so far, give the girls that were junkies enough of a taste to get them through the night, count everybody's rubbers, and slap around the girls who didn't have enough cash or condoms. If a girl had done especially well, or if she was new and expected to be romanced, they might give her part of the night off and bring her back to the bar.

The rest of the work force would drift back under their own steam an hour or so before closing time, hand over their money, and get something to drink and some food. Family members who had been babysitting might bring the kids by and return them to their mothers. Sometimes somebody would yell, "Let's have a party at my house," and the bar would empty.

Fluff had seen a dozen places like this one. She knew how to handle herself here. This was fine. It was just that hookers in Atlanta, like everybody else in the Free Christian States, lived under a legal code of strict racial segregation. The Laws for the Protection of Racial Integrity were not enforced as strictly in red-light districts as they were elsewhere — say, in restaurants or on public transit. But brothels usually didn't hire colored and white girls. If you ran a mixed massage parlor that got busted, the fine for racial pollution was so high, you'd never be able to reopen. Managers of segregated cathouses just got a slap on the wrist, unless it was an election year.

But Fluff had always hated working in the houses. She was not exactly popular with management. She guessed it was because of her attitude. You made more money on the street, doing tricks out of cars. People said it was dangerous, but she knew plenty of girls who had gotten raped or beaten in massage parlors. Besides, once you went to work in a place like that, you were just one step away from having a man who would run your life and take your money. She had never used her money to support anybody but herself, and she was careful not to get too close to girls who were in somebody's stable.

There was a kitchen in the back of the bar that turned out grilled sandwiches, barbecue, and limp fries. That was what most of these girls lived on. The smell of the barbecue made Fluff's mouth water. It smelled like home. She wanted to get a big plate of sliced pork smothered in that sauce, sit up at the bar and strike up a conversation with somebody, find out how business was in this town.

But the man sitting next to Doc said, "Aren't you going to introduce your charmin' companion?"

"Fluff, this is Slim. Mahalia's brother."

Fluff cudgeled her memory. Hadn't somebody mentioned that name? Ah ha! Wally. "You've been running on empty ever since Mahalia died," she had said, and Doc had been pissed off to be reminded. This Mahalia must have been her lover.

She put out her hand. "Pleased to meet you, Mister Slim."

He laughed. "Oh, aren't you a dangerous one. Throwin' misters around like you just a poor commoner, a goose girl gone to meet the king. Why don't you just call me Slim?"

Doc was laughing, and Fluff joined her, but she did not appreciate the rebuff.

"Seems to me like you lookin' a little too slim yourself, Fluff. How would both of you like somethin' from the kitchen?"

"That," Doc said with great relief, "would hit the spot. Thanks."

Slim turned his head, but an elegant Egyptian princess dressed in a black silk dress with oversized emerald lapels was already at his elbow, awaiting his command. She wore long, dangling earrings and a collar of green rhinestones. She had high cheekbones, a long, straight, supercilious nose, and a mouth that was so rich and full you wanted to bite her lips.

Fluff thought, he just has to show Doc that she's not the only one has a woman she can order around. The cool beauty of Slim's lady made her feel second-rate. She put both of her hands in her hair and tried to comb it out, give it some body. Just wait until they see me dressed up, she thought. Nobody will think they can outclass Doc then.

"Fluff," Doc said impatiently, "what do you want to eat?"

"Uh — the barbecue," she said. "Pork, if they got it. I sure hope they do."

The woman's lush mouth broke into a smile when she heard Fluff's voice. "Girl, you from *home*," she said. "Oh, when did you leave? Is it still the same?"

Fluff was surprised by this outpouring of love for her despised origins. "Well, I guess so. It rains so much in summer that the catfish walk out of the water."

Slim's woman clasped her hands in front of her body. "Do you all like *corn*?"

The question was uttered with a great deal of intensity, as if corn were salvation.

"I sure do," Fluff said.

"Yeah," Doc chimed in. "I like corn."

"Well, we got corn to-*night*, and I will bring you some *fresh*," the woman declared, and went off to order their dinner. They could hear her back at the kitchen window, saying curtly, "Nigger, get over here. I want you to do this fast, now."

"That's Hattie," said Slim, chuckling. He lit his own and Doc's cigarettes with a highly polished rectangle of sterling silver. "She left Georgia during the troubles, you know. Lost most all of her people. Just her and her baby sister come out alive, is all. They walked most of the way to Kansas City on bleeding feet. Movin' at night, runnin' from the dogs. Sometimes I think she so homesick, she gonna go back there anyway. Then I got to buy her magnolias, you know, and night-blooming jasmine, and gardenias. Just cover her bed with them. And love her all night long in all those cool white flowers. She put her face in them and smell them and kiss them and just cry to think of home. Crazy bitch. Ain't nothin' there to cry about, I tell her. But home is home."

"I know exactly how she feels," Fluff said. She was uneasy about her body's response to his persuasive, sensual voice, to the image he had just painted.

"You don't. But she wouldn't never tell you that. She just glad to have somebody here who knows what she's missin'. I know you be kind to Hattie, now, won't you, Miss Fluff?"

"*Here* is your *meal*," Hattie cried, putting steaming paper plates down in front of them. The tangy smell of the sauce made Fluff sick. She was so hungry she almost fell face-first into the plate.

"Child, slow down, we *got* silverware," Hattie said. "You going to choke yourself right to *death*."

"It's all right, I know the Heimlich maneuver," Doc said. "We've been on the back of that bike a hell of a long time."

"You got a motorcycle?" Hattie said. She took Fluff's left hand and squeezed it. "You lucky, lucky girl. I bet you have a lot of fun on that. But ain't it awful dangerous?"

She nodded and said "Uh huh, I bet" while Doc gave the table a lecture on motorcycle safety, but she continued to apply light pressure to Fluff's hand, which she did not release, and eventually Hattie put her arm around her as well. She smelled wonderful, like all of the flowers Slim had described, and Fluff had a mental image of leading her through the ferns, orchids, and palms of a jungle to a pool, a pool fed by a little waterfall, and sinking into the cool, clean water side by side. There would be butterflies. There would be a long, muscular thigh between her legs. There would be—

"Jesus, I think you're asleep already," Doc said. She was standing behind Fluff, shaking her. Hattie had withdrawn. "Wipe your face," Doc said tenderly, and turned her around in her chair to dab at her face with a paper napkin. "Poor baby. Listen, Slim has this hotel, all of his girls got rooms there. And they got a vacancy."

"I told Amber she should keep her hands out of her john's pockets," Slim said sadly. "But that ho had magic hands. Lift the fillings out of your teeth. She make some serious money before she snag a vice cop's wallet. That no-dick casper put my girl away for thirty days, no fine. We go to court, but it don't do no good. Judge says, you got to serve the time because you got no ties to the community and you don't show no remorse."

"But we got his picture," Hattie said. "Took it myself with my little Kodak. Take that film down to the one-hour booth, made us a mess of pictures. Dozens."

"Hundreds. We spend all the next day handin' them out, don't do no business at all, just give that boy more press than a movie star. He think he can put my girl away," Slim said. "If you do the crime I expect to pay the fine, but he tell the judge Amber is incorrigible, so I tell everybody on the street, no pussy for that paleface Marshall Dillon. He can suck my dick before he get laid in this town again."

They laughed together at the memory. Fluff wondered how long they had been together.

"So you all going to take Amber's room?" Hattie said. "She leave it nice and clean. If her stuff is in the way, you just put it downstairs, they show you where. Some of her dresses and things might fit you, Fluff."

"Oh, I wouldn't just borrow her clothes without asking," Fluff said.

"We all one big, happy family here, we share and share alike," Slim said.

It was an awkward moment. Fluff did not know what his connection was to Doc, but she knew she did not share it, and she did not want to be part of Slim's family if that meant becoming one of his money machines.

Doc deflected the tension. "We're going to be here for a while, so I have got to take this cookie shopping. I been promising her a real wardrobe ever since we met. Pretty girl like her can't live out of saddlebags forever."

"You know, Doc, I will never forget how good you were to my sister," Slim said. "A lot of her friends turned away from her. Even some of our own family abandoned her, treated her like a leper. Nobody loved Mahalia as much as I did except you, Doc. I would have made the time to take care of her, but I didn't have to, because you were already there. Doing a better job than I would have done. She told me once, Slim, you listen to me now, anything I want, Doc makes sure I have. She brings me everything I need. Stand on her head to make me laugh. And if she ever needs anything you make sure she has it, Slim. Well, I promised my sister that and I won't never forget it."

Doc took his hand. They were standing very close. He put his hand on her shoulder. "Thanks," she said finally. Her voice was thick with emotion. He let her go and took a step back.

"So you sure you know how to get to the hotel? Fine, then I check in on you all later."

"We'll probably be sleeping."

"Then I see you tomorrow. You know where my office is." He laughed. "Right here at the head table."

As Doc and Fluff walked toward the door, they heard Slim lecturing Hattie. "What you waiting for, woman, a weather report? Rain or shine, there's money to be made. We got expenses, you know. I can't keep you bitches for free. Get out there and earn your keep. No, you take your hands offa my neck, now. Don't want you messin' with me. Get on the stroll. You want to walk out that door or you want to fly?"

Getting her leg over the Medusa made Doc groan. "Is this place very far away?" Fluff asked anxiously.

"How the hell would I know?" Doc snarled.

"I was just hoping you could rest pretty soon. I know you're hurting."

"Oh. No, I don't think it's too far away."

Fluff did not try to talk to her during the drive. It was too windy, and if there had been a thought in her mind, it would have gotten shaken up so bad it would have hurt itself.

They found the hotel and wrestled their gear into the lobby. It took some arguing to get the desk clerk to give them the key to Amber's temporarily vacant room. "Look," Fluff finally said, exasperated, "we are not goin' away, and I don't think Slim would be very happy to come in tonight at midnight and find us sleepin' in the lobby."

"Don't you threaten me," he said, and gave them the key.

They were getting ready to hump everything up the stairs when a small bundle of enthusiasm hurled itself out of the lobby and into Doc's arms. She was not much taller than Fluff, and was the same shape and color as a ripe blackberry. Her hair was so kinky that Fluff would have been willing to swear a strand of it stretched out would be six feet long. She had a broad, flat nose and lips that looked like they had been turned inside out. This was not an Egyptian queen, Fluff thought.

"Rowena?" Doc said.

"You biker trash! Ain't I glad to see you? Ask me if I ain't glad to see you!"

"Okay, Rowena, are you glad to see me?" Doc asked, laughing and patting her on the back. "Ouch! Rowena, this is Fluff."

"Your girlfriend," the woman said, and took Fluff in her surprisingly strong, short, plump arms. Her skin was soft, and her hair pomade smelled like oranges. It was such a relief to have somebody label her relationship to Doc so simply, and just accept it. Fluff felt deeply ashamed for comparing Rowena unfavorably to Hattie. She squeezed her back as hard as she could.

"What did that useless desk-boy tell you all? You don't have to pack all this on your backs. You ain't donkeys! We got us an elevator." Rowena showed them where it was, and talked a blue streak all the way up to their room. Fluff knew she was probably telling Doc what had happened to all the people they both knew since they had last met. If she could only concentrate, she would probably hear a lot of useful information about these folks. But none of it made any sense.

Finally there was a door shut between them and the outside world. It was a small, tidy room. The bed took up most of the floor space, and there was a wardrobe and a sink. "Is the bathroom down the hall?" Fluff asked, dreading the trek, but reluctant to put her filthy body on those clean sheets.

"I don't think so," Doc said, dropping her load. "I think the plumbing here is just eclectic. What's this?" Fluff hadn't even seen the outline of the door. Doc turned the handle, and there was a toilet and a shower stall. "You go first," Doc said. "Let me adjust the water temperature for you. It's going to take me a while to get my boots off anyway."

Normally, she helped Doc with that chore, but tonight Fluff gladly accepted a reprieve. She was halfway into the water before she realized that she still had her underwear on.

"Don't grow any gills in there," Doc called. "I don't know how much hot water there'll be."

There was, by a miracle, enough hot water for both of them. When they were finally clean and horizontal, Fluff couldn't remember why she had been so desperate to lay down. She wasn't even sure she could fall asleep.

"So tell me about Mahalia," she said.

"I did."

"No, you didn't."

"What do you want to know?"

"Who was she? Was she your lover? How did she die?"

"She was my lover," Doc yawned. "She had the hunger, AIDS. Fadeaway. That's what killed her."

"Come on."

"No, really. I don't know how she got it. Needles. A trick. All that money she made and the girl never got the shots. She told me that she thought it wouldn't have made any difference. That black tattoo of an A in a circle with a bar across it wouldn't have shown up on her skin. So she wouldn't have made any more money. She thought making the johns use rubbers was enough. Hell, even I went and got my shots. With my very first stolen credit card!"

"She was a hustler?"

"Yeah. She was a hooker. Only that was before I met her. She retired when she found out she was sick. Slim gave her a stack of money, told her to just go out and enjoy herself. I met her in a stuffy dyke bar uptown. She was just dancing and dancing, all by herself because all the local butches were too dumb or too bigoted to dance with her. I thought she looked like a much better time than any of those boring white girls in their polyester business suits, so I sashayed right over and shook my big ass at her. Pretty soon we were doing a whole lot more than dancing. Goddess, she was a good time."

"Did you know she was sick?"

"Not at first. Slim was the one who told me. Thought he'd run off this weird white bulldagger who was messing with his sister. By then I knew something was wrong anyway. She was tired all of the time. And she'd been really sick once, pneumonia, of course. Last time we ever went dancing I had to pick her up in my arms and just kind of waltz around the room in time to the music. She was in so much pain, I wanted to put her in the hospital. We just couldn't take care of it at home. But she wanted her own things around her, her own clothes, and her music, you know. She said to me, don't you let them put me in one of them baggy hospital gowns. So I kept her home. Gave her pretty clothes and ice cream and a lot of Ativan and morphine. I don't know why the Goddess let it take so long. She was just so gutsy, she wouldn't let go. Her body kept going even after her spirit had left, she was that full of life. It was ... awful."

"I'm sorry," Fluff said. "She sounds like somebody I wish I could have met."

"Really?"

"Yes, really."

"Well. That surprises me."

"Come on, Doc. I don't know hardly anything about you. I like knowing about where you've been, meeting people that you know. I want to know everything about you, Doc. You aren't just a fuck to me."

"Haven't been much of a good fuck lately anyway."

"Stop it. We can rest up and take it easy now. You got to let me take care of you. I owe you, and I'd like to get out of your debt."

"I don't know, kitten. I don't think I can take it easy. I have some hard stuff to take care of and I have to do it soon."

"But not tonight," Fluff said. "Turn around, back up into me. That's good. Now just sleep. Sleep."

Toward morning, Fluff half-woke. Doc was — Doc was calling someone's name, and it wasn't hers. Or had it been a dream? The room was quiet, and she drifted back into unconsciousness.

17

D esiree could not have been happier. She finally had what she wanted, although her knight in shining leather had not come in the form that she had expected. But there were advantages to riding with Paint instead of one of the men. She wasn't afraid of Paint (well, not usually). But when she was frightened of Paint, it was thrilling, it was because she knew something exciting was going to happen. It didn't lay in her stomach like a lead ball of dread. And the sex was, well, it was what you thought sex was going to be when you were still a virgin, before you found out it was clumsy and messy and it didn't even hurt, not really.

Under normal circumstances, Paint and Desiree would have gotten a lot of harassment. But baiting Paint was not exactly as much fun as teasing Crystal about her friend Angel the Butch. She was likely to misinterpret the point of the whole thing and bury it between your third and fourth rib.

And these were not normal circumstances. Prez had withdrawn into a dream world. Every day's ride seemed to get shorter and shorter. Raven always took him away some place private as soon as supper was done. It left a big gap in the convivial man-to-man conversations around the fire. If you wanted a decision made, you still asked Prez, but it was usually Raven who told you what he wanted done.

Most nights, Paint was found in the campfire circle with the men, making everybody laugh, and Desiree would join her as soon as she finished helping Carmen clean up after dinner. Desiree would sit on the ground between Paint's legs, feeling warm and safe for the first time in her life. She liked to hold a long stick into the fire so its end would burn. She usually said nothing, just hugged herself and waited for what would happen when they were in their tent.

Mendoza's Traveling Discount Whorehouse, as Sunny, Dee Ann, Lydia, Rose, and Desiree (before she hooked up with Paint) had once been collectively called, had gravitated toward Raven, who everybody now called The Queen. The four single women had become the Loyal Subjects. They had appropriated the dead man's dented van, washed it, taken the mattress out and burned it, and hitched his bike to the back of it. Even Mendoza's Dobermans had become fanatically devoted to The Queen. One of the younger Angels had tried to muscle in on the four women's claim, blustering something about Mendoza owing him money, and Sunny had told him contemptuously, "Tell it to Prez." He took one look at her angry stare, another look at Raven's pitiless face, a third look at the quiet, intelligent, deadly dogs that flanked her, and gave it up.

The Queen never had to lift a finger. She was fed, her gear was packed and unpacked, her fire built, her tent pitched, and anything she wanted was fetched for her by one of the four. They even brushed her hair and did her makeup. The campsite that held Prez and The Queen and her Loyal Subjects kept getting further and further away from everybody else. Sometimes you could see Raven sitting with the female members of her court around the fire, and they were all talking about something, but Prez (and the dogs) were nowhere to be seen.

Shit, yes, it had been a long, strange trip home. But now they were at the top of the hill, looking down on Alamo, and Desiree was almost ready to get off Paint's bike and walk down to it. Her tailbone had turned into a vibrator, and she swore that a few weeks on this bike had made her more bowlegged than five years of fucking all comers.

The township of Alamo was laid out in nice, neat squares. Each block was divided into eight parcels of land, so that every house had a generous amount of space around it. The streets were labeled with numbers and a direction instead of a name. In the center of town was a big hall, used for public meetings. The bank, bars, and other businesses were mostly centered around Town Hall Square. Street numbering began there.

"Seems awfully neat for a lot of disorganized anarchists to come up with," Desiree said when Paint explained how to find her way around town.

"Well, there's a story that Alamo was founded by a bunch of Vietnam vets who used to be Mormons. You ever been to Salt Lake City? If you put the temple down right there, this would look a lot like it."

Vietnam? Mormons? Desiree didn't want to look dumb by asking about any of these mysterious topics.

"Yessirree," Paint said, "I'm just an immigrant from Deseret, myself. Grew up in a little mining town called Jasper. Nothing as far as you could see but tailings from the uranium mines, alkali flats, and sagebrush. I said to myself, there has to be more to life than horned toads and cottonwood trees. First time I heard the roar of a Harley, I knew what it was, and I ain't never had anything better than this between my legs. Except maybe you, lover-girl."

"Where did the money come from to build all this? How do people live?"

"We make money a lot of different ways. All my business is legitimate, of course. Mind you, I always get paid in cash, and I don't go checking the serial numbers on the bills. Let's see, the speed factory is underground so the feds can't spot it. Don't tell anybody I told you so, but it might be under the airport. See where all those helicopters are parked, and that big building, that's a hangar. Makes it easier to defend. We got a couple of caves growing mushrooms in the hills, some of 'em are mind-altering and some of 'em we sell to fancy French restaurants.

Some of the guys and the huskier gals work the oil rigs. Course, sometimes payrolls disappear on offshore Jap gas pumps that hire bikers. There's always some scam goin' on. We got a few crazy boys with their truck drivers' licenses, makin' money hijacking shipments of military hardware, computers, stuff like that, and selling them back to Uncle Sam. Lot of arms flow through Alamo. Nicaragua used to be a good customer of ours. We even got us a few farmers. Only thing we don't have is a Harley plant. But we're working on it. That's my little house right down there, the rose-colored one."

Desiree couldn't pick it out, but she said, "It's real nice."

It took them less than an hour to race to its front door. The house *was* real nice. There was a garage, which seemed to be full of airbrush equipment and bottles of paint and gas tanks, fenders, side case covers, even a few frames.

The door was opened by a very tan young man with long, straight black hair that he kept tied in a horsetail, like an Indian. He had a red bandana around his head. His torso was longer than his legs, making his body look a little out of proportion if you studied it real close. But he looked like such a rooster in his tight, white T-shirt and tighter faded blue jeans, who cared?

"Welcome home," he said.

"Desiree, this is Jim. You're gonna be really glad you skipped this run. I don't even know where to start. What a mess."

"Hi, Desiree. I just came over to say hello, Paint. Carmen called yesterday, said she thought most of the herd would wander home today, so I made sure your house got cleaned. There's some steaks in your refrigerator."

A tortoiseshell cat came around the corner of the house and rubbed itself possessively against Paint's leg. She threw Desiree a haughty look over her shoulder, then stalked off to roll on the lawn. "Hello, Agatha," Jim said. "Thanks for nothing. See if I ever feed you again." The cat came close enough to stretch out her neck and sniff at him. Then she ran away.

"Well, now…" Paint said. She chewed on her bottom lip.

"Be nice to have some company," Desiree said.

"You have to stay for dinner," Paint said. "Tell us all the news."

"Well, if you're sure it isn't any trouble…" Jim preceded them into the house. Desiree linked arms with Paint and whispered, "You know, honey, you're old enough to be his mother."

"I am that," Paint said complacently. "He's a good boy."

"Are we talking about a man you've had or a puppy you're thinking of buying?"

"You know, the two experiences are remarkably similar."

Desiree put potatoes in the microwave and Jim made a salad while Paint told him about their summer. He didn't have much to say, just raised his eyebrows every now and then and whistled a few times. "Sounds like this Raven is a force to be reckoned with," he said when she was done.

"I don't think she'll last two seconds in this town. You wait and see. We're going to have a vote of no-confidence within the week, and Prez and his witch are going to be out on their asses," Paint declared.

"I don't know," Jim said. "Shall I make some coffee?"

"You do that," Paint said.

They took their coffee into the living room. There was a fireplace, and Desiree stacked paper and wood there, and struck a match. Paint had decorated the room with Indian rugs and cow skulls. The furniture was all big, sturdy, and very comfortable, upholstered in natural, undyed leather. Paint poured everybody a little brandy to sip with their coffee, and they sat around feeling sleepy and too full of food.

Desiree thought, this guy is a hunk. What's wrong with me? I should be making moves all over him. Him and Paint must have had a thing going. She sure acted like it. Maybe not. Maybe they *are* just neighbors. If she wants him I don't mind. I'd be happy to make myself scarce. Or I guess we could do him together. If she really wanted to. Then Desiree decided that since she didn't really feel like doing anything with Jim, Paint would have to give her a good, strong green light before she got sexy with him.

Instead, Paint started talking to Jim about restoring the Rattlesnake that Carmen was trucking back from Harpy Farm. The conversation deteriorated into a detailed technical discussion of carburetors, tailpipes, alternators, and other frabbles and doojangles. Desiree went into the kitchen and washed the dishes.

She was nearly done when Paint and Jim walked through the kitchen. Paint showed him out the side door and came back to her. "Sweetie, you don't have to do that. I have a dishwasher."

"Besides Jim, you mean?"

"Yeah."

They both laughed.

"I think he would have been happy to stay if you'd winked at him," Paint yawned. "I would have been glad to disappear if you'd wanted to grab yourself a piece of ass. There's a spare bedroom. Come to think of it, I've got a big enough bed for three."

"Well, I was kind of waiting for you to let me know what the score was."

"I don't know." Paint looked sleepy and surprised. "I've had a very good time teaching that boy things he should have learned in school, but for some reason I just didn't want to bother with him tonight."

"I still feel like grabbing a piece of ass, though," Desiree said shyly.

"Do you, now?" Paint drank the last of her brandy.

Desiree lunged at her. "You better run for a soft surface, 'cause you're about to fall."

"I am, am I? Shit! I guess I am. Well — run this way."

The two women settled into a routine that pleased them both. At first, Desiree mostly did the housework while Paint cleaned her shop and started filling back orders for customized parts. But there really wasn't much to do around the house. So Desiree started hanging around the garage, handing Paint tools or mixing colors for her. When there was nothing else for her to do she would doodle on spare sheets of paper, playing around with some of the standard themes that Paint turned out — flames, dragons, naked warrior women, the Grim Reaper, monsters, and demons.

"I didn't know you could draw," Paint said one day.

Desiree jumped. She had not heard the older woman come up behind her.

"Oh, I can't, really, I'm just copying what you've done."

"Copy, hell. Your mermaid looks twice as good as the original. Guess you just have a way with tits, girl. Do you know how to cut a stencil?"

From then on, Paint began to teach her. "If I can get you going on some of the simpler jobs," she said, "I can take that old bike apart and start making it hum."

One evening, Carmen dropped by. They fixed her dinner and tried to entertain their unexpected guest. At first, she just moped around, but eventually the ice melted and she became animated enough to admire some of Desiree's sketches and laugh at Paint's jokes. It wasn't until the after-dinner pipe of weed that she told them what was really on her mind.

"I don't want to step on anybody's toes here," she said, "but something tells me the two of you are more than just friends. Right?"

"Actually," Paint said, "Desiree may be the only real friend I've ever had. But I think I know what you mean."

"I wish it could be that simple for me," Carmen said bitterly. She took a big hit of smoke, held it, and passed the pipe. Exhaling noisily, she continued, "I don't think I want another woman that way."

Desiree and Paint, who knew all about her affair with Harpy Farm's Chief, gave each other significant, skeptical glances.

"Come on, I can have a good time with girls. I know that. But the way it used to be with me and Michaels ... you know, him and Anderson never did come home. And I guess I should feel guilty for just leaving them. But it was like getting rid of something you don't want, you know, just shoving it away from yourself any old way you can. I don't want him back. If he was here he would probably say I was in love with Tina. And I miss her. But I don't want her that way."

"Sounds like you're having a hard time," Paint said finally.

"I *know* that," Carmen snapped.

"Maybe you just haven't met the right person yet," Desiree ventured. "Sometimes it doesn't matter if it's a man or a woman so much as ... who they are, you know, aside from that."

"And maybe there isn't anybody out there for me," Carmen said nervously. "Maybe I'm done with all that romantic shit. I feel so damn restless all the time. I can't stand to see any of the people I used to know. Don't want to read anything or clean my house or go shopping. You know, I bought that old bike of Mendoza's. I have to bring it around, Paint, maybe you can adjust the timing. The son of a bitch pops. But all I want to do is ride. I just want to ... I want the wind in my face, I don't want to think, I just want to ... go."

"Talk to Raven," Desiree said impulsively.

"That lunatic?" Paint protested.

"Well — come on, now, she's not just crazy. There's something else there. Look how she's changed Sunny, Dee Ann, Rose, and Lydia's lives. Those girls are not the same useless twats that they were when Mendoza handed us out like two-bit cigars."

"I don't know," Paint said, shaking her head. "Things have been pretty weird ever since we got back to Alamo. Prez turned up at one meeting and stayed long enough to extend the interim town council's term of office for thirty days, and left. If anybody could figure out how to confront him, they'd run his ass out of town. There just doesn't seem to be anybody who's a big enough stud to want to take on the job. They say some strange things go on at Prez's house, now that the Queen's moved in with her Loyal Subjects. She really is a witch."

"Well, I met a lot of witches at Harpy Farm, and I thought they were kind of sweet and wild and wonderful," Desiree said defiantly. "If anybody can help you, Carmen, it's Raven. She knows stuff that nobody else around here is going to know."

"Maybe I will talk to her," Carmen said, knocking the pipe on the edge of the ashtray. "I think we've been smoking the screen here, kids. Got another bud I can stuff in here? And let's have another round of that brandy."

✧

Doc extricated herself silently from between the covers. She couldn't wake Fluff up. If she did, the little busybody would want to come with her. And that was not a good idea. Doc dressed in quick, delicate, noiseless motions. She had to go talk to the Jaguars alone. She picked up her boots and jacket and tiptoed out the door. If she didn't come back from this meeting, at least Fluff would be with people who knew Doc, and she would have all the cash and merchandise that had been on the bike.

In fact, it wouldn't be a bad idea to leave Fluff something on paper, so she would know that Doc had thought of her at the last, and done what she could to provide for her. She tugged on her boots and then dug in her jacket for the little notebook she carried to record mileage.

When Doc wrote something down, she printed in capital letters. THIS IS TO STATE THAT IN THE EVENT OF MY DEMISE ALL OF MY PERSONAL EFFECTS ARE THE PROPERTY OF FLUFF. She read it over. Well, it was terse, but it would have to do. She signed and dated it and slid it under the door.

It was nine o'clock, but nobody greeted her on her way out of the hotel. There wasn't even anyone at the desk. She stopped at the lobby's pay phone and made a call. The person at the other end was extremely rude and unfriendly. And this was how they behaved when they expected *good* news, Doc thought.

Once on her bike, she began to think that actually, it would be kind of nice not to deal with these creeps any more. It wasn't like they were fun to be around, like Slim or the Angels. She had never met another bunch of people who were such stick-in-the-muds.

The Revolutionary People's Army, informally known as the Jaguars, probably because most of them were alumnae of that youth gang, had their headquarters uptown. Doc drove her bike through miles and miles of slums. The sight of so much human misery made her heart ache, but it also made her pat her left shoulder. She considered the .45 that hung there to be part of her personal war on poverty.

The building that the Jaguars had commandeered was a sprawling Victorian mansion, unfairly trapped by the spreading miasma of urban blight. Even after decades of neglect, its fanciful architecture made Doc itch to scrape and paint and fix it up. Originally the building had been placed in the middle of extensive grounds. These had long ago been sold to developers. But it still had large sheets of struggling grass around it, and several weeping willows and tiny Japanese maples.

She drove her bike as close to the front door as she could get it, backed up so it was pointed out of the driveway, and turned it off. The kickstand took forever to get down, a sure sign she was nervous.

She walked up the steps and turned the brass handle that rang a gong inside the house. The door snapped open, and a young woman wearing crossed bandoliers and toting an M-43 presented arms.

"I'm one of the friendlies," Doc said, holding out her empty hands.

"Huh."

Jaguar women were no joke. They didn't talk much to Doc, but she had a suspicion that they talked plenty to their men. The way she heard it, the only reason the Revolutionary People's Army concentrated its fundraising efforts on drugs, gambling, and produce instead of prostitution was because the Jaguar women would not approve marketing their sisters' flesh to the white bourgeois enemy. They also stayed away from loansharking. Loansharks were "Jew parasites" and "Hebrew vandals without honor who prey on the life blood of the helpless people of color who suffer in exile from Mother Africa." Doc thought that all the freelance Sicilian bankers she'd met would have laughed their asses off if they'd heard that piece of Jaguar propaganda.

"Take me to your leader," Doc said, and followed the woman up a set of stairs. The carpet was fraying so badly that she had to watch her step. Some kid had left a pull-toy, a duck on wheels, on the stairs, and that made her smile. It's hard to maintain a front of true revolutionary fervor unless you plan to die within the next twenty-four hours.

Colonel Jelly Bean had his office at the top of the stairs. Doc always thought of him as Colonel Jelly Bean because he had a large glass jar full of the multi-colored candies sitting next to the Koran, the complete works of Karl Marx, and the assorted memoirs of dead black leaders on the bookshelf in his office. She was always tempted to ask if there was a prize for guessing how many it contained. His real title was, of course, Colonel Akhmed Allah Akbar, Defender of the Poor, Protector of the Helpless, Uplifter of the Downtrodden, and all-around Savior of the Masses.

He was also mean enough to break Prez over his knee. The trouble with the Colonel was, he wasn't crazy. He loved money, he loved power, he loved women, and he knew what he had to do to keep on getting more of what he loved. He was ruthless to his enemies, and he had no friends.

He sat behind a mahogany desk with a glass top. Behind him were two more women with automatic weapons and bandoliers. He wore a plain khaki uniform, a red beret with a black jaguar patch, and no visible weapons. He had a hatchet-face and kept his head shaved. Doc had never seen him without sunglasses and short leather gloves. She imagined him wearing them in the bathtub.

On the walls were posters from Cuba, China, a really old one from some place Doc had vaguely heard of called Nicaragua — was it that napalmed crater in between Honduras and Costa Rica? — and the Black South African Socialist Republic. There was also a banner that said, "The People United Shall Never Be Defeated."

Right, Doc thought to herself. Get all the people together in an ice house. That'll unite their asses. I guess it's better than selling them horse. At least nobody ever caught the hunger from a pipe.

"Make your report!" the Colonel barked.

"Do you mind turning down the volume?" Doc looked around, saw a chair, and dragged it over. "Don't mind if I do," she said. "Sit down," she added, and suited the action to the word. She took out her cigarettes and lit one. "Don't you like this rug any more?" she asked, insolently waving the dead match around.

The Colonel tilted his head in her direction, and one of the women gave her a pristine crystal ashtray.

"Tobacco is the red man's revenge on the white man who stole his land," he began. This was one of his favorite lectures. Doc did not think she could stomach it today. She never trusted people whose vices were invisible.

"Really? That's a very interesting perspective on drug addiction, Colonel Defender Protector Uplifter and Savior. Would it be fair to say that ice is Japan's revenge on America?" She frowned, and dropped some ash into the dish in her hand. "Although why we should let them take over the world, I do not know, and I have a hard time seeing the Yakuza as the agents of karma. Personally, I'd rather deal with the old-fashioned Mafia. They're every bit as psychotic, but they feed you better." Doc tipped her chair back, and it groaned under her bulk. Goddess, it made her feel better to be reminded that she was a big girl. She exhaled smoke, careful to blow it at one of the women instead of at him. "But I suppose the poor must suffer for the sins of the rich. Haven't they always?"

"You dare to come here and speak to me this way? To trivialize the suffering of the oppressed and brutalized? I warn you, we will not tolerate you and your kind forever. The day will come when we will not need to traffic with the decadent dregs of this dying system. The capitalist warmongers are strangling in their own putrefaction. The genocidal poisons they intended to turn against my people are devouring them instead."

"And London Bridge is falling down. Yeah, yeah, yeah. Look, I told you a long time ago, I don't give a shit about your politics. All I care about is the cash. I have friends who make something you need. You give me money, I go set it up for you, everybody gets a little richer. I don't care if you want to take your money and use it to finance a revolution or," Doc began to choose her words very carefully, "go buy a yacht and throw wild parties where you can pick up teenage girls and teach them to field-strip your gun. It's none of my business. Just like my politics and my addictions and what I do with my cut are none of your business."

He smashed the desk with his fist. "That's about enough out of you, do you think I don't know the perverted—"

"Oh, I would imagine that what you don't know about perversion could be written on my little fingernail. C'mon, Akhmed. Don't you want to hear my report?"

"Yesterday," he said.

"Okay. This is my report. The deal is off."

There was a very chilly silence.

"Say what?" Akhmed finally drawled. Something alarmingly like joy was lighting up his features.

"The deal is off. Kaput. Finito. No can do."

"Let me understand this. You came to me making certain promises. Because of the nature of those promises, I extended myself for you. I took a gamble. And now you are telling me that I was wrong to extend myself for you. I am not happy. I am not happy at all."

"Yeah, well, I never promised to make you happy, healthy, or wise. I only promised to try to make you wealthy."

"I am a simple man. It takes very little to satisfy my needs. But the cause I serve is immense, and it consumes every resource I can conjure up. Surely you have more of an explanation to offer than this. You may not care about this failure, but I am accountable not only to my army, but to history."

Puh-leeze, Doc thought. Well, when all else fails, tell the truth. "The deal fell through because I tried to be a hero. The president of the Angel chapter I was dealing with had himself a hot little piece. Only it seemed to me that she was just a little too young for him, and he wasn't treating her very well. So I took her away from him."

"Just like that?"

"Just like that."

He waited. When Doc said nothing else, he gestured impatiently. "Well — so?"

"So he lost it. Lost his mind. Declared war, came after us, a lot of ugly things happened real fast. Would have made a great movie."

"And he is dead now?"

"No. If he was dead, things would be simpler. If he was dead, he would have a successor, and I could deal with that man. His own people did not support him in this vendetta, Colonel, and I have a feeling that he is not long for this world. But until somebody punches his ticket for that hellbound train, I'd advise you to sit tight. You have other suppliers."

"I should have sent someone else."

"Who?"

Doc imagined that he would probably never forgive her because he did not have an answer to that question.

"Be reasonable," she said. Now, that was an idiotic suggestion. "This is not going to put you out of business. It just means that you have to stay at the current level of production. I give this thing maybe three, four months to work itself out. Give it the winter. In spring — say, summer, to be on the safe side, to give everybody time to let bygones be bygones, we can try again."

"I gave you money," he said. "A lot of money. Money that I received in trust from people who believe in our cause. Where is that money?"

This was when everybody was going to forget their party manners. "I had expenses."

"Expenses? We do not subsidize incompetence. Surely you do not expect us to pay for your betrayal."

"It was a joint venture that would have been profitable to all parties. I expect you to share in the risk, just as you would have shared in the profits."

His facade dropped. "Bitch, I gave you a hundred thousand dollars. Now you give it back, or you're dead."

Doc didn't need to take the time to drop her facade, she just drew her gun. "Wrong again, asshole."

Both of the women covered her. Shit, Doc thought, I don't mind sweating at times like this, but why does it always have to run into my eyes when both of my hands are busy?

The telephone on Akhmed's desk rang. Everyone in the room jumped. He picked it up. He said to his two soldiers, "Do not take your sights off of her," and left the room.

"You ladies want to toss a coin to see who I take with me when he brings back reinforcements?" Doc asked. "I could use a bodyguard in the hereafter." One of them snarled silently at her, but the other one had knocked her beret askew getting into firing position, and her face was visibly wet with nervous perspiration. Doc divided her attention between the pair, but she gave more of it to the jumpier of the two. Nothing more humiliating than dying because somebody *else* had panicked, Doc thought. Of course, if my own stupidity kills me, I won't be embarrassed at all.

Akhmed had company when he came back, but this was not the kind of backup Doc had anticipated. She had never seen this woman before. She was almost as tall as the Colonel, and she was wearing the same uniform. She had the same oval face and knife-blade features, and while she hadn't shaved her head, it was damn close. Unlike the colonel, she did not scorn to sport a pistol at one hip. Doc grimaced at the heavy military holster. Takes for fucking ever to get one of those unsnapped.

Well, it took next to no time for her to unbutton her lip. "Do you know how many of our female children die from neglect, disease, and hunger? How many are raped? Beaten? Prostituted? How dare you come here and tell us about a white man's abuse of a white girl-child? What is her plight compared to the violence, starvation, and frustration that cripples and kills our young people? There is a plague ravaging our people, the plague of white privilege and white greed. Pity is a guilt-trip. We owe you and your entire predatory, evil race no pity whatsoever. You brought our money with you. If you hadn't, you never would have dared to come here. Put it on the table and walk out. Do it now."

Well, at least those two magic words, "Walk out," had been uttered. Doc reached into her jacket — slowly — and withdrew a thick manila envelope. She threw it onto the desk. The Colonel and his female alter ego dived for it. Doc got the hell out of there. Nobody told the bodyguards to shoot her, but she didn't think they would care to escort her down the stairs unless they could carry her out in a big, green trash bag.

In her haste, she almost bowled over a woman in a veil who was picking up the child's toy that had been left on the steps.

Most of the women in this house were in purdah. They went shopping in pairs, usually escorted by a male recruit. A woman had to personally satisfy the Colonel about her dedication to the cause before she got promoted to fatigues and an M-43.

Doc knew she was lucky to get away with a whole skin. She ought to call it even and walk away with no hard feelings. But once they got around to counting that money, they would be on her like white on rice. And the Colonel had called her a bitch. That left a very bad taste in her mouth.

So she shot out all of the front windows before she rode away.

✧

Carmen approached the house on the hillside with dread. She kept downshifting and downshifting until she was just crawling up the grade. She was wearing heavy leather jeans, a sweater under her jacket, a wool watch-cap that Desiree had knitted for her, and insulated ski gloves. But it was still just as cold as a well-digger's ass out here, or was that other simile more appropriate? Cold as a witch's tit? Her own tits were covered with goosebumps, and her nipples had contracted so much that they hurt.

All by itself, apart from its occupants, the official residence of the president of the Alamo Chapter of the Angels was intimdating. Almost everybody in Alamo had modern, ranch-style houses or duplexes. But Prez's house made Carmen think of the real Alamo. Its white adobe walls were tall and thick enough to repel anything except mortars, the windows were narrow enough to provide cover if you were a defender returning hostile fire, and its roof was covered with red Spanish tiles. The two wings were somewhat less imposing. They were two stories instead of three, and had big glass windows, so they looked palatial — regal rather than military.

On her way up to the house, Carmen passed the small cottage where the gardener, a dark Texan boy who kept Prez's collection of cacti and succulents thriving, lived. His wife did most of the cooking and cleaning, but lately she had been seen doing some athletic drinking at one of Alamo's bars, complaining that she wasn't being allowed into Prez's house to do her job.

Once in the circular driveway in front of the house, Carmen turned her bike away from the building. Prez certainly had a good view of his domain. From here, the lights of the town were beautiful. There seemed to be no ground, no horizon, just one huge sphere of black sky, and she was suspended on her bike with stars above her and stars below.

Why come at night, when she was bound to be jumpy? Carmen wondered. For that matter, why come at all?

But it was too cold for her to just turn around. The ride back would probably give her hypothermia. And it was definitely too cold to sit here watching scenery. Carmen put her bike in gear and went the rest of the way up the driveway, to the front door. A battered green van and Prez's Harley were parked out front. She frowned at that. If nobody was going to run that bike, they ought to drain the fluids and put it away for the winter. Damn shame to ruin a beautiful thing like that.

Prez didn't have any comets or Vikings painted on his gas tank. His bike was just one color — black, of course. But even in this meager light — just a few safety lights high up on the front of the house — you could see the glossy purple highlights that seemed to come from deep within its finish. Prez was an absolute bastard, but he had style. He didn't live like a biker, he *was* one, the quintessential outlaw on two wheels. You never doubted he would do anything to have his own way. It was that arrogant sense of absolute consistency and self-confidence that made other men follow him. It was either that, or kill him.

She parked her bike beside Prez's and walked up to the front door, pulling off her gloves and cap. She pressed the buzzer, but could not hear any doorbell ringing inside. She waited a few seconds, then wondered if she had pressed it hard enough. But before her hand could make contact with the button, the door opened, and Sunny motioned her inside.

Carmen smiled at her, then did a double-take. It *was* Sunny, all right. There was the long, sandy hair, the freckled face and the sensuous, sassy mouth, the slim body, the tits that were just beginning to sag. But she had never seen gray in Sunny's hair before. She must have stopped coloring it. Carmen had never seen her without any makeup, either. Sunny was wearing jeans, boots, and a T-shirt — not exactly the appropriate attire for a hot mama. She had cut her fingernails, too.

Sunny smiled back. Carmen didn't recall ever having gotten a real smile from her before. If the old Sunny turned the corners of her mouth up at you, it was usually because she had just been down on your man or gotten you into trouble with Prez.

"Wait here," this new woman said. She showed Carmen to the front parlor, then left her alone to study the parquet floor. Wrought-iron lamps the size of streetlights lit the room. The furniture was all black leather and brass buttons. There were some large brass vases full of dried palm leaves and other big, dead plants in the corners of the room. Carmen thought it was exceptionally ugly, the kind of place you brought people that you had to talk to and didn't want to offend straight up.

When Raven came in, she was dressed much as she had been on Harpy Farm. She was wearing black cowboy boots, a full patchwork skirt of black-and-purple velvet and silk, and a black leotard. Her hair fell straight to her waist like a sheet of jet. She had carefully drawn black lines around her eyes, making them look huge. But she had left her long, black velvet vest with the High Priestess's crescent moon patch at Harpy Farm. Instead, she was wearing Prez's colors. Carmen could not believe her eyes. She was so astonished and, yes, offended by this that she barely noticed the bulge at Raven's shoulder that meant she was packing. So she must know it was a capital crime to put on club colors if you weren't a member, and she was prepared for the consequences of this rash act. Then Carmen noticed that Raven's belt was a hangman's noose, made out of silver wire. That gave her another turn. When she saw the long leather strap that Raven carried, it took Carmen a moment to realize that it was studded with tacks, because there was something on the metal that dulled its shine and made it blend in with the brown color of the leather.

"Carmen," Raven said, greeting her in a warm voice that was completely inconsistent with her appearance. She dropped the strap onto a table. "I am so glad to see you. I hope you haven't had any trouble with the bike you bought from us."

"No," Carmen said. She had been rubbing the palms of her hands up and down the side-seams of her pants, trying to work the numbness out. She made herself stop. "It runs real good. Paint helped me give her a tuneup. And she runs, uh, real good now." She was relieved that Raven did not offer to embrace her. She did not think she could bring herself to touch the denim that had graced Prez's back.

"Would you like something hot to drink?"

Carmen hesitated. She would look like a complete idiot if she walked out now. She had no idea how to talk to this small, obsessed, and dangerous woman. But if she left, where would she go? Home was unbearable, it reminded her of Michaels. She wanted to pour gasoline over everything and throw a lit match into the middle of it.

"Yes," she said finally, softly. "I'm very cold."

"I'll make you some hot chocolate," Raven said, and took her into the kitchen. This room was like the ones that Carmen remembered from growing up, helping her mother cook and clean for the white professional couples who lived in the "nice" part of her hometown. It was warm, a place where secrets could be told and comfort given. She sat at the round oak table while Raven busied herself with an espresso machine, milk, chocolate, and cinnamon. Finally there appeared on the table a whole thermos of something steamy and spicy to drink. "Dee Ann made these," Raven said, and she put a plate full of shortbread next to the cocoa.

She sat across from Carmen and filled her mug. The delicious aroma and the cozy atmosphere of the kitchen almost made Carmen forget the deep groan she had heard as they walked from the parlor to the other side of the house. She was not sure if it had been a cry of pain or a cry of pleasure. Well, Prez had asked for it. He had traded Fluff for Raven, given away his demon and gotten the devil herself in exchange. She put it out of her mind and sipped and nibbled.

"Do you miss your husband?" Raven asked her.

It was nice to have someone put their finger right on her dilemma. Startling, but nice. She would not have to tell any lies here.

"No," Carmen replied. "But I don't know why. Once I just knew that I would never love anybody but Michaels. And it bothers me to have that change so much, so fast. I'm not sure I would put things back the way they were, but I'd like to know why they changed."

"Maybe some of your basic assumptions got shattered," Raven suggested. But she did not say what those might have been.

Carmen munched another bite of shortbread and thought hard. What had Michaels meant to her? Maybe that was the wrong question. Maybe Prez had shown her that it did not matter how good things were between her and her husband, because there was this big ugly thing going on between men and women all around her marriage, and no matter how happy she and Michaels were, that ugliness poisoned them, poisoned them slowly, in little ways they probably couldn't even see. When she had picked Tina up and taken her to the truck, she had discovered that she had more in common with Tina than she would ever have with Michaels, Anderson, the Prez, or any other man. And that had nothing to do with who she wanted to fuck.

Except that it did, in the end, affect her sexually. It made her feel that she did not dare fuck a man, ever again. Because no matter how good the sex was or how much he loved her, she would always know what was behind it, what surrounded it, and he would not know. And if he didn't know, then she was not safe. Her life was in danger, and she could not bear the thought of living side by side with someone who would not know how angry and frightened she was.

If she told Michaels all this, he would try to comfort her. He would try to make her feel better. But he would not share her feelings. My God, who would want to feel this way if they could help it? No, he would want her to just stop talking about it, stop thinking about it, pretend it wasn't there. And that was dangerous, stupid. It ought to be unnecessary.

She tried to tell Raven some of this, but it was hard talking about men with her. Carmen had a crazy thought that it would be easier to have this conversation with Doc.

"You're finding it difficult to speak your mind," Raven said.

"Yeah, I guess I am." Carmen realized there were no more cookies, and the thermos was empty. She could not drink another drop or eat one more bite.

"Are you afraid I'll try to convert you?"

"Oh, come on."

"Seriously. You are afraid of something."

Carmen decided to be blunt. "I'm just afraid of you, that's all. It doesn't have anything to do with you making me a dyke. If I am one, it's because of who I am, not because of anything I ever did with my best friend in high school or Doc or Eagle Wing or any other woman. But you're up to something scary here. I can feel it. I can see it in your eyes. Something ugly is going to come down real soon. And I don't want to be a part of it."

"You have good reason to hate Prez."

Carmen caught her breath. "Yes. I do."

"Don't you think you are entitled to exorcise it?"

Carmen caught Raven's glittering, mad black eyes and held them. She would not look down, she would not look away. She must see this thing, listen to what was *not* being said.

"I don't choose to exercise a lot of my rights," she said.

"Tina is entitled to revenge. She cannot take it for herself because she died in that farm house, died under Prez's violent hands. The Goddess needed her so she gave her a new life, but there is still an old rule that has to be kept, or the balance will be lost. A life for a life. A life for a life, Carmen. And you should be part of it. You are Tina's rightful proxy. As women it is our task to preserve the balance. Sometimes we can't, but we have to try. The earth, our mother, is sick and may die because we haven't tried hard enough. Men rule us because they are willing to be violent. They are too stupid to realize that our capacity to be violent exceeds theirs. Women have to stop being afraid of that potential, and learn instead to exercise it with wisdom and justice."

"I—" Carmen felt sick. She remembered the bloody, spiked strap. The groan. How did it make her feel, to hear Prez groan? She had had to listen to Tina cry out in pain for miles and miles and miles. Which plea for mercy rang the loudest in her ears?

"I don't know if I can," she finished. "I don't think you're wrong. But I don't know if I am able."

Raven smiled at her and changed the subject. "You're part Indian, aren't you?" Raven asked.

"Yes. My grandmother was Zuni."

"There's a retreat for Indian women who want to learn traditional herbal medicine and other forms of healing. Sometimes they let a few white students come. But it's mostly for Native American women, all tribes, because there aren't enough of them left for any one tribe to keep what it knows away from everybody else. Josie is going to die if she doesn't get help. We could take her there. When our work here is done."

"When would that be?"

"I think soon after Solstice. The day after. You could prepare her for a journey. There are some things she should stop eating if the treatment is going to help her, some herbs she should be taking. Sometimes the best thing to do when you're confused is to work. Having a task prevents you from making a mess of the rest of your life while you get things figured out."

"Yeah, I think I could talk to Josie about that. She's been to so many doctors. She says she just won't go any more. I'd have to convince her that this was different."

"You're a good woman, Carmen. The Goddess recognizes your strong heart, and She will help you find your path. You are not the only one who has changed. Michaels and Anderson will be here before the longest night of the year, and many of your questions will be answered then." Raven leaned forward and took Carmen's hands, pulling her to her feet. She drew a circle on her forehead, lightly touched each one of her breasts, and the crotch of her jeans. "It's not a pass, it's a blessing. That's what the High Priestess tells all the young Harpies. Just be sure not to tell Josie too much. We won't want anyone to be able to follow us when we leave."

"Your secret is safe with me."

"Then it's your secret, too, isn't it?"

Raven left Carmen to find her own way out of the house. At the front door, Carmen was halted by a shriek. It seemed to come from all directions. She almost went back into the house to track it down. But there was her bike, and her cap and gloves were already on, so she started her Harley.

She was at her own front door before she realized she hadn't felt the wind at all, and she'd been smiling all the way home.

18

It was early afternoon when Doc made it back to the hotel. She had stopped for lunch and a couple of drinks at a gay restaurant called Dick's Diner. It was nice to be back in the city where you could get comfortable while you got a little loaded.

The hotel was showing signs of life. There was somebody at the desk now — a different guy than the surly asshole they had dealt with last night — and when the elevator came down to the lobby, two of Slim's girls got out, talking about where they were going to eat breakfast.

As the elevator door opened, Doc could hear a banshee wailing at the end of the floor. She strolled down the hall to Amber's old room, and opened the door. Inside, on the bed, Hattie was trying to cuddle an extremely distraught Fluff.

"Your tits must hide quite a pair of lungs," Doc laughed.

Hattie shook her head. "Where the hell you been? Can't nobody sleep with this girl going off like a siren."

Doc resented having to come down from her warm, friendly glow and deal with this hysteria. "I'm not accountable to you, Hattie."

Fluff balled up the note Doc had left her and threw it at her. It hit her cheek, and stung. Surprised, Doc touched her face.

"What you expect, going off and leaving this poor little girl with nothing but your last will and testament?" Hattie asked witheringly. "Is that your style? Make her a widow before you make her a bride?"

"Oh, I didn't know Slim had married you." As soon as it was out of her mouth, Doc knew she had made a big mistake, but it was too late to take it back, so she just dug her heels in and braced herself for the storm.

"Slim is my man," Hattie said. "I know where I stand with him. If he leaves me alone, I know he's taking care of *our* business. You better look to your own mending before you go poking holes in the fabric of *my* lifetime."

She got off the bed like Hatshepsut descending from the royal barge, and left the room vibrant with her disdain.

"What the hell's the matter with you?" Doc demanded. "Quit carrying on, will you? Goddess, you're giving me a headache."

"But I thought you were — I thought you were—"

"What? Dead? Well, even if I was, all this blubbering and bellyaching wouldn't bring me back. Knock it off."

"You — are — such — a — jerk!"

Doc had never seen Fluff turn red with rage before. But she was insulated by alcohol and the euphoria of having come unscathed from the fiery furnace. When Fluff looked like she was about to unleash a torrent of angry words, Doc decided she just didn't need this shit. So she left.

✧

It took Doc about a week to acquire enough additional layers of insulation to return. Portland had a big gay community. There were five or six lesbian bars and dozens of places where faggots did their drinking. Doc figured it was important for her to visit every one. She hadn't been here for months. If she was going to set up any kind of business, dealing locally, she had to scope out the territory.

When she finally made it back to Slim's hotel, Fluff was gone, and so were all of their belongings. The unfriendly night clerk didn't know anything about where she had gone. Doc had already knocked on all the doors upstairs. Everybody was out working.

"It's time for you and I to develop a better understanding of one another," she said, and grabbed the clerk by his hair. She pounded his face on the desk a couple of times. "Did that help your memory any?"

He tried to come across the counter at her, but it was too high. All he did was slam the wind out of himself. Doc laughed. "Come on, I know that bitch of mine. She's compulsive. She must have left a note for me. Don't you want to help the course of true love run smooth?"

He was too busy lifting the hinged portion of the countertop to look for a note. Doc waited for him to get out from behind the desk, then punched him in the face. "Learning is a slow and repetitious process," she said, shaking her head, and stepped over him to rifle through his papers.

Doc found a large sheet of purple paper, folded into the shape of a swan. She couldn't get it open without tearing it. There was no salutation, just an address written in gold ink and the initial F, drawn like a feather. "That's just around the corner," Doc said out loud. "Hope she found a place with a big bathtub."

The desk clerk caught at her leg on the way out, and she stomped on his hand. "I think we're going to have to send you to remedial living," she told him. "You're not just rude, you're stupid."

She found the address in the note without much trouble. It was, as she had thought, just two blocks away from the hotel, around the corner. When she rang the bell, nobody answered. The front door of the building was not locked. The dead bolt had been ripped out of the door jamb so many times, there was nothing left to hold it in place. There was no elevator, and the apartment number was not on the first floor, so Doc climbed, cursing the stairs. Her leg had been getting better, but the last time she kicked that kid she had put her back out.

The apartment door had a poster tacked onto it, a Dixie beer ad that featured two girls on rollerskates. Their metallic silver bathing suits were decorated with little Confederate flags. Cute. Doc tried the door. It wouldn't open. The poster was meant to hide the fact that the door had a glass window in it. She could always break it. Instead, she used the little door jimmy that she kept on her keys. It was a simple lock, and popped easily.

It was only a studio apartment. The bathroom was on your right as soon as you entered the front hallway. It looked scrupulously clean, and there were four real towels (all different sizes and colors) folded over the racks. A kimono hung from a hook behind the door. The bathroom cabinet contained Alka-Seltzer, aspirin, a comb, a toothbrush, some toothpaste, and a lot of makeup.

Doc washed her face in the sink, groped for a towel, and blotted herself dry. Most of the dirt seemed to have come off on the towel. Well, it's hard to clean your own face, it's not like you can see what you're doing. Better not hang the towel back up, it wasn't clean enough to use again. She left it on the floor under the sink.

The hallway ended in the kitchen, and to the left was the bedroom. A small table with a yellow formica top was wedged in between the stove and the kitchen door. Doc edged around it and opened the refrigerator. There were several cartons of yogurt, a bag of apples, a box of chocolates, milk, cheese, bread, eggs, butter, and a packet of sliced ham. "We're going to eat good, I can see that now," Doc said to herself. There were even dishes in the cupboard — some plates and coffee cups — and some silverware in one of the drawers. "Aren't you a little homemaker?" she asked the empty air.

She got a cup of yogurt out of the refrigerator and had a spoonful. Brrrr, that was nasty. "Guess I still don't like this stuff," she said, and left the container on the counter with the spoon stuck in it. Fluff might be hungry when she got back home.

There was one closet in the bedroom. Where had all those shoes come from? The big pair of saddlebags and her camping gear were stowed on the top shelf of the closet. Fluff's outfits were hung up neatly, an inch of space between each dress. Doc swept them all together, took off her jacket, and hung it up. It was too heavy for the hanger, and made it bow. She closed the closet door before she could see if it fell on the floor or not.

One end of the sofa held a stack of folded sheets and blankets and a pillow. Must be a bed inside there. The sheets matched each other, but not the pillowcase. Doc pulled on the bottom of the pile of linen, and it toppled to the floor. With a groan, she collapsed on the sofa, then was sorry she had laid down without anything to drink.

"Haven't you been a busy girl? Decorated up a storm for somebody who's only been here a week," Doc said, propping her boots up on the arm of the couch.

Then she noticed the bookshelf on the wall opposite the closet. It was not very big, just two shelves, but it was freshly painted. She expected to see a few rows of Harlequin romances, neogothics, comic books, and movie magazines. Maybe even a murder mystery or two, for those rare occasions when Fluff felt intellectual. But there were no paperbacks. She sat up a little, and squinted to get a clearer view of the titles. *The Diagnostic Handbook of Gynecology*, *Beginning Algebra*, *Gray's Anatomy*, *Introductory Chemistry*, *The Physician's Desk Reference* (that would be helpful), *Understanding Statistics*, *The History of Immunology*.

They must have been here when Fluff moved in. Typical of the bitch, that she'd be too lazy to get rid of them. Doc thought about getting up, but before she finished thinking about it, she was asleep.

✧

When Doc woke up, daylight was just beginning to fill the little room. The front door was creaking. She removed her piece from her jacket and rolled off the bed, landing on the floor with her elbows braced, ready to shoot.

"Wait a minute, I think you got this all wrong," Fluff drawled. "Since you all are the one who broke into my apartment, don't I get to shoot you?"

Doc sat up and holstered the .45. She felt a little foolish. "Broke in? Whaddaya mean, broke in? I didn't break anything. Listen, you need to get some beer in that refrigerator."

"I don't drink beer," Fluff said. "It makes me belch."

"Well, I like to belch."

"Charming. Is that what you came all this way to tell me?"

This reunion was not going well. Doc sat up and reached for her smokes. "You got an ashtray in this palace?"

Fluff looked around. It wasn't a palace, was it? She hadn't been letting the other girls smoke here. Oh, well, it was Doc. She went into the kitchen and came back with a saucer.

"Here," she said.

Doc ran one hand up the inside of her leg. Fluff was wearing a black vinyl miniskirt and a tube-top of bright yellow spandex with leopard spots printed on it. She had on knee-high, black vinyl boots with impossibly high heels. Her wrists were loaded down with gold bracelets, and her gold hoop earrings were big enough to put a fist through.

Under the skirt was a pair of stockings and a garter belt, and nothing else except soft girl-skin and soft girl-fur. Doc clamped her big hand on the soft, tender part of the inner thigh and squeezed. Fluff got a little unsteady on her feet, and bent over far enough to put the saucer she was holding down on the arm of the couch. Doc's thumb was teasing her tense, red clit. But when it slipped into her cunt, Fluff hit her sharply on the back. So Doc slid further back, and put the wet thumb up Fluff's ass.

Somehow, in one of those awkward yet magical moves that make sex possible, Doc got Fluff sitting on her lap, facing her. She ran two of her fingers through the wetness of Fluff's crotch and twisted them up into her ass.

Fluff's cunt was overworked and sore. It was wonderful having someone that she did not despise touch her. It was even more wonderful to think that this time, sex might end in orgasm for her. Doc was licking her neck, nibbling it, and her free hand was rolling up the tube top to expose Fluff's breasts.

"Is my dildo still in those saddlebags you got in your closet?" she asked.

"Anything you left there is still in them," Fluff replied.

"Then go get it," Doc told her, withdrawing from her ass.

As Fluff went to the closet, she heard Doc pulling out the sofa bed. She yanked at the saddlebags. They were too heavy and too high up. When they slid off the shelf, they damn near brained her. She reached into one without looking, not wanting to intrude into Doc's belongings, just letting her hand search for what she had been told to find. However, she did have the presence of mind to hunt for the lubricant as well as the dildo.

The part of Fluff that was not aroused was full of misgivings. Doc had come into her place without permission, and just look at the mess she'd made. But if she didn't want Doc to come here, why had she left her that note? She had an uneasy feeling Doc was in trouble. And Doc had stood by her when she was in trouble, hadn't she? Fluff thought, I owe her. I have to reciprocate.

Besides, she wanted to get fucked. She wanted to be fucked mindless and senseless by somebody who would not let her control the entire process. The mind games involved in turning tricks were just too much sometimes. You always had to be in charge. The idea was to make them lose it as quickly as possible, and get rid of them before they got mad. You never wanted to feel anything with them because it was dangerous.

So she took the big, thick dildo and its folded, slightly scummy leather harness over to Doc, and made up the bed while Doc put it on. "Get up on all fours," Doc said, pulling a strap tight, adjusting the base of the dildo over her mons. "I want to have you from behind." So Fluff waited on elbows and knees, wondering why her bottom and her feet always got cold just before she had sex. She put her head down, trying not to think. Doc would not have to do anything to make her ready. Fluff could tell she was slippery already. Bored and anxious, she squeezed her ass-cheeks together, rubbed her thighs up and down to make one half of her wet sex chafe against the other, and fluttered the muscles inside her cunt.

Doc didn't seem to know there was such a thing as foreplay. Fluff was glad, this time, to feel the slick shaft simply and efficiently opening her ass. She was too needy to be able to tolerate preliminaries. But what about the next time? Fluff wondered if Doc would be patient enough to work on arousing her.

Then Fluff could not worry any more about the future. Doc was relentless. Her arms were so long, she could easily reach Fluff's throat while they were fucking. But what Doc wanted this time was her breasts. She used Fluff's nipples like reins to guide her course up and down the intruding instrument. Fluff began to touch herself lightly, trying to ease the overwhelming sensation of anal penetration, her body's reflexive need to expel the thing that was giving her pleasure. Finally she was masturbating frantically, irrationally terrified that Doc would come before she got off, afraid that something would change or stop or prevent her from finally, finally achieving satisfaction.

"Who do you belong to?" Doc demanded, making her hurt, making her tell the truth.

"You," Fluff gasped. "You," she hissed. "You," she shouted, and came, and came, and cried as if her heart were broken. This was not what Fluff wanted. This was not how she wanted to feel, and this was not where she wanted to belong.

✧

Fluff fell asleep without making any effort to appease the sexual need that had accumulated in her partner's loins. Doc thought about fucking herself, but she didn't want to get out of bed and go wash off her dick. That was one of the problems with ass-fucking. You couldn't just put another condom on it. So Doc rolled onto her stomach and beat off with the fingers of her right hand hooked just barely inside her own cunt. She used the palm of her hand to press up on her clit. It was always a contest to see if her wrist would give out before she got off. She had tried vibrators a couple of times, but she didn't like the idea of getting used to them. Electricity was not something you could count on when you traveled. Tonight, ligaments outlasted lust. Doc came hard enough to force a cry of pleasure out of her throat, and she went to sleep with Fluff's cold little butt pressed into her belly.

Doc woke up first. She took a shower, then went into the kitchen and started making breakfast. There were potatoes under the sink. The only kitchen knife was too dull to cut them, so she used the Buck knife on her belt. Things like that might have annoyed other people enough to discourage them from cooking, but Doc found the lack of material possessions comforting. Why bother to accumulate a lot of stuff? She wasn't going to be in one place long enough to make it worthwhile.

It also didn't bother her to be eating breakfast when most people were coming home for dinner. Doc liked having her day turned widdershins to the straights. It made her think of herself as a nocturnal predator, big enough and mean enough to survive in the dark, searching the night for prey.

She couldn't find a coffeepot. Now, *that* was weird. What was she supposed to drink for breakfast, milk? Apparently! She took a plate in to Fluff, woke her up, and put it on her lap. "Eat up," she told her when Fluff just sat staring dazedly at the fried eggs and potatoes. "We got to go out and get some coffee."

"I stopped drinking it," Fluff said.

"Yeah, well, I didn't. So you want to go to Craps?"

"That sounds about right," Fluff murmured. She cut into one of her eggs and dipped a potato in the yolk. "Honey, are you in some kind of ... bad situation?"

Doc looked at her like she was out of her mind. "What are you talking about?"

"Oh, come on, Doc, don't snow me. Why'd you leave me that note if you weren't in trouble?"

Doc smiled. "Baby, trouble is my business." She thought to herself, it's better for her if she doesn't know. I can't think of a better place to hide from the Jaguars than the middle of the ghetto. They'd never expect us to be here. And what Fluff doesn't know, she can't tell anybody.

But Fluff persisted. "I know that, Doc. So tell me about it."

This was annoying. Fluff had no right to know the details of her business. Doc had to protect her connections. "I was supposed to do a deal for these people with the Angels. I fucked it up, and they were pissed. But I gave them their money back, so it's all taken care of. Okay?"

Fluff twisted her mouth and gave her a sour look, but she went back to eating and stopped the cross-examination. I swear, Doc thought, women get nosier every year.

It took Fluff at least an hour to get dressed to go out. "The less you wear, the longer it takes you to get ready," Doc swore. "Look at you." Fluff was wearing a red and black camisole under a red circle skirt. Her black high heels had red rosettes. "You're going to freeze on the bike."

"I'm used to working outdoors, remember?"

Nevertheless, she did put on her fringed, white jacket before they went out the door.

"I gotta buy some clean clothes," Doc said on their way out the door. "All my T-shirts are falling apart."

"There's a laundromat down the block."

"I don't have time to sit all day in a laundromat watching my clothes go around and around."

On their way to the bar, they passed a Woolworth's, and Fluff asked Doc if she wanted to buy a coffeepot.

"I don't want to cart it around," Doc said irritably.

Fluff made a mental note to stop by that little corner market that was open twenty-four hours a day. She usually went in there about midnight for some hot chocolate and a chili dog.

They had a few housewares, there was probably a coffeepot somewhere in those dusty odds and ends. Getting the laundry done would be harder. She carried a bag full of her own stuff down to the Fluffi-Spin on the corner every Sunday afternoon. If Doc wouldn't help she'd have to make two trips.

Doc had taken them right up to Come 7 Come 11's door. Fluff slid off the Medusa and was inside before Doc got her kickstand down. Doc came in behind her, and raised an eyebrow. Fluff was sauntering around like she owned the place. Everybody turned around to greet her. Even the bartender had a smile for her, and the Vietnamese girls stopped their cutthroat poker game long enough to say hello. Doc saw at once what was happening. There was a new girl in town, and all the local businessmen were trying to get her account.

Doc located Slim and went over to his table. "Well, look who's back. Sure is a fine cat dragged you all in, Doc. Sit down. Take a load off."

Doc took his advice. Fluff came over to her with a drink. "You want something to eat, honey?" she asked anxiously.

Everyone in the bar, especially the men, were covertly watching them together. Doc said, "Maybe later. You visit with your friends," and sent her away.

Fluff made a circuit of the bar. She greeted all the men respectfully, but if they tried to engage her in conversation, she just giggled and said, "I have to get back to Doc." When she did come back, she brought Rowena with her. "You sure you don't need anything before I go?" she asked Doc.

"Where are you going? We just got here," Doc protested.

"Honey, I promised Rowena I'd keep her company tonight. I still don't know Portland very good, and her arthritis is bothering her so."

"You don't need to work tonight. Stick around. Let's have a drink."

"I'll be back before you know it," Fluff said, and blew her a kiss on her way out the door.

"Shit," Slim said, "if I went off for a week I know what I'd come home to. A house full of lazy, fat bitches sittin' around in their nightgowns eatin' chocolates, watchin' television, and playin' with themselves. You got yourself a real hard worker there, Doc. She's a good girl."

Doc felt a label descending firmly around her that she did not want. "I don't think you understand our relationship," she said, knowing that protest was futile.

Slim laughed. "Oh, I think I understand it better than you. Doc, you're my friend, so I'm going to tell you, you better go to school. Only thing worse than a ho that won't work is a man who don't know how to turn her out. If you don't run them, they run you. I'm talking to you like a brother, now."

"Okay, Slim, okay. Think whatever the hell you want. But I am not Fluff's pimp."

Slim lifted his shoulders and widened his eyes. "Ask around. You ask any of the brothers here, hey man, are you a pimp? And they tell you, no sir. I'm a musician. I'm an artist. I'm an unemployed bricklayer. Shit. A pimp is someone who is supported by the immoral earnings of a woman of pleasure, and that's illegal. You get less time for killin' somebody. No, we all just happen to have women who is working girls."

"And what would you say if I asked you, Slim?"

"Don't ask me, Doc, don't ask."

"I need another drink."

"Leave that shit alone. The rotgut they sell in this place will eat your liver up faster than cancer. Have a line of this. It'll clear your head." He took a gold box the size of a cigarette case out of his jacket and laid out two lines of coke.

"Sounds good to me," Doc said.

✧

Fluff stayed with Rowena for the first hour, but then they both agreed it wasn't working and split up. The only offer they'd gotten was a man who wanted to take both of them to a hotel and have them do a show together. When Rowena named her price, he rolled up his window and drove off.

So now Fluff was alone on a side street that fed into the highway that went across the river. There was still some commuter traffic, but she really should have been out here by five o'clock sharp. The wind was biting. She pushed her jacket off her shoulders as much as she could stand and kept walking. You just didn't want to walk too fast, that made it look like you were a good girl with a legitimate destination.

She was finally flagged down by a guy who said he wanted a blow job. When she slid into the front seat, he already had his dick and his money out. He tried to show her his tattoo, but she put a condom on him anyway. "Why are you doing that?" he asked. "Because I'm in too big a hurry to get this big luscious prick in my mouth to show you mine," she replied, and started sucking. Only a fool trusted that overpriced vaccination. The virus mutated too damn fast.

Blow jobs seemed to be the fad today. Fluff did two more quick and easy tricks who wanted to come in her mouth. Neither of them balked at the condom. There was even one guy who was so paranoid he wanted a hand job. She hesitated when he said he wanted to come on her tits. "Will you lick it up?" she asked on a whim, and when he said yes, she knew she'd hit pay dirt. She pulled her tits out and took his shaft in one hand. He came fast and easy, and then all it took was a little verbal humiliation, pulling his hair, tolerating the slimy touch of his tongue, and he tipped her a hundred dollars.

Then there was the motherfucker. Every day you had to deal with at least one. When Fluff realized he was the motherfucker, she told herself that meant it was a good day, that she was only going to run into this one asshole. First he wanted to fuck her. But he bitched about the condom. "No glove, no love," she said firmly, and he let her put it on. Then he didn't want her on top. She insisted, knowing better than to get pinned under somebody who outweighed her by at least a hundred pounds. And *then* he couldn't come.

Fluff had a routine for these situations. First she found the door handle and got a good grip on it. She put her head into gutter gums mode and gave him five sentences of extremely filthy encouragement. Then she shut up and let him stroke in and out five times in silence. Then she snapped, "Come on, *get off*. What's wrong with you? I'm not a sex therapist."

He said, "I want my money—"

She had the door open and was on the pavement before he could say "back."

This guy was a real head case. He opened his door to come after her. She showed him a knife. "Don't try it," she snarled. So he got back in the car and tried to run her down.

It took him a while to get the car up over the curb. By then, Fluff was up the closest set of stairs and in a doorway, where the car could not possibly touch her. So he shouted at her and finally drove away. All she could think was, thank God she had not been working beneath the underpass, where there would have been no escape.

She did not want to walk back to Craps, for fear he was still driving around and would find her. A cab passed, but the driver wouldn't stop. Some cab drivers brought passengers down here and even steered tricks to certain girls. But some of them refused to have hookers ride in their vehicles. It was true that if you'd had a bad night and you caught a cab home, you'd tell the driver you didn't have any money and offer to take it out in trade. That was standard operating procedure. But Fluff waved money at the guy and he still wouldn't stop, didn't even slow down. He had a chrome fish and a cross welded to his trunk lid. "Thank you, Jesus," Fluff yelled, giving him the finger.

Finally Fluff gave up and lit out for the bar on foot. She ran most of the way, and kept colliding with obstacles because she was glancing over her shoulder so often. Every time she saw a car the color of her crazy trick's vehicle, she ran up the nearest flight of stairs.

Three blocks from the bar she found Rowena and sobbed out her story. "How much you take in?" Rowena asked.

"Three hundred."

"Shit, I got forty dollars. Don't complain to me."

When they walked into Craps, she could tell that Doc was as high as a kite. Doc and Slim were playing pinball and just beating shit out of the machine. Doc didn't want anything to eat, but she stopped playing long enough to sit with Fluff while Fluff chewed the meat off a plate full of ribs. "Want to knock off early and have some fun here?" Doc asked her.

Fluff knew if she told her about the bastard who had tried to run her down, Doc would never let her out the door. And there would go any independence she had. But she was so scared, she chewed her lip and thought seriously about taking the rest of the night off. Then Doc said, "Have you got any money? I owe Slim for some coke," and Fluff knew she had better keep her troubles to herself and get back on the stroll.

She gave Doc a hundred dollars. "Will that cover it?" she asked. She felt as if every man in the place watched her do this, and crossed her off his list of potential conquests.

"Yeah, sure."

"I'll be back with the other girls," Fluff said, kissed her, and left.

19.

Prez's head lolled from side to side. The neat rows of punctures on his thighs, chest, and upper arms were scabbing over. Any movement pulled the new crusts away from the edges of the wounds, and made them twinge. Prez didn't care. He knew that the small, deep holes in his flesh would never be allowed to heal properly. The bitches would be all over him soon, too soon. They kept hurting him. His body healed in spite of them, to spite them. Prez was secretly proud of the way his flesh resisted infection and took advantage of every split second they left him alone to repair itself. He had been reduced to this, beaten down, exhausted, and confused until he could not really imagine escaping from them. A scar was a victory. He had lost track of how many new scars he had, an appalling number, or how they looked, crisscrossing his body like a map of perversity.

His tongue was as thick, dry, and sticky as an old, dirty boot-sole. "Water," he croaked. Rose came up to him and spit in his open mouth. He swallowed, amazed. That horse-faced bitch. He'd once told Anderson that he would rather hump a cactus than let somebody that homely suck him off. And now she hated him. That wasn't unusual. Most women hated him. But Rose let it show, she flaunted it. How dare she?

He had been put in this chair by Dee Ann. Prez had been taught, repeatedly and shamefully, that her big body was not made of blubber. Dee Ann was the one who moved him from place to place, who held him down while the other women strapped or tied him so that he could not get away. Assisted by the Dobermans, she guarded him when the others ate or slept. When he was in her grip, Prez imagined that she was an iron woman, wrapped in thick layers of suet and plush.

It infuriated him to be held prisoner by someone who amused herself with a big box of crayons and a coloring book. While he rattled his chains, she concentrated on staying inside the lines. The other women kept getting older and uglier-looking, regular hags, but Dee Ann became softer and more childlike. She sang to herself almost all of the time now — nursery rhymes and jingles from her favorite commercials.

Lydia, her enormous tits competing for space inside her T-shirt (they all wore T-shirts now), came close and dabbed some conducting jelly on his nipple. Prez tried to bite her, but she jumped out of range of his jaws. "You're slowing down," she said. She spoke with quiet satisfaction, as if taking pride in a job well done.

She put the alligator clamps on his nipple and stepped away, cupping a black box in the palm of her hand. "I don't like the way you look at me," she told him. That was all she needed to say. Prez understood what she meant. He would have to pay for the privilege of noticing her jugs. She was going to hurt his nipples, and keep her tits in his face the whole time, and make him think about the fact that it wasn't his mouth on her big nipples that made them get hard. No, it was his suffering that would excite her. Was that so despicable? Prez knew he was on trial, maybe already sentenced and condemned, because he liked to hurt women. But all of the women he had injured (or killed, sometimes) were women who had made him scream. It was only fair.

Their first day here, Raven and her court had found the chambers in the basement the Angels used to hold and interrogate club enemies and competitors. The black box that Lydia held now had been one of his favorite implements for discovering the truth. But the women never asked him any questions. He would have been glad to tell them anything, but they never asked him any questions. And they thought *he* was some kind of sick, sadistic monster.

Rose was looking at Dee Ann's coloring book. "This peacock is real nice. You made that look very elegant," she said, and gave the big woman back her book. Prez could not believe that he was being tortured, and Rose was too busy to pay any attention.

Lydia flipped a little switch and turned up some dials. He screamed. "You're cheating," she said scornfully. "It doesn't hurt yet. Behave, now, or I'll clip this sucker to the end of your dick."

Prez bit his lip. Sometimes screaming made them stop. So he had learned to start screaming as soon as there was the slightest pretext. If screaming was not going to make them stop any more, what would work? Despair made him want to dig his own fingers into his eyes, but his forearms were strapped to the heavy wooden chair, and anyway, why should he do their work for them?

Then the door opened, and Lydia stopped playing with the box.

She came into the room. Prez never saw her now without imagining a dark nimbus around her. It had been so long since he was allowed to have his head higher than her head that he had become convinced that Raven was actually taller than he was. She loomed, she towered, her mouth was big enough to swallow his face.

She took the box away from Lydia and gave her the spiked leather strap to put away. "Time for our music lesson," she said, and Dee Ann laughed.

She tortured him then, and Prez was glad. The pain was no greater, no lesser than it would have been if Lydia, Rose, Dee Ann, or Sunny had administered it. But they were often crass when they hurt him, and their eyes did not shine. They did not receive his pain with love. This was personal. Raven loved to hurt him, and the thinner, dirtier, and more damaged he was, the more she loved him.

"Howl for me, dog," she said gleefully.

Prez screamed for her. It burst from his chest as big as a hymn bellowed out by an entire choir. It was a cry of praise for her power and beauty. He did not mind being helpless as long as she saw his plight. His filth and his wounds simply made her seem more glorious. And he was hers. She had put out her small white hand and captured him within a cage of her slender fingers.

She made him scream until he was hoarse, then took off the clamps and put the box away. "I'm thirsty," he told her, and she cut him across the thighs and gave him his own blood to lick off the knife.

"Hungry," he complained.

"I don't want to feed you too often. It just makes you shit," she explained patiently. Prez was sorry, but he knew she was right.

"Want to fuck you," he said thickly. It was the longest speech he had made all day. He had hoarded the strength to make it.

Raven laughed. "You're incorrigible," she said. Then she leaned a little closer. "Soon," she promised him. "Not yet, but soon. Every dog has his day."

Prez clicked his teeth, but he did not even come close to biting her. Might as well try to bite a mountain — or a fish hook.

Then Raven left him, and all dread and wonder left with her. There was only Dee Ann and her toys, and his hatred of Dee Ann. Even hating her was boring.

Prez supposed he really should do something about getting out of here. There were business matters, political matters that he ought to be handling. Fun was fun, but you had to stop playing some time. His feet had fallen asleep hours ago. He wondered when they had last fed him. The food had tasted bad. There were so many things he had to do. Raven would understand. And he really ought to warn her about wearing his colors like that. If somebody saw her, they would shoot her. That would be terrible, to have her die alone, far away, where he would have no part in the hunt, couldn't see her fall and watch the blood spread out in a thick, slow pool or turn the body over and marvel at the difference between the tiny hole where the bullet went in and the crater where it blew its way out of her body.

It made him cry a few small tears, and he really didn't have any moisture in his body to spare. Prez's head sank onto his chest. He had to remember to explain it to her. But so much was always happening. They just didn't talk to each other anymore.

The cut on his thighs was still bleeding. His stomach hurt. He wanted the blood, even though it would evaporate the second it hit his tongue and leave a thick scum of iron-and-meat taste behind. If he asked Lydia, would she spit into his mouth again?

"Raven," he whispered, and slid into the uncomfortable, twilight state that he now thought of as sleep. He dreamed that his dick was long enough to put up her cunt and come out of her mouth. He was fucking her and he had the head of his own cock in his mouth. There was blood on it. He was going to come soon, and he wasn't sure how he felt about swallowing his own load.

"Raven," he said aloud. Dee Ann looked up from her coloring book and saw his erection. How it could keep on getting hard after the things Raven did to it mystified her. She didn't like being around when the hammer and nails and the board came out. It was too noisy. Too much like the factory where you looked at shoes going down the line all day and sometimes the foreman came by and showed you a shoe and screamed at you, and always the machines were banging and banging.

She flipped the pages of her coloring book. There was a picture of a bird with a harp for a tail. The shape of the harp made her think about Raven's waist, the way it curved in so sharp and nice. Rose said that Raven would like that picture. But she should color the other ones first to practice. Dee Ann looked at Prez. Would he be quiet tonight, so she could color without him bothering her? Sometimes he shrieked, and that always made her jump, and then the crayon went outside the lines, and you couldn't erase it.

He looked pretty restless. She decided to wait to do the special picture. She found one of a butterfly on a branch full of orchids. That was very nice. You got tired of all the bright bird colors. The orchids could be pale, maybe mauve, and she could do the tips of the petals in a different color. Periwinkle? Or she could color them cream, and put tiny brown and purple speckles all over them.

She sorted through her crayons, humming a song. "Wee Willie Winkie runs through the town, upstairs and downstairs in his nightgown." She couldn't remember the rest of it, so she started again at the beginning.

Prez shrieked as if eagles were eating his insides. Eagles — or harpies.

20.

Doc and Fluff settled into a routine. Every single evening, Fluff got ready to go to work. And every single evening, Doc would ask her to stay in. Most days, Fluff laughed it off and went out to walk her route. On the few days they stayed in, she tried to get Doc to take her for a ride out of the city, but Doc always made some excuse, and they wound up at Craps or a dyke bar downtown.

Fluff wasn't sure if she wanted Doc to accept her line of work or not. She hated it when they fought about it. She was grateful when Doc started coming out on the Medusa to fetch her back to Craps when the night's work was done. But she also knew that a lot of the men who paid her for sex were attracted to her because she looked so young. What would happen to her in another four or five years? She didn't want to be like some of the older hookers, pounding the pavement from dusk till dawn and feeling lucky if they got a hundred dollars.

It wasn't as if Doc seemed any happier when she stayed home. Fluff didn't feel like they really went anywhere together. Doc just did the same stuff she did if Fluff wasn't there. Fluff had spent so much of her life in bars that they bored her. She didn't like the noise and the smoke. Would you take a secretary out on a date by inviting her up to your office?

Besides, she couldn't really relax at Craps. Slim would tease Doc about letting her get lazy, and the girls she normally worked with would make bitchy remarks. Then Slim would get out the coke, and Doc never said no to that. When they got buzzed together, Fluff felt left out, but she didn't want to join in.

Fluff thought coke was overrated. The only time she had done it, she felt a few minutes of heart palpitations and a rushing sensation, started talking fast and laughing a lot, felt kind of warm and horny, saw a few sparkly lights at the edges of her vision, then spent the next two hours feeling like somebody had dropped her off a building. Why did people like it so much? It seemed to her if you were going to spend that much money you ought to get more for it. Since they came to Portland, Doc had put the price of a fur coat or a car up her nose and all it did was make her want to do the same thing all over again. It made Fluff shake her head, but she kept giving Doc money, although every now and then she found the courage to say, "I don't see why it's my job to get you fucked up."

Fluff usually sat with Doc and Slim for a half hour or so, then moved to another table and spread out her books and papers, read them, and took notes. Doc found this incomprehensible and irritating. She had been baffled when she found out that the textbooks in the apartment belonged to Fluff, and even more confused when she found Fluff doing algebra problems or memorizing the bones in the human hand. "Your tricks like to hear about higher mathematics, honey?" she asked, curling her lip.

But Fluff refused to be drawn into an argument. She just kept carrying her academic tomes and notebooks around, and taking them out whenever she could get Doc to leave her alone for a few minutes. She had her reasons, and they were nobody else's business, especially not the business of somebody who would just make fun of her. Fluff was already afraid she was not sharp enough to comprehend the data she kept forcing into her brain. Every time she got the right number to follow an equal sign or absorbed another fact, she beat back despair. What was in the books, she told herself, was real. That was the world where she wanted to live, where you drew conclusions based on solid information and everything you believed could be proved. Her life was a dream, a bad dream, and the sound of pages being turned over would sooner or later wake her up.

Doc absolutely refused to let Fluff read at the lesbian bars. Fluff didn't mind too much. Those places were too dark to see the print on the page anyway. It wasn't like Craps, where the bartender turned the light up for her and a couple of the kids had taken to coming by to get help with their homework. At the dyke bars, there was always loud music and a dance floor, even if it was tiny, and she loved to dance. Doc was a good partner, but sometimes her back was bothering her, and she would tell Fluff to find somebody else to show off with.

The first time this happened, Fluff studied the dancers, decided who looked hot, and asked one of them to be her partner for the next song. She had picked a tall woman with a cute snub nose who hid her short hair under a Confederate cap. She didn't wear a bra, maybe because she had hard little teacup tits. Fluff liked the way you could see her nipples under her T-shirt. But this boyish vision of poetry in motion was not pleased by Fluff's invitation. That was when Fluff discovered that "femmes," whatever that was, weren't supposed to ask butches to dance. So she asked the next dancer on her list, a very thin woman who wore a white shirt, black pants, a tie, harlequin glasses, and lipstick. That was when she found out that "femmes" weren't supposed to ask other "femmes" to dance, either.

At first, Fluff tried to ignore these weird rules and just be friendly to everybody. Of course, her notion of friendliness included taking women she found attractive (usually butches) out into the alley and fucking them up against a brick wall. Afterward, some of them were pissed off, but others followed Fluff around like homeless puppies, their eyes large and liquid with desire for more. This annoyed the piss out of Fluff, and she literally kicked them away.

A few of her conquests got upset enough to complain to Doc, which made the big woman roar with laughter. "You want me to make her stop doin' that? I'm not as dumb as I look!" she would tell them.

"But she hit me!" one of them whined. This was Rita, a Hispanic dyke who had been clean for two years, but still had a skinny, strung-out body. Fluff found her little, narrow ass quite attractive. Once, she had tried to get to know Rita better. There was only one way that she knew of to finance the kind of habit that Rita bragged about having, so Fluff figured they would be able to swap war stories about walking the street. But Rita didn't want to talk about "whoring." She blustered, "I was never into that shit." Apparently, you could still be a tough, strong woman if you were an addict, but not a hooker.

One night, Rita had been complaining to everyone who would listen about it being her twenty-first birthday. Fluff had asked her if she wanted the traditional festivities, and Rita had agreed emphatically. So Fluff took her over her knee, right there at the bar, and made her count every whack. Rita hadn't complained until Fluff put her back on her feet and declined to go someplace more private where she could stick her hands in Rita's pants. Fluff didn't know why she didn't want to fuck the birthday girl. Maybe it was because she suspected this number was going to be trouble; maybe it was just payback for Rita's attitude about whores.

So Rita took her case to Doc, and would not let up. Doc gave her a withering look, stood up, and took her shirt off. "Hey!" the bartender started yelling. "You can't do that in here. Put that back on!" She had been swabbing down the bar, and she started waving the cleaning rag around, spraying all the seated patrons with soapy water.

Doc ignored her. She turned around and let Rita stare at her back for a good sixty seconds. It had been a while since Fluff had beaten her, but her broad shoulders were still marked with plum-colored bruises. And there was an F, shaped like a feather, cut into her right shoulder. "The bitch is good at what she does," Doc said. "Don't come cryin' to me because all you got was a taste. You can't handle the real thing, Rita. And Fluff knows it. Everybody knows it."

"You're all a bunch of sick motherfuckers," Rita had declared, and stormed out of the bar.

Doc wanted to head out after her, but Fluff grabbed her by the back of her belt and pretended to put the big woman back in her seat. "I love you," Fluff said, kissing her on the nose, "but if you don't put your shirt back on we're going to have to call an ambulance for the bartender."

Later, snuggled up in Doc's arms, Fluff whispered, "Why do they get that way?"

"They who what?" Doc grumbled back. She had almost fallen asleep.

"You know, those girls I take outside, why do they get so pissed off? I never do anything they don't like. Or they come crawling after me, they have to know that's a real turn-off. I'm not the answer to anybody's prayers. I can't fix everything that's wrong with them or continually entertain their lazy asses."

But Doc refused to take the question seriously. "Don't try to pretend you don't know you're being bad," she yawned. "Just keep on being your bad little cherry-busting, heart-breaking self." She hauled Fluff's ass up against her stomach, and was immediately asleep.

Listening to Doc snore, Fluff was lonely. She wanted some-body to talk to besides Hattie. She wanted to know more about being a lesbian. How were you supposed to do it? What were the rules? Doc talked a lot about dykes and their code of honor and their superiority to straight men, but she never talked about the things that really interested Fluff — the intimate details, how lesbian relationships were supposed to work, what it meant to love another woman, how that changed you.

Fluff could not ask anybody else about how this was supposed to go. But she guessed it didn't matter too much. The bikers, jocks, and bar dykes that she and Doc hung out with were outcasts and rebels, but they wouldn't talk about personal stuff even if she had dared to ask them. If you could judge by the things that butches let her do to them in the alley or the bathroom, a lot of dykes liked having their nipples pinched real hard or their asses smacked, and they responded quickly to a girl with a bad mouth, but nobody put a name on it. There just wasn't any place to get new ideas or even some simple advice.

Most of the women she met at these lesbian bars were incredibly rude. She got tired of being treated like a straight interloper or Doc's pet moron — especially when she knew Doc was sitting there black and blue under her leathers. Fluff unleashed her sharp tongue a time or two, but that just made people think she was a shrew. Of course, Fluff was glad when they made a few friends over time — women in leather jackets, for the most part, who saved them a place at their tables and bought them drinks and laughed at Doc's stories. If Doc asked them to, they would dance with Fluff. But they were Doc's buddies, not hers. And they wouldn't really talk to Fluff, just flirt with her — warily, of course, with one eye on Doc's temper.

This isolation made what happened between her and Doc, in their bed, seem forbidden and special. She became obsessed with Doc's erotic secrets. She wanted to know everything about how Doc's sexuality functioned — what she had done with other women, what she hated, what she needed, what she was afraid to try. Doc was a library, and she wanted to read every book. Doc was also like a minefield that she had been ordered to sweep. Fluff wanted to be the best lay that Doc had ever had. It sounded crude when she put it that way to herself, but Fluff didn't trust sentiment, commitment, or honor. She trusted the greed for pleasure and comfort that she saw driving all human beings, the men who sought her out to put their folding money and their erect cocks in her hand, the short-haired women who showed their muscles off every time they tipped up a bottle of beer, posing along the walls and pool tables of the dyke bars, the hookers cozening their pimps for a smile or a chance to sit with daddy and buy him dinner, and Doc, whose protective shell was as thick and hard as her inner self, the self she gave up to Fluff, was needy, frightened, and wild. You could call that love. You could call it salvation. You could call it degradation. For Fluff, it was safety — to be the one who was wanted, the one who was pursued, the one whose hands could grant suffering and then take away all the pain they had inflicted, and a little of the older pain, the hurts you took just from living, besides.

Now that they had a fixed abode, Doc had revealed more of the contents of her saddlebags to Fluff. These items lived in a nightstand by the sofabed now instead of in the closet. Padded leather wrist and ankle cuffs were among those possessions, and several hanks of soft, cotton rope that were gray from use. Fluff had learned not to wait until they came home from the bars or she got off work to try to do what Doc called "a scene." She had a slight preference for Doc drunk over Doc buzzed on cocaine. The physical consequences of alcohol were not as dire, and drinking made Doc rowdy and loud instead of sinister, sarcastic, and paranoid. But all she was good for in either state was a quick fuck, if that.

So they usually played (another one of Doc's terms — it did not feel like playing to Fluff) in the afternoon. If they really got into it, they wouldn't go anywhere, just stay home and keep on fucking for the rest of the night. Doc liked being physically restrained. Fluff knew she would always say "No" when she saw the handcuffs or the leather cuffs. So they had an agreement — Doc got to say "No" three times, and Fluff got to ignore it three times. After that, if she kept saying no, Fluff would put the toys away. Doc learned not to exceed her quota of protest.

It was quite a challenge, to make somebody helpless on a foldout bed. Doc was a big girl. She could move the whole couch when she got active. So Fluff put bolts in the wall and the baseboard, and used them to supplement the ropes she ran from Doc's wrists and ankles down to the legs of the bed. Sometimes that was enough, especially if she had put Doc in a rope body harness that was so tight it cut into her skin, and then used more rope or chain to secure her to the bed. Just the stress of the bondage and the unfamiliar feeling of vulnerability was enough to make Doc wet. Fluff liked fucking someone who was literally helpless. It didn't look as mean as it was.

But the first time Fluff tried to handle Doc's whip, they had a lot of problems. It was a long, heavy, unbraided cat, and Fluff could not seem to make the lashes land any place except Doc's neck or kidneys. Once she got the hang of it, she found that it exhausted her. Doc didn't want any sting. She wanted heavy, solid blows that resonated deep in her flesh.

So Fluff made Hattie take her to the three adult bookstores and the one leather shop in town that sold toys. Hattie raised her eyebrows over Fluff's purchases, but she quietly bought herself a couple of magazines (*Surfer Lust* and *Co-ed Dorm*) and a white vibrator with many red attachments. Fluff came home with a riding crop, which she loved and Doc absolutely forbade her to use ever again, and a leather paddle which produced the correct sensation, except that Doc hated being hit on the butt. Finally Fluff gave up and had somebody make her a shorter, lighter version of Doc's flogger, and practiced with that until both of them were satisfied with her proficiency. She found that it helped to stand on a milk crate. It gave her enough height to make the whip land with crashing force. Doc seemed to think it was funny, but Fluff shrugged that off. Doc always had to find a way to needle you for giving her what she wanted.

She was, however, surprised when Doc balked at the sight of Fluff wearing her own dildo harness. At first, Fluff thought it was because Doc didn't want to have a dildo used on her. But a little conversation revealed the fact that Doc was upset because Fluff had made it on Rowena's sewing machine, and she didn't want Rowena knowing about her stuff.

Doc had introduced a new concept into Fluff's ideas about sex — the concept of "limits," which meant things you weren't supposed to do unless the other person was very excited and you thought they would probably forgive you the next day. One of Doc's limits seemed to be having other people know about the fact that she got tied up, beaten, and fisted. Fluff didn't know how to reconcile that with Doc's displaying her marks to Rita.

"Fisting" was another new concept. Until Doc told her, it never occurred to Fluff that her whole hand might not fit in every woman that she fucked. She had only gone through a couple of dozen women so far, but she had never found a vagina smaller than her hand. It gave you something new to look forward to, Fluff decided.

What was she supposed to do with all the new things she learned or suspected about herself? For example, Fluff was shocked to find that tying Doc up and hurting her made her own cunt get every bit as wet as Doc's. It was very different from servicing johns or Prez. Of course, there were a few disturbing exceptions to the rule that you never came or even got turned on with customers. And she had been so terrified of Prez that the fear had disappeared. She just couldn't live in a perpetual state of panic. So she substituted anger, and took it out on him, even though she knew that when he got what he wanted it made him even more dangerous.

Was it bad, did it make her a bad person, to enjoy screwing clamps onto Doc's nipples or whipping her? Was she going to lose her mind and start killing people someday? Fluff knew that she didn't enjoy random infliction of pain. When the whip went astray, she wasn't excited, she got fussed. But did that have to do with the fact that Doc didn't like it, or was it because she didn't want to be clumsy or incompetent?

And where was all of this leading them? How far could you go? Would there come a day when she would have to choose between being boring and being deadly?

Maybe Doc could have soothed some of her anxiety. But Fluff's pride prevented her from insisting that they talk this out. Besides, there were those glorious moments when she had no doubts. Times when they were covered with a single sheet of sweat, united in a struggle to wrest one more ounce of sensation out of Doc's flesh, compel the tongue to flick, slide, and probe for one more orgasm, make her arm pump out one more fuck, whirl the cat for another ten minutes, when she could not tell who was making which noise because they were one creature. That was, Fluff told herself, all the answer and reason that she needed.

✧

Doc saw a lot of the goings-on at Come 7 Come 11, and she embellished some of these events to amuse her cronies. The more adventurous women started asking Doc when she was going to take them to this fabled pimp bar.

One night, Doc pulled the Medusa over to the curb in front of Ricky's. This was one of the largest lesbian bars in Portland, and most of the crowd wound up there on Saturday night. But instead of being inside saving seats for them, practically all the women they knew were standing on the sidewalk arguing with the bouncer, Marlene. She was a ruddy-faced, square-set blonde, captain of the women's rugby team. Fluff had heard Doc's cronies say, "Marlene isn't so tough," but none of them ever challenged her authority. She had a police flashlight that she swung nervously as she talked to them.

"The owner says it's just getting too black in here," Marlene called out. "This is not a leather bar. Go do your drinking some place else." This did not make her happy. Her job was usually to keep obnoxious men out of Ricky's, not women.

"Fuck this," Doc said. "I know a place where we can go." And she gave them directions to Craps.

The pimps and their women made room for this crowd of bulldaggers with some amusement and some distaste. It made Fluff sick with dread. She did not want Doc's dyke friends so close to her working life. Nevertheless, Doc wanted them there, so they came. Craps became the place where they all stopped to eat before going on to the women's bars. In the beginning, Fluff simply didn't go out to work on nights when she came into the bar and saw other dykes sitting with Doc. Then she got mad. Who was paying for the drinks? And how was she supposed to keep on doing that if she didn't go out and earn some cash? So one night, she gathered up her courage, kissed Doc goodbye, and went out with all the other women.

When Doc's friends realized that Fluff was a hooker, nobody said anything derogatory, but their attitude toward her cooled considerably, while Doc seemed to acquire even more status, finally becoming their acknowledged leader. When Fluff realized that Doc's friends had stopped flirting with her, and most of them didn't even meet her eye, she got very angry. It reminded her of the unspoken rule that a pimp did not talk to another man's woman unless he was trying to woo her away and get her into his own stable. Fluff had often heard Doc say that women did not do the same fucked-up things to other women that men did. But when she told Doc how much this hurt her feelings, Doc just said, "What are they supposed to talk about with you, honey? Turning tricks?"

After that conversation, Fluff withdrew. Maybe she wasn't a lesbian. Loving Doc sure wasn't enough to make her a member of the club. She had been an outsider all her life. It was stupid to pound your head on a brick wall. When she went to Craps, if it was a night when she wasn't going to work, she would get Doc and all her friends their first round of drinks, then go sit by herself and do her lessons. If Doc wanted more money, she had to come and ask for it. Most nights, she didn't bother, just hustled drinks from her buddies. If Fluff was going out, she would sit with Hattie, Rowena, or Amber (just out of jail and not at all chastened) to get her morale up.

The only lesbian in their circle who didn't ignore Fluff was Nikki. Nikki was part black and part Japanese. The epicanthic fold of her eyes and her small, bronze, kittenish face made her look exotic, delicate, and even younger than Fluff. In fact, she was a busy, grown-up girl who took good care of herself and had little time for other people's problems. She was also the only other obvious femme. Most of the women that Doc called femmes dressed like everybody else except for hair that was a little longer or styled with hairspray, and maybe some lipstick. They might wear blouses instead of T-shirts, and flats or low heels instead of boots or Converse sneakers. But Nikki wore dresses and a lot of makeup. She even put glitter in her eye shadow. She had a long wool coat instead of a leather jacket, and she carried a purse.

Doc did not like her. Fluff had asked why, and Doc had explained that butches kept getting 86-ed from various bars for fucking Nikki in the bathroom. Fluff thought it was obvious that Nikki didn't drag them into the ladies' room in a half nelson, but Doc seemed to feel that if a girl asked you to fuck her, you were sort of obligated to do it, so if it got you into trouble, it was the femme's fault.

Privately, Fluff thought it pissed Doc off that Nikki wanted to get dragged off and done instead of sexually assaulting ambivalent butch women the way Fluff did. The fact that Nikki was both a bottom and a femme made her untrustworthy. And the fact that she would not settle down with one lover made her ... could it be? ... competition. Nikki had a rebellious and buoyant spirit. She wouldn't go away no matter how many times Doc hinted that she was unwelcome. In fact, she always greeted Doc with sweetness and joy, as if they were old and dear friends.

Nikki started coming over to sit with Fluff when she social-ized with Hattie, Amber, Rowena, and other female members of Slim's family. She asked them questions about their hair and clothes, invited them to go shopping, told them about movies she had seen. Slim's women liked her. She was open, friendly, pretty, and she did not condescend to them. One evening she got Fluff alone and asked her about working. Fluff tried to give her an honest picture of the ups and downs, but Nikki cut her short.

"How much can you make on a good night?" she asked.

When Fluff told her, she said, "Shit! I don't make half of that running that damned cash register at the supermarket, and the manager is always pinching my tail."

The very next night, Nikki took Doc aside and said, "I want to work with Fluff." When Doc didn't say anything, Nikki said, "Well? What about it?"

"What about what?" Doc asked impatiently. "If you want to work with Fluff, work with Fluff. It's up to the two of you, not me."

"But I don't just want to work for myself," Nikki said softly. "I want to be part of your family."

Doc gave her a look of scorn and distaste. "Are you out of your mind?" she demanded, and hustled back to her friends.

Fluff was appalled. None of the men there would have publicly humiliated a woman that way. A girl who was eager to go out for you was a gift from God. Turning one away would be like committing blasphemy. Very rarely, you might reject a woman who was agitating to join your stable, maybe because she was a troublemaker or because your main lady hated her, but you did it gently. The pimps had a saying that one enemy was one too many.

Nikki kept coming to Craps anyway, and she kept getting closer to Rowena and Hattie. She finally succeeded in persuading them to go out shopping and to see shows with her. They introduced her to other girls from other families. One day Fluff came in to work and saw Nikki seated at a table with King. He was a very black man who preferred formal evening wear to the rainbow hues of the other pimps' fancy suits. King's old lady, Belle, was bisexual, and she had her arm around Fluff's friend. Belle's former favorite looked like she had been crying, and King was petting her and feeding her peanuts.

Fluff nodded hello to Nikki, who looked very happy, and sat down beside Doc, who was visibly disgusted. "I always knew she was really a straight girl," Doc said, and spit on the floor.

"Doc, that's stupid," Fluff protested. "Nikki's with Belle."

"Yeah, and are you going to try and tell me that King doesn't help himself to Belle's girlfriends?"

"No. But if you had let Nikki come to work with us, she wouldn't have had to go to King."

"She didn't have to *go* with anybody," Doc said. "You never did."

"Not everybody is strong that way," Fluff tried to explain. "She wants to belong. She wants to know her place."

"Yeah, well, she's right back in it along with every other straight girl I ever met. King'll keep her in her place all right."

"Is that what you really think? That Nikki's straight? Is that what you think of me?"

Doc didn't say anything.

"Is it?" Fluff insisted.

"Come on, what is this? Are we going to fight all night? Can't you get over this?"

"No, I can't. You really don't think we're on the same side, do you? You like to see me all dressed up, and it makes you feel big and bad when the men here admire me and want me. But deep down you believe I want them too. When all I really want to do is make you feel that pride in me, make you want me. You'll let me touch you but you think I'm your enemy, don't you? And you have contempt for me. You don't think I'm a person the way you're a person. Do you?"

"Look, I'm not going to fuck Nikki just so you can have a little playmate on the street. If you want to be a pimp, you take her on. But I don't turn women out and give them away to men who are going to use them and abuse them. I am not that kind of traitor."

"It would have been nice to have some company. I like Nikki. What's the matter with that? Hooking is a job, Doc. You don't sell your soul. You sell your time. It doesn't have anything to do with who you are or who you love. You think I'm straight because I'm a hustler?"

"Honey, can you honestly tell me that you will never replace me with some prick?"

"Doc, that's unfair. I don't have any plans to replace you. And how do I know what's going to happen to me next? I love you. I've never felt this way about a man, but I've never felt this way about anybody before. And it isn't as if the lesbian community has opened up its arms to receive me. If anything I've been given the feeling that I don't belong. You'd think being a lesbian was some kind of wonderful privilege that you had to bribe and steal and sweat and scuffle to deserve. Guys who want to patch with the Angels have an easier time than I've had in the dyke bars of Portland."

"Look, honey, I know you're upset about Nikki. I'm sorry I said something bad about your friend. But don't let yourself get hysterical."

"Oh, I won't. I don't think I'm the one who's lost her mind," Fluff said, and left the bar. Doc didn't even call out after her. She went home and opened her books at the cramped kitchen table. Somewhere in these dry, slick pages there was a way out of here. She knew it. There just had to be.

Doc came home pretty drunk. Despite her advice to Fluff, she had not forgotten about their fight, and she wanted to finish it.

"What you want me to believe," she told Fluff, leaning on the door jamb, "is that you don't like what you do. That jerking those men off and sucking them off and getting fucked night after night means absolutely nothing to you. Except for the cash, and I hope you won't try to convince me you don't love that. I think I cope with it pretty good. The only assurance I have that you won't bring home a dose of something that could kill me is your word. And I trust you about that, even though you don't trust me enough to stop working for these pricks."

Fluff was tired of being ignored, belittled, and goaded. She said bitterly, "Am I supposed to believe you're going to take care of me? I wouldn't trust you to take care of a stuffed animal! Yeah, you trust me about being clean because you want to get fucked. You need to get laid as bad as any john. Only they pay me when they come. And all you do is drink liquor, snort coke, eat groceries, and sleep in a bed that *I* pay for. Somebody in this relationship has got to make some money. And I am tired of you bitching about where it comes from when you're so glad to spend it."

She hadn't even bothered to stand up to make this speech. Doc reached across the tiny kitchen table and slapped her. Fluff stood up, took one step to the kitchen counter, and grabbed a knife out of the drawer. For a few seconds they just stared at one another, breathing hard. Doc was mortified by the red hand print she saw coming out on Fluff's cheek.

She began to cry. "I'm sorry," she said. "I don't know what's wrong with me. I can't believe I hit you. I just got so mad. I'm sorry."

Fluff put down the knife. But she did not move to comfort Doc. "Why don't you go stay someplace else for a while and get your shit together?" she suggested wearily.

But Doc seemed not to have heard her. She staggered into the living room. Fluff finally went to see what she was doing. Doc was out cold, collapsed on the couch. She hadn't even bothered to pull the bed out, so there was no room for Fluff to lay down. She was so exasperated she wanted to slap Doc awake, but she dug her nails into her palm and made herself calm down. She didn't want to sleep with Doc anyway. So she put some clean underwear in her purse and went to spend the night with Hattie. She would stop by that all-night florist's stand first. See how Hattie liked some orange birds of paradise, gold Chinese lions, and blue nuns, instead of all those white funeral flowers Slim heaped upon her. Get some chartreuse, too. Hattie liked her liquor, but she wanted it sweet-flavored and in a pretty color.

✧

"If I didn't know you better I'd think you was trying to get me drunk," Hattie giggled, tipping up her glass to get the last swallow of pale green liqueur. It was her third drink, and Fluff was still working on her first one. Stuff tasted like mouthwash. But Hattie was talking some more. She was leaning over to finger the birds of paradise, running her long, slim fingers along their beaks, ruffling the beards of the Chinese lions with her long, oval fingernails, spreading open the blue-and-white faces of the nuns. "And you *are* a married woman, so you couldn't be tryin' to get me smashed and take advantage." Hattie rearranged her long legs and gave Fluff a look that was full of pure trust and adoration. Fluff bet that look was worth a million bucks in the front seat of a car. "Or is this just the luckiest day of my little old life?" the black woman drawled. Fluff let Hattie take her by the arm and draw her close.

"I've never been lucky, but I do know how to kiss," Fluff said, and reached for Hattie's face. The tip of her tongue was tiny, like a snake's tongue, slipping over and past the full bud of her lower lip. Fluff put her own tongue to work to get past the taste of chartreuse. The only contact between them were the tips of her fingers on Hattie's cheeks and their lips and tongues. Both of Hattie's hands lay at her side on the sofa, but as Fluff continued to kiss her, she began to knead the cushions with her claws.

"Oh, stop it, you stop it," she hissed, leaning forward for more. "You just stop that now, you wicked, wicked, wicked, oh, *you*!"

Fluff let her hands trail down Hattie's bare shoulders and upper arms, just barely touching her. By the time she got to her forearms, they were covered with gooseflesh. She repeated the caress, then dug her own nails into Hattie's back and began to bite her lips. Hattie moaned and tossed her head, but still her hands dug into the couch. So Fluff left her mouth, and sank her teeth into the smooth dark neck and shoulders.

"Don't bruise me up," Hattie said, in a flat voice that was completely different from the breathy, giggling, nonsense voice she had been using to encourage Fluff. "Slim don't like it."

"Oh, but I'm so careful," Fluff said, biting her again, more judiciously. "I'm sooooo careful, darlin'."

"Are you, now? Is that what you are?" Hattie laughed, sounding drunk and excited again. "Lord, the teeth inside that mouth, child, they are wicked, wicked, *pointy* things. You got a mouth fulla little knives. Oh, yes, oh, yes."

Fluff had been picking at the knot of her kimono, trying to get it untied without letting Hattie know she was touching it. This was very different from making love to Doc, who either pushed you away or stood up and immediately took all of her own clothes off. But she seemed to draw courage and knowledge from Hattie's skin, which was marvelously smooth and inviting. Now the knot was loose, and Hattie, who seemed unaware of the consequences of the gesture, shrugged one shoulder and let the red silk slide off her shoulder, neatly exposing just one breast.

Fluff stared at the plump, brown curve of her breast, the darker, bittersweet nipple that had a hint of pink at the very tip. Hattie made a little sound, to get her to look up. Once she had caught Fluff's eye, she put the tip of her index finger into her mouth. Slowly, slowly, she wet the tip of it, then lowered the finger to her nipple and circled it once, twice, making it shine. It was immediately hard, a miniature mountain peak surrounded by tiny dimples. Fluff went to take it into her mouth.

Hattie caught her, held her off. "Not so fast." She shrugged her other shoulder, exposing the other breast, and wet and hardened that nipple as well. Then she leaned back and squeezed her breasts together, pleasuring the nipples with the tips of her fingers. Her mouth was pursed in an "o," and her eyebrows were crooked in a salacious question.

"I don't like being teased," Fluff said. Her voice sounded as if it came from the other side of the room, the words coming out more harshly than she intended. It was a bad moment. She almost grabbed up her bag and jacket and left. Doc would call Hattie "a straight girl," and now Fluff got some inkling of what that meant, the potential for humiliation and rejection. She was suddenly sure that Hattie did not want her, could never be satisfied by another woman, and had only been leading her on for a joke.

But Hattie slid right over to her and pressed her warm torso up against Fluff's stiff little body. "Don't you be that way," she crooned. "You got me so hot and dizzy. There's just no air in this room at all. Don't you want to see what you're gonna get, now? Hush, come here, you be sweet to me, don't you go talkin' mean to me when I'm feeling so rich and sweet and fine." Hattie kissed her, stroked her back, picked up Fluff's hands and placed them on her breasts. "Love me now. Don't make me wait."

Fluff shivered under Hattie's warm and expert hands. She could feel tears starting behind her eyelids and squeezed her eyes shut, willing them back, refusing to let them fall. Why had she come here?

"You come here with me," Hattie said, standing up, extending a hand. "We don't have to ball on the sofa like two horny kids, I got a big bed just through this door, here."

Fluff followed her into the bedroom, and stood watching as Hattie moved around, turning down the covers, plumping up the pillows. Finally she could not stand the fussing and went to her, stood behind her, ground her hips into Hattie's ass. "I want you on your stomach on that bed," Fluff growled in her ear. "I want to see this pretty behind up in the air."

She slid her hands up her thighs, bunching up Hattie's kimono, and wedged one hand between her legs, then pushed.

"Oh, I just knew you were going to be terrible to me," Hattie giggled, tipping over, but not so fast that Fluff had to let go of her behind. She bent her legs at the knee and kicked a little, showing off her long legs. Fluff was probing her, and she responded with such a strong backward thrust of her hips that it almost threw Fluff off the bed.

"Ain't you going to take your clothes off?" Hattie panted.

"Don't I have enough to do?" Fluff replied, turning her hand, looking for resistance and finding only generosity, the kind of wetness and yielding that makes you want to stay inside someone forever.

Hattie sighed a little as her hand went in. Fluff moved it in circles, from her wrist, and let the tips of her fingers comb the swelling surfaces inside. Hattie's cervix was behind her knuckles. When she came, she arched her head and hindquarters at the same time, nearly ripping Fluff's arm out of its socket. Shaking her head, she slid off Fluff's hand, turned onto her back, and put one hand over her cunt to play with it. She was grinning.

"Well, I feel like I found myself a whole new playground," Hattie said, stretching like a big cat. "What do you think of my pussy? Isn't she fine?"

"Fine? We went beyond fine," Fluff said, standing by the bed to take off her clothes. She poised her naked body over Hattie's, stroked skin against skin, then slid down, spreading Hattie's legs and then her inner lips. The labia were the same color as Hattie's nipples, and in between them was a glowing funnel of pearl-pink.

Fluff had seen the vaccination tattoo on Hattie's hip. But even if it hadn't been there, she would have dipped her head and licked that glossy, salty place. Outside of this room was trouble and grief, misunderstanding and obligation. These seamless moments of joy, this little stretch of time when she could do no wrong, were priceless. To stop was to step back into harness. She needed this to salvage her pride. Hattie was making her feel beautiful again, and Fluff figured that was worth about fifty million orgasms and a half.

"You gonna dip your mouth into my chocolate box?" Hattie teased. "Tired of using your fingers, you gonna just put your whole head in there?"

Fluff licked the wettest part of her cunt, spread the moisture up over her clit. "This sure doesn't taste like chocolate to me," she said. Hattie's stomach shook with laughter, and then it shook with delight.

Fluff stayed down there, wheedling and commanding, until Hattie just could not stand it any more. Her clitoris felt like it had been peeled. "If you don't leave that alone I'm never going to have a use for it again," she declared, and hauled Fluff up by her hair. She emerged complaining but beaming with triumph. Hattie grabbed at her before she could wipe her face, and licked her cheeks and lips. "Bet you don't taste like chocolate, either," she said huskily, "but I want it worse than I ever wanted dessert."

Fluff almost stopped her, then bit her tongue and put her hands back on the sheets. She never let the women that she dragged out of the dyke bars touch her. Sometimes she was even reluctant to let Doc try to make her come. But Doc was far away, Doc had nothing to do with this. It would spoil everything if she was petty and withholding.

Besides, Hattie was very good. "Oh! I never! You sure you never did this before?" Fluff asked her indignantly.

Hattie raised her head to glare at the blonde girl. "Who said I never did this before? Somebody spreadin' lies about me?"

"I see," Fluff said, touching her head, rocking her hips. "I see—"

"See Jesus for all I care, just shut up for a minute," Hattie responded. Her mouth resumed its tiny, clever motions. Her long fingers slid into Fluff's wet slit. "Now where's that spot you hit? Made me think I was going to take off like a helicopter."

This was genuinely taboo. It was something she had never let Doc do. But Fluff found that the guilt simply enhanced her pleasure. The worse she felt about it, the more she knew she was being bad and unfair, the better it felt. She became angrier and angrier with Doc, and less and less inhibited with Hattie. She came more than once that way, and each orgasm seemed to make her hotter for the next, until Fluff finally realized that Hattie was about to get her entire hand up inside her cunt. Then everything closed down, hard, and it hurt so much she screamed.

Hattie pulled away from her and scooted up to the head of the bed. "Stop it," she snapped, and slapped her. "You're hysterical." Fluff stopped screaming, but there were tears on her cheeks, and she couldn't help but cry. Hattie stared at her, then she started to cry, too. They fell into each other's arms and sobbed for a long time.

Finally Hattie pulled herself away and went to fetch some Kleenex and the chartreuse. "I swear we must need to get loved up more often," she said, shaking her head. "We're actin' like crazy women." She drank from the bottle.

"I think I just need to make love with you more often," Fluff said, running her nails down Hattie's back.

Hattie puffed up her cheeks and blew all the air in them out, dismissing the compliment. "Now we're right back where we started from. You are a married woman, and I ain't exactly uncommitted."

"Don't make me leave yet," Fluff said. "Please. Not yet." She kissed her thighs, her hands. "Please."

Hattie narrowed her eyes. "Wish I could be sure you were runnin' *to* me instead of *away* from Doc." Fluff buried her head in the sheets. Hattie sighed, rested a hand on her shoulder. "Come on, now, don't you get me started again with the water-works. It's bad for my complexion. You stay as long as you want to, it's fine by me. Just don't pull any more tricks out of your sleeves."

She got into bed with Fluff, pulled the covers up over them both, and switched off the lamp. Fluff rolled over to Hattie in the dark and cupped a hand over her closest breast. "I'm not wearin' any sleeves," she said.

"I knew we were both in trouble. No teeth! I said, *no teeth!*"

✧

When Doc came to, she felt pretty shaky, but she didn't recognize what she was feeling as a hangover. It was one of her axioms that *she* never got hung over. She was expert at recognizing the symptoms in other people, and mixing them up hellacious remedies, but Doc could hold her own liquor and she knew when to quit, thank you.

She opened a can of Coke, poured a third of it down the sink, dumped in a few glugs of Jack Daniels, then used the results to swallow two aspirin. It made her feel much better. She dug into her saddlebags and got out a roll of bills, what was left of the funds she had confiscated from the Jaguars and the profit she had made this summer. Fluff was right about one thing. It was time for her to get off her ass and go to work. Her old coke connections might have ties to the Jaguars. So she would go through Slim. He could set her up for a quantity buy, and then she could start doing something besides drinking at the dyke bars.

Doc had a shower, dressed, and was on her way to Come 7 Come 11 before she thought to wonder where Fluff had spent the night. Oh, well, the girl was a workaholic. She'd be at Craps, either to study or to hook, and they could kiss and make up then.

Slim raised one eyebrow when Doc told him that she wanted to set herself up dealing coke, and asked him to help her. "I won't be competing with you," she explained. "I won't work out of here, just the gay bars."

Slim visibly relaxed. "I got to make a phone call or two," he said, and left the table. When he came back to her, he looked a little nervous again. "The man want to see me in person," he explained.

"Can I go with you?"

"Don't be as dumb as you look. You wait here."

A few hours later, Slim returned and gave her a name and an address. "It's all set up," he explained. "You just got to go over there and pick it up."

Fluff walked in with Hattie on her arm. Doc waved at the two of them on her way out.

"She don't seem upset," Hattie murmured. "Maybe she ain't the jealous type."

Fluff just laughed. She had had too much fun to worry about Doc right now. "I have an idea," she said, gesturing for Hattie to bend over so she could whisper in her ear. "Let's get our asses out of here and make a little money, then go play hookie at the Hyatt. Slim won't care if you're a little short one night."

"He wouldn't care if he got invited to play hookie with you all," a silky male voice said. Slim was standing behind Fluff.

She looked over her shoulder at him and gulped.

"Don't you be corrupting one of my best workers, now," he warned her. "Doc give you a loose rein, but I keep my fillies on a check rein."

He crooked his finger at Hattie, and she went away with him, sat down at his table, took out her manicure set, and did his nails. Fluff was left alone with her memories. Their tropical colors quickly cooled, and she did not think she wanted to pore over her textbooks under Slim's baleful eye.

The fleet was in. Tonight would be busy. But those sailor-boys didn't have cars, and most of them were too cheap to spring for a hotel. They wanted to save all their money for booze. She hated doing tricks outside. But they were fast and easy to please, as if they could not wait to get their obligatory piece of ass and rush back to their boyfriends.

But she was not going to be run out of here. Fluff turned her back on Slim and Hattie, took out her compact, and took her time wielding her lipstick brush, eyebrow pencil, and blush. The results were pleasing. "You look like a girl who's about to make a lot of money," she told the little mirror. She snapped the compact shut, threw it back into her bag, shook out her hair, and headed for the door.

21
_◇

White Owl and Moon Rabbit sat cross-legged, close to the small fire that lit and warmed the tipi. Most of their conversations had taken place in this cone of waterproof canvas, where a shift of the wind could send smoke back down the ventilation hole, and you could not forget that snow was falling outside even if the cold, wet flakes were not landing on your skin. Now that cold had driven most of the Harpies indoors, privacy was hard to come by, and White Owl didn't think it would be good for the new High Priestess if some of the older Harpies heard her odd questions about the traditions she was trying to teach her.

The new wing that was to have been added to the big house was incomplete. The beams had been placed, and two walls had been built, but then the lumber had run out. Harpy Farm did not have the means to mill its own timber. There was a cash surplus from sale of the marijuana crop, but the High Council was blocking attempts to use it to buy the wood it would take to finish building.

This had made the passing women and the ex-hets livid. Some of them now believed that Raven's vision of complete integration and equality had been forgotten when she left the farm, and would never be implemented. Once, they would have looked to Wally to solve this problem and scavenge the necessary supplies. But Wally was so angry about the Harpies' reaction to her romance with Leaping Salmon that she had withdrawn from all but the most basic and necessary responsibilities.

When someone approached her to ask for help, she had said harshly, "It took me and the guys a whole week to find those beams and drag them in here, and we got no fucking help. I smashed my hand, and Tony got a sprained ankle, and nobody even said thank you. So work it out yourselves, ladies."

Before the first freeze, one of the ex-hets, Sahara's lover, Bridget Li, a Korean woman who had come up with some ingenious ways to teach young, restless Harpies their alphabet, had suggested that Harpy Farm's outcasts go into town and sell or trade something for the wood. The idea of them doing business with outsiders was controversial. The debate got bogged down in an argument over what exactly should be bartered or sold. Should they try to find a buyer for the surplus from the fish ponds? Should they wait until spring and plant another half-acre of sinsemilla? Should they sell some of the quilts and jewelry and other crafts that Harpies made to keep themselves from going crazy, locked up inside all winter?

Meanwhile, the ex-hets and passing women who had been moved in to the big house by friends or lovers refused to leave. The women who had moved their trailers or tipis left them as close to the house as possible. And Software, a strange but happy and *very* talkative little soul who had pink-and-green hair, had even built a lean-to, using a corner of the unfinished wing for two of its walls. She was cold, she told everyone, but she felt she had to keep reminding the born-Harpies where she belonged. Her computer, of course, could not stay in the lean-to, so Sahara made room for it in the toolshed.

Moon Rabbit wished that White Owl would give her more practical help resolving dilemmas like this one, and concentrate less on making her memorize the calendar of the Great Mother, all Her names and attributes, the paraphernalia necessary to conduct various rituals, the texts of blessings and sealings and healings and summonings, the recipes for herbal concoctions that would help open mundane eyes to sacred matters, and on and on and on. There was no end to it. By comparison, catechism classes with Sister Mary Sacred Torment of Jesus had been a piece of cake.

White Owl was proportioned after her namesake. Her hair had once been as black as Raven's, but now it was a mixture of gray, a little black, and white. Most Harpies said that her hair had turned white when she witnessed the death of her lover, and she never said they were wrong. She wore a dress made out of deerskin, decorated with beads and paint. Moon Rabbit was amazed when she saw White Owl walking through snow in her moccasins. But she had spent most of her life out of doors, either farming or climbing mountains to find a place to talk to the Goddess, and her feet were as hard as the split hoof of a goat.

Moon Rabbit found it necessary to bundle up more. She wore overalls and hiking boots, a thermal undershirt, and the long, black velvet vest that Raven had given her. She had added only one thing to it, an inch-square microchip that Software had given her. It had four blinking, colored lights on it that you could turn on or off by pressing one of the corners. Over the vest, Moon Rabbit wore a down parka that she'd won playing cards with Wally and the guys. It was warm enough in the tipi to leave the parka unzipped and its hood down, but just the whistle of the wind outside made her reluctant to take it off.

Today, they were arguing about the Winter Solstice sacrifice. Moon Rabbit had been shocked to learn that she was expected to sacrifice a rooster during the longest night of the year. She had tried to reconcile herself to this necessity. After all, White Owl had pointed out, she had had no trouble eating fried chicken on the one day this treat had come hot and crisp from the kitchen. She had even gone to visit the bird, to convince herself that it was a lower form of life that would feel little, if any, pain when its life ended.

There in a wire mesh poultry run was the rooster. He was a fine, black bird that stood nearly as tall as her knee. He had rust-colored tail feathers, a rust-red belly, and a pure red comb that seemed unusually plump and flamboyant, full of his vitality and virility. No doubt about it, she thought, as he jerked his head, scratched the ground, and turned a glittering, uncomprehending eye upon her, he is a pompous and silly creature. But his death will not make spring come any quicker, and it will not make me more powerful, or keep anybody from catching influenza.

Moon Rabbit had already decided that she was going to explain this to everyone at Solstice, and urge them to give the Goddess honeycombs (which were even more rare and valuable than meat) and toast Her with wine instead of with blood. On a farm, of course women would not be squeamish about butchering pigs or killing chickens, but she could barely justify shedding blood so they could have the animals' flesh to eat. Sacrificing the rooster, no matter what White Owl said about the necessity of demonstrating that the male principle was subservient to and existed only at the whim of the female principle, seemed cruel and wasteful.

She explained all of this as best she could. When White Owl tried to resume the argument, Moon Rabbit made an abrupt gesture with her hand. "I don't want to talk about it any more," she said. "We've both told each other how we feel. Repeating ourselves will not make us understand one another better. Let's just accept the fact that we disagree."

White Owl grabbed the toes of her moccasins and rocked back and forth and laughed until she coughed. Moon Rabbit tried to pat her on the back, but White Owl motioned her away. She did accept a sip of hot tea from the thermos. Wiping her eyes, she said, "Spoken like a true high priestess. You know, my dear, your role here is not really to tell everybody what day of the year it is or use the proper knife to cut the proper color cord, depending on the holyday you are celebrating, and face the right direction to salute whichever aspect of the Goddess rules that day. Wolf Clan and Apple Blossom keep the calendar quite nicely, and the members of Snake Clan will always be only too happy to perform whatever magical hooeykaflooey you loftily delegate to their capable hands." She leaned closer, and her voice got low and conspiratorial. "Your real job is to tell the truth."

Moon Rabbit was skeptical. "But everybody here is remarkably honest," she said testily. "I never heard such blunt, outspoken women in my whole life. And why have me memorize all the other stuff if my job is really as simple as that?"

"Because your people need the comfort and release of celebrating their devotion to their Great Mother," White Owl said. "She has so many faces, and gives us so many different ways to come to Her, because She wants all of us to be able to find some way to love Her. Some way to let Her into our hearts. Because if we don't let Her, there is nothing She can do to help us. Speaking the truth is not an easy thing. It's very different from being loud about your opinions. It's usually dangerous. Any truth, spoken forthrightly, carries its own authority, but your people will suffer less if they love you and believe in you enough to act promptly on what you tell them. Provided, of course, that you have kept your own eyes clear and your own heart strong so you are a straight channel for the truth, instead of secretly working for your own self-interest."

"If the truth isn't just my opinion, what is it? How can I distinguish the truth from my own self-interest?"

"Truth serves justice," White Owl said. "And justice is another word for kindness. It is a passion for dealing fairly with everyone. It isn't enough to make sure no one gets cheated. You must also make sure, as much as you can, that no one feels ill-used. Because if we are going to exploit one another, if we don't love one another, then why are we here? We forfeit all right to Her good earth."

Moon Rabbit loved the Harpies. She was bound to them because they had known her before her miraculous healing.

The Harpies were her witnesses, living proof that something wonderful had happened. But she also loved them because they did not try to talk her out of this memory or cloud her vision about the future. They were curious to know what had really happened to her, what she really saw. She loved them for their bravery and even for their ignorance of the outside world. Here, they were people. Outside, they were women. Which place would anyone in her right mind choose?

So it bothered her that she did not know more about them. She genuinely wanted to do a good job for them, and would have tried to be the most productive weeder or milker or baler of hay, if they had asked her to do that instead of being a high priestess. Sometimes she wished it was her job to work in the garden, dairy, or fields instead of taking on this mysterious position of infinite responsibility.

"So why are we here?" Moon Rabbit asked. "How did we get here?"

"This land has been women's land for a hundred years," White Owl said. "There was a group of women who wanted to get out of the city and live with each other. One of them had enough money to buy the land. Some of them found that they didn't enjoy life in the country, including the woman who had money, and they left. Not all of the women who stayed were very good farmers. It took a long time for us to be able to feed ourselves. Once, it is said, the land was held by only three women living in a tent, and they had to walk a mile and a half for water because there was a drought. But when the woman who had originally bought land for Harpy Farm died, she left all of her money to the settlers, on the condition that any woman who came onto this land would not be turned away. So the first Harpies could dig a well, put in some permanent buildings, build a road and a windmill."

"But that doesn't tell me why," Moon Rabbit said. "And if the first women who came here were from the city, why is there so much hostility between old Harpies and new ones who weren't born here? If it weren't for refugees, this place wouldn't exist."

"Well, that's a wise thing to remind everybody of now and then," White Owl said. "People get used to living with their own kind. They get set in their ways. Outsiders bring new ways, new ideas. The tube of lipstick that Fluff gave Clam has caused more trouble than a time bomb. Everyone is upset about Leaping Salmon sleeping with Wally because she was supposed to succeed her mother as Chief, and because they don't want their own children initiated into perverse sexual practices. Harpy mothers don't like Software because they are afraid their daughters will want to dye their hair pink and green."

"Some of them have," Moon Rabbit giggled.

"Yes, I know, and I wonder who helped them," White Owl said severely. "Food coloring is expensive, you know."

"But it doesn't last as long as India ink, which is what they were going to — oh, never mind. Seems to me that Clam acted far too much like her namesake until she found some way to make herself look a little different and get some attention. And why should a bunch of dykes object to their children witnessing a loving sexual relationship between two women, even if it's based on a fantasy that a lot of them don't share? I hate this term, passing women. Where did it come from?"

"A passing woman is a woman who can pass for a man," White Owl explained. "It's also used in the sense of not being committed to being female, of 'passing through' that identity. Harpies think that very masculine women like Wally or Doc, or women who have taken male hormones like Tony and Leigh, must hate being women. They think they are trying to be men. And since every Harpy knows it was men who drove us out, men who are so cruel and selfish that sane women have to leave and come to this farm, well, it's like fraternizing with the enemy."

"But it's not very consistent, is it?" Moon Rabbit said. "I challenge you to tell me who's more butch, Doc or Eagle Wing.

Women who live here get to do all the things that men say we aren't supposed to do. That's the whole point of Harpy Farm. Where I come from, any woman who picks up a power tool can be accused of 'acting like a man.' What about this phrase, ex-hets?"

"Former heterosexuals," White Owl defined. "While passing women are liable to have been dykes outside, ex-hets were not. Therefore, their ability to love other women is questionable."

"Well, that's bullshit," Moon Rabbit snorted. "Bridget Li is one of the ex-hets, and she's been a dyke all her life. I'm an ex-het, and I find it very easy and comfortable now to sleep with other women."

"Ah," White Owl said. She cleared her throat. "This is a delicate matter. You can tell me it's private, and I'll mind my own business. But do you love the Chief?"

"No," Moon Rabbit said without thinking. "And I find her assumption that I should sleep with her just because I am the High Priestess to be very annoying."

"Well, you see, usually Harpies don't have sex unless we are in love. Everyone knows you do not love Eagle Wing. Sleeping with her when you do not love her is dishonest, isn't it?"

"I'm not sure this *is* any of your business. First of all, I don't agree with you that all the sex on Harpy Farm is romantic. One reason these girls go so crazy in winter is because they can't sneak off into the bushes for a quickie. If you ask me, Harpies are a lot more promiscuous than they're willing to admit. If they're not going to be celibate until true love comes along, why should I?"

"Is the ideal of love a terrible thing that we should destroy?" White Owl asked.

"No, but I can't tolerate hypocrisy, especially not when two people who *are* in love are being made to feel they are outcasts."

"An excellent point," White Owl nodded. "And perhaps one that should go beyond this tipi."

"Are you hungry?"

"Oh, yes. I was hungry hours ago." White Owl put her hands up to let the younger woman help her to her feet. "You're a quick student, my dear, please don't despair. And don't be too impatient with us. As unpleasant as it is to hear gossip or watch someone be ostracized, we don't punish women for being different the way women are punished outside. We have no prisons, no insane asylums, and very little space to get away from fellow Harpies that we dislike. Yet there's very little theft, almost no murder. We are essentially gentle people."

"Gentle, but bossy," Moon Rabbit laughed.

White Owl mooed, the Harpy response to that accusation. She might be as bossy as an old cow past her milk, she thought to herself, but she wasn't dumb. If this much fuss was going to be made about a rooster, she would let somebody else talk to Moon Rabbit about the fate of newborn boys.

✧

After dinner, Moon Rabbit waited for the plates to be cleared away. But before anyone could leave the dining room or take the tables apart, she stood up and said firmly, "The Goddess has said this to me."

She was pleased to see that there was no hesitation at all about the nearest Harpy opening the big book that was used to record such pronouncements. By now, Harpy Farm had dozens of these books in its library, and she had found them amusing and enlightening reading. Some of her favorite declarations included a recipe for eggnog, a poem about taking a shit outside in the middle of winter, a list of unacceptable children's names, and an elegy for a woman who was celebrated for her ability to chop onions without crying and lift hot pans off the stove with no mittens.

"You have not finished the work I gave you to do. I am not pleased. I warn you not to forget the words of My last revelation to My servant Raven. If the new wing of the big house does not have four walls by the end of spring, all of your buildings will have only two walls standing by the end of summer. From the born-Harpies, I ask for a renewed commitment to this project. And from the immigrant Harpies, I ask for patience. I appoint four women to study our obstacles and remove them: Bridget Li, Wally, Eagle Wing, and Software."

She saw everyone exchanging dubious glances. "What say you to the appointment?" she asked. In turn, everyone said, "Aye," although Wally's agreement was shrieked out under the influence of Leaping Salmon's hard stomp on her toes, and the Chief looked like she would rather agree to drive one of the honey wagons. Still, Moon Rabbit knew, she had to be part of the committee. Innovation was no good if people couldn't accept it. Eagle Wing would force the newbies to come up with a plan that other Harpies could accept.

"The Goddess has also said this to me," she continued. "Most of you prefer to couple under cover of darkness, or concealed in green foliage. You dally in the river, on the beaches, or you take refuge beneath a blanket. All of you recognize this need for privacy, and if no real privacy is possible, it is the custom to turn your head and cover your eyes and ears, and ignore what can't be hidden. This is a gift we all give each other, except for those sacred occasions when bacchanalia is declared, and we celebrate our mutual fertility and the joy of the flesh. Now I declare that pleasure is a good thing, an experience which I want all of My daughters to have, and no one is to be punished for the way she obtains pleasure, unless her partner is unwilling. Of late, there has been considerable unkindness toward some of you who lost the protection of secrecy through no fault of their own. So I ask all of you to consider if secrecy has served you well. Perhaps you need to speak more openly with each other about matters of the flesh, and reach a truer understanding of what pleases each of you. When you feel yourselves becoming serious and critical, beware. I love games and I love athletes more than I love those who keep score or referee the players."

After this was faithfully copied, Moon Rabbit left the room and went into the kitchen to get herself some more tea. "I'm glad you said that," Chlorella said. Her large body and lantern-jawed, bearded face might have gotten her categorized as a passing woman if she had not shown such an affinity for kitchen work. It was hard to hold someone at arm's length who made ice cream in the summer and dried-fruit cobblers in the winter. "Maybe now I'll quit getting teased about where the wooden spoons have been."

Later that evening, Moon Rabbit went up to Eagle Wing's room for a long and rather painful conversation with her. The first thing she told Eagle Wing was that she was making a mistake by pushing Leaping Salmon to join Eagle Clan. "For now," Moon Rabbit told her firmly, "she belongs with Wally. They are good for each other. Leaping Salmon is not ready to be a leader. If you force her to try, she will make a bad one. But if you let her go now, maybe in time she will come back to the course that you desire for her. If the loss of status bothers you, then it's time to make Wally and her friends choose a name and form a clan, and give them a formal structure. You forget that you are the one who gets to say what is normal around here and what is not. Stop feeling sorry for yourself and use the power that means so much to you."

The second thing Moon Rabbit told the Chief was that she would no longer be spending her nights in Eagle Wing's bed. "When I first started sleeping with you, I needed the comfort and the human contact. I am grateful to you for all the healing attention you gave me. But I am not injured or sick any more. I have to toughen up. And I need more free time to get to know other women here, so I can understand our culture. I'm not angry with you, but I don't love you, and I think if I continue to spend this much time with you, we'll start to hate one another."

To her surprise, the Chief did not argue with her, just listened calmly. She cried a little bit at the end, but then she gave

Moon Rabbit some blankets and a pad to sleep on. "If you ever want to come back, you're welcome," the Chief said, embracing her.

"Provided you're alone."

The Chief laughed. "You make a lot of assumptions for a sexual radical. If I'm not alone, you might have to work a little harder for my attention, that's all."

On her way out the door, Moon Rabbit realized that the Chief's response to her had been perfect. Her interest was piqued now, and she probably would be back.

The difference between this "divorce" and her last angry confrontation with Anderson made her heart swell with even more love for the women of this farm. She hugged the bundle of quilts, turned on her flashlight, and went out into the night to find White Owl's tipi.

✧

Doc had trouble finding the address that Slim had given her. It was near the port, an area she didn't know well, and it just wouldn't have been cool to ask him for directions. But she had finally found the street and was checking the numbers. Were they going up or down? Shit, maybe she was going the wrong way.

A car engine started up, but it wasn't until Doc passed the alley where the car was parked that she realized someone was gunning the engine. The car hit her broadside, and the Medusa went down with sickening ease. It slid across the street screaming. The drivers of oncoming cars slammed on their brakes, and for a miracle none of them hit her.

Doc had managed to get away from the bike, but she felt something crack in her leg when she hit the pavement. She could not stop herself from skidding along the asphalt. It was all she could do to hold her head up. She wondered what she was going to run into. Then she slid under a parked panel truck, and stopped. For a long time, she just lay there under it. It was leaking oil, but she hurt too much to care.

She heard car doors opening and people running away from her. Then they ran toward her, cursing. The car doors shut, and the vehicle cruised by. She thought to herself, over and over again, I am invisible, I am invisible.

Her leg was probably broken, and the Medusa that she loved so much was trashed. Doc could not figure out how to get up, much less get home or get medical treatment, and she frankly wasn't sure she wanted to do any of these things. She stayed under the truck for about an hour and cried.

Finally she was sure nobody was coming back to shoot her, so she crawled out from under the truck, dragging her injured leg. The back of her jacket had a big hole burned in it. Her jeans were shredded, and the heels of her boots were gone. She leaned on the truck and tried not to pass out. Where was she? Were there buses — taxis — anything?

Then she saw a familiar figure strutting down the street, wearing silver tights and a silver halter top. The girl had her jacket down over her arms like a mink stole, her blonde hair was fluffed out and wild, her mouth was cherry-red, and she was just too hot. You wanted to beg her for the privilege of giving her everything you owned. Even from here, Doc could hear her whistling, "I'm Popeye the Sailor Man."

"Fluff!" Doc called, but her voice did not carry. The girl stopped when she was a block away, wary of the dark figure that crouched by the truck. Doc cleared her throat. "Fluff!" she croaked. "It's me, Doc, I need help, honey."

How could anybody run on those stilts? Fluff was there in seconds, trying to wrap her jacket around Doc, touching her face, asking so many questions that none of them made sense.

"Did you see my bike?" Doc asked.

"You need a doctor!"

"Yeah, but I'll still need one after I find the Medusa. I think she slid down this alley. Help me."

Doc's weight on her shoulder was crushing. Fluff staggered up the street, helping as best she could. When Doc saw the silver and magenta frame crumpled on its side, she roared like a wounded lion. She let go of Fluff and tried to run to the bike, but without support on that side her leg failed, and she wound up on the ground. Fluff tried to help her up, but Doc ignored her, crawling over to the damaged machine.

"Turn it off," Doc hissed at her. Fluff found the ignition and turned the key. Doc was in no shape to keep track of it, so Fluff pocketed it. "Oh, you poor baby," Doc said, "you're so fucked up. Look at you. Just look at you."

Fluff left her and went back to the street. She got a cab by stepping in front of one. "Wait here," she told the driver, handing him a fifty-dollar bill. "My friend's bike just went down, and we gotta get to a hospital."

"Shit!" he said, and got out of the cab to help her.

Between the two of them, they got Doc up and into the car. Without asking, the driver took them to the city hospital's emergency ward. He tried to cheer them up with stories about his younger days of racing dirt bikes, but all it did was make Doc cry, so Fluff told him if he didn't shut up he wasn't getting any tip.

"Try and help somebody and see what you get," he grumbled.

They waited in the emergency room a long time. A mere broken leg didn't seem important compared to gunshot wounds, stabbings, and drug overdoses. Doc was in shock, and claustrophobic besides. She hated waiting even if it was under the most pleasant circumstances. She kept saying, "There's nothing really wrong with me. I just got shook up. Let's go home. I want to go home *now*."

Finally Fluff got up and went to see the nurse behind the front desk. "When is my friend going to see a doctor?" she demanded.

"That's up to triage. We have to take the most serious cases first."

"Well, fuck that," Fluff said. "I saw you haul six people through here who can get all the treatment you like, they're still going to die. All I need is some x-rays and a cast."

"I'm sorry, miss. Your, uh, *friend*, will just have to wait."

Oh, ho, Fluff said to herself. So that's it. "You homophobic cunt," she said, speaking pleasantly and clearly. Then she went around and behind the desk, into the hallway that led to the examination rooms.

"Hey, you can't go out there!" the nurse shouted.

But Fluff grabbed one of the doctors by his white sleeve. He was a young man with short brown hair that stayed in place because it wasn't very clean. The lenses of his glasses were dirty, and he had dark circles under his eyes. She waved a hundred-dollar bill at him and stuffed it into the pocket of his lab coat. "Can you look at my friend for me?" she asked. "There's another hundred for you if you can get us out of here in a half hour."

He gave her a startled look. "Where's your friend?"

"The waiting room, otherwise known as Dante's Inferno," she grimaced.

He laughed. "Bring him in to room 220."

She didn't bother to correct the pronoun. A wheelchair was sitting in the hallway outside a room where a doctor was examining someone on a table. She wheeled it away. The nurse at the front desk gave her a dirty look when she pushed it straight into the waiting room. "Get on this thing," she told Doc. "I found you a doctor."

"Will he be able to pay any attention to me so soon after he's shot his wad?" Doc asked.

Fluff was too tired to get mad. It just added a few more drops of acid to what was already in her stomach. She got Doc into Room 220, and stoically stood by while the doctor wrote up a request for x-rays. He went with them to make sure the pictures were taken promptly, and within twenty minutes, he was explaining them to Doc. Fluff heard the phrase "hairline fracture," and then they were cutting Doc's pantleg off at the knee and wrapping her calf in plaster bandages. She gave the doctor another hundred for a pair of crutches, and told him, "If you'd clean your glasses once in a while, I bet all kindsa girls would be givin' you money." He looked at her as if she had just stepped out of a UFO.

They took a cab home. Fluff peeled and cut Doc out of her rags, put aloe on her burns, bandaged her feet and hands, gave her some codeine, and put her to bed. She was about to take some of the same medication and go to sleep herself, but she was worried about Doc's bike. She didn't know if anything could be done with it or not. She found a twenty-four-hour towing service in the yellow pages, called them up, told them where the bike was, and asked them to deliver it to an authorized dealer whose address she also found in the yellow pages. Then they wanted a credit card number, so she used one she had stolen. Amber was not the only ho in town who had magic hands.

✧

When Doc woke up the next day, Fluff said, "Can I ask you about your bike?"

"No," Doc said. "I don't want to talk about it!"

She sounded so fierce that Fluff was frightened. She spent the day at home, trying to entertain Doc, but she was still in enough pain to make her irritable. So Fluff gave her more codeine, went out to the pawnshop on the corner, and bought a portable TV.

Over the next week, it became clear that she would have to go back to work. Doc's leg was going to be out of commission for a while. She could not have ridden her bike even if it had been intact. But they couldn't be without transportation. So Fluff bought a car.

When she came home with it, she expected Doc to be pleased about getting out of the house. "Goddess," Doc said, "you want me to ride around in a cage? What will you think of next, darlin'? All right, I suppose I have to go see this ... *car*."

"You are so strange," Fluff said. "I honestly think you'd act more cheerful if I asked you to come see a turd."

When they got downstairs, Fluff ran over to the little green sportscar and patted its fabric top. "Isn't she sweet?" she asked. "Why the hell did you get an MG?" Doc grumbled. "I'll never fit in that thing."

"It has more leg room than you would think." Fluff helped her into the car. Then Doc complained that it was going to be awfully cold.

"Well, as it happens, the heater does work," Fluff said indignantly. It was getting hard to be patient. "I checked it out before I bought it. But even without a heater, we'll be warmer in here than we were on the bike."

Then Doc was on her case for driving too fast, for not watching traffic closely enough, for stopping at yellow lights instead of punching them. Fluff bit her tongue and concentrated on getting them to Craps. Seeing her friends would make Doc feel better. Anything had to be better than being cooped up in the apartment with a little, bitty TV and a broken-hearted biker who had lost her wheels.

She parked Doc at her favorite table with two pals and went to get them all a drink. In the process she greeted her own friends and told them what had happened. When she got back to Doc, she was surprised to find her, if anything, more depressed than ever. And her friends had split, leaving her alone.

"I hate all these people staring at me like I'm a cripple," Doc growled. "But I suppose you want me to stay here while you work."

"Rent's due next week."

"Yeah, right. Rent's due. Fine."

Fluff went off, but she didn't do very well that night. The bounce seemed to have gone out of her step, and the night was unusually cold. Hattie walked with her for a while, and finally said, "Girl, what's wrong with you? You acting like you're at a funeral. Nobody's going to give you money to look at them like that, you look like somebody been beating you."

"She doesn't beat me," Fluff said. "Actually, I'm the one who beats her."

Hattie laughed. "You mean you spank her in fun, I know all about that. That's a different matter, sugar. You don't seem happy to be yourself. And that's not right. You are a *fine* woman. You just need somebody to make you aware of how fine you are."

"And who is that somebody? You want the job?"

"Slim don't do me the way Doc does you," Hattie said evasively. "When I bring home the bacon I get a piece of it and a thank you, not a kick in the rear."

"What's that supposed to be, a commercial?" Fluff jeered. "Slim just does not appeal to me."

"You makin' a lot of money, or you was," Hattie said. "A girl like you could go far with the right management."

"I don't want a manager."

"Well, then, you just go off by yourself and manage your own affairs, since I can't tell you nothin' you don't know already," Hattie said briskly, and walked away.

It took six hours for Fluff to pull in two tricks, and she finally gave up and went back to the bar. Doc greeted her impatiently. "I thought you were never coming back. Let's go home."

After that night, Fluff could rarely persuade Doc to leave the apartment. "I don't want you chauffeuring me around like an old woman," Doc would bark.

It was probably just as well that she made herself scarce around Craps. When Slim found out what had gone down between her and the Jaguars, he was not amused. He summoned Fluff to his table, dismissed Hattie, and told her all about it.

Doc had kept back a tenth of the money the Jaguars had fronted her. Normally, they would have put a hit out on her immediately. But most of the Jaguars' soldiers were embroiled in a power struggle between Colonel Akhmed Allah Akbar and his Amazon clone, Lieutenant Colonel Fatima, so Doc became a low priority. They did offer a reward for news of her whereabouts.

"There ain't no love lost between the Revolutionary People's Army and me and mine," Slim told Fluff. "We had a lot of problems with them hassling our girls, trying to hustle us for protection money and all that shit. I think anybody here would just laugh if they heard Doc gave those tin soldiers some grief. But poor people don't walk away from cash."

The desk clerk that Doc had beaten up at the hotel heard about the reward and snitched her off. In a weird piece of misjudgment, Colonel Akbar gave the snitch the reward money and told him he could have another thousand if he got rid of her. This man was in fact not very eager to confront Doc in person again, so he had been following her in his car, looking for a chance to run her down.

It turned out that Slim's wholesaler was the clerk's brother. Slim had gotten him the hotel job as a favor to his connection. The big brother had heard all about the dyke who had assaulted his kid brother, and when Slim called to set up a buy for Doc, he had made him come over. Under the guise of asking questions about Doc's trustworthiness, he had gotten enough of a description to verify her identity.

It was the hotel clerk who had been waiting for her. After colliding with her bike, he went back to the Jaguars, picked up his extra thousand, and started talking big all over town about being a "hitman." But the truth was that after finding the crashed bike, he hadn't dared look very thoroughly for Doc's body.

By then, Colonel Akbar had gone down in defeat before his sister's onslaught. Fatima no longer cared much about locating Doc — she was, after all, the one who had let Doc walk out in the first place. But she found the boastful asshole who had accepted Jaguar money for a job he hadn't done, and got a thousand dollars' worth of entertainment out of him.

"Real nice of Doc to give us all a warning," Slim bitched to Fluff. "The Revolutionary People's Army is a bunch of crazy motherfuckers. We let her drink at our bar? We're hiding her from the people's justice! So they wouldn't have thought nothing about coming down here and machine-gunning the whole place. Every time I think I can trust whitey it turns out I'm just another ignorant nigger getting used to shovel shit."

Fluff didn't bother to make excuses for Doc. Slim didn't expect her to. He was probably mad because he felt guilty about unwittingly setting Doc up to get killed. Anyway, she was pretty pissed off herself. She had asked Doc flat out if she was in trouble, and Doc had lied to her. If the Jaguars would shoot up a whole bar to get revenge, wouldn't they have loved getting their hands on her, Fluff? What if she had been on the back of that bike when they tried to kill Doc?

Things had deteriorated between them to the point where Fluff didn't even bother to tell Doc that she was upset. She spent as little time at home as possible, and when she was there, she pretended she was a babysitter. Doc seemed to have lost the power to get up on her crutches and do for herself, unless it was to take herself to the bathroom. So Fluff fetched and carried for her, adjusted the TV, got her blankets or pillows or took them away, ferried in food and drink — a lot of drink — and escaped as soon as she could to go make more money.

The only thing she would not provide was sex. Doc hinted a couple of times that she was horny, and Fluff made jokes about not taking advantage of an invalid. She knew these remarks would hurt Doc's feelings enough to turn her off. It wasn't nice. But she didn't understand herself why she didn't want to make love. So how could she explain it? Maybe when Doc's leg healed it would all go away.

Fluff was taking some idiotic chances at work. Sometimes when she added up the odds she was running, she got really scared. She was even turning van tricks, and any old whore will tell you that she got to live long enough to be old because she never stepped into a van. But Fluff needed money. The vague daydreams she had spun over the pages of chemistry equations and statistical tests had coalesced, but without money, knowing what she wanted would do her no good at all.

She didn't know anybody else who had done what she planned to do. But when she looked around, all she saw were people who were trapped. Their lives were not going to change. If she was going to escape, she had to do something unthinkable. She had to march into the very stronghold of the enemy. She was going to school.

22.

Anderson and Michaels rode into Alamo the day before Winter Solstice, although, as Doc had predicted, they didn't know what day of the week it was, much less how the earth was aligned with the sun. They stopped briefly in the hills above town, let their bikes idle at the side of the road while they assessed this place they had protected and helped to grow, this place that was no longer home.

"It's so fuckin' cold I almost wish I was in a car," Anderson yelled over to Michaels. The wind was wicked.

"Bite your tongue, man," Michaels scolded. His knuckles were blue. It had been stupid to go on this run with nothing but fingerless gloves. He couldn't feel his face move as he talked.

"*You* bite it," Anderson dared him. Under his leathers he wore plentiful evidence of the sharpness of Michaels's teeth.

"Oh, I will," his buddy promised, shaking dark hair out of his eyes. "That and more besides. We're going straight through town and up the hill to Prez's mansion, am I right?"

"You are. Let's finish our business here and get the fuck out." A freak gust of wind made the volume of his speech suddenly alter from a shout to a whisper, but the short, dark man could still hear the grim note in his buddy's voice. It was enough to make his scrotum draw up against his belly, rings and all. He had seen Anderson angry. They'd even lost their tempers together a time or two. That was fun. Anderson wasn't angry now, he'd gone cold, cold as a starving man cutting off his own finger to use for fish-bait. This wasn't about having fun.

"I'm with you," he said fervently, committed to fight and, if necessary, die at his friend's back.

Anderson nodded. "Together," he affirmed.

They cruised down the hill, gathering speed. It was so early that the streets were empty. It seemed as if everyone in Alamo was dead. But the one person who should be dead was still alive, and that mistake would have to be corrected.

It took them less than half an hour to make the trip to Prez's front door. It opened and Raven stepped out, as if she had known they were coming. "Gentlemen," she said. "You are just in time for the sacred drama. Will you help me set the stage?"

Raven clearly felt herself to be in charge. She led them through the house, down to the basement. Michaels wondered if Anderson would dispute her authority. As they trudged down the stone steps, the stairwell lit by gas jets, Michaels felt weirdly ashamed that women had seen, explored, and appropriated this place. He had been here a couple of times, once to interrogate a truck driver who was suspected of kidnapping, molesting, and killing a little girl, Smitty's daughter, once to call in the colors of an Angel, Foxy Bob, who had tried to make off with the proceeds of an entire chanterelle shipment, a couple times to punish offenses that he thought were mostly bullshit, just so Prez could get his kicks. It was the kind of thing you didn't want your old lady to know about, to say the least.

Raven led them down a hallway to the soundproof door of a room. Outside the door, Mendoza's Doberman pinschers craned their necks for Raven to caress. They gave Michaels the creeps. The damn dogs were smarter than a lot of men he'd met. They didn't even act like dogs, they didn't whine or jump on her. They were fanatics, a pair of good German soldiers, and Raven was their commanding officer.

For a window, the room had a one-way mirror. The two men looked inside. Michaels felt every single hair on his body lift straight up in protest. That slobbering, bleeding, filthy prisoner could not be … had to be … Prez.

Now came the confrontation he had been waiting for. Anderson gave Raven a glacial stare. "He's mine. Let me take him."

"No."

For the first time, Michaels noticed that she was wearing Prez's colors. Another horripilation ran from his scalp to his toes. Anderson bowed his blond head. He twisted his big, red hands together, crushing his own knuckles. "Why?" he said. The question was a harsh whisper.

"You don't have the balls for it," Raven replied. Looking through the one-way mirror at Prez, she laughed. Michaels wanted to be a million miles away from that awful, innocent, bubbling sound of mirth. He plucked at Anderson's belt. It took all the courage he had to pause before fleeing to try to take his friend with him. But his hands seemed to have lost their power. Anderson probably did not even feel his touch.

"This is not a simple execution," Raven explained. "It is revenge. His crimes are crimes against women, and the hierogamos is our ritual. No matter how bitter your heart is against him, your flesh is brother to his flesh, and sympathy will stay your hand when he must continue to suffer, if justice is to be done."

They were moving away from the doorway, back to the stairs. "Stay," Raven told the dogs, and Michaels could have sworn they saluted her with their black-and-tan muzzles. Those dogs used to be good for a few laughs. Now look at them. Shit.

Anderson would not give up. "I *have* to be part of this," he told her. "I loved Tina."

She gave him a look of surprise. "But you are. I have a lot of work for you to do. Both of you."

After making themselves some breakfast, the two men borrowed the keys to the green van from Sunny and drove it into the hills behind Prez's mansion. Raven had given them directions. They followed the black ribbons she had tied to shrubs along the road. When the ribbons turned to red, they parked, unloaded the necessary gear, and hiked into the woods. There was a nice, wide trail. A quarter of a mile in, they found a natural clearing. The women had used mortar and field stone to build a small fire-pit in the middle of it. A neat woodpile had been stacked up a safe distance from it. There was a white ribbon on the tree that Raven had selected, a big oak that stood at the far side of the clearing.

Anderson bent, cupped his hands, and gave Michaels a leg up into the tree. They discussed where cuts should be made, and then the bigger man handed up the chainsaw. While Michaels lopped off branches, Anderson put on a pair of work gloves and hauled them away. It took hours, but when they were done, the living tree had been transformed into a single upright with a bar across it, a T-shaped cross. Anderson took the chainsaw back and tossed Michaels a big, iron hook that the women had taken from the Angels' dungeons. Michaels used a cordless drill to start a hole for it, then screwed it in.

"I feel sorry for him," Michaels said, after he had swung to the ground. He was looking at the grotesque thing they had made. It reminded him of a gallows. Anderson gave him a questioning look. Michaels realized his use of the male pronoun was a little odd. "I mean the tree. It'll never be green again. No more acorns in the spring, no new leaves. Won't change colors next autumn."

"It'll carry a different kind of harvest," Anderson promised him. "I think the tree is glad to help us. Aw, listen to me. I sound like Raven." They wrestled the heavy power tools down the trail to the van, and drove much too fast on the bad road that led back to their bikes, and freedom.

When they arrived, Carmen and Josie had joined Raven, Dee Ann, Lydia, Rose, and Sunny. The ground floor of the house was full of the smell of cooking. Women were coming in and out of the kitchen with plates of chili and tortillas. Carmen only needed one look at the two men to know they were lovers. They had come in walking in step, hip-to-hip, and now they stood close together, wondering if it was okay for them to get some dinner. She put her food down, went over to Michaels, and kissed him.

"What's that for?" he said. Anderson was staring at both of them.

"It's the nicest way I can think of to say goodbye," she responded. When he tried to talk, she put her finger to his lips. "I know what's going on," she said. "Don't make me pretend that I'm a fool. We really loved each other. I'm sorry that wasn't enough." She touched Anderson's hand. "Be good to him," she said, evading Michaels's attempt to touch her, and left them to rejoin the other women.

"Your part here is through," Raven said. "But you are welcome to stay here and wait for us. Go and eat. You've earned a hot meal."

They went into the kitchen to sample the chili and wound up eating at the table there. They weren't unwelcome, exactly, just unimportant. Aside from Carmen and Raven's brief speeches, nobody spoke to them. Michaels rubbed his booted foot against Anderson's calf. "Eat up," he said. "I got plans for you."

Anderson snorted. "Talk, talk, *biiig* talk," he drawled.

"I'll remember that," Michaels warned.

"I hope so," Anderson replied.

One by one, the women came into the kitchen and put their dirty dishes in the sink. The two men tried to ignore them, but it was hard to turn your back on any of them. They were spooky. Michaels realized he wasn't used to women being so serious, focused, intent on getting a job done. "Fuckin' war party," he finally said to Anderson, who grunted his agreement. They gave up trying to talk, reached for each other's hands, Michaels's left to Anderson's right, and just held on to each other while they ate.

When they came out of the kitchen, most of the women were gone. Only Carmen and Raven remained. "Be good boys. Stay inside tonight," the High Priestess warned them again. She even shook her finger at them. Anderson snarled involuntarily at that.

Michaels felt for his keys. "You girls got wheels? Carmen, want to take my bike?" It was a major concession for him, but he wanted her to know he appreciated her kindness, didn't have any ill will.

"Thanks," she said, grinning, "I got my own."

Anderson clamped his hands over Michaels's shoulders, squeezed the suddenly tight muscles. This confident woman in leather didn't look any different from the Carmen that he remembered. But Michaels was no longer her point of reference. She did not position her body in space to stay close to him, did not flick her eyes over at him to check on him, did not monitor him at all.

"Let me show you where your room is," Raven said. She was wearing a European racing jacket with quilted shoulders and a narrow collar. Prez's colors hung loosely around her torso. The two men followed her toward the back of the house. She stopped just outside the bedroom door. "Your things are in the corner, over there," she pointed. Both of them strolled over to check it out. Too late, they heard the door shut and the lock click.

Anderson ran for the door and slammed his body into it. The fucking thing was three inches thick, ship planks reinforced with iron bars. God *damn* Prez and his Spanish decor. "Can we jimmy the bolt?" Michaels asked. But the dead bolt was seated deeply into the jamb.

"Well, I'll be fucked if I stay here all night," Anderson bellowed.

"Yeah, probably," Michaels said. "Nevertheless, I think we should find a way to leave. Good boy, my ass. I ain't *her* good boy."

"No windows," Anderson said, turning to look at the far wall. "No connecting door to another suite."

The two of them combed the room, looking for something they could use as a lever to force the door. Sometime during this hunt, they heard dragging footsteps go past their door.

"Who the fuck could that be? Are they back already?" Michaels stupidly asked.

"Shut up," Anderson cried. "That isn't them. It's Prez. They've let him out. He's on his way to meet them."

"Jesus, it's bizarre. We came here to off the bastard, but I feel like I should warn him," Michaels said. "What the hell is wrong with me?"

"She was right," Anderson said. "We don't have the balls for this. But I am getting out of this place!"

He dragged the mattress off the bed and began to pound on the frame, trying to wrench a piece of steel loose from it. His hands were bruised, then cut. Michaels cleared his throat. "How about a key?" he asked. "Think we could do any good with that?"

"What the hell?" Anderson turned. Michaels did, indeed, have a key in his hand. It was tied with red, black, and white ribbons. "Where did that come from?"

"It was hanging inside the toilet," Michaels said. "I found it when I raised the lid to take a leak."

The damn Harley steered like a pig. But it was still his mount, his beast, it would go where he willed. There was sweat in Prez's eyes, down his sides, between his thighs. He kept seeing colored snow, hearing a high buzzing noise, and knew these were signs that he could pass out at any moment. No. No.

His clothes fit badly. He slid around inside them like a bitch on the back of a seat with no sissy bar. His jacket trapped the smell of his body. When he dipped his head, it reminded him that he used to like getting a whiff of his own armpits and musk. Now he smelled sour and rotten. When he had finally managed to shake and stuff his body into the pile of clothing that Raven had left for him, and reached for his leather jacket, he had been enraged to see the darker sections on the back, where his colors had protected it from being bleached by the sun. He was going to get them back now, and that wasn't all. Payback. Party time.

Something cold rasped against his neck. It was Raven's noose, the plaited wire girdle that had hypnotized him and led him into her trap. She had come into his cell alone. Against its white, tiled walls, her black-and-purple clothing made her look like the ominous bird of prey whose name she had taken. She took the noose from around her waist, slowly, slowly. It would have taken some women less time to get all of their clothes off. Then she approached him, slithered over holding it out, like an offering, and he had bowed to her and let her drop it over his head without her asking. Then she leaned close enough to him to let him inhale her scent. She smelled excited, like a carnivorous flower.

After she dropped the noose around his neck and drew it just tight enough to hold it in place, she put a knife between his teeth and told him, "You have passed every test. If you can cut yourself free and join me at the top of the hill, I am yours, and you can do anything to me you want."

"Why?" Prez had croaked. The women had not hurt him for a week. He had been given food, and plenty of water. He was still weak, but he was like kudzu or bamboo. You could cut him back and cut him back, but if any part of him was left, the attempted killing would simply make him grow back faster.

"I am not that different from you," she said, smiling. "Why would I enjoy watching you suffer if I didn't want to suffer myself? I only punish men who aren't strong enough to punish me. I have had enough of playing at being your jailer. I have had enough of drugging you and torturing you. Now it's your turn, but only if you're strong enough and wily enough to capture me."

She gave one final tug at his neck, then she was gone.

Lost in the strength of that memory, Prez had let the bike waver to the right of his lane. He turned his nose away from the soft shoulder of the road. He almost ripped the vile noose off and threw it into the wind. But the thought of what he could do with it later made him change his mind. The look on her face ... It was stupid of her to give him a knife. He still had that, too. He had managed to saw apart the heavy leather straps, don jeans, a sweatshirt, and boots, stagger up the stairs, mount his bike, and pursue her. Wouldn't she be surprised? Well, she had asked for it.

And she must really want it, too, because there were signposts along the way. His headlights picked out the fluttering tails of colored ribbon. Did she think he wouldn't be able to hear the sound of another bike, up ahead? He wondered how she had been able to con some dude into giving her a ride. Well, if Prez had to, he would take him out, too. Though he couldn't imagine any Angel being crazy enough to defend her.

He almost missed the turnoff. If he hadn't known better, he would have thought they waited for him, let him get a glimpse, as if they were leading him on. Well, that was just like a bitch. Flirting, teasing, then pretending to be surprised by what they got. "Ask me for trouble, and your prayers will be answered," he said aloud.

The road was a lot rougher. He was gasping for breath. His hands were slippery on the grips, his feet cramping on the pegs. Every bump in the path seemed to bounce his kidneys up to his ears. He hurt inside, outside, everything hurt, and it was her fault, her fault, the only thing that could fix it was to make her hurt more.

He passed a green van, parked between some bushes, camouflaged with branches that had been pulled down from nearby trees. Wasn't that Mendoza's van? Was he here? Had he given Raven a ride? No — Mendoza was dead, yes, he was, and *that* memory made Prez laugh, the only real laugh he'd had since Raven got her claws into his back.

There was a fire up ahead. Singing. He cut his engine, parked, crept on foot through the trees. They, the Loyal Subjects, they were all holding hands and dancing in a circle, naked, going around and around to the left, singing around the fire. Raven was naked, too, and her skin called to his skin, made his injured and outraged tool hurt itself again by erecting inside the abrasive denim of his jeans.

"Come here," she called to him. Her voice was unearthly. She was not a woman, she was a musical instrument, a wild thing. Could it really be that simple? One corner of his mind noted the presence of Carmen and Josie. *They* weren't part of Raven's court. But that was not as important as the fact of their nakedness, their vulnerability. When women took their clothes off it meant only one thing.

Raven held her arms out to him. She was wearing a wreath, evergreen, mistletoe, ivy, and holly. In her hand she held another crown, obviously meant for him. And so he went to her, stumbling into the firelight, feeling amazed and nearly blinded by the bare tits, bellies, snatches, thighs of his tormentors.

"You came here of your own free will," Raven said, and placed the wreath upon Prez's head. She pushed it down, and something sharp broke his skin. But he was distracted by the hands she ran up and down his body. "You are mine," she said. "The first part of the ritual has been fulfilled. And now you must race with us. The stakes are your life, or mine."

The women began to keen. It was a ghastly sound. They advanced upon him, arms outstretched, teeth bared. Without thinking, he ran. He was in no condition to realize that they were giving him a head start. He simply fled.

Then they were after him. But before the women coursed Raven's dogs. They ran in silence, synchronized, rising and falling together, and if he could not shake them, they would bring him down. Prez felt for his knife, then felt again. It was gone.

He tripped. The dogs did not come on any faster, but the gap between them closed. He blundered into thorny brush, veered off, and then he could hear their panting. Behind the dogs came the rising note of vengeance and triumph he had heard by the fire. Then one Doberman had him by the calf, the other had his sleeve, and he was down on his back, screaming, "Don't let them kill me!"

But the dogs had not been ordered to kill, merely to fetch. Their teeth did not even graze his skin. They kept him there without passion. Then the one they loved appeared, touched them briefly, and praised them with a few short words. They did not wag their tails, but Prez knew that they were satisfied. They went to their places at her heel.

Raven stood before him. She threw his knife up into the air, caught it, flipped it, caught it again. "Do you remember this knife?" she asked. "Answer me, fool! Straw man! Answer me."

Why should he remember it? It was a Ka-Bar, a good blade, lots of dudes packed them.

She shook her head. "You're not going to die this ignorant, I promise you that," she said, and gestured to her coven. "Take him."

They laid hands upon him, and their strength made Prez realize how frail he was. He had been running on nothing but rage and spite and blind hope. He *had* been a fool. And so he did not fight them. They would make a mistake. Chicks are easily distracted, especially in the dark, in the woods. Little noises freaked them. He would save his energy until he got a chance to make a break.

They hauled him back to the fire, half-carrying him. Lydia, Dee Ann, Rose, and Sunny were matter-of-fact. They had been through intensive training for this moment. Josie and Carmen were every bit as grim, but not as practiced. To compensate for that, they were if anything rougher with him than the Loyal

Subjects of the Queen. When Raven sent them away to fetch Prez's bike, they went at a run and wheeled it into the clearing. When they brought him to his Harley, Prez began to drag his heels. The women were only too happy to force him onto his knees and make him crawl the rest of the way. Carmen was astride it, gunning the engine. Prez had never liked the sight of a woman on a bike, unless she had her arms around the driver or was turned the other way. What was the name of that bitch he had persuaded to sit on his dick, facing him, while he took both of them straight down the highway? She had sultry brown eyes and long red hair that kept getting in his face, but her cunt had been narrow and deep, his favorite shape, and her legs were strong. She did all the work of fucking while he kept the bike up to speed. What had happened to her? Had he run her over, given her an OD, or was she one of the hand-me-downs that he'd given to Anderson?

"The tailpipes are plenty hot," Carmen reported, killing the engine. Then Raven took Prez by the hair and forced his mouth onto the exhaust pipes. The scalding chrome tubes sealed off his screams. She wondered what Anderson and Michaels, hidden in the trees, would think of this violent parody of cocksucking. It was a common biker ritual, maybe something one of them had done to humiliate an enemy.

Their presence did not offend her even though she had forbidden it. Let them watch. Later, let them speak about what they had seen. A woman telling this story might be punished, might not be credible. Nobody would think a man could invent it. She was bringing an ancient myth to life here. If it did not become a legend, she would have failed.

The inside of Prez's mouth was horribly burned. He could not stand. The women simply picked him up and carried him to the tree. With Dee Ann's help, Raven vaulted to its crosspiece. As the women suspended him between earth and sky, she took the free end of the noose, which had been finished off in a small loop. This she slipped over the hook, and they let him go.

Because it was fashioned out of wire, the noose did not immediately slip tight enough to strangle him. There was not enough compression to close off his carotid arteries and produce unconsciousness, then death. But it sharply limited his air supply. Prez thrashed like a hooked fish. Maybe it was then that he realized Dame Fortune was not going to give him any second chances.

From the top of the cross, Raven looked down and relished her handiwork. Lydia fetched a wooden crate from the fire-pit. Dee Ann stood on it, holding Prez's arm against the horizontal branch. Raven bound his upper arm, forearm, and wrist with red, black, and white cords. They bound his other arm in the same way, then she leapt to the ground. Carmen and Josie caught her and cushioned her landing.

They bound his waist, his thighs. They placed one foot on top of the other and tied his ankles. Now Prez could get enough leverage to raise himself a half-inch and ease the pressure on his throat. He struggled to breathe. Now that it no longer mattered, he fought for his life.

Lydia put the first nail through the palm of his left hand. Rose wielded the hammer for the second nail, which neatly pierced his right hand. These were not the first nails that Prez had felt pierce his flesh. They were, after all, just slightly bigger than needles. Still, he ranted and wailed. He knew that his body would never be able to plug these holes up with new tissue.

It took both Sunny and Dee Ann to place the spike that was long enough to secure his feet. Carmen made herself listen to and absorb his cries of anguish and dread. She touched her own face and found that it was wet. The only way she could make herself stay and watch was to keep repeating Tina's name.

Then Raven walked over to her and handed her the knife. "An eye for an eye," she said calmly. Carmen took the blade, willing her hand not to shake.

She understood now that the ritual had made all of them culpable. No one woman could ever take the blame alone for

Prez's death. She stepped closer to the hanging, gasping man. Dee Ann ripped his shirt open. Carmen took one of his nipples between her fingers. It was thick with scar tissue, reluctant to stretch away from his chest. She yanked harder. He barely noticed this additional pain. But he noticed the knife. "Do you remember it now?" she asked, running the edge lightly along his taut flesh. A little blood seeped. Suddenly she wanted to see it run in sheets. It was easily done. She heard Josie gasp behind her. Raven's court sighed with approval, and Raven herself laughed with glee. Now he understood, and she cut more slowly, wanting to make him beg. But Prez did not grovel. He cursed his pain, his fate, but he did not whine for mercy.

Raven dropped the bits of flesh into a little leather pouch. Carmen did not see what she did with it because the priestess took Josie out of the circle, back to Prez's bike. In the meantime, the women in the circle flogged him with evergreen branches. When Josie and Raven returned, they were carrying a motorcycle battery.

Once again, Raven mounted the cross. She attached a length of plastic tubing to the battery, clamped it off, and turned it upside down on the branch. Then she descended, and opened his pants. He stopped howling and looked down at her. Was he actually smiling? Josie squirted some lubricant onto the end of the tube, and Raven worked it down into his urethra. She went slowly, but there was bleeding. Still, he made no sound. Even when his cock hung swollen in a bloated mockery of an erection, he simply stared at her. Yes, he was smiling now.

Raven bound his cock, secured those cords to the ones that encircled his waist. Now he could not dislodge the catheter.

"I take your life," she said, "in the name of everything living. You are a despoiler. You have squandered and ruined every good gift our Mother gave you. My hand is only one of many that pushes the wheel. You harvest no more, no less, than what you have sown."

Then she undid the clamp. Prez could see the battery acid flowing through the plastic tubing that impaled his sex. And now he said all the things that pride had kept behind his teeth. He proclaimed them at the top of his lungs. But it did about as much good as he had done in his lifetime.

✧

Carmen rode ahead of the van, on point. Raven had tied the medicine pouch that contained Prez's nipples to the left handlebar of her Harley. She found that she liked the fact that it was there. Carmen was tired, but satisfied. It was important that they put a few hundred miles between themselves and Alamo before they found a place to rest. She could do that. She could probably do anything. Tina's Ka-Bar was a comfortable, square weight on her right hip.

Everyone else was huddled in the van. Sunny drove. Rose sat beside her in front. There was enough room on the clean mattress in the back for everyone, even the dogs, to get comfortable. Lydia wrapped Dee Ann in a quilt and held her hand while she snuggled into her pillow. Josie was propped with her head in Raven's lap.

"I'm proud of all of you," Raven said. "We were so good, we didn't even have to use the anesthetic." No one replied, but her praise made them glow.

"I'm sleepy," Josie complained.

"Then sleep," Raven said, touching her hair. "We'll be on the road for a couple of days, no more."

"Will they be able to help me?"

"I don't know," Raven said. "I believe so."

"Anything is better than just waiting," Josie sighed. "It's awful having somebody you love just sit and watch you die."

"Yes," Raven said. "Anything is better than just waiting."

✧

Dawn came slowly. It touched the tops of the trees first. The longest night of the year was over, and the sun would reclaim her hegemony over the hours of the day.

One mutilated tree was reluctant to accept illumination. It bore a burden too heavy to be natural. The corpse seemed to be twisting in pain. But of course it was quiet, helpless, its purpose fulfilled. For the first time in his life, Prez waited.

23 ⋄

Doc knew that things were going badly. In the beginning, she had been Fluff's hero. No fair maiden on the planet was a big enough dope to ask Doc to rescue her now. She hated the cast on her leg, couldn't bear to think of the accident, refused to accept the fact that her bike was gone, couldn't stop blaming herself for being in this mess, and didn't see a way out of it.

Gratitude made Doc queasy. If you had to be grateful to somebody, you were dependent upon them. Her instinct for survival dictated that she try to bluff anybody who might think she was beholden to them. Doc had a million ways of making people feel that they had not done her any favor at all — or that they had in fact fucked up instead of doing something nice for her — or that they had done something that was nice but unnecessary, maybe even foolish.

But one day, Doc's outraged pride overcame the con artist in her, and she decided that she had been a couch potato for long enough. She got up, and vowed as she struggled to her feet to start exercising. This cast wouldn't be on forever, and it would be humiliating to be more of a cripple after it was removed than she was now.

She went into the kitchen and took stock of the shelves and the refrigerator. There wasn't much to work with. Fluff had not been keeping many groceries in the house lately. Well, who could blame her? Not only was she paying the bills, she was taking care of her belligerent and lazy girlfriend. It was like working two full-time jobs. Doc was filled with a sudden tenderness for Fluff, who had been so good to her. A pretty girl like that deserved better. She would have to find a way to persuade Fluff that things would not always be so awful.

Doc stumped back into the living room, put some money in her wallet, and humped herself on crutches to the front door. She was out of the building and on the street before she realized that she had no idea where the grocery store was. So she flagged down a cab and told the driver to take her to the Friendly Farmer's Food Factory. There had to be one of those in Portland.

Once there, she spent two hours shopping. The store was packed with people who seemed frantic to amass huge quantities of food. Crazed strangers kept elbowing her and running into her cart, then apologizing profusely when they saw her crutches. Outside, there were long lines for taxis. Doc had to wait nearly another hour to get a cab home. Then she realized she would have to talk the driver into helping her get her purchases up the stairs.

Luckily, this time she'd gotten a woman cabbie, a competent-looking forty-year-old with long, gray hair who used language worse than a longshoreman's. When Doc said shyly, "It'll take me all day to get this up the stairs on my crutches, and I'd really like to surprise my girlfriend with a nice dinner when she comes home," the woman laughed and told her to just worry about getting herself up the stairs. She brought up the groceries in only two trips, running up the stairs, carrying six plastic bags at a time.

Doc was glad she'd thought to buy a disposable, aluminum-foil roasting pan, because there wasn't a pot in the kitchen big enough to hold the roast she had bought. She hummed as she bumped and lurched around the kitchen, sticking garlic cloves and peppercorns into the huge hunk of beef. Her armpits were beginning to ache from pressing on the padded handles of the crutches.

So she took a beer into the living room and watched a little TV while the roast spent its first hour at 375 degrees Fahrenheit. She looked at her watch. In about two more hours, Fluff should be home, and a feast would greet her.

Doc kept going back into the kitchen to bother the roast. She found a bottle of red wine and unscrewed its cap. It wasn't great wine, but maybe giving it some extra time to air would improve its flavor. Were you supposed to baste roasts like you basted turkeys? She opened the oven door and splashed some wine on the mound of meat.

During commercials, she peeled potatoes and carrots. Eventually she shoved them into the oven alongside the roast, and added more wine. The house was smelling really wonderful.

Finally, the meat was tender. The juice inside the pan smelled delicious, and tasted better. The vegetables offered no resistance to a fork. Everything was ready. But where was Fluff?

Doc sighed and turned the oven off. She covered the roasting pan with a sheet of aluminum foil. Maybe she should make a salad. Fluff couldn't always keep regular hours. She was probably having a busy night. It wouldn't hurt things to keep them warm for a little while.

Doc waited another hour. Her stomach was growling. There was no more beer. She jockeyed the disposable pan out of the oven with two dish towels. It bent under its heavy load and spilled hot grease over her hand. She dumped it onto the top of the stove and speared some potatoes and carrots onto a plate. When she cut into the meat, she could tell it had dried out. Well, there was no sense in letting all this food go to waste. She left the pan sitting in a puddle of spilled meat juices, and took her plate and the bottle of wine into the living room.

She had finished her meal and was almost done with the wine when the door of the apartment opened, and Fluff came in. "Something smells real good in here," Doc heard her drawl, but she didn't bother to turn around and look at her. She had had so many happy fantasies about what she would say to Fluff, how Fluff would smile at her when she revealed her plan for their future. But now all she felt was disappointment and rage.

Fluff could sense that Doc was in a terrible mood, and sighed. She went into the kitchen and helped herself to food. "This was a wonderful thing for you to do," she told Doc, coming into the living room to eat.

"Yeah, well, it probably tastes like shit by now," Doc said morosely.

"I'm sorry, if I'd known you were making something special I'd have been here sooner."

"It's not anything special. I don't know how to cook. I just thought I would try to save you some bother."

"Thank you," Fluff said, mashing up her potatoes. "What are you watching?"

Doc didn't answer her, just stared at the tube. Fluff kept on eating, but she felt a sick sense of dread. She wished Doc's temper would explode so she could stop waiting.

"Where were you?" Doc finally blurted. She spoke loudly so she could be heard above the television, but it came out even louder than she had planned, and Fluff jumped. When Doc saw Fluff acting afraid of her, it filled her with shame. She couldn't help but remember the time she had slapped Fluff. And she became frightened, because her inclination was to move in on people who were afraid, bully them, shake them down, take whatever she could from them. She did not want to feel that way about her lover.

Fluff knew that Doc would not believe her if she told her where she had been. She had finally taken Nikki's advice and gone to a meeting of Co-Dependents Anonymous. She hadn't realized until she got there that the meeting was held in a church. When she saw that, she almost walked away, but how could she tell Nikki she was afraid to go inside a church? She set her chin and went in with everybody else. The size of the crowd frightened her. Most of them were wearing office clothes. Fluff knew she didn't exactly blend in wearing a black satin evening gown with rhinestone flowers on the bodice, but it was her best dress.

They seemed to do everything by numbers — "Five Organizing Principles," "Twelve Steps," "Six Diagnostic Measures of Co-Dependency." Regular attendees took turns reading these edifying, canned pieces of rhetoric from xeroxed sheets that had been covered in plastic. The official speaker told his life story. Fluff was impressed by his ability to blame other people for his weak-minded mistakes. Every time he used the word "alcoholic" or "addict," she cringed. They came out sounding like cuss-words, just full of bile.

Then the meeting leaders called on people who had their hands up. One woman wanted to complain about other people who brought "literature that was not conference approved," whatever the hell that was, into meetings. She droned on and on about it. Exasperated, Fluff put her hand up, and squeaked in dismay when they actually called on her.

She introduced herself. Having everyone greet her in unison made her heart pound until she thought she would faint. But then she heard her own voice, contemptuous and amused, saying, "I don't give a flying fuck about approved literature. I'm in such deep shit that I'd read anything anybody thought would be helpful. I'm in love with somebody who treats me bad. Maybe she's an alcoholic. I don't know, even if she is, I doubt that's the whole problem. I don't think she means to be abusive, but she can't seem to stop herself. And I don't know what to do."

All the group did was listen, but for some weird reason just saying that out loud had made Fluff feel better. She was surprised at herself for being brave enough to tell a bunch of straight people that she loved Doc. But nobody seemed to treat her any different. The people were a little distant, but not in a nasty way. It was more like they were shy.

After the meeting, people stayed to drink instant coffee and chat. A woman that Fluff would never have dreamed was a lesbian had come up, introduced herself, and told her there were gay CDA meetings. She gave her a pamphlet about it. There was a table full of pamphlets. Fluff scooped up one of each of them, and stuffed them into her bag. On her way home, she cranked up the heat in her MG and decided that she should probably try another meeting. Those people might be assholes, but they were not walking the knife-edge of desperation. They obviously knew something about life that she did not.

Fluff knew that Doc would laugh at her adventure. And she didn't feel strong enough to jeopardize the comfort, the fragile hope she was feeling. "Well, I wasn't out having some wild affair," she told Doc coldly.

"Says you."

"Are we back on this?" Fluff asked steadily. "Because I think I've already heard what you're going to say a bunch of times. If you want to break up, why don't you just tell me so? Spare us both the effort of having another fight if you would, Doc. I'm tired of making you unhappy."

Doc could not believe that her attempt to thank Fluff for being so sweet and to seduce some of the magic back into their lives was turning into disaster.

"What did you do, find yourself a sugar daddy?" she accused.

"Oh, stop it. Just fucking shut up. I never told you I was anything but a whore, and I will not apologize. I don't make you feel bad about being a dyke."

"That's what you think," Doc retorted.

"Well," Fluff said calmly, taking another bite and chewing it slowly, "I'm sorry to hear that. I certainly never wanted it to be this way. I still find you fascinating, Doc. I look at you and I just want to get inside you. Follow you around. See if I can't get you excited. But there's no reason to keep on doing this if all we're going to do is injure one another. I don't hate you, and I don't want you to hate me."

Doc did not like the way this whole discussion was going. Fluff seemed way too willing to let her slip away. "Look, all I asked you was where you'd been," she said, trying to get the conversation back on track. "You're two hours late. It's a reasonable question."

Fluff replied with a brief, sour laugh. "And all those times you've come in drunk, did I ever once ask you where you'd been? Do you know how many times you've told me to meet you some place and you show up late, or never show up at all? That day you almost got killed, I had no idea where you were going. You been running ever since we got to Portland, Doc, and you never told me why. If I had known how bad things were I might have been able to help you, but you thought I was too dumb to be trusted with the real, hard fact of your predicament. And now you want me to tell you where I've been? What is this, a curfew? Besides, it doesn't matter what I tell you, you won't believe me. You think all I do when I'm not with you is chase after men and fuck them and suck them and take their money. I don't owe you any explanations at all. And I think it's a big mistake for me to try and have a serious conversation with somebody who's been drinking."

"I have been running since the day I met you, sweetie. Maybe you've forgotten whose fault that was."

"Doc, Doc." Fluff was really sad. "I think we're about even on that one. I'm real sorry I sucked you into my problems and fucked up your life. I was just so desperate it made me stupid. And I had no more idea what the consequences would be than you did. But I think I've made amends for that by now. I think we ought to wait and talk about this when you're sober."

"What the hell is this stuff about me drinking? All I did was have a few beers while I was waiting for you. And I'm not drunk now!"

"But you're never sober," Fluff said. She sounded like she was trying to explain something to a small child. "Either you're drinking, or you're smoking pot, or you're doing coke, or you're hitting up some speed. You think I don't know about that? I ignore it, that's all, Doc. But after all that time I spent with Prez I can recognize the signs."

"So what? I take care of business. I never do anything I can't handle."

"Doc, you are not handling things at all. Look at us. Look at your life!"

"Well, excuse me, but you seem like a very unlikely candidate to be giving me a temperance lecture."

"Look, I give up. There's no way I can control anything you do. But I have to start taking care of myself, and taking care of my life. So this is what I want to do. You can stay here until you get that cast off, then you can find a new place to live. I found this apartment and I want to keep it. We'll share the bed because we have to, but I don't want to make love with you. I'm tired of bossing you around in bed and getting treated like trash outside of it. And I am not giving you any more money. We are going to split the rent, split the food bill, and you can start buying some gas for the car."

Doc knew that Fluff had not said anything unfair. But she had never had someone leave her before. And that was what Fluff was trying to do, leave her. The fact that she was doing it so sanely and humanely just made it worse. Doc felt like she was being offered charity. She had wanted to climb out of that trap, and now Fluff had shoved her right back into it.

"You think you've been mistreated," she said quietly. "You think I haven't done right by you. But baby, you don't know how lucky you've been."

She saw her hands go out and wrap around Fluff's neck, and could not stop herself. Even with a broken leg, she was so much stronger than Fluff that she had no problem at all getting her down on the bed. "You tired of bossing me around in bed?" she crooned. "See how you like the other part, then."

Doc tore open Fluff's dress and squeezed her breasts hard enough to bruise them badly. She couldn't believe the little bitch wasn't screaming and pleading with her to stop. She risked a glimpse of Fluff's face. It was dead-white, frozen, and it seemed to Doc that the girl was jeering at her, mocking her with her superiority. She lifted her big body enough to get her hand between Fluff's legs, tore off her underwear, and jammed as much of her hand as she could into Fluff's cunt. She had not expected it to be so tight. It was as small as the rest of the girl.

"Now you tell me you don't come this way," Doc snarled. "But I'm going to fuck you until you *do* come, whether you like it or not, just because I say so."

Fluff could not remember the last time they had had sex. The lack of privacy in the studio had meant that she rarely even masturbated. She was terrified and furious, but Doc's hands knew a thing or three about women. Fluff knew she would come any time Doc really wanted her to. She also knew that would damn her again in Doc's eyes, prove that Fluff had been lying every time she said she did not enjoy sex with her tricks.

"This is mine," Doc said, her arm pumping, "so you give it to me *now*," and Fluff came in spite of herself. But Doc kept on making her do it, fucking her until she was so sore she was screaming from the pain, and Doc did not seem to be able to tell the difference between that and an orgasm.

Doc was so engrossed in what she was doing that she had forgotten to protect any of her vulnerable points. Fluff stiffened the fingers of her left hand and brought them sharply into Doc's throat. It didn't cut off her air for very long, but it startled her and gave Fluff enough time to escape.

She was crying so hard she could barely talk, but she had something important to say. "Why didn't you ever do that when you loved me?" she sobbed. "I would have been happy to give it to you, to feel pleasure in my cunt instead of having

300 ❖

it be like a numb, dead animal. But you never would, would you, because you thought it was dirty, and you still do. I won't live this way! I hate you. Get out of here. I hate you!"

Doc found that she could walk perfectly well without her crutches. She left with nothing but the clothes on her back. All of her gear was still in her saddlebags, and it would have been too painful to see them or handle them now.

On her way out of the apartment, she tripped over something that Fluff had left in the hallway, propped against the wall. It was a holly wreath tied with red ribbon and decorated with little, gold bells. There was also a shopping bag full of gift-wrapped boxes.

Oh, yeah. That's why the store had been so crowded. It was Christmas Eve. Great. The very armpit of the year.

24.

Prez found himself floating in a dark void. So this was death. He was glad it was quiet. Things had been so noisy for a while. His throat and chest had hurt. No — best not to think about the pain. He did not want to remember all of that just yet.

Where were the flames? Where was the devil?

If he wanted to, he knew he could move, but what was the point? Against this emptiness, motion would be meaningless.

Little points of light came out of the darkness, and from somewhere a breeze sprang up. It was not forceful enough to be a real wind, but it was very cold, so cold that he thought he should swim or fly just to keep warm.

Then something appeared that made him freeze again.

It was Her, the Woman. She wore a short garment over Her breasts. It was made of chain mail that glittered like the skin of a sea serpent. She had a fish's tail, and in Her hand there was a trident. Or was it an ax? Or just a whip?

"My consort," She said tenderly, or was She being ironic? "You have been lost. I see My priestess made you travel a long, hard path to come to Me. She is very devoted to Me, is she not? And so creative. You were valorous, My hero. Yes, you are My hero. There is no devil here. You are the one who wears horns for Me, and dances to show Me his strength. Touch your head if you do not believe Me."

Prez stared at Her. When he touched his temples, he was surprised to find smooth points there, like the budding horns on a baby bull.

His name disintegrated and fell away from him. It was lost, like a number too long to remember. He was only ... other, different from Her. But dependent. Her creature. He wanted to tear the armor from Her body and ravish Her, but the fish's tail made consummation of that desire seem unlikely. He would have to cut a place to bury his need.

"Still so bloody-minded?" She asked. "My stag, My stallion. Haven't I given you the animals to hunt, and a whole world to roam? Haven't I given you enough women to rut with? And still you are so full of anger, you would destroy everything. You are angry because by yourself you can make nothing live. This is true for the women, too, but it does not make them hate you. You have not done well, My consort. You still have many lessons to learn. You have done terrible things to make yourself powerful. You are the embodiment of the sins of all men."

He screamed at Her.

"Yes," She said wearily, "that was the first thing I ever heard you say. And we keep coming back to it."

He was naked. His sexual flesh was pointing to Her, aching, and he was furious with himself for wanting Her.

"I love you for your courage and your will," She said. "You are bold and vital. I wish everything I made had your strength and joy. Even your arrogance is beautiful. But I swear there are times when I wish I had been able to think of a way to do without you. Now go, where your anger can harm no one, and be devoured by your fear."

Suddenly Her fish-tail made perfect sense, because they were up to their necks in water. When he tried to swim toward Her, She turned Her back on him, dived into the water, and disappeared. Her body was a sinuous green streak of speed and muscle, and there was no way he would ever catch Her.

He tried to swim, but quickly grew bored, and floated instead. There was nothing to swim toward. Finally even floating was fatiguing, and his head slipped below the gentle waves. His first mouthful of his enemy was as warm and salty as his own blood. But it was, he knew suddenly, Her blood. This was Her womb. It was going to drown him, but he would never die here. Never.

Then his naked feet were greeted by things that made him swim as passionately as he had lived.

25.

Sometime in the spring, Doc found herself at Craps. She wasn't sure why. She hadn't been in a bar for a couple of months. She'd gotten thrown out of nearly every dyke bar in town and several of the men's bars. She had vague recollections of fights, broken bottles, police car lights, running along rooftops and fire escapes, and coming to in alleys and once in jail, but very few names or faces were connected with these violent fragments of memory. She had no idea when, or how, the cast had come off her leg.

After she'd left Fluff's apartment, Doc had gone on a binge, perversely reasoning that she would show Fluff that she could handle her liquor. Once she sobered up from that bender, she decided to avoid booze. The blackouts scared her. But she felt so low and worn out that she had to score something to bounce back. Coke was too expensive, so she settled for speed. When that got too crazy, and she noticed she hadn't eaten anything for a few days, she would try to calm herself down with a quart or two of red wine. Because wine was something you had with dinner, right? It was almost as good as eating. But drinking made her sloppy, it wasn't safe to get that loose, so she had to go back to the speed to get her edge.

It was a vicious cycle. Being strung out on speed would make her jumpy, irritable, and paranoid. When the isolation got unbearable, she would go to bars looking for company. But in order to stay there, she had to drink. Then it was easy to find camaraderie and sex, but who wanted a bunch of lushes for friends? They never did anything besides camp at the bartender's elbow. She would start fights with them out of sheer boredom. Drunk broads were lousy in bed. It felt cleaner to be alone, so she would try to purify herself by shooting speed. Doc wondered why had it taken her so long to figure out that the person she was trying to get away from was simply herself.

Doc shuddered when she remembered one particularly gruesome night when she'd spent all her money on crank and forgotten to score a new needle. She had turned her arm into hamburger, trying to hit a vein with a point that didn't just have a burr in it, it was obviously bent. Finally she had thrown the needle on the floor and cut her arm open, then poured white powder into the wound, pressed it shut to try to drive the drug into her bloodstream. Even as she watched herself do this, she was thinking, at least I'm not smoking ice, you get hooked really fast when you do that. Denial was a maze without a heart. You could wander in it forever.

She had gone to her first Alcoholics Anonymous meeting the day she'd gotten out of jail. She had spent too much of her adolescence in the custody of the state. If her game had gotten so rusty that she could be cornered and picked up by the cops, something was very wrong with her life, and radical measures were obviously necessary.

Most of the gay groups met in the Rainbow Coalition Church. She had gone to a few of those, but didn't seem to connect with any of the men there. They weren't the kind of leather daddy faggots she could turn into buddies. There were lesbian groups meeting at the Women's Building, and Doc went to a few, hoping to see some dykes, but all she found were gay women, and she wasn't about to spill her guts in front of any of those girls.

She preferred meetings at the Star of Hope mission that fed homeless people in the red light district. The place appealed to her sense of irony because the clergy who ran it often looked worse than the bums. She felt right at home talking about drinking with old winos.

Now and then a Harley boy turned up at these meetings, and one of them, a stocky, balding dude named Bulldog, had dragged her off to meet his club, a bunch of ironed-out, dried-out bikers, headwires, and perverts called the Mutants. Most of them went to Addicts Anonymous meetings, and they didn't just talk about drinking there. These men and women had survived everything — heroin, wings, coke, PCP, gold dust, getting holes drilled in their skulls so they could punch a button and stimulate the pleasure centers in the brain.

A few of them snickered the first time Doc referred to her higher power as the Goddess. Then Bulldog did the same thing. They laughed at him, too, until somebody else made himself an easier target by talking about Lord Krishna. Doc didn't figure Bulldog for one of your radical faery types. So she cornered him and asked him why he had embarrassed himself that way. He said, "Because nothin' is more important than staying alive. And if you quit coming to these meetings, you'll die."

"You're a real friend," Doc had told him, meaning it. "But you don't have to call on a deity that you don't believe in. I won't disappear on you. There's more leather in this group than you'd find at a Chicago stockyard. I'll keep coming back." Like they always said at the end of the meeting when everybody stood up and held hands, it works! Or at least, you hope it does, because there's nothing else left to try.

Doc had gone to a meeting of some kind every single day for a month. But she still wasn't sure how she felt about being straight and empty. Deep in the stubborn core of her heart, she did not believe that anything on earth was more powerful than she was. She could not really believe she was helpless in the presence of alcohol or drugs. It seemed to be the equivalent of confessing that you would always be a victim, and Doc knew that today's victim was tomorrow's road kill.

Kicking had been awful. The fact that you were prepared to detox rather than continue to be an addict was one of the ways you could tell just how bad being hooked was. The dramatic part was over, the days when she had paced the floor, sweating ice water, starving, hating noise, hating light, throwing up, having burning, shaking bouts of diarrhea, trying to sleep, hallucinating, getting up to pace the floor some more. She never wanted to go through that again. But every day she woke up and wanted to get high. Every day she went to bed amazed that she had not had a drink or taken any drugs. Maybe it got easier.

Doc had to admit she felt better than she had in years. Her pants were even a little loose. She liked remembering what she had done two days, even a week ago. But that searching moral inventory they kept talking about doing, well, that was going to be a bitch. What was she supposed to do, give the Jaguars their money back and say, "I'm ever so sorry"? Apologize to the feds for that load of Brazilian rock that had somehow never made it to New York to enrich the coffers of the CIA? Track down every dumb jock in high school who had paid a sawbuck for an ounce of her patented blend of oregano and pencil shavings, who was so excited he could wet his pants over the prospect of "blowing his mind"?

Despite Doc's uncertainty about her own motives, this visit to Craps must be important, because she had put on clean clothes and her new leather jacket. Well, it was almost new. Rolling drunks at the Pony Express bus terminal didn't give you as big a selection as shopping at Ishi's. She'd even gotten her boots shined. A girl was entitled to a certain period of mourning, after all, and then you had to wash your face, comb your hair, go out the door, and get on with your life.

So that must be why she was at Craps, to see Fluff and try to end this chapter of her life. Maybe she would ask Fluff to forgive her. Well — maybe not. Doc tried very hard not to have any grandiose fantasies about how this was going to go. She noticed that when she went up to the bar and asked for coffee (she was damned if Fluff would ever be able to say to her again, "You've been drinking"), everyone moved away from her.

Doc turned around with her coffee cup in hand and leaned on the bar. She could not break the habit of never turning her back on the room. Slim was at his favorite table with Hattie. He gave her a completely neutral look. So Doc took her coffee and walked over to him. "How's business?" she asked.

"*My* business is good. Family-type holidays is always good for this business. Daddy can't wait to stop spendin' time with his family and come visit mine. What about *your* business?"

"Well, I think I'm going to have to take an entry-level position somewhere and start all over," Doc said. "I really lost it this winter."

Slim nodded. "You got that straight. But you know what, Doc? I still got a warm spot in my heart for you!" He rocked back in his chair and laughed so hard, Doc thought he would piss. Hattie gave Doc a look of complete mystification. "You a real rascal, Doc," Slim guffawed. "And I *have* missed you. It seems like just yesterday when I was ready to kill you, but fortunately at the time I couldn't seem to find you. No harm's done. We can call it square." He reached for his cocaine kit. "Allow me to propose a toast to our friendship."

Doc shook her head and raised her coffee cup. "I'll have to toast you in this, Slim."

He raised his eyebrows. "You ain't going to turn into some kinda preacher's kid on me, are you, Doc?"

She laughed. "As a matter of fact, I was a preacher's kid. Did you know that? I grew up with hellfire and brimstone and the back of my father's hand. Wasn't he surprised when I grew up to be as tall as he was? By the time I was twelve I was too big to hit. It didn't mean he didn't try, though, and I was so scared I might hurt the old man I hit the road instead. Juvenile authorities caught up with my ass and stuck me in a home for incorrigible youth for the longest time. Do you have any idea how hard it is to minister to the sexual needs of two hundred and thirty-four incarcerated teenage girls, not to mention their teachers, parole officers, social workers, and guards? By the time I got out of there I was a shadow of my former self."

Slim laughed. "And I think I got it rough with eight women. Sometimes I think my dick's gonna fall off."

"You ought to learn to use your tongue," Doc said. She blew on her coffee, tried a sip. "Goddess, this stuff is awful."

"Now, you know us macho black dudes don't eat pussy," Slim scoffed, and winked at her. "Don't you make me laugh, now." He was laying out lines of cocaine with the precise hand of a Hopi medicine man making a sand painting. "You looking for Fluff?" he asked, turning his head away from the mirror to talk.

"Might be."

"Yeah, I 'spect you might. She ain't been in here much, Doc. But she was in here lookin' for you last night. Had two rough-looking white boys with her. Said she'd be back tomorrow. That's today." He bent over his mirror.

Doc couldn't stand to watch what he was doing with that razor blade. The gold straw was just inches from her hand. It would be so easy to say, "Guess I'll have a little of that after all." Self-loathing rose in the back of her throat like vomit. Where did it come from, this corrosive hatred that kept trying to eat up her life? Uh-uh. "Thanks, Slim, I gotta get some smokes," she said, and ambled over to the machine at the front of the bar.

Three cups of coffee later, the atmosphere in the bar had thawed a little, and she was chatting with Rowena about how her kids had come through the chicken pox. King and his entourage showed up, and Doc excused herself to go over to their table and say hello to Nikki. The tawny-colored kitten face broke into a smile, and Nikki (ignoring a dirty look from King) got up to give Doc a hug that nearly cracked her ribs.

"I was worried about you," she said, and Doc was surprised to find herself believing it.

"Well, it was nice of you to care," she said softly. She could feel her cheeks getting pink from embarrassment. She tried to think what she could say to apologize for the sarcastic remarks she had made about Nikki behind her back.

"A lot of people love you, Doc."

Well, what the hell were you supposed to say to *that*? Doc gave her a wounded look, mumbled, "ThanksI'llseeyou-around," and went back to Rowena's table.

"You get religion?" that shrewd, rotund woman asked her suspiciously. "Ain't no halo in the world big enough for your head, Doc."

"No, I'm just trying to mend a few fences before I jump 'em," Doc said. Her voice was full of tension. So Fluff was hanging out with two men. Why? She certainly had a score to settle with Doc. Were they supposed to settle it for her?

Doc really wanted a drink. She went up to the bar and said to LeRoi the bartender, "I'm going to come back there and show you how to make coffee."

"Be my guest," he said, flicking his towel at the bar. "It's a girl's job anyway."

"Any job you ever had was a girl's job," Doc scoffed.

"Puh-leeze, they call us *women* now," he retorted, fluffing up his hair. "We even got us a movement. Or hadn't you heard?"

"Shit, no, I'm just an old diesel dyke who wants to get me some pussy whenever I can. But I heard you feminists are horny bitches." She dumped the grounds, found a clean filter, and spooned coffee into the basket.

"Shush your filthy mouth. I want me a husband," LeRoi told her firmly, laughing a little.

"My, how radical of you," Doc said drily, and poured water into the top of the coffee machine.

"Well, Doc, I see you got yourself a day job at last," she heard somebody say. It was a familiar male voice, but not one she had ever expected to hear in this place.

"Anderson!"

The rangy blond man was laughing at her, standing on the other side of the bar, resting one arm on Michaels's shoulder. Doc saw at a glance that their relationship had changed dramatically. For one thing, the short, dark stud had his hand on Anderson's butt. And neither of them were wearing colors. Anderson had gotten his ears pierced. And Michaels had had one of the epaulets of his jacket set with rhinestones. Bikers are so subtle.

She jumped over the bar to wrap her arms around both of them. There was a lot of back-pounding and shouting. That, at least, hadn't changed. You had to send a Harley boy to the chiropractor to convince him you were glad to see him.

Then the two men separated, and she saw who was behind them. Doc suddenly realized that one of the problems with having no expectations was that you had no speech prepared. So she just gaped at Fluff, like a rube with his first porno magazine.

"I'll give you a hug, too, if you let me," Fluff said. "I was hopin' you would turn up before these two gentlemen left town. I knew you would be glad to see them."

Doc said, "You don't have to do that."

"I know."

Fluff came over and briefly embraced her. Doc had forgotten how good her hair smelled, and how well that little face fit against her broad chest. Doc kept her arms at her side, paralyzed by too many happy and ugly memories.

"Let's all sit down," Fluff suggested quietly, subdued by her contact with the big woman she had adored and despised. There just wasn't anybody else like her, goddammit. Fluff might be able to love somebody else, but she would never be able to replace her. It was unsettling.

They had brought a bag of donuts with them. Anderson and Michaels ordered Irish coffee, Doc already had java, and Fluff produced a peppermint tea bag from her purse and asked for plain hot water.

Doc had a chocolate donut and let the boys catch her up on current events in biker land. The description of Prez's execution was chilling. But she was glad to know that Raven had the ice to keep her promise. The fact that he was finally dead made the whole universe cleaner. Fluff looked transformed with joy and relief. Doc was equally glad to hear that Raven and her unlikely co-conspirators had gotten away, and taken Josie with them.

"Of course, when we sailed into town and told everybody that Prez was dead, it caused quite an uproar," Michaels snickered.

"Everybody who had a Polaroid was up there," Anderson continued. "My God, a lot of people hated that man. We even got us an anthropologist from UCLA with a video camera. He hung there a whole day before they could clear the crowds and take down the body. Of course, it left a big gap in the leadership. Especially when me and Michaels resigned. They didn't know what to do. Losing three officers in one day?"

"So who's the Prez now?" Doc asked.

"Scott Campbell. Who else? Everybody had had enough of Prez's antagonistic, flashy style. They wanted somebody steady. With his wife gone, Scott needs something to do to keep his mind off it. Prez let everything slide. Scott's going to have his hands full putting Alamo biz back together again."

Doc chewed on her lower lip. How long could Lieutenant Colonel Ms. Jelly Bean aka Fatima stay mad? She had always liked Campbell. He was a reasonable man. You could do business with him.

"So who's the new treasurer?"

Michaels was squirming, he was so excited about being the one who got to tell her. "Paint!" he whooped. Doc's reaction did not disappoint him. She literally fell off her seat.

"She can't hold office in the club — she's not a member!"

"They *patched* her," Anderson crowed. "And do you know what she said when they asked her to make a speech before the vote?"

Doc and Fluff said in unison, "I think I'm old enough to be your mother."

"That's right! And it's true. She's been sorting out candidates for years now. Do you know how many of the bros got into the club because Paint gave them a nod? How could they tell her no?"

"I can't believe the old guard will stand for this," Doc said.

"Maybe not," Michaels agreed. "But would you want to go to war with Paint?"

"Not me," Anderson said. "Not with sweet little Desiree, who thinks she's the reincarnation of Annie Oakley, standing at her side drawing a bead on your family jewels. Would you, Doc?"

"No, not today, thank you," Doc demurred. "Well, what about sergeant-at-arms? Don't you have two kids, Anderson?"

"My kids are going to live with Paint and Desiree," Anderson said. "Just for a little while, until the end of the year. Did you ever meet James White Wolf? He hardly ever comes on the runs. Anyway, he's their next-door neighbor. Jimmy's a good man even if he is a lone ranger. I put him up for the vote and they let him have it."

"Think he'll do a good job?" Doc demanded. For some reason, the idea of Paint wearing a set of the Angels' colors made her briefly see red.

"I really don't care," Anderson cheerfully admitted. "I'm tired of counting hand grenades, Doc. I'm sick to death of teaching gumbies how to calibrate their sights, running inventories on helicopter fuel and air-to-ground missiles, planning raids on Texas coca farms and the next battle with El Diablos, calling on good women and telling them that their men have bought the farm. No, sir. Me and my man are feeling the call of spring."

"The call of the wild," Michaels interjected, and howled like a coyote. It made everybody in Craps jump.

"We're heading up to Canada," Anderson explained.

"Yeah, well, just don't try to drive through Vancouver," Doc warned.

"That's a pretty easy detour to make," Michaels said, "considering that it glows in the dark. Once we get past that, we're gonna see what's left of Alaska."

Doc's hand closed involuntarily on a throttle that wasn't there. "That sounds like a good ride," she said wistfully.

"Then we're thinking about buying some land," Michaels continued. "We ought to have enough cash when Paint sells our holdings in Alamo, the houses and the stock and everything. We should ask you some questions about that. Do you think we could put something together like Harpy Farm? There haveta be other dudes out there like us who could use a home base."

Doc instantly saw them living very close, indeed, to Harpy Farm. At last, a way to turn all those baby boys into folding money. "I don't see why not," she said with her saleswoman's smile. "Alaska. Damn. I wish I could go with you."

"You can," Fluff said, and tossed something shiny onto the table. Doc picked it up. It was the key to her Medusa.

"I wondered where that had gone to. But it's no good to me now, Fluff. You know I lost my bike," she told the two men. "Got hit by a car, laid it down. Nothing left but scrap metal."

Fluff laughed. "It's sitting at a garage on Morris Street, and I would dearly love to stop paying the storage charges. I had your bike towed and fixed up, Doc. I kept trying to tell you but every time I brought it up you forbid me to talk about it. I even had the side case covers and the valve covers chromed. It was going to be your Christmas present."

Doc felt tears come to her eyes. "Would you two excuse us?" she asked.

"Sure, let's go play pinball," Anderson said, scraping his chair back.

"I got a better game to play but I need *your* balls to do it," Michaels snickered.

"Then you better give me more than an Irish coffee," Anderson warned.

"So, baby, thank you," Doc said, turning the key over and over in her big hands. "But why did you do this for me? I wasn't very good to you, Fluff. I'm sorry things got so fucked up."

"You're not the only one who has a lot of regrets," Fluff said. "I missed you. I wanted to go after you. But from things I heard through Nikki it seemed like you needed to be left alone."

Doc put the key down and lit a cigarette. "I thought a lot about what you said," she admitted. "About the booze and the dope. I really did. I haven't had a drink for forty-two days, six hours, and eleven minutes. I haven't had anything else, either. But I don't know if I can quit forever. To tell you the truth, I'm not sure I want to. You know the life I lead. I'm the last advocate of free enterprise in America. If it's illegal, if people want it and they aren't supposed to have it, it's my sacred duty to make sure they can have it. For a price. The biz is in my blood, Fluff. I just can't see myself settling down and getting a job in a warehouse or a gas station." She didn't find it necessary to tell Fluff that she was currently supporting herself washing dishes in a diner, or mention that she had been picking pockets and living in gas station restrooms before that.

"Yeah, well, you have to figure all that out for yourself," Fluff said. "All I know is, it was a mistake for me to do what I did with you. I thought I was being a good girl, taking care of you, but what I really did was treat you like a child and rob you of your self-respect. I'll never do that again."

"I hurt you," Doc said. "I'm so ashamed of that. There's no excuse for that kind of violence."

Fluff pressed her hands together. "No, there's not. But I don't want to be angry with you forever. Maybe we can forgive each other and just try to do things better the next time." Her chest hurt, making it difficult to talk. "It was hard for me to do without you, Doc. When I couldn't blame you for all of my troubles I had to start figuring out my own shit. I was so lonely, but the last thing I wanted to do was make the same mistakes with somebody else. There certainly was no shortage of offers to take your place." She gave a significant look around the bar. "I don't like being single, but it's better than being straight."

Doc finished her coffee, thinking hard. Finally, she said, "You want to come with me to Alaska?"

Fluff shook her head. "No, baby. I'm going to school. I'm gonna be a bachelor of science."

"*What?*"

"I got accepted to college, Doc. After you left, I got some tutoring and took an equivalency exam. I have a high school diploma now."

"That's wonderful."

"Well, it isn't much, but it sure surprised me when they told me I had passed the test. So then I thought, well, apply for college, all they can do is turn you down. They have a pretty good pre-med program at the University of Oregon. So maybe you'll have to call *me* Doc someday."

Doc raised her eyebrows at that. Fluff sounded so happy and excited. She remembered her own enthusiasm, going into the army nursing program. Of course, that was long before she got kicked out for sleeping with the captain's wife. Well—you couldn't really call what they were doing in the middle of the parade ground "sleeping."

"I'm going to miss you," Doc said. "It's lonely goin' on somebody else's honeymoon. Does your school start in the spring?"

"No, the first semester starts in the fall. But I have a lot of studying to do before then. I'm not really ready to do the work. I have a lot of catching up to do."

Doc knew that if she pressured Fluff, she could probably get her on the back of her Medusa. Then she looked at Fluff's determined chin, and thought, maybe not. "Well, I don't want to fuck up your education," she said dutifully. "Seems like spending time apart from each other has been good for both of us."

"Yes, it has." Fluff had put her teabag back into her cup, and she was mashing it with the spoon. Pretty soon it was going to pop open and there would be little pieces of peppermint all over the bottom and sides of the mug.

"Could you stop makin' that racket?" Doc asked. "You taking some kind of class to get you ready for college?"

"Oh, I'm sorry. No, I'm not. I just have four or five books I ought to read."

"Well, shit!" Doc exploded. "There's room for a few books in my saddlebags. Fluff — give me a chance to show you I can be good to you. Don't let me go off feeling this way. Please, baby. If you want to break my heart I guess you're entitled. I know you are. But please give me another chance."

Fluff looked away from Doc, surveyed the room. Hattie was sitting next to Slim just two tables away, running the curved end of a tiny file under his nails. He had his legs stretched out in the position of a man well satisfied with the care he is receiving. In front of Hattie were bottles of cuticle-softener and clear polish and the brush she used to buff his fingertips to a high shine. From the top of her long and superior Egyptian nose, Hattie gave her a look that said, I got mine right here. Ain't nothing in the world more important than that. Don't let yours slip away, now.

Fluff leaned forward, took Doc's face between her hands, and kissed her. The moment her lips touched Doc's, they opened, and Fluff's tongue slid into a sweet, welcoming mouth that could not seem to get enough of her. "Oh," Doc said. "You bitch. Oh."

Fluff sat back down. From her chair, she could smell Doc's arousal. Or was that her own flesh, eager to go home? She said, in a hard, flat voice, "There won't be any room for my books in your saddlebags unless you leave the dope and the Jack Daniels behind."

Doc tamped a cigarette on the table, hitting it hard enough to make it jump out of her hand. "You drive a hard bargain, honey."

"I had a good teacher. And I'm *not* your honey."

Doc laughed. "Then I got a condition, too. We do this clean and sober, but you don't mess with my biz."

"And you don't mess with mine," Fluff said, pointing at Doc with her spoon. "I have to be back here by the tenth of September, or I will mail your ass to Mars. And if you ever lay a violent hand on me again, you'll find out what prime rib feels like bein' sliced extra thin."

"Then let's get the hell out of here," Doc said, pushing back her chair. "Hey, Anderson! Michaels! Come on, honey, what are you waitin' for?"

*Alyson Publications publishes a wide
variety of books with gay and lesbian themes.
For a free catalog, or to be placed
on our mailing list, please write to:
Alyson Publications
40 Plympton St.
Boston, MA 02118
Please indicate whether you are interested in
books for gay men, for lesbians, or both.*